KILLING

A SAM RIVERS MYSTERY

MONARCHS

Also by the author

Gunflint Burning: Fire in the Boundary Waters
Opening Goliath
Lost in the Wild
Wolf Kill
Cougar Claw

PRAISE FOR *KILLING MONARCHS*

"In *Killing Monarchs,* Cary J. Griffith combines monarch butter-flies, a Mexican cartel, and compelling characters—both human and canine—to deliver a chilling thriller you won't want to put down. Sam Rivers and his wolf-dog partner, Gray, make a terrific, crime-fighting duo!"

—Margaret Mizushima, author of the award-winning
Timber Creek K-9 Mysteries, including *Striking Range*

"What do murders disguised as overdoses, endangered monarch butterflies, and international heroin smugglers have in common? U.S. Fish & Wildlife Special Agent Sam Rivers and Gray, Sam's rescued wolf-dog hybrid with a nose for narcotics. As the bodies pile up in the Land of 10,000 Lakes, Sam and Gray are on a mission to stop the killer before he claims his next victim. A gripping thriller highlighting the ironclad bond between man and his best friend, *Killing Monarchs* had me turning pages all night long. Sam Rivers and his faithful wolf dog are my new best friends."

—Brian Malloy, author of *The Year of Ice* and *After Francesco*

"Both thriller and mystery, *Killing Monarchs* mixes an elementary-school science project with scorpions and drugs. Totally surprising is how butterflies flit into this fast-paced and tantalizing story. Cary Griffith has laid out another fabulous tale, based on solid knowledge of the natural world, with a provocative sense of the deviousness of humankind."

—Mary Logue, author of *The Streel* and *The Big Sugar*

"*Killing Monarchs* is an exciting, thrilling, and suspenseful page-turner! Griffith weaves together an intriguing mystery with fascinating environmental concerns, young adults facing the reality of their past, and the dangerous world of drug cartels. Sam Rivers, a U.S. Fish & Wildlife agent, is a captivating character, and, as a K-9 handler, I especially enjoyed Rivers's sidekick, the extraordinary wolf dog, Gray. Together, Rivers and Gray make an outstanding team. Readers will be rooting for them and stay up late to find out what happens next. *Killing Monarchs* hooked me from the first page, and I couldn't put it down. I highly recommend this series!"

—Kathleen Donnelly, author of the award-winning National Forest K-9 series and K-9 handler for Sherlock Hounds Detection Canines

"With one sharp eye on the world of nature and another carefully watching the evil antics of two-legged species who roam the earth, Sam Rivers is one part teacher and two parts crime solver. *Killing Monarchs* floats like a butterfly and stings like a scorpion. Prepare to be schooled."

—Mark Stevens, author of *The Fireballer* and The Allison Coil Mystery Series

KILLING

A SAM RIVERS MYSTERY

MONARCHS

CARY J. GRIFFITH

PUBLICATIONS
adventure

Cover design: Travis Bryant
Cover photos: Vladimirkarp/Shutterstock (monarch) and John McLaird/Shutterstock
Author photo: Anna McCourt
Editors: Mary Logue, Holly Cross, and Jenna Barron
Proofreader: Emily Beaumont

Library of Congress Cataloging-in-Publication Data
Names: Griffith, Cary J., author.
Title: Killing monarchs : dd/ Cary J. Griffith.
Description: First edition. | Cambridge, Minnesota : Adventure Publications, [2023]
Series: A Sam Rivers Mystery
Summary: "As a special agent for the US Fish & Wildlife Service, Sam Rivers has researched
and studied a variety of animals. He's visiting sixth graders at Hopkins Elementary to
share photographs of the Monarch butterfly, and he's brought along his drug-sniffing wolf
dog, Gray, to give students a demonstration of his partner's remarkable skills. Gray finds
a sample drug packet, hidden by Sam, but that's not all. The wolf dog keeps following
his nose, leading Sam to a utility room where they discover the school's janitor, dead. Local
police write it off as a drug overdose, but Sam is no stranger to crime scenes. He suspects
foul play. When Sam and Gray come upon a second victim, the coincidences are too great
to ignore. Sam starts turning over rocks, and what slithers out is more insidious than anyone could have foretold. Sam's instincts tell him there'll be more deaths, but those instincts
put him at odds with conventional law enforcement. Armed with his knowledge of the
natural world and his wolf-dog companion, Sam must uncover answers to questions that
few others believe exist"— Provided by publisher.
Identifiers: LCCN 2022054436 (print) | LCCN 2022054437 (ebook)
    ISBN 9781647551759 (pbk.) | ISBN 9781647551766 (ebook)
Classification: LCC PS3607.R54857 K55 2023 (print) | LCC PS3607.R54857 (ebook)
    DDC 813/.6—dc23
LC record available at https://lccn.loc.gov/2022054436
LC ebook record available at https://lccn.loc.gov/2022054437

10 9 8 7 6 5 4 3 2 1
Copyright © 2023 by Cary J. Griffith
Killing Monarchs: A Sam Rivers Mystery (book 3)

adventure

Published by Adventure Publications
An imprint of AdventureKEEN
310 Garfield St. S.
Cambridge, MN 55008
800-678-7006
adventurepublications.net

For my wife, Anna, great nurturer of milkweeds and monarchs, from spring shoots and eggs to bursting pods and butterflies.

And for the grandkids: Ryder, Cormac, Mylo, and Pieta. It is an honor and blessing to watch you emerge in a metamorphosis all your own.

DAY 1

Wednesday, May 21

CHAPTER ONE

There were three in the car. Domina drove, Jon Lockhart sat in the front seat, and Tiburon, the muscle, in back.

They traveled north on Minnesota Highway 169 to the Highway 7 exit. At this hour of the morning the streets were empty, but Domina approached the top of the exit carefully, signaling a left well in advance of the light. As she approached, the light turned yellow and, rather than risk it, she slowed to a stop.

"You could have made that light," Lockhart said.

"No reason to push it. We got time."

"How long?" Lockhart said.

"Five minutes to the drop-off. Take you another five to get into position behind those bushes. Then Tibby and me circle the block, park, and knock on Jerry's door."

"Tibby" was Tiburon, hunkered in the back seat, staring into the rearview out of obsidian eyes.

Domina wore a pair of custom-made Gaspar black driving gloves and a lightweight jacket with a dark sheen. Her jet-black hair was long on top and shorn butch on both sides, in the style of certain women she hung with in Morelia, south of the border.

"What if he's early?" Lockhart said.

"Jerry Trailor wouldn't show up early to a clusterfuck of beauty queens."

"You sure about the bushes?"

"I checked." Domina remembered them from previous pick-ups and had scouted the place. "No way Jerry's going to see you back there. It's a blind spot."

"Just make sure he doesn't look around," Lockhart said.

"Jerry's not the kind of guy to look," Domina said, remembering. "Jerry rolls."

Lockhart sniffed and said, "Just make sure."

Lockhart wore a light gray hiking shirt over a black tee, faded jeans, and a pair of Keen hiking shoes. There was a wide-brimmed hat on the seat beside him and a black day pack balanced on the floor between his legs. He'd acquired the gear from an outlet outside of Dallas eight hours after crossing the Mexican border. The left side of his face and ear looked like he'd been caught between two surgeons having a skin fight. Otherwise, he could have easily passed for a tourist heading out Highway 7 to Minnetonka or Deep Haven or farther west to check out wild country. But the hiking disguise had been unnecessary because in two days' driving they had not been stopped. Now, less than a mile from their destination, Lockhart swore he could smell something like wet iron, something like blood. But maybe it was the idea of watching Jerry Trailor die.

Domina exhaled, waiting for the light. "Jerry's going to tell you whatever you need to know. But he doesn't know jack about your money."

After a pause, during which Lockhart was careful not to betray his intentions, he said, "We'll see."

A crescent moon hung off the eastern horizon like a sickle waiting to drop. The way west, where they were headed, was a cavernous maw.

The light changed and Domina turned. Two blocks from the school she pulled to the curb. "Five minutes."

Lockhart opened the car door and said, "Tell him to be careful with the pack."

"Tibby grew up with stingers," Domina said. "He'll be careful."

Inside Ms. Mansfield's sixth-grade classroom, Jerry Trailor stared at the 2-pound brick of brown heroin, trying to think. Twice a year he fielded shipments from *Las Monarcas,* the Monarchs, a Michoacán drug cartel. But before, it had always been meth.

Yesterday afternoon, he'd only had time to tuck the shipment into Ms. Mansfield's refrigerator, careful to change the lock. Then he'd gone out to Walmart and picked up a bottle of Johnson's Baby Powder.

Every six months he got a little freebie, courtesy of the Monarchs. He'd carve out six, maybe seven good hits and replace the ground crystal with baby powder, nobody the wiser. Stealing from Monarchs was risky, but no way they could track so little replaced so well. And they hadn't.

After getting the Johnson's, he'd texted his old pal Suthy.

"Coming into a little extra jack. Maybe we should head over to Shakopee and get some rooms at the casino, do a little partyin'?"

Suthy was in.

But now Jerry stared at the brick of heroin and thought, *Baby powder will show up on this stuff like snowdust on sand. No way I should touch it.*

But Jerry knew plenty of girls who would jump at a chance for a taste. Jump and kneel and do just about anything else he could imagine, which was plenty. The idea caused a hot fog to swirl below his solar plexus, clouding his mind.

Think . . .

Nobody'd miss a couple, three, maybe four good hits, nicked off at the corners. Two for me. One for Suthy. And a half each for the chiquitas.

He stared at the brick the way a kid stares at a birthday cake with sweet buttercream frosting, candles, and well wishes. It was a gift. A hot-girl gift.

But he had no way to conceal it.

But on a brick this size, who would notice?

Think . . .

He glanced at the clock's minute hand, same clock on the classroom wall when he was a kid. Same goddamn black-on-white marks he stared at before recess and end of school and last day, waiting for that minute hand to tick, waiting for that freedom bell to ring. Now, it clicked onto the black four, telling Jerry he'd better decide. In 10 minutes, he had to be at the school's side door, looking relaxed, fist-bumping his old friend Domina, business as usual, just more product passing through.

Jerry knew the smart move. Jerry always knew the smart move. He just had trouble making it.

Lockhart hustled up the street through the dark, approaching the school from its rear. He crossed through shadows to the remote side entrance and crouched behind the row of bushes.

The morning was still and black. An hour before dawn was supposed to be the coldest time of the day, but it was already 70 degrees and humid, crazy climate for Minnesota three days before Memorial Day weekend. It was as though Lockhart had walked across the street to his colonial *casa* in Morelia, Mexico, instead of the dark side entrance to Hopkins Elementary.

When he had imagined his homecoming, he had always imagined it cold, the ice man cometh. But now Minnesota had gone all global warming on him and he was going to have to improvise. *Now,* he thought, *the devil rides a hot wind, bringing grim reckoning.*

The idea did nothing to assuage the throb that spread across his scarred left cheek. He reached up to rub it and thought, *Fuckin' Minnesota.* The irony of a perfect Twin Cities spring making his burn scar ache should have made him smile. But Jon Lockhart wasn't the kind of man to smile about anything.

He heard Domina's car approach along the dark side street.

There was a faint click from inside the school's side door. It pushed open . . . 6, maybe 7 inches.

Lockhart remained still, his back pressed against the redbrick wall. The door's narrow opening faced a small walk that stretched 30 feet to the side street.

The door narrowed to a 1-inch crack.

The car pulled to a nearby curb and the idling engine turned off. A pair of car doors opened and shut. Then steps started up the walk. When they grew close, the door swung open and Jerry said, "Hey, Doms. You bring this heat from Mexico?"

Even though it had been five years, Lockhart, hidden behind the bushes, recognized Jerry's voice.

"The only things I bring from home are these guns," Domina said, turning her arms and flexing her biceps.

Domina and Jerry laughed, familiar.

Domina—"Doms"—was short and solid through the shoulders. Beneath her driving jacket, her stout arms were covered with tattoos, one of them a crucifix with a highly stylized image of Jesus, hands and feet weeping blood. Doms wore black jeans, a black Billie Eilish T-shirt, and an oversize dark-blue hat with "A's" emblazoned above the bill, for Oakland. The bill was turned off-center, resting on ears with black steel earrings piercing her cartilage.

Tiburon was two heads taller than Doms and wore a dark-blue Twins baseball cap with the bill turned sideways. His Jack Daniel's T-shirt was too tight for his ample chest and belly. The pack hung over one shoulder, riding on his back like Quasimodo's hump.

Jerry thought the way Tiburon's hat was turned sideways made him look stupid. But he didn't know the man, so he only nodded and said, *"Hola, compadre. ¿Qué pasa?"* like a wannabe Mexican gangster.

Tiburon shrugged.

"How ya' been, Jerry?" Doms said. Doms had been raised in Iowa by Mexican immigrants, so she sounded Upper Midwestern. But if she wanted, she could affect an accent as thick as a Michoacán *Monarcas.*

Doms reached out, and she and Jerry did some kind of secret handshake, slapping each others' palms.

"I been hangin'," Jerry said.

"Tiburon's my mule," Doms said, pointing to the pack.

"Damn straight," Jerry said, holding out his fist toward the big man, ready to bump knuckles. But Tiburon only stared.

"He's not so good with the English," Doms said.

Jerry dropped his fist and shrugged. "No problemo. I ain't so good with the Mexican."

The three disappeared inside and the door swung shut.

Jon Lockhart waited 30 seconds. Then he pushed off the wall and hurried to the side entrance, reaching into his pocket for a key. He put his good ear to the metal and heard voices echo down a hall, turn a corner, and fade.

Once inside, Lockhart saw a long, poorly lit hallway with rows of lockers down either side, ending at a pair of closed glass doors. In front of the doors, there was an opening, and down the left he heard Domina talking, and then someone, Jerry, laughed.

Lockhart followed without a sound.

"Here it is," Jerry said, stopping in front of a classroom door with "Ms. Mansfield" posted on the wall. Jerry's chrome chain hung almost to his knee. His long-sleeve work shirt was rolled up to his elbows, revealing the start of tattoos that ran to his shoulders, one of them an ornate cross, just like Doms's, from their time in the Arrowhead Juvenile Detention Center in Duluth, when they thought the shared Jesus would keep their gang safe. Jerry made a kind of flourish, pulling on the chain until the keys jangled out of his pocket.

"What happened to the piercings, Jerry?" Doms asked.

A long time ago, when they were both in juvie, Doms presided over Jerry's first piercing. His left cheek. One of the kids in the yard held a match to a 2-inch shingle nail until it turned white hot. Doms could still remember how Jerry had tried to act tough about it, like he could handle the pain. And for five seconds, while the hot metal burned through his cheek, he kept still. But as soon as they pulled the nail out, Jerry howled and danced like a jumping bean.

A half dozen onlookers laughed like a pack of hyenas.

Before they got out of juvie, he did it two more times: one in the lip, another in the ear lobe.

But that was more than four years ago.

"Policy, man," Jerry said. "The school district won't hire you with face piercings or too many tattoos. These tats are bad enough," he added, nodding to his arms. "Got to wear a long-sleeve shirt during the day so the brats don't see." Jerry inserted the key into the door and let them in.

Amber Mansfield's sixth-grade classroom was dark and empty. The ambient streetlight revealed three rows of seats, each with a writing surface, pointing toward the room's front. A recessed ceiling light bathed a large teacher's desk in half-glow. Behind the desk an oversize poster was taped to the wall—*The Miracle of Metamorphosis*. The poster contained four large close-ups: a monarch butterfly egg; caterpillar; pupa; and finally an adult butterfly, wings open, resting on a yellow flower.

"*Es un signo, puta,*" Tiburon said. It's a sign, bitch.

Jerry fished his iPhone out of his breast pocket, flicked on the flashlight beam, and said, "What'd he say?"

"He likes the poster," Doms said. "He thinks it's a sign."

Doms and Tiburon were members of the Monarchs. It was about being kings, but it was also the name of the large orange butterfly that overwintered in the mountains of the Mexican state they called home.

"Oh," Jerry said, remembering the affiliation. Jerry was only a contractor.

"*¿Qué dice?*" Tiburon asked. What does it say?

"'*El milagro de la metamorfosis.*'"

Tiburon didn't know "*metamorfosis.*" But he said, "*Sí. Somos milagros macarra.*"

"What?" Jerry said.

"He said, 'We're badass miracles.'"

"Damn straight," Jerry said, turning to acknowledge Tiburon's comment. But the big man was considering the poster. "The fridge is down here."

"Damn, Jerry," Doms said. "I never thought you'd bow down to the man." It was a joke, because whenever possible Jerry Trailor took the path of least resistance, played the angles, maximized personal benefit, and minimized pain.

"Sometimes you gotta give an inch," Jerry said.

"I guess," Doms said.

"Because later, you take a mile," Jerry added, and stopped in front of the half fridge.

"I hear that," Doms said. Then Doms turned to Tiburon, and even though Tiburon didn't understand English, some kind of acknowledgment passed between them. But Jerry didn't see it.

Jerry sorted through his keys, found the right one, and crouched. There was a lock on a clasp and, once it was opened, Jerry pulled on the fridge door and extracted a box. On the cardboard side was printed, "Monarch Butterfly Preserve, San Isidro De Las Palomas, Michoacán, Mexico. Fragile. *Frágil."*

Jerry returned his keys to his pocket and placed the box on the counter next to the fridge. Then he pulled a white plastic trash bag out of his pocket and said, "We gotta be careful. We don't want any of these ugly little bugs damaged or there might be questions."

Jerry used a box cutter to slice through the plastic tape. Then he opened the flaps, took off the thin cardboard covering, and shone his light on a sea of green monarch butterfly pupas. Each of them was about the size and shape of a finger digit. They were a shiny emerald, with a black stripe near their top center, along an edge marked by tiny gold dots; they were iridescent and startlingly beautiful, if you forgot they were alive.

"Creepy little mothers," Jerry said.

Doms glanced into the box and said, "Not if you think about what they become," considering the orange butterflies. Then Doms noticed something about the box—the edge of tape—and picked it up to have a closer look.

"I guess, but looks like money to me," Jerry said. "The kids can't get enough of this shit. The school district pays to have these ugly bugs shipped from Mexico, and you guys get to move a little product. Easy peazy." He handed Doms the white plastic garbage bag, but Doms didn't take it.

"You already open the box, Jerry?"

Jerry shrugged and said, "I had to look, Dommy."

"You shouldn't have opened it, Jerry."

"It felt a little funny. Heavier. I was worried, so I had a look. But I didn't touch nothin'."

Domina's face turned cold and still.

Jerry smiled, a little nervous, and said, "You didn't tell me it was heroin, Dommy." He was still holding the white bag for Domina to take, which she did, slowly.

Then Jerry carefully gripped the box, tipped it, and poured the pupas into the bag. "They're definitely disgusting," Jerry said.

When the pupas were all out of the box, Domina said, "Damn, bro. You shouldn't have done that," still talking about Jerry opening the box.

Once the emptied box was back on the counter Jerry reached in and took out a thin piece of cardboard. Under the false bottom, the 2-pound brick laid wrapped in heavy plastic.

"No biggie. It just didn't feel right. I wanted to make sure, in case there was a problem."

"How long we been doin' this?" Domina said.

Jerry shrugged. "Four years."

"We ever had a problem?"

"We never moved 2 pounds of heroin. It was always meth, and only a pound."

"What difference does it make?"

"Street value, Dommy. This much heroin is worth a lot more than meth."

"So what?"

"It's just a lot of jack. A lot more than a meth shipment. Especially on the street."

"What we get on the street shouldn't make any difference," Domina said. "To *you*."

She wasn't happy, but Jerry continued. "Just sayin', given the merchandise, maybe my payment's a little thin."

Domina looked at him until Jerry glanced away.

"Just sayin'," Jerry said.

After an uncomfortable silence, Domina said, "Let's get these bugs back in the box. Then I gotta check out this shipment. Somewhere safe. You got a place . . . out of the way?"

"Yeah," Jerry said. "I got the dungeon. Nobody goes to the dungeon. But are you thinkin' I took something?"

"Just sayin' I gotta check, now that I know you opened it."

"Sure. Check," Jerry shrugged. "But I'd never take nothin'. You know that, Dommy."

"Gotta check, Jerry." Domina knew Jerry; he was a liar, a cheat, and a punk. But he was one of those guys you liked because he made you laugh. "If everything's okay, we can talk. Maybe we got something else for you."

Jerry nodded. "Okay."

They wadded newspaper and used it to fill the space where the heroin had been. Then they reinserted the cardboard square and carefully poured the pupas on top of it. They folded down and retaped the box and returned it to the fridge.

While Jerry was locking the fridge, Tiburon opened his backpack and carefully slipped the 2-pound brick inside, beside two different-size jars. Something alive scuttled inside the jars. Tiburon's hand jerked out like he'd stuck a fork in a wall socket. But Jerry didn't see it.

After the fridge was shut and locked, Jerry led them out of the classroom and down a very long hallway into a stairwell. They walked down two flights of stairs into shadows. On the right, there was a metal door marked "Utilities."

Jerry unlocked the door and said, "Welcome to the dungeon," and walked in.

It was a narrow room with low pipes overhead, maybe 7 feet from the floor, and a huge boiler near the right back wall. The boiler had been replaced long ago by more modern HVAC technology.

Down the left side of the room was a workbench with tools strewn haphazardly on racks and across the workbench surface. Jerry walked down and made space on the bench and said, "You can check it out here, Doms. But I'd never take nothin'."

There were two old wooden school chairs sitting at a scarred wooden table holding an ashtray filled with cigarette butts.

"Have a seat, Jerry, while I take a look," Domina said.

Jerry let out an irritated sigh and sat down. He reached into his breast pocket, pulled out a lighter and a pack of Kools, and lit one. Then he inhaled and filled the space with smoke.

Domina unzipped the backpack and carefully extracted the brick.

"They let you smoke in school?" Domina said.

"Nobody comes down to the dungeon."

Domina was careful with the plastic, peering closely at the folded, taped ends. Through the clear plastic she examined the brick and noticed what appeared to be small nicks at the corners. *Jerry, Jerry, Jerry,* she thought, without betraying her suspicions. The corners could have been nicked in shipment, even though care was taken with biological cargo. There was no way to tell for sure. She was still hoping Lockhart was just going to scare her old friend. Scare the hell out of him, get some information, and then they'd all walk. Jerry would learn a lesson, and Lockhart would understand Jerry didn't know shit about Lockhart's money.

But Domina didn't know Lockhart, and over two days of driving the only thing she'd learned for certain was that the man trusted no one and was a son of a bitch, a real *puta*. If Lockhart thought Jerry had stolen any product, however insignificant, Domina's old friend could be enduring a whole lot more than pain.

So, for now all she did was look up and nod to Tiburon and say, *"Está bien. Listos."* Okay. Ready.

Then the big man walked back to the dungeon door and opened it.

Jerry, startled, watched a man with a hideous half-face walk into the room.

CHAPTER TWO

"What the hell?" Jerry said, standing.

The guy was about Jerry's height, 5 foot 9, with the left side of his face and part of his ear looking like melted candle wax. And he entered the room like he'd been expected.

"What the hell?" Jerry repeated.

"Sit down, Jerry," Lockhart said. "We need to talk."

Jerry didn't sit because the moment he heard Jon Lockhart's voice he remembered it. When he was a kid, he believed there were fiends in the world who could do a lot more than scare you. When he turned 17 and started working for Lockhart, helping him peddle meth in Isanti County, he knew he had finally met one.

Jerry stepped away from the table.

"Sit down, Jerry," Lockhart repeated. "We don't want any trouble. We just need to talk."

Tiburon came up beside Lockhart and pulled a long black handle out of his front jeans pocket. He squeezed and a blade popped out of it like a glittering tusk.

"I guess you remember me?" Lockhart said.

Jerry looked at the blade and managed a slight nod. "What gives, Doms?" Jerry said, a tremble in his voice. But he didn't look in Doms's direction. He kept glancing between Lockhart and Tiburon's knife.

"Lockhart says he knows you, Jerry." Then she turned to Lockhart. "It's all here."

"Sure it is," Lockhart said. "Jerry wouldn't steal from *Las Monarcas,* would you, Jerry?"

Jerry shook his head, too frightened to answer.

"It's okay, Jerry," Lockhart said.

But it wasn't and everyone knew it.

"Sit down," Lockhart said. "I need to ask you some questions."

Jerry paused. Lockhart and Tiburon blocked any chance of escape. Jerry sat down. His cigarette was in the ashtray, sending a thin trail of smoke into the dank dungeon air.

Lockhart glanced at Domina and made a deliberate nod in Jerry's direction. Domina reached into the pack and pulled out a roll of medical gauze. Tiburon moved toward Jerry's chair, knife ready. Domina walked over to wrap Jerry's arms to the chair's arm rests.

Jerry jerked his arm up and said, "Hey, Doms, what the hell?"

"Precautions, Jerry," Lockhart said. "Let's face it, we've got a situation here. I don't need you doing something crazy. We just want to talk and it's safest for everyone if you stay in your seat."

"I'll stay," Jerry said. "You don't need to tie me down."

Tiburon took another step forward, the blade flashing in the poorly lit room. He had an opaque expression that convinced Jerry he would have no problem using the blade, if necessary.

"Humor us, Jerry," Lockhart said. "It's just a precaution. Our little talk will take five minutes and then we're gone."

"You don't need to do this," Jerry said. "I'll tell you whatever you need to know. Promise."

"Like the promise you made five years ago, in Isanti?"

Jerry's face paled. "That wasn't me."

Domina managed to roll the gauze around Jerry's arm, circling the solid oak twice. It was woven fabric with a mildly adhesive backing, strong enough to bind the worst wounds.

"I was a kid," Jerry said. "A stupid punk. I didn't know nothin'. And that wasn't my idea. It was Maury."

Five years earlier, Maury Trumble had introduced Lockhart to the others. Lockhart, 24 and two years out of prison, made an impression on the group of 17-year-olds. First, he befriended them. Then he convinced each of them they could make serious money peddling meth to their friends. Lockhart knew how to handle teenagers. By the time they realized they should get out, departure was not an option.

Lockhart looked serious. "I wondered if it was Maury."

While Lockhart talked, Domina moved to the other arm and fastened it down with a couple of twists of tape.

"The ankles," Lockhart said.

"You don't need to do that."

"I know, Jerry. Like I said, we'll all be outta here once I get my information. That's the least you can do, don't you think?"

Domina crouched down and fastened Jerry's ankles to the chair legs.

"I'll tell you . . . whatever you need," Jerry said.

"All I need's the truth, Jerry. The truth will set you free."

Jerry looked like his last meal was seconds from reappearing. He nodded. "I'll be straight."

"That's good, Jerry. Because if you aren't straight, things could get unpleasant."

Jerry didn't say anything, but he was thinking, *Don't fuck with him. Tell him what he needs to know,* because fear was welling up in him like a poisonous fog.

"So back then," Lockhart said. "Up in Isanti. It was Maury who told them? About me?"

Jerry paused. "Maury got caught," he said.

"Maury?" Lockhart said.

Maury Trumble came from a wealthy family. Unlike the others, Maury dealt meth for the rush, and to solidify his 17-year-old reputation as a bad boy.

Jerry nodded. "Maury got caught. They scared him. He gave up all our names."

"Why didn't I know about it?"

"Nobody knew. They picked us off one by one. Everybody but you, because you were out of town. Up north, or something."

Lockhart remembered. He had gone up to Lake Vermilion to do a little gambling at a casino but had told no one. He'd taken a woman, but if she had a name, Lockhart couldn't remember it. He just remembered partying at the casino and then coming home three days later to something different, something that made the hair on the back of his neck stand up. "So what happened then?"

"Maury got to us in lockup . . . in jail. He told us not to say or do anything and he'd figure out an angle."

"Good old Maury. I bet he figured out an angle."

"Next thing we knew, we were pleading guilty to reduced sentences and everybody but Lonnie was supposed to walk."

"Lonnie was 18," Lockhart said.

"Yeah. The rest of us were 17."

"Juveniles," Lockhart said. "And Lonnie agreed to take the fall?"

Jerry didn't say anything. He looked away. Then, "Lonnie didn't know. Maury told him he was part of the deal. He'd get probation too. That we'd all walk."

Lockhart thought about it. "But Lonnie didn't walk?"

Jerry didn't answer.

"So the deal was to give up the 24-year-old leader, someone old enough to charge and convict, and everybody walks? You gave me up, Jerry? You ratted on me?"

"No!" Jerry said. "I didn't say nothin'. One minute I was headin' out to get something to eat, and the next I was pulled over and cops were swarming my car."

"So how did you get to be part of the deal?"

"Maury set it all up. He told us if we didn't talk, we'd be doing hard time. They'd try us as adults."

"So you must have done something. Signed something or told them about the operation. They don't bargain if they don't get something, Jerry."

"None of us got out! Maury set us up . . ."

Jon Lockhart held up a finger.

Jerry stopped.

"We'll get to Maury in a second. What did *you* tell them, Jerry?"

"Nothin'," Jerry said. But it was a lie.

"Jerry, you be straight with me, it's all going to be fine. If you don't tell me what I need to know . . . then we've got a problem. And we don't want that, Jerry. *You* don't want that."

Jerry looked away. "I . . . I told them my part, about the house outside of town. And the operation."

"And me. You told them about me."

Jerry finally nodded, just once.

"So it was Maury who had all the angles figured out?"

"For himself," Jerry said. "Maury walked. The rest of us did time in juvie. When they couldn't get you, they got Lonnie. Went to Stillwater."

"But you told them everything you knew. Right, Jerry?"

"They already knew," Jerry whined. Tears would have come if he thought it would have done any good. But he knew weakness would trigger Jon Lockhart. Weakness was an invitation to cruelty. So he tried to fight it, but his eyes started to glisten and he could feel his throat tighten.

"I figured something was going on," Lockhart said. "When none of you answered my calls. And then when Maury finally answered, there was something about his voice. He sounded like a carny barker with a mark." Lockhart was looking at Jerry, but he was remembering the call from five years ago.

He'd used a burner phone outside a convenience store on the edge of Virginia, up on Minnesota's Iron Range. There was a slight click, then another, and then Lockhart's neck hair stood on end. It took four rings before Maury answered. At the same instant, a picture formed in Lockhart's mind of an unmarked car hidden behind a sumac thicket and a man wearing earphones, listening in on Maury's line. Lockhart imagined more agents watching out the back window with pistols holstered to their belts. They were waiting for him.

It could have been from watching too many cop shows on TV, or an overactive imagination stimulated by paranoia. But Lockhart respected his prison sense. It had served him well.

He told Maury he'd meet him at the farmhouse in four hours.

It was grouse-hunting season. He bought a license and threw a weathered 12-gauge into his trunk, along with enough shells to look convincing. Then he hiked to a hilltop less than a mile behind the farmhouse, with one bare break in the oak savanna. If he stood just right, by the trunk of one of the ancient trees, he had a clear view of the old house. A pair of binoculars brought the ramshackle grounds in close. In less than 10 minutes, a stranger stepped out the back door. Someone he didn't recognize, with a buzz cut and a crisp new hunting vest. No gun. Like him, Lockhart thought, a hunting disguise.

If Lockhart had had a high-powered rifle and a little less savvy, he might have used it. But Jon Lockhart didn't take unnecessary chances. One day he would settle the score with Maury. And the others.

"So what happened to my money, Jerry?"

Jerry looked at him. "What money?"

"I had a lot of money in a hidey hole, Jerry." Lockhart stared and waited.

Jerry knew it was one of those moments. A crossroads. But he didn't have anything. So he went with the truth.

"We didn't know nothin' about any money. None of us ever saw any money."

Lockhart considered it. "The papers didn't say anything about recovering it. Bust like that would have been used for law enforcement advertising. I laid low for two months before going back to that farmhouse and checking, but my hole was empty. Somebody stole all my money."

Jerry looked at him, scared. "I'm tellin' ya, we didn't find any money." He was whining again. "Maybe one of the cops took it?"

"Maybe one of your friends, Jerry?"

Jerry thought about it. "Maybe," he said, recognizing opportunity. "But if they did, they never talked."

There was a pause, an edge-of-the-world kind of silence.

"I believe you, Jerry," Lockhart said. Then, "So I need to talk to the others, but I'm having trouble tracking them down. You got addresses?"

Jerry paused. Maybe he could get out of this. "I . . . I don't know. I don't know where any of them are. After juvie we lost touch."

Jerry was a bad liar.

"Got a cell phone?"

Jerry thought. If Lockhart got his phone . . .

"Shirt pocket," Domina said.

Jerry flashed a look as Domina came forward and pulled out an old iPhone with a cracked screen, handing it to Lockhart.

Lockhart looked, slid a finger over the screen, and said, "Passcode."

Jerry paused, then said, "six . . . sixes."

"Nice," Lockhart said. Then he pulled up Jerry's phone list and started flipping through the contacts. The only number he found interesting was Suthy Baxter. "*Suthy* Baxter?"

Jerry looked scared.

"That Kurt?" Back then Kurt Baxter had been one of Lockhart's 17-year-olds.

Jerry didn't say anything.

"Kurt get a nickname?"

Jerry cursed in his mind. He raced through possible answers, but none of them sounded half as convincing as the truth. He thought, *Maybe . . . maybe if I give him this one thing. Then, after they leave, I can call Suthy and warn him.* So, he said, "Yeah, I guess. In juvie."

"If you lost touch with . . . Suthy," Lockhart said, "why is his number in your phone?"

Jerry paused. "I haven't talked to him since . . ." but Jerry knew if Lockhart checked, he'd find the text message to Suthy. Recent.

Lockhart was already there. "Jerry, Jerry, Jerry. So what about the others?"

"I don't know. I don't know where they are."

"Like Suthy?"

"No," Jerry said. "Like . . . I don't know nothin' about where any of them are."

"So where's Suthy?"

Jerry hesitated. "Cambridge."

"Still in Cambridge. Got an address?"

"I don't know," Jerry said. "We just text once in a while. That's all."

"Don't you still have family in Cambridge?"

Jerry nodded.

Lockhart paused then, thinking. "I can't trust you, Jerry. I didn't know it back then, but I know it now."

"No," Jerry said. "I told you everything. Everything I know. Straight."

Lockhart turned to Domina and said, "Get the small jar." Then he turned back to Jerry and said, "You weren't straight about Suthy, Jerry."

Jerry remembered that tone, like the frayed ends of electric wires.

Domina gave Tiburon the order and he turned to the workbench, set his knife down next to the pack, reached into it, and pulled out a small jar. There was something inside the jar, but Jerry couldn't see. Tiburon handed it to Lockhart, and then Jerry saw something move, something ugly and alive.

Lockhart brought the small jar to within a foot of Jerry's eyes. "This is my friend Oscar."

It was a large scorpion, huge in the jar. Its fat claws were raised menacingly. Up close it was more than ugly. It was terrifying.

"Oscar's an emperor scorpion," Lockhart continued, "the biggest scorpion in the world." He moved the jar a little closer.

Jerry turned his face and arched his back to get away from it. His legs and hands strained against the tape.

"It's in a jar, Jerry," Lockhart chuckled. "It can't hurt you." Then he handed the scorpion back to Tiburon.

Jerry was scared. Lockhart was ice. They had said it back then. You didn't know what he was going to do. He was dangerous. He was . . . a fiend. The ones you knew were out there, waiting. The panic was starting to choke him.

"Oscar's big claws are for show, because his sting is like a wasp," Lockhart said. He turned and nodded to Tiburon and the big man brought out a larger jar, with smaller creatures inside it, things Jerry didn't want to see or know about.

"These are different," Lockhart said. He kept the jar far enough away from Jerry's face so he could see it. Inside, several smaller scorpions scuttled over the tops of each other, struggling to climb the jar's sides.

"These are very common in the place I've called home for the last three years. These guys are a little more deadly than their big cousin Oscar. In Mexico, they kill a thousand people every year. If they stung a full-grown man like you, Jerry, first you'd feel a nasty bite, like a bad wasp. Then you'd start to feel fire inside your veins, moving up your arm. These guys don't have venom, Jerry, they have truth serum. Because when it comes to stinging, everyone tells the truth. You want to get stung, Jerry?"

Jerry shook his head.

"Then tell me, Jerry . . . tell me where the others are. Let's start with Suthy's address in Cambridge."

Jerry paused. Somewhere under the fear he considered giving up Suthy's address, but, if he did, Lockhart would have confirmation of his lie. So he stuck with his prevarication, a bad choice. "I don't know. It's been five years. I don't know where they are."

"But you just told me Suthy was in Cambridge."

"He's the only one," Jerry said.

"And you don't know his address?"

Jerry shook his head.

Lockhart turned to Domina and something passed between them. Then Domina let out a sigh and turned to the roll of surgical gauze. With Tiburon's help, Domina taped Jerry's mouth shut. Then both of them stepped back.

Lockhart used chrome surgical forceps to extract one of the scorpions and maneuver its tail over Jerry's right arm, over the weeping Jesus.

"Maybe he'll help you," Lockhart said, about Jesus, lowering the tail until it was close enough to sting.

The strike was silent, but Domina could have sworn she heard a *pffftt* . . .

The first sting made Jerry's eyes roll up in his head, but only for a fluttering instant.

Domina had known it might come to this. She had always liked Jerry, but when she found out about Jerry's role in Lockhart's business five years earlier, she wasn't surprised. When she learned Lockhart would use the scorpions, she assumed that if it was necessary, it would only be one sting, a significant lesson. Now she watched Lockhart move the bug in a second time, and before Domina could do anything about it the bug was finished.

Pffftt . . .

"Then again," Lockhart grinned, about Jesus, "maybe not."

For Jerry, it felt like the white-hot shingle nail that pierced his cheek years earlier. Only the pain didn't abate; it spread. He screamed like he had back then, but all you could hear under the tape was a terrified moan. The venom left two tiny red bumps smaller than mosquito bites. But it felt to Jerry as though someone had taken a red-hot poker and shoved it up his vein, lighting his arm on fire.

Lockhart got Suthy's address . . . and everything else Jerry knew about the others, which wasn't much.

The only one Jerry had kept up with was Suthy. In addition to his address, Jerry knew he was getting some kind of college degree and would be housebound the next couple of nights, studying.

Lonnie DeLay had gotten out of prison a few months back and lived across the St. Croix River, in Hudson, Wisconsin.

All Jerry knew about Maury Trumble, who after the incident had more or less disappeared, was that his parents bought him a place somewhere in the St. Croix River valley, on the Minnesota side, near Hastings. An orchard.

Domina wrote it all down.

Then they reaffixed the tape across Jerry's mouth and Lockhart turned to Domina, tossed her a small baggie of white powder, and said, "Cook it."

The heroin, if that's what it was, was a surprise. "What's this?" Domina said.

"A little something to help Jerry with his pain," Lockhart said.

Tiburon turned to the pack and pulled out a lighter, some rubber tubing, a syringe, and a big metal spoon.

Domina wondered about the dose, if on top of the scorpion bites it'd be too much. She paused.

Lockhart said, "Do it."

Domina didn't like it, but Lockhart was running the show. Domina heated a dose of the powder in the spoon until it turned to liquid.

"When you wake up," Lockhart said, "I don't want you to breathe a word of this to anyone. You understand?"

Jerry nodded, but just barely. Because he wasn't sure he was going to wake up.

Domina avoided her old friend's eyes, because she did not have a good feeling about what Lockhart might have put in the powder. She did not feel good about any of it.

"Give it to him," Lockhart said.

Domina flashed Lockhart a look. They hadn't talked about this before picking up the shipment. The only thing they'd discussed was scorpions. They were supposed to scare Jerry. To scare and punish him. That was all.

"Trust me," Lockhart said. "It'll make him feel better."

Domina knew Lockhart wasn't the kind of man to trust. She turned to Tiburon, but the big man's face was stone.

There was no other move. Domina turned to her old friend's arm, glancing at the cross that bound them in juvie. She turned to the other arm and said, "This is going to help you, *puta.*"

Jerry was too scared to look at anything. His eyes squeezed shut and he felt the warm liquid empty into his left arm.

The rush was unlike anything Jerry Trailor had ever felt. Even in the first days he had joined Lockhart's meth trade, when a good dose of crystal made him feel immortal. For just a second, those days flashed for him like scenes from an accelerating kaleidoscope—faster than anything he thought humanly possible. A flash before his terrified eyes.

Then, darkness.

Domina stared. "Jerry," she said, loud. "Jerry!" She slapped him across the face.

"Don't leave any marks," Lockhart said.

Domina turned and Lockhart shrugged, "Guy like Jerry would have talked."

"He could have kept his mouth shut," Domina said.

"He was a liar. He deserved it. Besides, this way they'll find an OD with white heroin. It's better all the way around."

Domina thought about charging. She imagined a rush with fists. She felt pretty sure she could beat Jon Lockhart, beat him bloody. But she paused, because she knew it wasn't worth it. And she suspected Tiburon would prevent it. And her old friend Jerry had been a punk. Lockhart had the power, so Domina swallowed and turned away.

They untaped Jerry, dropping the used bandages into the pack. They wiped down everything they'd touched, including the baggie, the rest of which they stuffed in Jerry's breast pocket.

"A keepsake, Jerry," Lockhart said. Then he looked up and said, "Let's go."

At the door Lockhart paused and used a cloth to make sure the knob was unlocked and clean. They stepped into the hallway, closing the door behind them.

Domina turned at the door and, with Lockhart and Tiburon in front of her moving away, made the sign of the cross. *Old habits die hard,* she thought. *But not as hard as Jerry Trailor.*

CHAPTER THREE

In the darkened room, Sam Rivers flashed the photo of an oyamel fir onto the screen. The tree was 70 feet tall, and every branch, twig, and frond were covered with monarch butterflies, transforming the normally deep-green fir into orange-skirted brilliance.

The kids and a few parents exclaimed with awe. Sam heard an "incredible" and "ooh" and then Mac McCollum, his portly fellow special agent who had squeezed himself into one of the undersize desks, said "whoa!" loud enough to eclipse everyone.

Mac never held back.

Sam stood in front of the class in his official khaki greens, wearing work boots. The boots added an inch to his 6'2" height. His black hair was cropped short, with hints of gray at the temples. There was a small scar over his right eye and another on his left hand, remnants of altercations in the field. The scars and two-day beard growth gave him a rugged look, but everyone was staring at the screen.

To give the monarch-filled tree a sense of scale, a Mexican wildlife agent, Miguel Verde, stood at the bottom of the tree, dwarfed by the massive orange brushstroke towering above him.

Sam explained the tree full of butterflies marked the end of one of the most extraordinary migrations in nature.

"It was an hour climb up the mountain to reach this place," Sam said. "On the way up, we began seeing butterflies. Just a few at first, then more the farther we climbed. After a half hour, the air started filling with them, more and more filling the trees, until we finally came to several trees like this one up top." Sam broke off, remembering the scene. He turned and peered at the 12-year-olds, Mac, and a few parents. "You remember the first time you saw something different in nature? Something unique and remarkable? The moment I saw this tree was like that. Magical. It made me feel alive in a way I wasn't feeling before I saw it."

Sam wasn't sure the adults understood, but a small blonde girl with pigtails and glasses sat in the front row and stared at the screen as though hypnotized. Several of her classmates peered with similar intensity.

Sam Rivers had always felt a visceral appreciation for wild places. He still remembered seeing his first wolf, moose, bear, and rare woodland caribou. He had been raised in Northern Minnesota, and the one thing he knew for certain was that special manifestations of flora and fauna had always summoned a state of reverence that made him feel—for a few stolen moments— grace and awe. That's just one of the things Sam, special agent with the U.S. Fish & Wildlife Service (USFW), appreciated about being in the wild.

Even Gray, the wolf-dog hybrid who had been fidgeting beside Sam, stared up at the image on the wall, with one blue eye and one yellow, and for a moment paused. That made Sam smile because Gray was one of those animals who never stopped surprising him.

Sam continued displaying pictures of the remote mountain forest, narrating as the images appeared.

Six weeks earlier, Mac had asked Sam to speak to his niece Amber Mansfield's class. Mac knew Sam had been to the Michoacán butterfly preserves, and he suspected Sam would appreciate an excuse to leave his Denver, Colorado, office early. After the long Memorial Day weekend, Sam was expected on Isle Royale, where he was going to help wolf researchers consider the best way to reintroduce new blood into their isolated pack.

Today was Wednesday, six days before Sam was due on Royale, which would have given him plenty of time for a side trip to Defiance, up on the Iron Range, where he had been looking forward to spending a few days with Diane Talbott, his occasional girlfriend. It had been a great plan, and the moment Sam agreed to talk to the kids, he phoned Diane.

After the initial hellos, Sam said, "What are you doing Memorial Day weekend?"

"Uhh," Diane paused. "I've been meaning to call you."

Normally that would have been a good response, but her tone conveyed something different.

"I was going to call *you* earlier," Sam said. "But some stuff came up on the Western Slope and I had to be out of pocket for a while."

They both knew it was an excuse. When it came to cell phone coverage, even the Rockies' Western Slope wasn't a total dead zone.

"That's okay, Sam."

Uh-oh. It wasn't "okay," and Sam knew it.

"Sam," Diane said, "I met someone local."

Diane Talbott was an attractive woman, and he knew there was no want of Iron Range men—single or married—who would love to spend time with her. But she'd chosen to be single for most of her adult life and Sam considered their long-distance relationship a convenient way she could have the best of both worlds. Diane liked her alone time, and Sam—divorced for two years—still needed his.

"A guy?" Sam said. It was a stupid question.

"Sam."

"Who?" Another stupid question.

"Sam, you don't know him."

And it didn't matter, Sam knew. But he couldn't deny it swept through him like a nor'easter, for a moment knocking him off-center, which had prompted the stupid questions.

He was surprised by how quickly he righted himself.

"I guess a bird in the hand . . ." Sam said.

About a thousand miles separated Sam's Colorado home from Diane's place outside Defiance, which he figured was too great a distance for a sustained relationship . . . at least for them. Sam didn't blame her. But it would be difficult forgetting the image of the well-contoured journalist, particularly when she stood in front of him wearing nothing but wool socks. And that made him realize how much more their relationship had been about bed than breakfast.

". . . is worth two in the bush," Diane said.

Sam told her he would miss their visits, but he understood. He thought he heard Diane sniffle, but it was more likely a weak connection. Then they both wished each other good luck and hung up.

This morning over breakfast Sam had broken his news about Diane to Mac.

"Sorry to hear it," Mac said. "You can come up with me and Margie and the kids and her entire extended family to the lake. Your presence would be welcome, considering her two Libertarian brothers think they pay my salary and never tire of telling me so. Maybe if you were along, they'd back off."

"It's a tempting offer," Sam said. "But I've met Margie's brothers." Then, "Maybe I'll take a slow drive up Superior's North Shore and do some hiking. I'm overdue for some wilderness time."

"You don't need to spend any more time alone, Rivers," Mac said. "You need to figure out something that requires my assistance so I can postpone my visit with the Libertarians."

"Why don't you come with me? We could do a little backpacking."

"For starters, that won't pass Margie's excuse test. And then there's this," Mac said, patting his belly, "which interferes with physical exercise."

While Sam finished one egg over medium, a piece of dry toast, and a little juice, Mac worked his way through a big stack, a three-egg omelet, two pieces of buttered toast, and a pile of bacon. The "lumberjack special" was about as close as Mac got to physical labor. Which was okay, since he was looking at retirement in the not-too-distant future.

"Gotta hit the head," Mac said, pushing away his plate.

Mac had a large leather bag with a strap that he carried everywhere because he thought it made him look hip and urban. Sam called it a man-purse, or murse. While Mac was in the bathroom, Sam took out a scent poke of heroin and hid it in the bottom of Mac's murse. A heroin poke was a wrapped, thumb-size baggie that contained trace amounts of the drug. Sam used it to train Gray and for demonstrations. And for occasional displays of public embarrassment, when they could be arranged.

Back in the classroom, Sam explained why he had made his late-fall trip to the monarch butterfly preserves in Michoacán, Mexico. "Gray and I were invited to Mexico to help wildlife biologist Miguel Verde reintroduce rare Mexican wolves into the countryside of Northern and Central Mexico. Miguel heard about our efforts in the States, and he thought we might have some useful advice on how to proceed and what to expect.

"Since I have always been interested in visiting the overwintering site of the monarch butterfly, Miguel showed me around. But as often happens in our line of work, we stumbled onto the unexpected, something that makes the work you kids are doing here with your monarch butterflies very important."

"Cool!" one of the kids said. He was skinny with uncombed hair and an agitated demeanor, as though he'd skipped his morning Adderall.

"Neil," Ms. Mansfield said, silencing the overexcited boy.

The rest of the kids liked to hear they were helping the butterflies, and that it was *work*. The parents, too, appeared interested.

Sam's next image showed a field of stumps, maybe 10 mature trees felled. Around the stumps the ground was covered with what looked like a river of faded orange blood.

"If you understand the ecology of oyamel firs, you understand why the monarchs have chosen to overwinter here. The fir trees help absorb sunlight and keep the butterflies warm. Without the trees, butterflies can freeze to death, as these did after the felling of their homes."

When the kids realized the ground was covered with dead butterflies, they fell into stunned silence.

"That's awful," Mac said.

"Over the next few minutes, I'm going to share a crime story with you. Like many of the crimes we get involved with—as special agents with the U.S. Fish & Wildlife Service—this one started with a protected area and species and involved greed and ignorance and maybe a little cruelty, and a man who lost sight of what was important in life. But it has a happy ending."

Sam flashed more pictures onto the screen until he came to a police booking photograph of a middle-aged man with a balding pate and sideburns starting to gray. There were two images on the screen: mug shots of a front and side view.

Gray sat beside Sam. He was wearing an orange service dog marker around his collar. Normally he stood still as a regal statue, but he was fidgeting. As Sam paused in his story, the wolf dog came out of his sit and started to sneak down the classroom's side aisle like a furtive 12-year-old. But sneaking is difficult for a wolf dog who stands 37 inches at the shoulder.

"Gray!" Sam said.

Some of the kids smiled.

Gray turned and glanced at Sam, then turned back around and continued walking.

"Gray!"

Gray stopped at the half fridge and began pawing the locked door.

"Sorry about this," Sam said, starting into the aisle.

"Maybe you didn't give him enough breakfast," Mac said.

More kids smiled, and Neil said, "My dog likes fish chews. My mom keeps those in the fridge."

A couple of kids laughed, and Sam turned to Ms. Mansfield and said, "What's in the refrigerator?"

"Just some water and soda," Ms. Mansfield said. "And the monarch butterfly pupas."

Gray's behavior was odd. He had been fed, so it wasn't food. And the wolf dog knew he was going to perform. Before class, Sam had coached him with another heroin scent poke and let him know they would be looking for it, and the one in Mac's murse. But something in the fridge triggered his nose. Sam put Gray in a sit and said, "Can you open it?"

"Normally I can, but Jerry changed the lock," Ms. Mansfield said, with irritation. "He's our maintenance engineer."

"That's a name for *janitor*," the blonde girl said.

Some of the kids chuckled.

"Celeste!" Ms. Mansfield said.

"Can we get him to open it?" Sam said.

"Sure. I'll call him."

Ms. Mansfield glanced at the wall clock and saw it was 9:50. "Ten minutes to recess," she said. "We can get him up here then."

"Since Gray decided to interrupt my story, maybe we'll take a moment to demonstrate his drug-sniffing skills."

Neil's hand shot into the air.

"Neil," Ms. Mansfield said.

"Is he a wolf?"

"He's a wolf dog," Sam said. "A hybrid. His father was an arctic wolf, and his mother was a malamute."

"What's wrong with his eyes?"

"The different colored eyes are caused by a condition called heterochromia."

"Does it give him special powers?" Celeste asked.

Sam grinned. "I've worked with him long enough to make me wonder," Sam said. "But no, he has normal eyesight."

The classroom eased, but definitely conveyed appreciation for Gray, which caused Sam to add, "In many states it's illegal to breed or sell wolf dogs. That's not the case in Minnesota. But there are plenty of professionals, me included, who think it should be illegal. Gray was a rescue animal. He was the lone survivor of a breeder who did not care for the animals and whose only motivation was money."

Sam was quick to point out that he did not recommend wolf-dog hybrids and that they could be problematic pets, but that you had to consider each animal on its own merits. Early on he recognized Gray was not only extremely intelligent but also had a superb sense of smell. Lately Gray had grown adept at finding the most common illicit drugs. And that skill set, as well as others, made Sam recognize his value in the field.

Sam explained how they used Gray's scent-tracking skills last fall in the Minnesota River Valley to track some very bad people and bring them to justice. He also explained how scent-tracking dogs could be trained to follow trail scents, scents over and under water, and to sniff out cadavers.

When none of the kids reacted, Sam said, "Cadavers are dead people."

"Ooh," Sam heard. And "creepy."

"Usually, scent-tracking dogs specialize in sniffing out specific substances like drugs or gunpowder or plastic explosives. But Gray here is one of those rare animals who has a nose that can be used to sniff out just about anything, given the proper training."

Sam paused, peering at his friend. In addition to Gray's multicolored eyes, his long hair was a mix of gray, black, white, and brown. His legs were preternaturally long, and he had paws designed to chase whitetail over deep snow. In many overt and subtle ways, he was a remarkable animal. But most importantly, he'd come into Sam's life at a time when both of them needed each other.

"While he was a rescue animal," Sam concluded, "I often feel he rescued me as much as I rescued him."

It was a good time to demonstrate the wolf dog's drug-sniffing skills.

"Once I give Gray the signal he will begin searching. At that point he becomes pretty much obsessed and doesn't stop searching until he finds something, or I call off the hunt."

Before class Sam and Ms. Mansfield had secreted a heroin poke behind some books in a rear bookshelf. Now Sam waved his hand forward and said, "Find." The wolf dog's nose became hyperactive. Gray searched down the row, over desks, onto the floor, jerking excitedly from side to side. Some of the kids reared back and Neil squealed. Eventually Gray found his way to the books, pawing at the exact location where the poke was hidden.

The kids loved the demonstration. While they were exclaiming about Gray's skill, Sam signaled Gray to continue searching. Gray shifted and again turned from desk to desk, making his way to Mac, whose murse sat on the undersize writing surface in front of him.

Gray stared at Mac, then the murse. Then Mac, then the murse. Mac and the wolf dog were eye to eye.

"What's going on, Rivers?" Mac said, worried.

Gray reached up and placed a massive wolf paw on Mac's leather bag.

"I should be asking you the same question, Agent McCollum."

"I got nothing in there but my wallet and . . ."

"Fish chews?" Sam said.

The kids started laughing.

When Sam checked Mac's bag, he pulled out the second heroin scent poke. Gray's tail wagged and Sam rewarded the wolf dog with touch and praise before turning to Mac and saying, "Agent McCollum, you're busted."

"Rivers," Mac said.

Then the buzzer rang and Ms. Mansfield said, "Fifteen minutes. Then we will hear the rest of Agent Rivers's story."

The kids scrambled out of the classroom.

CHAPTER FOUR

As soon as Gray was finished with the demonstration his attention returned to the half fridge. Sam was still smiling at Mac, who had finally extricated himself from the desk.

"That was a lame stunt, Rivers."

"I always suspected you had a dark secret, Uncle Mac," Amber Mansfield said.

Sam glanced over at Gray, who was keeping vigil in front of the fridge. "Amber, do we have time to fetch that key?"

"Sure. I can call Jerry. He should be down in his office."

As she walked to the front of the classroom, a woman came through the door.

"Dr. Rodriguez," Amber said, greeting her.

"Sorry I'm late." When Dr. Rodriguez saw the empty desks, she said, "Did I miss it?"

"Only the drug-sniffing demonstration," Amber said. "You would have enjoyed it."

Sam assumed that Dr. Rodriguez was a parent. When she turned and glanced in Sam and Mac's direction, she paid cursory attention to the adults. Her gaze focused on Gray pawing the fridge door.

"I bet I would have," she said, turning toward the big hybrid.

Sam was about to tell Dr. Rodriguez she needed to be introduced.

Then Dr. Rodriguez said, "Gray?"

Gray turned to consider her. Unexpectedly, his tail made a slow wag.

"How do you know . . ." Sam started. Then he remembered.

Last fall Gray had been shot—grazed, really—in the Savannah Swamp south of Shakopee. After a rare cougar-human predation, Sam had been asked to review the tragedy. With the help of Gray, Sam uncovered much more than the alleged predation. When Gray was following a trail into the swamp, a murderer lay in wait, taking aim at the hybrid with a 9-mm. The slug sliced the top of Gray's rear flank. Sam rushed Gray to a late-night veterinarian who stitched Gray's wound. That had been Dr. Rodriguez.

She came close and spoke softly to Gray. Sam was about to tell her she *still* needed to be introduced, but whatever she said made his tail wag faster.

It was unusual behavior for the wolf dog. Gray had strong pack animal instincts and Sam was his pack, at least for now. Anyone outside the pack was regarded with suspicion.

"And Agent Sam Rivers," she said, turning to him.

She had green eyes. Sam remembered them because they were uncommon, and when she worked on Gray they focused with startling intensity.

"Doctor," he nodded, shaking her hand.

"Carmel," she said. "Carmel Rodriguez. And I told you that magnificent animal was going to fill out."

Last fall, after she'd finished doctoring Gray, she'd weighed him and predicted he was going to add another 30 pounds to his frame. At the time Gray had been a year old and Sam doubted her opinion. But in the intervening months, Gray had gained 27 more pounds, not an ounce of it fat.

Sam also remembered something else. "I thought your name was . . . Susan?"

She paused. "I used to go by my middle name," she said.

Gray's attention returned to the fridge.

Before she could explain, Amber, who had been trying to call Jerry, said, "He's not answering."

Sam turned to her. "Got his cell?"

"This *is* his cell. He's supposed to pick up. Maybe it's turned off. Or he's out of juice? He should be down in his office. If you want that key, we'll have to go get it," Amber said. "Or you and Mac will. I have to stay in the classroom."

"We can get it," Sam said.

"Gray doesn't look like he wants to leave that fridge," Carmel Rodriguez said.

"Wonder what's up his nose?"

"Maybe deception," Mac said, "given your recent little stunt."

"Deception is odorless," Sam said. "Though I wouldn't be surprised if Gray could pick it up."

Sam put Gray in a heel and had to leash him to pull his attention from the fridge.

Mac trailed behind.

"Where can we find him?" Sam asked.

Amber considered how best to explain the route to Jerry's utility room.

"Is that the dungeon?" Carmel said.

"Do you know it?"

"Jennifer's told me about it. The kids tease about the place. Never been there, but Jennifer told me where it is."

"Nobody ever goes down there, so the kids try and scare each other about it. It's at the end of the other wing. Can you show them?"

The elementary school had two, single-story wings, except for one set of stairs that went down to the dungeon.

Once in the corridor the wolf dog seemed to take on a new interest and began following, then leading Sam, pulling him in front of Carmel and Mac.

"Looks like Gray knows the way," Carmel said.

"Not sure what he's doing," Sam said.

"Hybrids can be unpredictable," Carmel said. "Personally and professionally, I don't recommend them. But sometimes they surprise you. And, as I recall, this one was a rescue animal?"

"That's right."

"From the hell kennels of Angus Moon," Mac said.

Mac had been part of the cleanup crew at Angus Moon's backwoods kennel. There was a broken-down trailer at the end of a twisted drive and narrow cages with dirt floors where Moon had bred wolves with the largest dogs he could find. Moon was one of the most diabolical men Mac and Sam had ever encountered. He murdered without conscience and took pleasure in treating his animals with a brutal hand. In the end, Gray, a puppy, had been found chained to his mother's dead body.

"He seems pretty well socialized for being born into a hell kennel," Carmel said.

"We've spent a lot of time together and I've worked him pretty hard," Sam said. "We're learning as we go. But a lot of it is just character. He was born this way. From the moment I first met him I knew he was special."

"I understand the special," Carmel said, considering Gray. "I see them once in a while. I mean dogs, not hybrids. But they're almost always mixed breeds, sort of like Gray. He's definitely handsome."

Gray led them around a corner and started toward a distant stairwell. "This is how he acts when he's following scent," Sam said.

"He's definitely on the trail of something," Carmel said.

Gray led them to the top of the stairs, and they descended two flights into the poorly lit cellar, stepping in front of a door marked "Utilities." There was a narrow slice of light beneath the door's threshold.

"What was his name?" Mac asked.

"Jerry Trailor," Carmel said.

Sam knocked. "Jerry?"

Gray was focused on the door.

They waited a few moments, listening. But there was nothing. Then Sam tried the knob, found it unlocked, and pushed the door open.

A man sat at a table, his head sagging on his chest. A syringe was stuck in his left forearm. His face—what they could see of it—was pale as the underbelly of a bottom-feeding fish. Jerry Trailor, if that's who it was. There was an eerie stillness in his body and the room. Death. Sam recognized it. So did Carmel.

"Oh God," Mac said.

CHAPTER FIVE

M ac and Carmel looked on in stunned silence. Sam stepped into the room. Gray started to follow, but Sam handed Gray's leash to Mac and said, "Hold him."

Sam had witnessed scenes of premature and unexpected death, but he had never grown used to it.

Carmel took a step toward the victim.

"Wait," Sam said.

Carmel paused, then said, "I was just going to confirm, but . . . he's gone."

Most civilians, Sam knew, would have turned away. "We just need to be careful. Technically, it's a crime scene, especially since it's in an elementary school."

Even though the victim appeared to have been dead awhile, his face was contorted into a death mask of pain. Sam thought he caught a whiff of something—tobacco smoke with a strong overlay of perspiration. But there was something else in the dungeon. Fear? Something.

Whenever Sam encountered a scene like this one—like the field of stumps in the Michoacán mountains or the kill scene last fall in Savage, Minnesota, or Angus Moon's north woods compound—controlled fascination swept through him like an adrenalin surge. He leaned into the room, stepping forward. As Sam neared Jerry, the smell of sweat was strong.

The victim sat in an old school chair. He wasn't *at* the table; he was angled toward it. Sam looked at the scene, imagining how it might have happened. A workbench ran against the wall. It was unkempt, with several tools spread across it. Sam eyed a large soup spoon, probably a cooking spoon, next to a disposable lighter. He imagined Jerry at the workbench, pouring a quantity of something into the spoon, using the lighter to heat it to a liquid, and then using the syringe to suck it up. Sam watched him cross over to the table, pull out the chair, sit down, tie off his elbow with the rubber tubing, surface a vein, and use it as the delivery channel for whatever he put inside himself that—unexpectedly, Sam assumed—caused his death.

But the imagined scene didn't feel right. The position of the chair was wrong, for starters. The way it was angled beside the table. If he used his right arm to inject himself with whatever (heroin?), he should be nearer the table. And why didn't he do it all at the table, where he could sit, rather than standing at the workbench?

The rear of the room contained a hulking boiler, clearly no longer operational. To the side, a more modern HVAC unit had replaced it. There were shadows behind the old boiler, probably a nest site for dust balls and mice, given the dank mix of smells.

Sam reached down with his index and middle finger and touched the victim's neck. Clammy.

"He's been gone awhile," Sam said.

"It's horrible," Carmel said. "In Hopkins . . . my daughter's school."

"I agree," Mac said.

"Definitely ugly," Sam said. "Mac, can you go up to the office and tell them to call the police and then cordon off the top of the stairs. We don't want anyone coming down here, particularly kids."

Mac nodded. "I'm on it."

"Tell them we don't think any kids are in danger. We're pretty sure it's an isolated incident," Sam said, trying to find the right words. "And it's not an emergency. There's no reason to make a scene."

Mac nodded again and handed the leash to Carmel. Then he turned and disappeared.

"Carmel, can you keep Gray back? I don't want him nosing around until somebody local has a chance to look at things."

Carmel nodded. She was quiet and attentive and had remained in the door's threshold.

"Are you okay?" Sam said.

She gave a quick nod. "Just shocked."

"Understandable," Sam said. "Me too."

When Gray heard his name, he looked up at Sam, awaiting his chance to join in the hunt. Sam had partnered with a lot of dogs over the years. They'd provided solace and, though they couldn't talk, they'd been among his best friends. But he had never met any that were quite as earnest or intelligent as Gray. "It's okay, boy. You'll get your chance." When he thought the dog understood, he continued.

Sam bent over Jerry Trailor's body and peered at the dead man's face. Sam thought he looked startled, as though he may have been surprised by the dose. Sam examined the syringe and the victim's left arm. Tattoos covered his arm from wrist to elbow, disappearing under his rolled-up sleeve. Apart from the needle hanging out of a vein, Sam thought Jerry's skin appeared clean. Serious junkies would have some needle marks, but Jerry didn't have any, at least in his left arm.

Sam took a close look at Jerry's right arm. It, too, was tattooed, the most prominent a crucifix with Jesus weeping tears of blood. There were two very small beads of dried blood on the top of the supine Jesus, spaced close together. A heroin addict would use a vein from under his arm. Sam leaned in to have a closer look and saw minor, red irritations around the blood.

Maybe he tried here first? Sam wondered. But given the placement, it didn't make sense. Sam also noticed the right forearm was slightly larger than the left. Probably right-handed, so the choice of his left arm for the needle seemed correct.

Sam turned to the workbench, but the only odd items were the cooking spoon and lighter. There was a pack of Kools on the table next to an ashtray filled with butts. It was another confirmation that no one visited the dungeon because smoking in schools was forbidden. Moreover, unless the school's administration looked the other way, the guy could have been fired for smoking in the school. Sam guessed if parents found out about it, the man would have been crucified.

Not that it mattered . . . at least for Jerry Trailor.

Maybe the absence of tracks was another indication the victim was an inexperienced drug user, which would support the idea he got in over his head and shot up a lethal dose by mistake. But Sam knew he could have been using some other part of his body for previous doses—his groin, between his toes, maybe an ankle or foot or anywhere else he could surface a large enough vein. The medical examiner would look over the rest of his body and the authorities would check his records and see if he had any drug-abuse history. That might better explain the overdose.

"I can't see that he's used," Sam said. "At least recently, apart from this time."

"Can I have a look?" Carmel said. She was still in the doorway. Gray was staring at Sam, waiting for his chance to enter the room.

Sam was surprised by Carmel's request, which must have shown on his face.

"I was a med student before I transferred to vet school," she explained. "We did human anatomy our first year. Some of the cadavers we dissected were drug users."

Another surprise. "Sure," he said. He came forward and took Gray's leash. "Just be careful you don't touch anything."

"I know. A crime scene."

Carmel approached Jerry's body and spent the next couple of minutes examining him. Like Sam, she placed her fingers on his neck, but otherwise touched nothing.

"He's been dead awhile," she said.

"Rigor?" Sam said.

She nodded. "And temperature. The rigor is starting. I suspect he's been dead at least three hours. Maybe more."

That could put the time of death before dawn. Sam wondered when Jerry started in the morning. "Anything else?"

"If he's a user, he's never used this arm. At least before this. His right arm has some curious marks, on that crucifix tattoo, but they look like bug bites. Maybe mosquitoes?"

"I agree, except when mosquitoes sting, they suck blood and replace it with an anticoagulant. That's what makes it swell and itch. There's usually a larger irritation."

After Sam mentioned it, Carmel recalled the chemistry of the ubiquitous pest bites. "That's right," she said. "Maybe spider bites?"

"Maybe. But it's an odd place for spider bites. On top of his arm, he should have felt it or seen it."

"Maybe while he was sleeping?" She peered in closer to look at them. "But they look more recent than something that happened last night."

There was a long chrome chain hanging out of Jerry's front pocket, with its end linked around a belt loop. Judging from the bulge in his pants pocket, it held keys.

"Gray's dying to get in here and have a look, but first I want him to take a look at that half fridge," Sam said. "Can you take him while I search for the keys?"

Carmel took Gray's leash while Sam turned to the workbench, found a pair of needle-nose pliers, and stepped toward Jerry. He used the pliers to coax the keys out of Jerry's pocket, unclipping the key ring, using the needle nose to hold it.

"Let's go have a look."

"We're just going to leave him?" Carmel said, about Jerry.

Sam turned. "He's not going anywhere. We won't be gone long."

By the time they returned to the classroom the kids were ambling back to their desks. While Sam moved down the aisle to the half fridge, Carmel gave a sweet wave to a dark-haired girl near the front of the classroom and then walked over to Amber Mansfield. Carmel turned her back to the class and told Amber what they'd found.

Amber's hand went to her mouth, trying to conceal her shock.

At the half fridge, Sam worked through the keys, while behind him, an excited Neil asked, "Are we going to get our monarchs now?"

"Not yet," Sam said.

"Neil, get back to your seat," Amber said in teacher mode. "Class, something has come up and Agent Rivers is going to be busy for a while."

Not hearing the rest of Sam's story likely meant they would be doing classwork.

"Aw, come on," Neil said.

Amber's Medusa stare silenced Neil's outburst. Then, "I know it's disappointing, so for now, let's do a free read. Find your books and continue reading *Hatchet,*" she said. That made some of the kids happy. Neil, clearly a nonreader, groaned.

Gray was beside Sam, still demonstrating intense interest in the contents of the fridge. Sam finally opened the door and counted bottled water, a couple of Frescas, and a box, reading the side lettering—"Monarch Butterfly Preserve"—and the rest of the label. He pulled it out and set it on the counter, and Gray followed it with his eyes.

"We'll check it, buddy. Just a sec."

Sam carefully examined it. The box had been opened and retaped at least once. Maybe a couple of times. Sam took one of Jerry Trailor's keys and used the sharp end to cut the seam. After opening the flaps, he lifted off a thin cardboard covering.

The box was full of iridescent green monarch pupas. They shimmered under the classroom lights. He parted some with his index finger and felt a false bottom, squishy under his finger's pressure. He lifted the box, but there was no extra weight in it. He bent a corner of the false bottom and saw wadded newspaper beneath it. He fingered down beside the newspaper until he touched the box bottom. Clearly it held only monarch pupas.

He moved the box down for Gray to examine it, and when he started to raise his paw to affirm it was the item of interest, Sam pulled it away. "That's okay, buddy," he said to Gray, who seemed to frown.

Sam placed the box on the countertop and folded down the box flaps. Then he returned it to the fridge.

Sam wondered if Jerry had trace amounts of heroin on his hands when he transferred the box to the fridge. Drug-sniffing animals like Gray could locate heroin from a few molecules.

Sam recognized the Mexican town from the lettering on the side of the box: San Isidro De Las Palomas. It was a gateway to the nearby mountaintops where the monarchs overwintered. He remembered a charming cathedral and some houses and a hotel, La Englaterra. There were a few cafés. He and Miguel had eaten at two of them. It was a pleasant place.

Sam would have to ask Miguel about the Monarch Butterfly Preserve. The name was generic enough. But something about it, about buying monarch pupas from Michoacán—other than the extra hassle of getting them across the border—didn't seem right. As Sam remembered it, monarchs didn't lay eggs as far south as Michoacán, which was in Central Mexico. They waited until they reached milkweed plants in Northern Mexico or more likely the Southern US. As Sam recalled, they only overwintered in Michoacán. Maybe someone was caging them and breeding them in San Isidro?

The Michoacán origination of the pupas seemed odd.

Sam's cell phone vibrated, and he picked up. "Mac?"

"You still down there?"

"No. But I can be in a couple of minutes."

"Detective Marschel is here. We're on our way. And the EMTs are right behind us."

"We'll meet you. I've got the key," Sam said, and hung up.

He walked up to Amber Mansfield and with his back turned to the class said, "I'll have to take a rain check on telling the rest of my story."

"That's fine," Amber whispered. "I'm so sorry. I didn't know him that well, but I'm shocked. Just shocked."

"I've got to meet a police officer," Sam continued.

"I'll go with you," Carmel said.

The kids who were looking up from *Hatchet* heard only whispers. But they could read adult faces; something was awry, and it was serious.

CHAPTER SIX

Sam, Carmel, and Gray came around the corner and saw Mac with a taller, younger companion in street clothes. Sam figured the first officer on the scene would have been a blue coat, but if this was a detective, better.

The officer must have been 6 feet tall, with her shiny black hair pulled tight to her head. Her ears were set off with a pair of delicate pearl earrings. She had an aquiline nose that reminded Sam of Diana Ross, from the Supremes, when she was younger. Except the detective was taller and fitter. She wore a short tan skirt with a red blouse, opened at the collar, and a pair of cordovan pumps. Her legs looked like they'd seen plenty of gym time.

As they approached, she considered Gray with a wary eye.

"That was pretty fast," Sam said. "Detective?"

"That's right. Raven Marschel." She shook Sam's hand like a golf pro with a power grip. "I was on my way into work. The station's just a few blocks from here." After dropping Sam's hand, she said, "Got some ID?"

Sam took out his badge and opened it. Normally an ID check was perfunctory, but Marschel examined it.

The top of the badge was covered by a pair of wings spread above an oversize blue "US." Beneath it, a large ring circled a duck taking flight over a jumping trout. Printed inside the ring was "Department of the Interior—U.S. Fish and Wildlife Service." The bottom of the badge was marked by a big blue banner that declared "Special Agent" in oversize lettering.

While she examined his ID Sam noticed a gold wedding band on her left ring finger.

"Fish and Wildlife?" Marschel said.

Sam nodded. "I'm out of the Denver office and Agent McCollum's from St. Paul."

"Can't recall I've ever worked with Fish and Wildlife."

Most cops had a vague notion of what USFW officers did and respected it. Some didn't know but respected them as fellow law enforcement officers. Others didn't know and didn't care. If Sam were to guess, he would have placed Marschel in the middle group, but you could never tell with first impressions.

"If it's a crime and it involves wildlife, we get involved," Sam said.

"Do you remember last fall?" Carmel said. "An executive was killed by a cougar in Savage, Minnesota. At least, allegedly. It turned out to be a murder."

Marschel thought about it. "I remember. It was his wife, wasn't it?"

"These guys and Gray," Carmel said, indicating the wolf dog, "solved that murder."

"Didn't the woman get away?"

"There were three involved with the murder," Sam said. "One is dead, one in prison, and, yes, the wife got away. For now."

"Huh," Marschel said, noncommittal. Then she turned to Carmel and asked, "Who are you?"

"Dr. Carmel Rodriguez," she said, offering her hand.

Marschel shook it and said, "You know the victim?"

"No. My daughter's a sixth grader. I was helping the agents find the utility room where Jerry, the janitor, was found."

The detective considered it. Then a policeman turned the corner and they all watched him approach.

Detective Marschel greeted him as "Spencer" and told him to stay at the top of the stairs. "Watch for the EMTs. Don't let anyone else down."

Spencer nodded.

Sam started to introduce Gray to Marschel, but Marschel cut him off. "Show me the victim," she said.

With regard to dogs, some people loved them, some didn't, and some didn't know because they'd never shared a life with one. Again, Sam gave the detective the benefit of the doubt and assumed she'd never had a dog, because once you had a dog and got to know it, what kind of person wouldn't like them?

Sam started down the stairs with Gray. When Carmel and Mac also started down, Marschel stopped and said, "We don't need everyone down there."

"There's plenty of room," Sam said. "And you might be interested in their impressions." When the detective paused, considering, Sam added, "Dr. Rodriguez examined the body. You might be interested in her professional opinion."

With piercing hazel eyes, Marschel reconsidered her. "Okay," she said. "But we don't need the dog."

"Gray is a drug-sniffing dog," Sam said. "He was actually the reason we went to find Jerry Trailor. Gray sensed something long before any of us. And if there's heroin in that room, he'll find it."

"Heroin?" Marschel said. "We haven't seen that in a while. Be strange to see it surface in an elementary school. You think that's how he died?"

"There's a syringe sticking out of the victim's arm and cooking paraphernalia on his workbench."

"Could be meth."

"Could be," Sam said. "But I don't think so."

Marschel peered down the stairs into the shadows and appraised the width of the hallway. But she ignored the dog. "Okay," she said. "Let's go have a look. But everyone stays out of the room."

Marschel led the way, and Sam and Mac exchanged a glance that said, *prima donna*. They followed her down the stairs and Sam stopped at the door to unlock it.

"Was it locked?" Marschel asked. "Before? When you first came down here?"

"No," Sam said. "The door was closed, but it was unlocked."

"Odd if he was shootin' up with the door unlocked."

"Good point. But I don't think he got many visitors," Sam said. "It's remote from the classrooms and the rest of the building."

Marschel said, "Remind me. Why were you coming down here?"

Sam explained about Gray's demonstration, the half fridge, the need to let Gray see what was inside, them coming to get the key and finding the victim and then returning to open and search the half fridge.

"Find anything in the fridge?"

"Just some soda and a box of monarch pupas from Mexico. But there's something about that box; otherwise, Gray wouldn't have been interested. Could be that Jerry Trailor stowed the box in the fridge and had some heroin residue on his hands. Maybe," Sam shrugged, but he wasn't feeling certain about it.

"What from Mexico?" Marschel said.

"Monarch pupas, or chrysalises."

Marschel's gaze still held a question.

"The pupas of the monarch butterfly," Sam said. "The kids are doing a unit on metamorphosis and the pupas are for their unit. After a week they turn into butterflies."

Marschel frowned. "My grade-school science is a little rusty."

Sam explained the life cycle. Egg to caterpillar, caterpillar to pupa, pupa to adult butterfly. "Metamorphosis," Sam said. "That's the term they use when an animal, postembryonic, goes through a change that transforms its structure. Like when a tadpole becomes a frog."

"So, just pupas," Marschel said, without much interest. "Nothing else in the box?"

"That's it," Sam said.

Marschel wondered about it. Then she dug into her pants pocket for a pair of surgical gloves and pulled them on. "I don't suppose you wore gloves?"

"We weren't expecting a crime scene," Sam said. "But we didn't touch anything."

"Except the victim's neck," Carmel said.

"Except the neck," Sam said. "To make sure he was dead."

"You couldn't tell if he was dead?"

"We thought he was gone the minute we opened the door. Dr. Rodriguez suspects, judging from skin temperature and stiffness, the victim died before dawn."

"Anybody else go in?"

"Just me. Then Dr. Rodriguez, who confirmed the death. We should let Gray nose around, see what he can find."

Marschel glanced at the dog, then back into the room.

Regular law enforcement sometimes considered U.S. Fish & Wildlife personnel out of their area of expertise when investigating street crimes. What they didn't understand is that wildlife crimes always involved humans, often occurring in remote places where Detective Raven Marschel might have struggled like a Cub Scout lost in a cattail swamp off the River Styx.

"Stay here," Marschel said.

When Marschel turned and entered the room, Mac and Sam exchanged another glance. This time Mac mouthed, "friendly," and frowned.

Carmel watched Marschel work.

With Carmel's attention elsewhere, Sam couldn't help but glance at her. Her long, black hair was pulled back and cinched behind her neck with a turquoise clasp. There were wisps of gray at her temples. If she wore makeup, it was subtle. She reached up and scratched her neck beneath her left earlobe. Her fingers were weathered and strong with short-clipped nails, a veterinarian's hands. No rings. There was a recent cut on her left arm where one of her clients must have taken issue with poking or prodding.

After Detective Marschel's careful tour of the room, she stopped in front of Jerry Trailor. She noticed a bulge in the victim's breast pocket and the top of an iPhone. She pulled out the phone and set it on the workbench, next to the drug paraphernalia.

"We'll need to check the residue in that needle. I'd be surprised if it was heroin," Marschel said.

Gray was fidgeting, still awaiting his turn to nose through the room. "Let's let Gray have a look," Sam said.

Marschel considered Sam, then Gray, skeptically. Then she stepped back.

"Don't let him touch anything. Just come in and look around."

Sam took Gray off leash and said, "Find."

Already intent, Gray didn't need to be told. He paced down the length of the workbench, sniffed, and stopped directly beneath the spoon. Sam bent down and rubbed his head. "Good boy," he said. Then he gestured with his hand for Gray to continue.

Thirty seconds later, after a quick spin around the table, Gray stopped in front of Jerry Trailor, his nose pausing less than 2 feet from the victim's breast pocket, staring at it. He started to raise a paw to the pocket, but Sam pulled him back.

"Looks like there's something else in the victim's pocket," Sam said.

Marschel stepped forward, felt deep into the pocket and fished out a small baggie with white powder. She moved over to the bench and examined it up close, under the overhead light, peering at it carefully. "Goddamn it," she said. "I think you're right. It's back."

"Heroin?"

Marschel nodded, just once, irritated. "For the past two years I've been part of a metro-wide drug task force. We stopped the heroin trade in the Twin Cities . . . at least for a while. The Cities have been as free of heroin as I've ever seen them in my 20 years as a cop. We knew it would make a comeback. We were just hoping it'd take longer than six months."

"That looks pretty pure," Sam said.

"You know heroin?"

"We've stopped our share of shipments."

"Definitely look's pure," Marschel said. "In fact, it's so pure I could have probably smelled it myself."

"That'd take some nose, detective," Mac said.

Marschel flashed Mac a glance.

While they talked, Gray moved to the back of the room, sniffing.

"Looks like Gray's still got something up his nose," Sam said.

Gray stopped in front of the old boiler, arching his head up. He sniffed, and then raised his front paws to rest on the boiler's side, near its top.

"What is it, boy?" Sam said, pulling a chair over to the boiler and stepping onto it. The top of the old furnace was covered with dust balls and dirt. Near the boiler's edge, atop years of grit, sat a 2-inch square of aluminum foil, shiny and new.

"Can you hand me that needle nose?"

Marschel gave Sam the pliers and he used them to grip the edge of the foil, depositing it in the detective's gloved hand. Marschel carried it to the workbench and teased the foil open. Inside she found several brown, semi-powdery pieces a little larger than a corn kernel.

Marschel looked closely and said, "Maybe hash?"

Sam considered it. "Or brown heroin. We busted a guy packing some in through the Coronado National Forest, down in Arizona. Looked just like that." Sam turned to consider Jerry. "Maybe he was more of a user than we thought? Or a dealer?"

After finding the foil, Gray's intensity diminished.

"I think that's it," Sam said.

"He has classic drug-sniffing skills," Carmel said. "It takes a special animal." Clearly, she admired Gray's capabilities.

"So you know drug-sniffing dogs, Dr. Rodriguez?" Marschel said.

"I volunteer for Minnesota Search & Rescue. I provide free veterinary services to the working dogs, if they need them."

Another surprise, Sam thought.

"You're a veterinarian?" Marschel said.

"Yes," Carmel said.

"How many human corpses have you examined?"

Carmel explained about being a med student and dissecting cadavers, some of them drug users.

Marschel turned back to consider Jerry Trailor and said, "This guy's definitely a junkie. I bet he's got tracks somewhere else. This time he played with fire and got burnt."

"I don't think so," Carmel said. "He doesn't have the usual physical signs."

"He's got the gangster look," Marschel said. "Tattoos up both arms, baggy pants, pocket chain. I'm guessing he's got a record."

"Intravenous drug users," Carmel said, "particularly heroin users, are usually skinny. This guy looks like he was healthy enough. And he doesn't have a red nose. No cuts, bruises, or scabs, at least that we can see. If he's a user, he hasn't been using long."

"We'll see," Marschel said.

"So you agree? An overdose?" Sam said.

Marschel considered Sam. "We have a baggie of heroin in the victim's front breast pocket, a cooking spoon with a lighter on his workbench, and a needle sticking out of his arm. Going out on a limb here, but I'd say yes."

"What about those marks on his right arm?"

"Looks like maybe he got bit by a mosquito."

Sam explained about the chemistry of mosquito bites, which made Marschel's hypothesis doubtful.

"Huh," Marschel said, again without much interest. "Maybe some other bug. All I know is it's not a needle mark." She pulled another pair of surgical gloves out of her pocket, walked over, and handed them to Sam. "Put these on. You can help me get his wallet."

Sam pulled on the gloves and walked over to the victim. Sam managed to get his hands under Jerry's armpits—he was definitely stiff—and lift him, long enough for Detective Marschel to extract Jerry's wallet.

Marschel found Jerry's driver's license and noted the name and address. "We'll check out his apartment. See if he has a record." She set down the wallet and grabbed the phone. She switched on the iPhone, but it was password protected.

"My tech guy's out until next week. Guess we'll have to wait on the phone."

They made sure Jerry was stable in the chair.

"Mac and I could help with the follow-up. And as you can see, Gray's got an excellent nose." It was as close as Sam ever came to offering his assistance. Usually, he was asked. And usually, the request was made by someone who knew about his expertise and capabilities. Sam had five days before he was due in Isle Royale and, while he loved the North Shore and had long wanted to explore the Superior Hiking Trail, finding out what happened here, which wasn't as clear to Sam as it seemed to be to Marschel, was much more compelling than a simple hike, regardless of its purported beauty.

"I think we'll be okay with our local resources," Marschel said. Then she thought of something. "Unless you got somebody who can get into this phone. Like . . . today."

Mac and Sam looked at each other, and Sam said, "We got Wheezo."

CHAPTER SEVEN

Domina drove a 1994 midnight-blue Chrysler LeBaron. Lockhart sat in the passenger side. Tiburon was in the back seat. The car had been a gift from Ernesto Fuego. After Domina had managed to get her first 2 pounds of brown heroin across the border, Fuego paid her a bonus. The odometer showed more than 214,000 miles, but the engine had been rebuilt and Domina—who had always liked the LeBaron's sharp-edged, boxy look (and the name, which she thought befitting of a member of The Monarchs)—thought the car "purred like a Mexican panther."

But now she wasn't really hearing anything. Domina wasn't feeling anything because of what went down with Jerry.

The three of them were heading south on Grand Avenue in Minneapolis, 10 blocks to 47th Street.

When Fuego had given Lockhart the names and addresses of the people who would be moving product, Domina had been in the room. Lockhart thought it was a breach of organizational hierarchy, but now he wondered if Fuego had shared anything else with a woman Lockhart considered only his driver.

"How does Fuego know this guy?" Lockhart said.

Domina kept her eyes on the road. "Silent partner."

"The silent partner is an American?" Lockhart said.

"No idea. Fuego doesn't like questions."

Lockhart glanced at Domina, but her face didn't change. "I don't like working with people I don't know," Lockhart said.

Domina knew Fuego recruited Lockhart because of his Minnesota connections. But she also knew, after spending time with Jon Lockhart, that he was a loner and a scumbag. You didn't kill ex-partners for familiar transgressions; you punished them and used their shame and sense of personal debt to leverage their assistance.

"You still know people in the Cities?" Domina asked, feeling certain she knew the answer. "People who can move this stuff?"

Lockhart paused. "It's been a while. All the guys I know are on my short list."

"You mean the others we gotta see? About your money?"

Lockhart didn't like questions, especially from a driver.

"Yeah," Lockhart said. "Old business partners. Like Jerry." He knew mention of Domina's old friend would, for the moment, silence her. Now they both continued looking ahead, watching for their next turn.

Lockhart had a plan. After their initial foray into his former home territory, he was going to wean himself from *Las Monarcas*. They'd been necessary, to get him back into the States and to Minnesota. But he was keeping his eyes open to opportunities. The authorities had his prints; he couldn't do anything about that. But he could make over his identity. Eventually he would rid himself of his minder driver and the mute muscle Tibby. And there wouldn't be anything Ernesto Fuego or the Monarchs could do about it.

He just needed to understand all the connections. Once he had the network, the rest would be as easy as cutting the head off an octopus. For the moment he contented himself with the image of writhing arms.

Five years ago, Lockhart had been careful before returning to the farmhouse to recover his cash. He'd stayed away long enough to let the crime-scene people process the place. He'd shaved his beard, dyed his hair, and acquired a fake ID, using it to buy a new set of wheels. Finally, after two months, he returned to discover his cash, more than $250,000, missing. He tore the place apart but never recovered a dime. He left in such a rage he didn't notice the flashing lights until they filled his rearview mirror. He thought about trying to outrun the cop, but that would have been the stupid play.

He eased to the shoulder. After the customary wait, during which his plates were run, the officer approached the vehicle. Lockhart tried to be cordial, but it was unnatural. The officer sensed Lockhart's discomfort. Suspicion rose off the officer like heat waves off a tarmac.

After a few cursory suggestions about minding his speed, he was finally issued a ticket. The close call made Lockhart realize it was time to leave Minnesota, tucking the memory of his stolen money into one of the gray folds of his brain, the way a loan shark files an IOU, knowing someday he'll return.

Now his money was due, with interest.

Domina had let Lockhart's mention of his old pal's name simmer. Finally, she glanced at Lockhart and said, "Taking care of your former business partners the way you did Jerry is gonna get around. I don't think Fuego's gonna like another body."

Lockhart's response was quick as a snake strike. "I didn't do Jerry," Lockhart said. *"You did."*

Domina, clearly bitten, said, "I didn't sign up for this shit."

"What makes you think Fuego doesn't know our plans?"

Domina thought about it. Fuego was a shirttail cousin on Domina's mother's side. Fuego had told her she was *familia.* Lockhart was family to no one, as far as Domina could tell.

"Fuego thinks more bodies are okay?"

"Fuego thinks more ODs on fentanyl-laced heroin is good for the business of promoting Mexican brown heroin. Everyone steering clear of the white stuff will have a substitute. But you don't need to bother yourself with the details."

Domina considered it, but she doubted Fuego knew the details. The idea of doing three more guys the way they did Jerry didn't seem good for anyone, especially for business.

Lockhart may have sensed Domina's suspicions because he turned to Domina and said, "Fuego also knows theft cannot be tolerated."

True enough for Fuego, Domina knew. But she wasn't sure the boss would appreciate a string of bodies associated with his new business venture, especially because bodies raised questions and interest.

Domina kept her eyes focused on the road, remembering her old friend Jerry. Jerry might have been a punk, but he didn't deserve the needle. Domina thought about pulling the LeBaron to the curb and walking. Just disappear. But it would be for Jerry, and there was nothing gained carrying a torch for a dead man. And Fuego and *Las Monarcas* knew too much about Domina. When Domina needed to move south, to wait for some Iowa legal troubles to blow over, Domina's mom told her about Fuego's import/export business. *In textiles,* she'd said.

So walking was not an option. Besides, she liked her car and she had prospects. So she tried to put the memory of Jerry behind her. But the next time Lockhart wanted an old partner dead, he could handle the needle himself.

At 47th Domina turned right and drove two blocks to Garfield, then headed north and came to a stop in the middle of the block, in front of a worn two-story stucco with peeling wainscoting and a sagging screened-in front porch. Through the screen they could see the silhouette of someone sitting on an overstuffed couch, smoking.

"This is it," Lockhart said. He looked at his watch. One o'clock. Then he turned to Tiburon.

"You armed?"

"*¿Estas armada?*" Domina translated.

"*Sí, siempre,*" Tiburon said. Always.

"*Este listo.*" Be ready.

"*Siempre.*"

Domina told Lockhart and he said, "I hate first meetings with people I don't know, especially with this much product."

Lockhart popped the car's door lock and got out. Domina and Tiburon did the same. When all three were headed toward the house, Tiburon with his backpack, the screen door opened and a thin, clean-looking kid with short hair and a two-day beard considered them. He wore a dingy green Rage Against the Machine T-shirt and a pair of dark blue jeans. He looked like he was in college. He had a cigarette in his right hand and held the door open with his left.

"Greetings," he said.

Lockhart came up the scarred walk. The front yard was mowed, but dry. "Rich Matthewson?"

"I am," he said, flicking his cigarette butt into the yard.

Lockhart was the first up the steps. Matthewson shook his hand and then greeted Domina and Tiburon the same way, nodding with a muted smile. "Come in," he said.

Then the four of them disappeared into the house.

"Can you believe this heat?" Matthewson said.

"Definitely hot," Lockhart said.

The front room was dark. The shades were drawn, but behind them, the windows were open. There was a red velvet couch with most of the velvet worn away, sitting against the front wall. A low coffee table sat in front of it, scattered with the remnants of pizza takeout, a full ashtray, and a couple of magazines, including *Variety*. A Marlboro Lights pack was sitting next to the tray. Some kitchen chairs sat around the low table. The room was trimmed in a dark wood patina that must have been more than 50 years old. There were small speakers set on end tables in both front corners. Against the side wall sat a full electronic drum set. Behind the drums hung a stage poster: "U2 360° Tour, Chicago, July 5, 2011."

"Have a seat," Matthewson said. He dropped onto the couch, reached over, pulled another cigarette out of the pack, and lit it. Matthewson was nervous, but he was trying to be cool.

"Got roommates?" Lockhart said.

"No." He glanced at Domina and Tiburon. The big man with the backpack looked a little tense. Rich tried to smile, but it was forced.

Tiburon ignored the kid and glanced away, checking out an entry in the left side of the back wall that led to the kitchen. There were stairs in the middle of the wall, heading up to a second level. To the right was an entry to a bathroom and a hallway that bridged two side bedrooms.

"The only name I was given was Lockhart," Matthewson said.

"I'm Lockhart. These guys are colleagues."

"Fair enough."

"We alone, Rich?" A long time ago, when Lockhart was serving time, he had a cellmate named Tony who was going to remake himself as a salesman, once he got out. Tony sent away for a Dale Carnegie course and the first thing he learned was the importance of "building a relationship," the cornerstone of which was the repeated use of a person's first name, friendly like. Whenever Lockhart met someone new, he remembered it. But because Lockhart was Lockhart, it was more intimidating than friendly, which he thought was also okay.

"Yeah," Matthewson said. "No roomies, like I said. Unless I get lucky at the bars." He laughed, definitely nervous.

"Young, good-looking guy like you. Bet you get lucky all the time," Lockhart said.

"I have my moments," Matthewson grinned.

There was nothing about Rich Matthewson that indicated he might be a user, Lockhart thought. Users were trouble. You could never trust a junkie.

"You mind if my friend has a look around, Rich?"

"Be my guest," Matthewson said, glancing up at Tiburon.

"Busca," Domina said. Search.

While Lockhart and Matthewson talked, Tiburon went into the kitchen. He peered out onto a scrubby backyard. Patches of spring grass and weeds were coming in green. A huge elm tree anchored the left side of the lawn. There was a standalone single-car garage out by an alley. Tiburon turned into a stairwell and the others could hear him as he checked out the basement, then rose to the kitchen, then continued through the rest of the house.

"How do you afford a place like this by yourself?" Lockhart asked.

"It was my grandpa's place. Gave it to me in his will."

"Nice."

Matthewson told them he was a drummer, a musician, part of a group who got gigs locally, though it was a little slow right now. They talked about how he knew a lot of people in the music scene.

Tiburon finally came back into the room. When Lockhart and Domina glanced up, Tiburon nodded.

"This here what we're about, Rich," Lockhart said. "This requires some care." But Lockhart could already see Rich Matthewson was a salesman. The kid was likable.

Lockhart was all about holding onto himself. He didn't like anyone. But he recognized affability and its importance in the sales process.

"As I understand it, you have a pound of brown heroin and you're looking for somebody to move it," Matthewson said.

Lockhart looked away, something flashing across his eyes.

"Now that's the kind of thing you've got to be careful about, Rich. Supposing, let's say, the room is bugged or your neighbor's working in the side garden outside your window and you're talking that openly about product?"

"The room's not bugged. And my neighbors are both at work."

"That was a for instance, Rich."

"I'll give you a for instance," Matthewson said. "Ever since that big bust last year this town's been a desert. If you don't want to say it by name, let's just say . . . if it was water, this is Death Valley. Everyone in this town is parched and ready for a long drink of cool water."

"That's good," Lockhart said.

"Yeah," Matthewson grinned, happy with his analogy. "I know a lot of people in the music scene. Take people my age, in their 20s. We're still trying to figure it out. Experimenting. Truth is, most of the people I know are casual users. They'd love to get their hands on a little taste. Just to try it. There's pent-up demand. And if this stuff's good, a pound . . . I mean, a gallon will be gone inside a week, depending . . ."

"That's good, Rich," Lockhart said. "For now, we're keeping our profits low. We're all about building a foundation and a network that can last. This is the ground floor, and we want to let people give it a try, more or less at cost. Let them know there's more where this came from. Once we have a solid foundation, we start raising prices."

"Like I said, it's a desert. Has been for six months. People are going to be lining up."

"What about your neighbors, Rich? What will they think when they see a lot of increased foot traffic coming and going?"

"You never shit where you sleep," Matthewson said. "I'm out in the clubs all over town. All the time. I'm what you call a full-service guy. If this stuff's good, I'll probably break it into smaller amounts and farm it out to friends I trust and know can move it."

"That's the idea, Rich," Lockhart agreed.

"So this is on credit, right?" Matthewson said.

From Lockhart's perspective, credit was unheard of, particularly with heroin. But Fuego had told them, "These first two shipments we can afford to be reasonable. We need to move it fast, before anyone else comes in and starts staking out territory."

So, credit.

But Lockhart didn't like it. He just nodded. "You cross us, Rich, we put you on a cross."

Matthewson laughed, hoping it was a joke, then realized it wasn't. He sobered a little and said, "I'm good for it. Hell, I've got this whole house as collateral. And I'm tellin' you, it's a desert."

Definitely a salesman, Lockhart thought. He looked up at Tiburon and indicated he should put the brick on the table.

Tiburon swung the pack off his shoulder, unzipped it, and pulled out one of the bags of heroin, setting it on the coffee table.

"Whoa," Matthewson said. "My God, that's beautiful."

"It is. And there's more where that came from."

The kid picked it up and weighed it in his hands. "It's a beautiful thing."

"So now that we're friends, Rich," Lockhart said. "Who's the connection?"

Matthewson looked up. "What do you mean?"

"My guy gave us your name and address. How do you know him?"

Domina frowned. She'd been quiet while Lockhart and the kid conducted their transaction. Fuego didn't like questions. Domina didn't like Lockhart. And now the prick was fishing for something Fuego had told him wasn't his concern. He was trying to understand Fuego's network. Domina tucked it away, like a good card in a poker hand.

Matthewson shrugged. "Friend of a friend and my friend's not talking. He just told me 'a guy he knows.'"

"Sounds a little risky, Rich."

"Not really. This is a very old friend. We've been buddies since the 7th grade. He's cool."

"You can't always trust old friends."

Matthewson looked at him and said, "I can trust this guy."

Lockhart shrugged.

"Is there a problem?" Matthewson said.

After a moment, Lockhart said, "No."

Lockhart didn't like it. When they got into the LeBaron, a pound lighter, Domina started the car, and as the engine purred, she said,

"It's your show, Lockhart." She checked her rearview mirror, getting ready to pull away from the curb.

Jon Lockhart looked away and didn't say anything. He could tell his driver disapproved of his inquiries. But he thought, *Fuego can go fuck himself. And so can this bitch, who thinks she's a player. In time, I'll be dealing both of them out of the game.*

CHAPTER EIGHT

At Hopkins Elementary, Sam, Mac, Detective Marschel, and Gray had spent the morning hip deep in the aftermath of Jerry's death. They helped get the victim out of the building and into an ambulance that took him to the morgue, where an autopsy would be performed. Carmel hung around until they got Jerry out of the dungeon and up the stairs. When she found out Sam was looking for a place to stay with Gray, she recommended an Extended Stay America. It was near her clinic and dog-friendly. She even offered to show Sam a good place to run Gray later, if he wanted.

"That'd be nice," Sam said.

Mac gave Sam the leering eyebrow raise, which he ignored.

Then Carmel returned to her clinic and they followed Marschel to the Hopkins police station, where the department fast-tracked the phone, checking it for prints before allowing Sam to take it.

Sometime during the morning, Marschel eased up on the prima donna act, which Sam and Mac appreciated. At the station, Marschel had an easy rapport with her colleagues, who called her Swish.

"Swish?" Sam said.

"I played high school ball in Hopkins," Marschel said.

Then, during the downtime of attending to the details surrounding the victim's death, Sam learned Marschel did not know much about the USFW (but was interested), and she'd never grown up with dogs (but was interested).

"If your guy can get you into that phone, check the victim's contacts and messages," Marschel said. "I'd bet my right ear his dealer is in there somewhere."

"I'd rather not wager an ear," Sam said.

"Nancy boy," Marschel said.

"Just sayin', Swish."

Detective Marschel grinned. "If you find someone interesting, let me know. I've got the day from hell. Week from hell. If you want to help, I don't mind you checking people out. It helps to have an extra pair of hands and feet. But don't try and be a hero, Rivers."

"Never." Everything Marschel suggested and asked was common practice.

Raven Marschel thought about Sam's case last fall. "If what I remember about that case over in Savage is true, you were pretty hard on local law enforcement."

"The sheriff's chief deputy was the murderer. You think I should have gone easy on him?"

"Sheriff Rusty Benson," Marschel said, remembering. "I didn't know his chief deputy, but I know him. He's on the metro-wide drug task force. Seems like he's used to running his own show. And he likes the stage."

"I saw he was reelected," Sam said.

"Barely. As I recall, you didn't hold back on your comments about the sheriff and his office."

"To tell you the truth, Detective, I try not to get involved in local politics, particularly when it's law enforcement. And I didn't get involved in the Scott County sheriff's race. But when the evidence was staring the sheriff right in the face, he was an obstructionist. There were some moments I had to call a spade a spade."

"I remember."

"And I remember Rusty Benson as a capable politician," Sam said. "He fought me every step of the way and when I finally took matters into my own hands and went around him—because he refused to work with us—he started making threats and tried to throw me off the case. Then we proved his chief deputy had committed murder, and he did a 180. He explained to the media how the crime had been solved, insinuating he had been in on it from the beginning."

Marschel grinned. "You've gotta love Rusty's razzle dazzle."

"Except when you're involved."

Marschel explained how last December, when they'd made all the drug busts, Sheriff Rusty Benson held a press conference and explained how his office had participated in the investigation from the beginning, as well as how several of the criminals were apprehended in Scott County and there had been significant seizures.

"That part was funny," Marschel said. "Sheriff Benson was only made aware of what we were doing. He let us do all the footwork and take all the risks. And he didn't know what was seized, only that drugs and money were found. But he referred to it as 'significant seizures.'"

"Guy has a future in politics," Sam said.

When they ran Jerry Trailor through the Minnesota Bureau of Criminal Apprehension's (BCA's) database they found something interesting. Jerry had been adjudicated for the possession and distribution of a controlled substance in Isanti County five years earlier, when he was 17. He received a felony count and served 12 months in the Arrowhead Juvenile Detention Center outside Duluth.

"Told you," Marschel said. "Once a junkie, always a junkie."

"All we know is he served time for selling a controlled substance," Sam said. He was more sanguine about whether or not offenders, particularly juveniles, could be rehabilitated.

"It was heroin," Marschel said.

"If the school would have known this, I doubt he would have gotten the job," Mac said.

"Agreed," Marschel said. "I've long believed everyone should have access to these juvie records. As it is, you can commit murder, and if you're young enough and get a good lawyer, a future employer won't be able to find it."

Most juvenile records were only available on special law enforcement databases.

"You do anything stupid as a kid, Marschel?" Sam said.

"What's that supposed to mean?"

"Kids do stupid things," Sam said. "They're learning, experimenting. When I was young, I set a leg-hold trap at a den I knew was being used by something. Set it and walked away and got busy playing. I waited three days to check that trap. When I returned, I found a foot in it. Whatever it was sacrificed its paw for freedom."

"That wasn't selling or using drugs," Marschel said.

"Some would argue it was worse, regardless of whether or not I could be convicted of anything. I couldn't get the thought of that animal out of my head."

"An animal," Marschel shrugged.

"Like us," Sam said. "In fact, it probably had about 97% human DNA."

"You a tree hugger?" Marschel said. She didn't wait for an answer. "It was a rodent."

"It was a stupid kid thing."

"Not the same," Marschel said.

Sam wasn't so sure. And Marschel never did answer the question about doing something stupid as a kid. But everyone does. Even star basketball players nicknamed Swish.

In fact, Wheezo could have been a poster child for minors who make bad choices. As a kid he had severe asthma and was never far from his inhaler. He was forbidden to participate in sports, which turned out to be a blessing. Wheezo (neither Mac nor Sam knew his real name) had a knack for working with computers. As far back as he could remember, he'd come home, fire up the latest technology, and begin exploring. Unfortunately, in the ninth grade, he figured out how to hack into a fledgling cell phone network, sharing access with his school buddies, who used their newfound intelligence to amass $60,000 worth of anonymous texting and phone calls. It didn't take long for the authorities to figure out the brains behind the operation. Wheezo had a rep. It was a stupid kid thing.

His introduction to law enforcement and the courts turned out to be a blessing. He began working with their technology departments and never considered returning to his miscreant past. Now he was in his late 20s, married, with one kid and another on the way. By all appearances, an upstanding young man. But his friends knew he still had a rebel's heart, which was just one of the paradoxical reasons he was good at what he did.

They met at Carmichaels, a local restaurant west of Lake Bde Maka Ska on Lake Street.

"I'm starving," Wheezo said. He wore a pair of black framed glasses over intense gray eyes. His two-day beard growth and buzz cut made him look like a teenager.

"So have something," Mac said. "I've heard the food here is pretty good."

There were windows across the front and part of the east side, filling the place with early afternoon sunlight. The tables and chairs were natural wood with chrome legs that sparkled in the afternoon sun. And it was air-conditioned.

"Who's got the tab?" Wheezo said.

"Who said anything about a tab?" Mac said. "We just want you to open this iPhone and then you can head back to the office. Don't you have work to do?"

"It's almost 3. Supposing it takes an hour to get into this iPhone, by the time I get back to the office, it'd be quittin' time. Besides, I'm hungry."

"Didn't you have lunch?" Sam said.

"I'm still growing."

Around the age of 19, Wheezo outgrew his asthma. Once he realized he could exercise without threat of asphyxiation, he began making up for lost time. Now he was a triathlete. Tall and thin, he consumed food like a disposal. And with abnormal amounts of endorphins washing through his brain, he had the relaxed demeanor of a long-distance runner.

"So how long is it going to take to open this thing?" Mac said.

Wheezo had the phone in his hands. "Hmm," he said. "An iPhone 4s." Then he looked up at them and said, "I'm so damn hungry, it's difficult to concentrate."

"Okay, bright boy," Mac said. "If the USFW spots you for a second lunch, how long will it take you to open it?"

Wheezo shrugged. "A good estimate is hard to calculate on an empty stomach."

"Oh for God's sake," Mac said. Then he stood up. "So looks like we order up front and they bring it to you, unless it's pastry." Truth was, Mac had been eyeing the pastry shelf.

Sam got coffee. Mac got one of two remaining caramel rolls, a monstrosity called a "pull-a-part" that could have been quartered and fed four students in Amber Mansfield's sixth-grade class. Wheezo ordered the ahi tuna burger with a side of fries and a Coke.

While they waited for Wheezo's food to come, he took another look at the phone. "An iPhone 4s," he said, and grinned.

He turned on his laptop, pulled a USB iPhone cable out of his pack, and inserted one end into the phone.

"Funny thing about the 4s," he said. "Apple got a lot more sophisticated with the 5. You can't get into the latest iPhones without a subpoena and help from Apple—and they don't help. But these earlier versions . . ."

Once the computer was up and he'd entered his password, he booted up a law enforcement forensics application designed to skirt iPhone security, at least for earlier versions of the phone. Without plugging the USB end into the laptop's port, he held down the iPhone's home button. Then he plugged the USB end into his laptop, entered a few commands, was prompted by a couple of options, and after answering, the phone's icons came up on his screen.

"A known backdoor into the iPhone 4," Wheezo said, handing the phone to Sam.

As if on cue, his food arrived.

Mac looked at Sam. "We've been Wheezo'd."

As Wheezo worked through his tuna burger and Mac his pull-a-part, Sam began examining Jerry Trailor's phone and text messages. By the time Wheezo had finished, Sam had cross-checked Jerry's text messages with his contact list and recent phone calls. There were three people who appeared interesting.

"Can you get into the BCA's criminal records database?"

Wheezo sipped down the last inch of Coke. Mac still had a small piece of the roll sitting on his plate. He was taking a rest, looking like a diabetic on the edge of a fugue state.

"How was that caramel roll?" Wheezo said.

"About the best I've ever tasted."

Wheezo looked at Sam. "I've heard this place is known for their baked goods."

"Can you get in?" Sam said.

"I'm feeling a little peckish," Wheezo said.

"Peckish?"

"Hungry."

Mac rolled his eyes. "After that tuna burger?"

"That was, like, an appetizer."

"Where do you put this stuff?" Sam said, considering Wheezo's frame.

"I ran 6 miles this morning and I'm swimming tonight."

"Don't you have a family?" Mac said.

"They come with. They love to swim."

"They love to watch you do laps?"

"We play around. Then they keep playing while I swim a mile. Then we play around a little more. Perfect evening."

"I wonder if Mrs. Wheezo feels the same way?" Sam said.

"Do you know the beauty of a kid who spends an hour in the pool?"

"No idea."

"That pool does something to him. When he gets home, he drops into bed like a bag of rocks."

"I bet his dad is tired, too, who ran 6 miles and swam another," Mac said.

"Not so much," Wheezo said. "It's my chance to spend some alone time with Mrs. Wheezo." He raised his eyebrows.

"Isn't she pregnant?"

"Four months. So what?"

"When Margie was pregnant, it was hands-off."

Wheezo was surprised. "Not Mrs. Wheezo. She's always frisky. And I've got to say, there's something about a pregnant wife. They're so, fecund."

Mac looked at Sam.

"I think he means rich and fertile," Sam said.

"I don't want to hear about your fertile wife," Mac said.

"How did we get from 'Can you access the BCA database?' to hearing about your pregnant wife's sex life?" Sam said.

Wheezo shrugged. "Just, still hungry. I get distracted when I'm hungry."

"Are you familiar with extortion?"

"In the abstract. My crimes involved fraud and robbery."

Mac rolled his eyes. "While you get into the database, I'll go get you that last caramel pull-a-part."

"While we're waiting for your caramel roll, run these names through the BCA's database." Sam handed over a sheet of paper with the names. "I want to see if any of them have a record."

"I'm on it," Wheezo said.

Within moments Sam was gazing at the juvenile record for Kurt "Suthy" Baxter, who at the age of 17 was adjudicated for a felony—possession and distribution of a controlled substance. He'd served 12 months in the Stillwater Juvenile Detention Center.

Suthy Baxter was one of three people with whom Jerry had been in recent contact, by both voice and text. But he was the only one with a record.

One of Jerry's latest texts to Suthy Baxter said, "Hey, coming into a little extra jack. Let's head over to Mystic Lakes Casino, do a little partyin'." So Jerry may have been a dealer? That was interesting. If so, it sounded like Jerry's buddy Suthy would know. Definitely a person of interest. He had a 763 area code. When Sam had Wheezo check it out, he used a reverse phone directory to pull up Baxter's address. 1025 25th Street, Cambridge.

Mac returned with the pull-a-part. It was slightly smaller than Mac's head. Wheezo smiled.

"I thought you couldn't concentrate when you were feeling peckish?" Sam said.

"Sometimes," Wheezo said, tearing off an outside layer of the gooey roll and biting off a chunk. "Sometimes it has the opposite effect," he said, his mouth nearly full. Wheezo grinned, bits of roll peaking from the corners of his mouth.

Sam noted the address and briefly thought about calling him. But if he picked up and they had a conversation, Suthy would be tipped off.

Sam called Marschel and told her about the contact.

"Okay," Marschel said. "You heading up to see him?"

"Can't just yet. Still have to check into a hotel and run Gray. I'm thinking an early morning visit would be best. Around 7? Before he goes to work, if he goes to work."

"Makes sense. Surprise him."

"You in?"

"At 7? You'll have to be on the road by 6. You go ahead and be a hero on this one, just keep me in the loop."

"Will do."

"As soon as they're done with the autopsy and drug analysis, I'll let you know. But my ear is tellin' me it's heroin and an OD by a practicing junkie."

"That ear's pretty smart," Sam said.

"It's like a superhero thing," Marschel said, and hung up.

By the time they'd finished at Carmichaels, it was almost 4:30. Wheezo ate the last bite of his roll, closed his laptop, and headed out the door. After Sam checked in at the Eden Prairie Extended Stay America, he was going to meet Carmel Rodriguez at Anderson Lakes Park Reserve to run their dogs.

"Close enough to quittin' time," Mac said. "I'm going home."

"Sounds good," Sam said.

"So does meeting up with that veterinarian," Mac said. "You going to try and hook up?"

"Hook up?" Sam said. "That doesn't sound right."

"You're a known slut, Rivers. Remember Diane?"

"I'd known Diane since I was a kid. She was practically an aunt to me."

"An aunt with benefits? That's sick."

Sam looked away, shaking his head. "I'm going to run Gray with her. That's all. She's showing me around."

"I bet. Did you see she wasn't wearing a wedding ring?"

"I noticed."

"I could tell you were interested."

"Anyone would think Carmel Rodriguez was nice to look at. Even a grandpa like you. But in the final analysis, Mac, I'm a working stiff. What's left, when romance turns south?"

Mac recognized a rhetorical question, so he shrugged and waited.

"Work," Sam said. "In the depths of the bad time with Maggie, the only place I could find solace, such as it was, was on the job, in the field. Didn't matter if it was the sun-baked plains east of Denver or the middle of the Rockies or the Western Slope or Northern Minnesota. Flora and fauna, Mac. It has always been my mantra, when the chasm of life opens and threatens to swallow you whole. Getting out under the sun and stars has always kept me sane. And it helps to have a partner like Gray."

Mac let out a sigh and said, "Rivers, anyone ever tell you you're full of horse shit?"

"You, when I get too philosophical."

"I'd love to stay and be educated in the ways of sensitive men, but I got a lawn to mow."

"You want to head up to Cambridge in the morning, before rush hour?"

"Are you kidding? You'll have to leave before 6."

"I'll call you after I talk to Suthy."

"Do that," Mac said. "Figure out some way to get me out of the office. I like the sun too. But because it's warm and spring in Minnesota. Not 'cause of all that other crap."

CHAPTER NINE

A t the hotel, Sam showered, fed Gray, and they were out the door before 6. They turned onto Anderson Lakes Parkway, heading toward the reserve. Carmel had said the reserve would be an excellent place for Gray to stretch his legs—plenty of trails and very few people, and those who hiked it were usually dog people. She had two dogs she liked to run there most nights. If Sam and Gray were okay with company, she could give them a tour.

That sounded just fine to Sam. Gray, too, Sam noticed, seemed to appreciate the vet. Sam wondered how he'd like the vet's dogs.

Sam and Gray saw the reserve sign up ahead and turned. There was a short road that curved right to a blacktop parking area with 20 spaces and only three cars. Carmel was waiting with her two dogs beside a red Expedition. She had a brown dog, maybe 60–70 pounds, and a smaller one, around 40 pounds, spotted black and white like a dalmatian. Both dogs appeared to be mixed breeds.

Sam parked his jeep two slots away from Carmel's Expedition.

Gray glanced at the two dogs and made a low-throated growl.

"No," Sam said, scratching Gray's neck and then pulling, just enough to snap Gray out of his aggressive instincts. Gray stopped and turned, enough to tell Sam he understood.

"Good boy."

Then the wolf dog's attention swung back to the new dogs.

When Sam got out of the car, Carmel smiled. She wore jeans and a simple white muslin top, what Sam's ex-wife Maggie would have called a tunic. Maggie had worn them to tactfully cover weight gain. Sam couldn't tell if Carmel was employing it for the same purpose, but he didn't think so.

"Just a sec. Let me get Gray on a leash. We need to introduce them."

Carmel glanced around to make sure they were alone. "I know these cars," she said, indicating the other two vehicles in the lot. "Once we get on the trails, we can take them off leash, if Gray's okay with it."

"That'd be great," Sam said. He turned to the passenger side of his car, opened it, and leashed Gray before he came down off the seat.

Carmel's dogs strained against their leashes, trying to get a whiff of the new dog.

"How is he with other dogs?" she said.

"The only time he's rumbled is when he's been provoked. How are your guys? Besides cute and handsome."

Carmel smiled. "This is Frank," she said, indicating with a nod the big brown mix. "And this is Liberty," she nodded toward the black-and-white spotted one.

Gray was pulling his leash taut, staring at the two with interest.

"Okay if I move forward?" Sam said.

"Sure."

They closed the 10 feet between them. Gray stood still, his tail wagging. That was a good sign, Sam thought. Liberty moved in toward Gray's back side and sniffed, low. Frank went nose-to-nose with Gray. Frank was 6 inches shorter and arched his nose up. The wolf dog's height and weight were a clear advantage, probably one of the reasons Gray was still moving his tail in a tentative wag.

Sam and Gray had encountered dogs in other parks that weren't well socialized. If they were big enough, they'd sometimes go after Gray. But the wolf dog was all sinew and muscle, and not averse to mixing it up, if the occasion required it.

Gray, Frank, and Liberty became friends about as quickly as three dogs can, in part because Carmel had the same control over her dogs as Sam did over Gray. Carmel and Sam were alphas, Sam thought, at least where dogs were concerned. Carmel led them down a side trail and they disappeared into vibrant green. The spell of warm weather precipitated an early spring, causing a green explosion only people who live in four distinct seasons get to appreciate. Everything was new and, Sam thought, *shimmering*.

"Something's happened in the last week," Carmel said. "There's been a sudden shift. It all feels different."

The day had been unseasonably hot, but since it was still early in the year, the evening was starting to cool. It was warm, but moderating—perfect, really, Sam thought, for walking dogs in the Minnesota woods. Particularly since the bugs hadn't yet emerged.

The trail opened into an early spring field filling out with foxtail grass, milkweed, sumac patches, thistle, mustard, and the usual patchwork of Minnesota wild. Carmel looked ahead and saw they had the path to themselves.

She bent down, unclasped her dogs, and said, "Let 'em run."

Sam was happy to oblige. And so was Gray.

Frank shot forward like a bullet, Liberty in pursuit, and Gray followed with his long-legged stride.

"Looks like they're on the hunt," Sam said.

"I'm not sure mine would know what to do, if they got lucky," Carmel said.

"They ever get lucky out here?"

"Not in the winter, so it's been a while. But now, suddenly, it's spring—practically early summer—and they're feeling it. But I can tell they're out of practice."

"Gray too."

"It was a long, hard winter," Carmel said.

"After work in Denver, Gray and I head out to the nearby foothills, sometimes Green Mountain, and once I get off the path and make sure we're alone, I let Gray run. It's great exercise for both of us," Sam said. "But last winter was tough for me too."

Carmel told him that she had lived in Denver as a kid. She'd attended the third and fourth grades in Lakewood, a Denver suburb. Her father had brought their entire family up from Monterey, Mexico. He was also a veterinarian and had to work through the licensing process to become certified in the States. Once he did, he moved the family to Hopkins, where his sister and a brother had already settled.

Sam felt comfortable with Carmel, at least enough to explain how he'd ended up in Denver at 17—homeless, without his high school diploma, bereft and adrift. There had been an incident with his father resulting in a threat to prosecute Sam for attempted murder. It had been a bogus charge, but Sam's father was an Iron Range attorney with connections and the ability to make the charge stick. Sam didn't share all the details, only that the logical choice was to leave. He changed his name and spent the next 17 years creating a new life. Two years ago, he had finally returned home to face the charges and clear his name. He ended up discovering much more than redemption. Sam helped uncover murder and insurance fraud, and ultimately rescued Gray.

The dogs turned into the field and were exploring a gradual slope, hunting for birds, rabbits, squirrels, or whatever else their noses could turn up. If you were an observer of dog behavior you could already tell the three dogs were beginning to form a pack, sorting out the hierarchy, moving in a kind of hunting unit across the slope. They were working at it, trying it on, seeing how it felt, sizing each other up.

"So what about your name?" Sam finally said. "I could have sworn last year, when we met at your clinic, your name was Susan? Dr. Susan Rodriguez."

She paused. "Susan was my ex-husband Carlos's idea. My maiden name is Carmel Susannah Martinez. But Carlos thought it would be better if we had Anglo names."

"Why did you need Anglo names?"

"To fit in. Carlos thought it would be better for business," Carmel said. "He thought people would be more willing to bring their animals to a vet named Susan rather than Carmel."

"Was Carlos right?"

Sam had a sudden sense there was still something between them. Conflict could be a connection, particularly among the long-married.

Carmel paused, watching the dogs on the slope nosing back and forth through the cover, and said, "Carl," almost in a whisper. "He actually goes by Carl. We argued about it so much, and I'm so damn stubborn, it's been hard to accept his perspective and call him by anything other than his full name. But it's just, his perspective. Irreconcilable."

When Sam's wife filed for divorce, she listed the reason as "irreconcilable differences."

"Sometimes irreconcilable is all that's left."

Suddenly Frank stopped and Carmel could see his tail shift to a rapid wag. "Frank found something."

Sam turned and noticed Frank's position and tail. "Definitely something."

"I hope it's not a skunk. Usually whatever he finds easily evades him, particularly in cover like this."

Suddenly a cock pheasant rose less than 3 feet in front of Frank's nose, screeching and flapping out of the green. Frank, startled, flinched, and then began bounding after the bird.

"Frank!" Carmel yelled.

It took several more calls from both of them before Frank— and Liberty and Gray, who had taken up the chase—returned from over the hill.

"Frank's first bird," Sam said.

"First bird of a new year. And a beautiful male."

After a few moments walking, Sam said, "So has it hurt your business? Being Doctor Carmel Rodriguez?"

"Not at all."

"So Carl was wrong."

"I think so. But he'd never admit it."

"Stubborn?"

"It's taken about a year for both of us to accept the divorce. He's a lawyer," she said, as if that explained something. "It's been a struggle, particularly with Jennifer. He's a good father; he has her half of the time. And she loves him. And it's important."

"Definitely," Sam said, who knew firsthand about bad fathers. He could understand, from what he sensed about Carmel, how her former husband might have found it difficult to accept the divorce. Though every marriage consisted of an x and a y, and the only people who fully understood the variables were those who were part of the equation.

"So the divorce was your idea?"

She flashed him a look. The question was, perhaps, too personal. But it had popped out of Sam's mouth before he could engage his better judgment.

She paused before answering. "It was his idea. But it grew on me."

"But he had trouble accepting the divorce?"

"There's some backstory to it, but yes."

There always was, Sam knew.

They walked and watched the dogs working the hillside. Milkweed was starting to push up with the mix of everything else on the hillside. Sam noticed it and reminded himself about the peculiarity of a box of pupas being sent from Central Mexico. He needed to check on it.

Far up ahead, the trail disappeared into dense timber. There was a very light breeze that shifted across a stand of poplars. Their bright-green leaves waved like tiny flags in the dusk light.

Carmel told Sam she wasn't sure where the trail led, once it entered the woods, but that it might get swampy down by the lake.

"We can handle swampy," Sam said.

They continued, watching their dogs sniffing across the hillside. Sam told Carmel about his work with the USFW. Carmel asked, casually—though it didn't feel casual—if Sam had been married.

"Once," Sam said.

They walked for a while in silence, the question shifting something in their conversation, from pleasant to poignant, though Sam wasn't sure in what way it might be poignant. When it came to reading women, he was like a man rendered sightless, trying to learn braille: attentive but slow.

After a few moments of silence, Sam said, "And the divorce was her idea."

"Oh," Carmel said. "Sorry if I was being too . . ."

"Personal? Nah. It's been more than two years."

Sam told her about Maggie and their seven-year marriage and what went wrong, as far as he could tell. He had been too remote, too closed down. Frankly, back to his childhood, he was still trying to understand those scars. It had taken him a while, but at least for the equation of his marriage he had a clear sense of his own variables. He thought, while he was telling her, it felt easier than it had been before on the few occasions he'd shared what happened.

Finally, Sam finished and said, "Okay, let's hear the rest of your story."

Carmel smiled and said, "Fair enough."

They walked a few more paces.

"Before the breakup, Carl was seriously busy at work. We were both busy. He had an important case he was arguing in front of a judge. Turned out the opposing counsel was an old girlfriend. From high school. He told me about it. No big deal. This was a big case, and he was working all kinds of hours for the client, preparing for it. Then the day they were scheduled to go to court and make their opening arguments, his client told him he wanted to settle. Carl tried to talk him out of it. He hates losing and he thought settling looked like defeat and they had a good case. But he finally accepted it and fought for the best settlement he could and got it."

She paused. The dogs were still working the hillside, still moving forward toward the edge of trees.

"And then he happened to meet up with the opposing counsel, and she invited him to lunch. After a couple of hours and a few drinks, they checked into a hotel."

Uh-oh, Sam thought. "Carl told you that?"

"Not at first. Carl kept the affair secret. It went on for a while. Finally, he asked for a divorce. One minute we're talking about Jennifer's fifth-grade teacher's conference over dinner at Chuck E. Cheese, and the next, while our kid's off playing games, my husband asks for a divorce."

"That's where he did it? Chuck E. Cheese?"

"That's where he did it. In retrospect, I knew something was going on. But I loved him. He was my husband. I wanted to fight for him. And I did, as well as I could. But he was so adamant. He was certain she was the love of his life. And he didn't tell me about the hotel thing, until I kept putting him off about the divorce. Finally—I think it was tactical—he told me about that day and what happened. Until then I thought it was an emotional affair, that he'd get over it. Naïve," Carmel said, remembering it. "But when he told me those details, I knew in my head I was done. It took a while for my heart to catch up."

At the edge of the woods, Sam said, "That's tough."

"It was."

"What happened with the old girlfriend?"

"He married her. A month ago."

"But he's angry?"

"He was angry because I fought him for child support. He's a very successful lawyer. He thought, since he was going to have Jennifer half the time, there was no need for money to change hands."

"But that's not how it went down?"

"No. He pays me child support. I didn't try for alimony."

In his own divorce, Sam and Maggie walked away without any financial ties. They didn't have children and they both had similar salaries, so there was no reason to exchange money. Sam took Charlie, their dog, because Maggie knew he needed the dog. Otherwise, they walked.

"What happened to Charlie?"

"Cancer," Sam said. "Before I visited the place I grew up. In Northern Minnesota. Sometimes I think my return home to reconcile with my past had more to do with Charlie's death than the end of my marriage."

"It's tough to lose a dog."

They walked a few more paces before Sam looked up toward the path ahead and said, "Any idea where this goes?"

"I don't know. I usually go in a different direction."

The trail made a sharp turn into fresh green. It appeared to run down by a lake, and when they took it, they followed the lake's perimeter for several hundred yards before turning to the right, up through another pasture, where they watched some deer crest a rise and disappear.

The dogs could not keep themselves from careening into the water, at least the edges of it. It was muddy down by the shore, but the dogs enjoyed the water, and Sam and Carmel enjoyed the view out over the lake.

On the way back to the car, Sam's cell phone went off. He looked at it and recognized the 612 area code, but not the number.

"I'd better take this," he said, answering.

"It's Raven," Detective Marschel said. "You enjoying the evening?"

"I am," Sam said, surprised. Then he explained that he and Carmel were running dogs in the Anderson Lakes Nature Reserve.

"Nice," Marschel said. "The lab results for that heroin came back. They were interesting."

"It was heroin?"

"Two kinds; the stuff in the foil was brown. The stuff that junkie put up his arm was a more refined white. Very pure. Your dog was right on."

"He usually is."

"The lab guys also told me the white was laced with enough fentanyl to put down an elephant."

"Fentanyl? That stuff's dangerous."

"Yup. Like morphine, only much stronger. Heroin producers sometimes use it to cut product and make it go a little farther, make more money, and give a dose an interesting edge."

"You mean a lethal edge."

"Exactly, if you don't know what you're dealing with. Most of the stuff like this we've seen is European."

"Apparently Jerry Trailor didn't know what he had."

"Guessing not."

"What about the brown?"

"Probably Mexican in origin, though they aren't sure. Could be Asian. They're going to send both samples off for more testing. We'll know in a day or two where it was refined."

"Did you hear anything on the autopsy?"

"Not yet. Said it'd be tomorrow."

"We've got to find his source," Sam said. "Before someone else has a too big taste of the white stuff."

"Definitely. In the meantime, I'm calling up the DEA. I think it'd be good to issue a press release about it, telling users there's some dangerous stuff on the street."

"Good idea."

"Maybe if we get the cop network going, they can pass the word. Meanwhile, you need to let me know what you find in Cambridge. First thing. And be careful, because whoever made this has connections. Fentanyl can be tricky to come by."

"Will do," Sam said, and ended the call.

By the time they returned to the parking lot it was almost dark. They followed the dogs, which seemed to sense the right way. The dogs were settled into a comfortable pack, their tongues hanging out of their happy mouths.

"That was nice," Sam said.

"Very nice."

"So where are we going for dinner?"

Carmel grinned. "There's a restaurant I've been meaning to try. Up the road."

"That'll work," Sam said.

He had been so busy with Jerry Trailor's death, the post-investigation, and their hike in the reserve he hadn't thought about food. But suddenly he felt hungrier than he could remember having felt in a long, long while.

CHAPTER TEN

At the AmericInn, Domina stretched out in a room adjoining Tiburon's. She was trying to get her head straight. She thought about calling Fuego, but there were problems with contacting one of the senior members of *Las Monarcas*. She did not want to sound like a snitch or be considered a complainer, and by going over Lockhart's head she would be violating protocol. The complaint part wouldn't have bothered her if Fuego hadn't spoken to Domina before they left and told her about Lockhart's side concerns in the Cities, that they would also be addressing some of Lockhart's "past business issues." But why kill anyone if it was unnecessary? It was bad for business, and Domina doubted Fuego would have condoned it.

Domina had been working for *Las Monarcas* for almost three years, and she had come to understand that sensitive topics were almost always conveyed in vague language punctuated by body gestures. In this instance, Fuego had shrugged and turned his head to the side as if to say, "We will humor the American as long as his concerns don't interfere with our own." But Domina was still new to the language and wasn't certain she had understood correctly. And besides, maybe Fuego had known about the killing and condoned it for disciplinary reasons?

For now she stretched out on her bed and tried to ignore the image of the needle going into her old friend's arm and the way Jerry had closed his eyes rather than look at her.

She would have talked to Tiburon about it, to get his perspective. With various gestures of his own—mostly head shrugs and eye rolls—she and Tiburon, she thought, felt the same enmity toward Jon Lockhart. But Tibby was from a bad Tijuana barrio and had a past he did not talk about. Tibby was a *Las Monarcas* enforcer, and in the final analysis, Domina thought, Tiburon would do what was asked, however repugnant or extreme.

In North Minneapolis, they stopped at Juanita's, a Mexican restaurant off Central Avenue. Someone had told Tiburon it was authentic Mexican, and the big man had a big appetite. Lockhart didn't protest, because over the last year, south of the border, he'd developed a taste for good guac and enchiladas, Northern Mexican style, with a little heat.

They had dinner and weren't disappointed. Tiburon also ordered the enchilada plate and a burrito on the side. Marita, a heavyset Mexican waitress born in Guadalajara but living in the States for five years, chatted up Domina and Tibby, at one point telling Tibby he had the appetite of a shark (*Tiburón* was Spanish for shark) but the heart of a *niño*, a boy. If anyone else would have said it, Tiburon might have made a scene. But Marita was flirting with him. Sometimes it happened, with women of a certain type— those who looked like they'd walked out of a Botero painting.

Then they continued north to Cambridge, up Highway 65, until they came into town. They made one stop, on Main Street, at a place called the Pizza Station, where Domina ordered a simple cheese pizza and waited. The restaurant's staff was wearing engineer-style denim hats with *Pizza Station* emblazoned across the front and colorful Pizza Station shirts. Domina followed a hallway to the bathroom. Inside, she opened a side closet and found bathroom supplies and on top an old Pizza Station hat. She stuffed the hat into the back of her pants, smoothing it flat so it wouldn't be noticed.

Five minutes later she was back in the car with the pizza inside the box.

"*¿Qué obtuviste?*" Tiburon said. What did you get?

"*Solo queso,*" Doms said. Only cheese.

"*Ai,*" Tiburon said, disappointed.

"*¿Todavía tienes hambre?*" You still hungry?

"*Un poco.*" A little.

Domina shook her head; the man was never sated.

It was already dark. They followed Lockhart's iPhone to 1025 25th Street, Suthy Baxter's residence. They drove by the house, a small, nondescript beige square on a block of similar working-class homes. There was a faint light glowing in the door window and a window on the right front of the house, covered with blinds. Big elms towered over the street, and there were plenty of mature shrubs and bushes around the surrounding homes, good cover for staying out of neighbors' sight lines.

"You sure he's in there?" Domina said, continuing down the street and turning left, starting to circle the block.

"Your pal Jerry said he'd be there, that Suthy told him he had to study the next two nights so he'd be ready, come the weekend."

Domina remembered. "What makes you think the guy's going to let me in?"

Lockhart turned and said, "Cuz he was the kind of kid who never said much and went along. He'll open the door."

"That was five years ago. Maybe he's changed."

"People don't change. He'll let you in."

Domina believed people could change because she had, but she didn't say anything.

They parked around the corner from Suthy's house and waited.

The pizza was in the back seat by Tiburon, and the inside of the car smelled like melted cheese. Lockhart and Domina were still full from Juanita's margaritas and big plates of food, but while they waited Tiburon helped himself to two pieces.

"Not all of it," Lockhart said. "We need the box to at least look like it's full."

Domina told Tiburon and Tiburon grunted and closed the box.

They waited until the only light left on in the neighborhood was in Suthy's front door window.

"Okay," Lockhart said. "Jerry said he lives alone, so when he comes to the door, show him the pizza delivery and then the gun and tell him to let you in."

"Wish I had a shirt from the place," Domina said, taking out the hat and fixing it. When she looked in the rearview mirror, she said, "The hat looks stupid." But she shrugged. "Just make sure Tibby covers the back."

"We'll make sure. But Suthy Baxter's going to let you in. Trust me."

No way Domina would ever trust Jon Lockhart. But she said nothing and got out of the car with the box and her Glock stuck into the front of her jeans under her KISS T-shirt. Then she walked through the dark to the corner.

Lockhart slid over and took the wheel. He drove past 25th street, turning into the alley. He stopped behind the house long enough to let Tiburon out of the car.

Domina, with the gun and pizza, crossed the street and turned left at the corner, continuing down the sidewalk.

The crickets were chirruping in the warm night, but otherwise the street and all the houses were quiet. Domina guessed the two lights on at 1025 were a front hallway light and to the right, a small living room light peaking around the blinds. A hallway was good, because once she was in the door, she could make Suthy backpedal and get him out of sight.

She turned up the broken walk, carrying the box in front of her. To the left of 1025 was another high row of lilacs, already leafed out in the warm spring. To the right was a low shrub, but the surrounding houses were dark. Before she reached the front steps, she lifted the lip of her T-shirt and pulled out her Glock G27, a .40 caliber subcompact that was portable, but square edged and showy when the person at the other end looked down and saw the barrel hole. No one expected a woman to have a gun, even a brawny woman like Domina. She would need to make sure he saw it.

The doorbell had a two-beat gong. The Glock's nose stuck out from under the pizza box, clearly visible. Somewhere in the back she thought she heard a TV. Someone inside approached the hallway and an outside light came on.

The door opened.

"Pizza from the Pizza Station," Domina said, in perfect English.

A small, thin guy wearing a too-big Minnesota Wild hockey jersey hanging over baggy pants—*almost like a wannabe gangster,* Domina thought, *but without the attitude*—peered at her through the front storm door. Then the kid looked down at the box and saw the gun. Then he looked back up at Domina, frightened.

"Don't close the door," Domina said quietly. "I just need to use your phone. Then I'm outta here. Seriously. The phone. Then I'm gone."

The kid was stunned. He looked like he might be weighing his options, so Domina said. "Seriously. Open it," a little stronger. She moved the Glock forward an inch.

Suthy Baxter started to reach, hesitated, and then Domina thought she saw something flash across the skinny kid's eyes, something like nerve. And then the kid took one quick pivot and suddenly the door slammed shut.

Shit, Domina thought, dropping the pizza, trying the storm door. Locked. Then she heard movement inside, across the floor. *Shit!*

Inside the house, Suthy darted away from the front entrance. He fled down the hallway, into the kitchen, sprinting toward the back door. He wasn't thinking. He was running. *Get out. Into the neighborhood. Scream.*

He blew through the back door and took two quick steps, breasting the huge maple beside the rear walk, sprinting toward the alley and garage, his mouth starting to open and form that first piercing *hellllpppp!*

But he hit something solid and there was a pain like a hammer blow on his shin and he launched forward, his belly hitting the ground in a hard flop, his arms out to his sides, his hands scraping the ground in a skid. His hands were spread too far out to support him and the air blew out of him like a bellows, "Ummppphhh!"

For a tenth of a second, he lay there, stunned. He lifted his head, starting to push up, knowing he had to run. Then he felt a sharp crack on the back of his skull—but only for an instant—and the world went dark.

DAY 2

Thursday, May 22

CHAPTER ELEVEN

S am and Gray were on the road around dawn. The day was another odd one, 20 degrees warmer than normal. It might as well have been August, and Sam thought the rare Minnesota spring morning was something to behold.

But not for Jerry Trailor.

Sam didn't know if Suthy Baxter was a working stiff, but if so, the early morning hour would be a perfect time to catch him unaware. If people didn't know they were going to be interviewed, particularly druggies, they didn't have time to fabricate correct answers.

The drive took an hour. By the time he pulled to the curb in front of Suthy's place, it was 6:45. The sun was well off the horizon, but the house was dark. He wondered about it because most of Suthy's neighbors' homes shown lights inside, their inhabitants apparently getting ready for work. Maybe Suthy worked a night shift and was sleeping in? Or maybe he was at a girlfriend's house?

"Wait here," Sam said to Gray.

Gray knew the routine.

Sam walked up the cracked cement to the nondescript front step. There was a small window to the right. When Sam peered through the front door's windowed top, he saw a hallway that led into the house. The vestibule was dark.

He rang the doorbell and heard the two-tone gong.

When no one appeared he knocked loudly and waited. Nothing.

To the right of the house, there was a low hedgerow. To the left, a stand of leafed-out lilacs. Sam turned to consider the neighbors and, while their windows shown light, he couldn't see or hear anyone. He figured they were probably having coffee, breakfast, maybe showering, watching the morning news, just waking up.

Sam stepped off the front stoop and moved to his left, behind the lilac wall. On the left side of the house, he found two more dark windows. One contained opaque glass, probably a bathroom. The other was covered with blinds. The backyard was simple, like the front. There was one small step in front of a back door and a cracked cement path that led to a detached garage positioned on an old alleyway. There was a mature maple in the middle left of the backyard. The patchy grass beneath it was covered with sticks and bark and a couple of places that looked like they'd been skidded over, like a kid sliding into home base.

Sam peered into the back door window. He saw an old stairway going down to a basement and to the right a corner of the kitchen, what had been behind the window covered by blinds when he'd walked along the home's side. He could see a stove and an old linoleum floor and an open doorway leading into another room. But it was all dark. He knocked a couple of times to be sure. Nothing.

Maybe he wasn't home?

There were two big windows to the left; Sam guessed either another bedroom or a family room? Both windows were covered by blinds, but there was a crack on the right side of the blinds, large enough to glimpse inside. Sam cupped his hands to shade his eyes and peered into the room. As his eyes grew accustomed to the shadows, he saw a person sitting in a chair with his head hung low. Still as stone.

Sam moved his head from the window, startled, and then peered again. As his eyes focused, he was pretty sure he saw something in the body's left arm. A syringe? The posture, the slump, the syringe; it was Jerry Trailor all over again.

Damn.

Sam rapped on the window frame, but the body didn't move. He knocked again, more urgent and intense. If the body was breathing, the rise and fall of Suthy Baxter's chest, if that's who it was, was imperceptible.

He turned out the lining of his right front pocket and used the cloth to reach up and try the back door. Locked. He hurried around to the front. This time the knob clicked, and he pushed and, once it was cracked, he used his elbow to push it all the way open.

"Hello! Anyone home?"

Sam hustled down a hallway into the rear dark room and saw a body slumped in the chair. He found the light switch and flicked it on.

The kid was dead. Just like Jerry Trailor. A syringe stuck out of his left arm with rubber tubing around his elbow, and a cooking spoon, lighter, and small baggie of white powder were on the table in front of him next to a phone. He was still as dirt, as anything that no longer breathed life.

To be certain, Sam used two fingers to press against the kid's neck. It was clammy and stiff and felt to Sam as though there hadn't been a pulse for a long time, probably all night.

Twenty-four hours and two ODs. Probably from the same stuff.

A small storm of *ifs* blew through his mind. If he'd come yesterday, if he'd called him and told him about Jerry. If they'd been able to find the source. If they could have gotten the word out. If he would have reported it to the Cambridge police so they could have checked on the kid. If any one of a number of different actions had been taken, the kid might still be alive.

And he looked like a normal kid in a normal house, not a chronic user or one of those street junkies who are half human, half need.

Sam paused for a moment, thinking.

When he took a closer look at the kid, he noticed grass stains on the knees of his pants. He examined him more carefully and noticed the heels of both hands were also stained with what looked like rubbed away grass and dirt. And then Sam remembered the skid marks in the turf beside the big maple in back. So Suthy Baxter, if this was him, tripped and fell and came back to cook some heroin and shoot up? Junkies didn't make sense, Sam knew. But he didn't even take a minute to wash his hands? It prompted Sam to make another careful examination of the victim, which is when he recognized a large knot on the back of the victim's head. Sam tried to reconcile it with tripping and falling, but why the back of the head, if the hands and knees indicated a front fall?

Looking the kid over, Sam noticed the kid's right arm. There were tattoos—what looked like a dragon snout peaking from under the sleeve of his Minnesota Wild jersey, and one of some kind of vine that looked like ivy roping around his forearm. But atop an ivy leaf he noticed two black dots, almost iridescent. Dried blood. Just like Jerry Trailor.

Sam bent over for a closer look and had the strangest sensation the kid was trying to tell him something. He glanced at the face, but it was hung down and the eyes were squinted and there wasn't anything glistening out of the creases of his lids.

But something.

Sam glanced back to the forearm. He reached into his pocket and pulled out his wallet and extracted his USFW photo ID, hard plastic. Then he bent over the two dots and carefully moved the edge of the card over the spot nearest the victim's hand and it flaked away whole, a flake of dried blood.

The drop rested atop the victim's arm.

Sam thought for a moment and then turned out of the room into the kitchen. He pulled a tissue out of a box on the countertop and used it to rummage through a few kitchen drawers until he found a plastic sandwich baggie. He took the baggie back into the room and with the edge of his ID coaxed both drops of dried blood onto the tissue, folded it twice, put it in the baggie, and pocketed it. Then he took a photo of the victim's forearm.

Sam could stay in the house, beside the dead man, and wait for the authorities. But he knew the first people on the scene would be Cambridge police, and he didn't want to be tied up with some locals who didn't know him and could, technically, hold him for breaking and entering. Apart from the dried drops of blood, he'd altered nothing.

Once he was certain he had photographed everything, he dialed 911, moving toward the front door.

He told them his address and that he was looking through a back window and he was pretty sure he saw someone who was unresponsive sitting in a chair and could they please send someone to check it out?

While Sam related the information he stepped to the front door, peered through the small window, saw the street was clear, and used his pocket lining to quietly open the door and step onto the stoop.

The dispatcher asked his name and Sam told her and he said, "Hurry, because I'm pretty sure he's in trouble."

She kept Sam on the line, talking. In less than two minutes Sam heard a siren, and in less than another minute a squad car pulled up behind Sam's Wrangler and an officer hurried out. There was another siren in the background, *probably an EMT,* Sam thought.

Gray was in the car, watching. First, he stared at the policeman getting out of the car, then Sam, then back to the policeman.

The officer was young and earnest and had a haircut that looked like he'd just gotten out of boot camp. He was nervous and there was already a little sweat on his forehead.

Sam introduced himself, and said, "Officer ...?"

"Caldrot," he said, shaking Sam's hand. "You're with who?"

"An agent with the USFW," Sam said. "I was going to speak with Suthy Baxter about an incident that happened in the Cities yesterday. A kid who overdosed on heroin. But when I knocked, he didn't answer. When I looked through a back window, I think I saw him slumped in a chair, with a needle in his arm. Just like the kid down in the Cities yesterday."

Another squad car turned the corner, no siren, but lights flashing. Officer Caldrot waited for the more senior officer, judging from the man's gray hair and ample middle, to approach the front walk.

As the other officer approached, Caldrot said, "He says he thinks there's a guy in the back of the house, unconscious."

"So maybe he had a late night?" the officer said.

"I knocked on that window pretty hard," Sam said. "If he was okay, he'd have heard it."

The other officer glanced at Sam, considering him. "Who are you?"

Sam told him and explained about the OD investigation and the bad heroin, and that it appeared this kid may have got some too.

The officer was suspicious. "Got some ID?"

Sam pulled out his ID card and the officer squinted at it. "Rivers?"

"Sam Rivers."

After a moment the officer said, "I see that," handing the card back, irritated. Finally, he turned to the door and knocked. There was no response, so he tried the knob and when it opened, he pushed on the door and yelled inside. "Hello?" He paused, waiting for an answer. "Hello?" he called again, and then walked inside.

"I think the room is straight back," Sam said.

The officer entered, called again, and made his way to the back room. Caldrot followed, Sam behind him. By the time Sam got to the room's threshold, the officer's fingers were feeling for a pulse on Suthy Baxter's neck.

"Looks like an overdose," he said. "Feels like he's been dead awhile." Then he turned and looked at Sam. "Who's this?"

Sam repeated more details about Jerry Trailor and how he was following up on a similar incident yesterday and he thought this was probably Kurt "Suthy" Baxter. He explained how he'd gotten the name and address and was just pursuing leads, trying to track down the source of the bad heroin, and that was about all he knew.

"I'm trying to figure out why Fish & Wildlife is involved? I know some of your local guys. They're, like, game wardens," the senior officer said.

Sam explained about speaking at the school and how Detective Marschel, from Hopkins PD, authorized him, and since Sam had some free time before heading north, he agreed to help out.

"So why didn't you call first?" the senior officer said.

"I thought if he was using, it would be better to surprise him."

The officer thought it all sounded a little . . . fishy.

There was a knock at the front door and Officer Caldrot turned to let in two EMTs.

"You are?" Sam said to the senior officer.

"Campenelli," the officer said, but he didn't extend his hand. "Sergeant Campenelli."

"Sergeant, do you mind if I make a call to Detective Marschel? She'll want to know about this."

He still looked suspicious. As Caldrot returned with the two EMTs, one of them moving forward to check out the victim, the sergeant said, "Go ahead. But stick around. I'm going to have more questions."

Sam nodded and backed up to the room's threshold. "I don't think you should move him until your guys have a chance to check him out, maybe dust for prints. If he died the way the victim died yesterday, there's some bad heroin on the street, and if we can find out where they're getting it maybe we can prevent another one of these from happening."

He punched in Marschel's phone number and waited.

The EMT paused over Suthy Baxter, looking at the sergeant.

"Just make sure he's dead," the sergeant said.

The EMT moved two fingers to Baxter's neck.

Sam looked at his phone to check the time: 7:07.

Marschel picked up on the third ring. "Yeah?" she said. She didn't sound happy.

"I'm in Cambridge," Sam said. "At Suthy Baxter's place. He's dead."

There was an expletive. Then, "Another OD?"

"Looks like it," Sam said. "Just like Jerry Trailor. Slumped in a chair, syringe in the arm."

"Damn."

"There's also a cooking spoon, the tube around his elbow, a lighter, a small baggie of white power, just like Trailor. I called 911 and the local police are here."

"Shit. That dog of yours had a chance to nose around?"

"He's in my jeep. We're just getting started here, a Sergeant Campenelli and Officer Caldrot and two EMTs."

"Pffffft," Marschel said. "We don't want them touching anything. I know the sheriff up there. He should be the one having a look at this."

"Call him," Sam said.

"Do I need to tell someone to hold on? That it's a task force matter?"

"Just a sec."

Sam moved the phone away from his ear and said, "Detective Marschel doesn't want anyone to touch anything until the sheriff's office has a chance to look around."

Sergeant Campenelli appeared miffed. "The sheriff? Did you tell your guy it's an OD?" he said.

"Yeah. Just like yesterday. But now it involves Hopkins and Cambridge and, well, it's interjurisdictional." Sam was blowing smoke, hoping to buy time.

The sergeant considered and Sam said, "I don't think you should move him until everyone involved has a chance to take a look."

Sam heard Raven Marschel's chatter in his phone, moved it to his ear. "What?"

"Let me talk to him."

Sam said, "Detective Marschel would like a word."

Now it was a scene, with Officer Caldrot and the two EMTs looking on and waiting and Suthy Baxter still slumped in the chair.

"Yeah?" the sergeant said into the phone.

There were some words and the sergeant breathed once, heavy, and said, "Call him." Then he handed the phone back to Sam.

"I'll call the sheriff," Marschel said. "Broom. He's one of the good guys. Meanwhile, don't let anyone touch anything."

While they waited, Sam walked out to his jeep to check on Gray. He leashed him and brought him down out of the car and Gray walked over to Sergeant Campenelli's cruiser, lifted a leg, and peed on his front tire. By this time the officers and the EMTs were on the front stoop. Campenelli frowned.

"Sorry," Sam said, appearing sheepish. But he was pleased by Gray's choice of piss sites, almost as though Gray knew territory was involved and he was staking their claim. After Gray was done, Officer Caldrot and one of the EMTs approached Sam and admired Gray, asking about him. Sam explained about his lineage and the EMT asked about the eyes, one yellow and one powder blue, and Sam explained it was a condition called heterochromia.

"Can he see okay?"

"Sure. Doesn't alter his sight. Sometimes I think it gives him special powers," Sam shrugged.

The officer considered this, wondering if it was a joke. Then in the distance they heard a siren and waited for the sheriff to arrive.

CHAPTER TWELVE

The Isanti County sheriff's cruiser turned the corner, cut the siren, and pulled to the curb, the lights still flashing. Sam could see an older, dough-faced guy in the front seat, passenger side, wearing a pair of teardrop sunglasses over a thick walrus moustache. The lights were cut with the cruiser's engine, and the chubby guy opened the door. The driver, a young deputy, got out from the other side and started around the cruiser's front. The sheriff stepped out of the front seat one tree stump at a time, with a little effort, and then glanced at the crowd on the front stoop. Once out, he moved his legs a little, stiff, apparently getting his circulation back. His khaki uniform was tight as a drum top but clean and crisp this early in the morning. When he came up the walk, he sauntered like a sheriff. The younger deputy walked a little behind him.

"Sergeant," he nodded to Campenelli, then Officer Caldrot and the two EMTs. "Whadda we got?"

Sheriff Broom had straight, pegged teeth, lightly tinted from a career involving daily draughts of office coffee.

"Looks like an overdose. This guy thinks it's bad heroin," Campenelli said.

The sheriff turned to Sam. "You the Fish guy?"

"USFW," Sam said. "Sam Rivers." He reached out his hand and the sheriff took it, but more from courtesy than interest.

"Sheriff Broom," the sheriff said, considering. "This is Deputy Hardy."

Sam shook Hardy's hand, too, and nodded. Her blonde hair was cut short and had a shimmer, Sam guessed from some kind of product. She wore starched khakis and a pair of teardrop sunglasses identical to the sheriff's, and she didn't smile.

"How do you know Detective Marschel?" the sheriff said.

If Sheriff Broom was a good guy, Sam wasn't feeling it. He seemed, like a lot of sheriffs, mostly politician. First, the sheriff was going to pay respect to his local colleagues and constituents. Then he'd turn his attention to the out-of-towners.

"I met her yesterday," Sam said. "She needed a hand and I agreed to help out."

"Huh," the sheriff said. "She told me you were the real deal and when she checked she found some high-profile cases to back it up. Something in the Cities last fall? And there was that incident up on the Range winter before last."

"I've worked some investigations in Minnesota," Sam said, surprised by Marschel's homework. "Some got a little press."

"I don't remember the Cities deal, but I remember that murder up on the Range. Near Defiance? Didn't you work with Sheriff Dean Goddard?"

"Yes," Sam said. "It was outside of Defiance. And yes, the Vermilion County Sheriff and I were both involved."

The sheriff considered it. "The sheriff had a tough reelection, as I recall."

Sheriff Goddard had been caught with his pants down, more or less. At least in pictures. Sam was very glad Dean Goddard held onto his job. But Sam wondered if Sheriff Broom was one of those people who had a more conservative moral perspective about Dean Goddard's extramarital affair (even though Dean's marriage had long been over).

Sam and Sheriff Broom were just making small talk, but Sam could see the sheriff was waiting for Sam's opinion.

"That investigation on the Range involved murder, insurance fraud, and five members of the Iron County Gun Club, one of them my father. After it was all over, I felt lucky to have Dean's help."

Sheriff Broom held Sam's gaze with some intensity, but Sam couldn't tell what he was thinking. "And I think Vermilion County is lucky to still have him in the sheriff's seat," the sheriff finally said. Then he smiled, but just a little. "So, we got some bad heroin here?"

"Looks like it," Sam said. "Yesterday we found an elementary-school janitor in pretty much the same situation down in Hopkins. This guy, Suthy Baxter, if that's who it is, was in the victim's phone."

"Think he's the supplier?"

"I think they both died of the same bad heroin, but all I see here is a small baggie. I'd like to get Gray into the house to be sure." Sam indicated with a nod to Gray, who had returned to the jeep and was staring at the gaggle of men.

Sheriff Broom glanced at Gray and then turned back to Sam. "First heroin we've seen in a long while. Detective Marschel tell you about our operation last fall?"

"She said you pretty much dried up product for the entire metro area. But now we've got some coming back. White and brown. And the white is laced with fentanyl, if this is the same stuff that killed the other victim."

"He any good?" the sheriff said, indicating Gray.

"If there's more heroin, Gray will find it."

The sheriff turned to have another quick look. "Looks like an unusual animal."

"Part wolf," Officer Caldrot said.

"Let's go have a look," the sheriff said. "Then we'll bring in the reinforcements."

The sheriff led the way into the rear TV room, followed by Sam and the deputy, the two local officers, and the EMTs. Sergeant Campenelli, Officer Caldrot, and the two EMTs looked on from the doorway.

When the sheriff saw the syringe sticking out of the victim's arm, the tubing, the cooking spoon, and the small baggie of white powder, he said, "Poor kid. Rolled the dice and came up snake eyes." He turned to his deputy and said, "Can you get the crime-scene guys out here? Looks pretty obvious, but we'll want to dust for prints and see what else we can find."

The deputy turned out of the room.

The sheriff was silent for a minute. Then he bent over and took a better look at the kid's face, which was hung down and turned to the side. "What did you say the name was?"

"Suthy Baxter."

"Let's wait until the crime-scene guys get here and we can see if he's got a wallet and some ID. But I think I know this kid. Or maybe it's his brother? Kid I knew was Kurt Baxter, but looks a lot like him."

"He was listed in the National Criminal Justice Reference Service as Kurt Baxter. Suthy's a nickname."

"Who was the victim in Hopkins?"

"Guy by the name of Jerry Trailor. About the same age as this kid, I'd guess," Sam said.

"Jerry Trailor," he said, familiar. He stood up, looking out the rear window, though it was covered by blinds. "Four, maybe five years ago, these two kids were part of a gang cooking meth. Can't remember the details. Have to look it up. But I remember these two. Went to juvie. They were both 17. I remember one of them walked. A Maury," the sheriff's gaze trailed off, trying to remember, but couldn't. "Had a good lawyer." He was recalling it, slowly. "I think one of them went to prison. Tough for an 18-year-old, but what are you gonna do?" Then, "Have to check our records to be sure, but I'm almost positive this kid and Jerry Trailor were part of it."

"Would be good to know," Sam said. "Could check out their old friends too."

"Providing we don't find the mother lode here. Find anything in Hopkins?"

"Nothing. Only stuff we found was on him, so we're thinking he was just a user. But far as we can tell, not a regular user. Unless the ME finds tracks some place we couldn't see. The ME's report should be in sometime today."

"Well," the sheriff said, considering, "Neither one of them are using anymore."

Over the next couple of hours, the crime-scene techs took over, found the victim's ID—a wallet on his bedroom dresser—and confirmed it was 22-year-old Kurt Baxter, same age as Jerry Trailor. They dusted the place for prints and turned it upside down, looking for more product, but couldn't find anything except a little weed. Didn't look like the kid was a regular user of anything, other than a little pot. Definitely not an intravenous needle user, unless, again, the ME found less obvious places on the kid's body where he poked himself. There were the grass stains on his knees and hands and the bump on the back of his head, which the ME would double-check. But so what? The kid fell and somehow hit the back of his head.

While the techs were finishing up, a car turned the corner and rolled up to the curb. Another twenty-something got out, nicely dressed, walking up toward the house, clearly shaken. He introduced himself as Ronnie Baxter, "Suthy's older brother."

The sheriff and Sam Rivers were standing in front of the house. Gray was still in the jeep.

Ronnie Baxter was pale, quiet, and thoughtful. A neighbor had seen the commotion and phoned him. Ronnie worked down in the Cities at a Best Buy and was on the floor when he got the call. He explained that he was four years older; he and Suthy had never been particularly close, especially after the meth-lab business and Suthy's stint in juvie. But Ronnie thought his little brother was back on track. He was living in their childhood home (their parents were both dead) and going to school at Anoka-Ramsey Community College, here in Cambridge. He was getting his nursing degree. This didn't make sense, according to Ronnie.

"I did not see this coming. Not at all. I thought he was clean. Maybe a reefer now and again, but that's it. He was into the whole nursing thing."

"Did you know his friends, where he might have gotten it?" the sheriff said.

"No. No idea. If I had to guess, maybe somebody from his time in the juvenile detention center? But that was a while ago. And I didn't think he was in touch with those guys. Maybe somebody in the nursing program?"

"Did you know Jerry Trailor?" Sam asked.

"Yeah. I knew him. A real low life. You think he had something to do with this?" Ronnie's eyes darkened at the mention of Jerry.

"He OD'd yesterday, down in the Cities," Sam said. "Same thing. Overdose on bad heroin. I'm guessing it's the same stuff."

"Not surprised with Trailor. I never liked the kid. I bet that's where Suthy got it. But I'm surprised because I didn't think they hung out much anymore. I didn't think Suthy hung out with any of them anymore."

"You mean the others in the meth business?" the sheriff said.

"Yeah. The others he got mixed up with back in high school, when they were cooking out at that farmhouse outside of town."

During the two hours they'd been busy with the techs and the crime scene, Sheriff Broom had recalled additional details about the meth-lab bust, five years earlier. There had been four kids, all buddies, one of them 18, the sheriff couldn't remember all the names. The 18-year-old went to prison. A kid by the name of Maury was the rich kid. Maury Trumble. The dad had some kind of business down in the Cities and had moved the family up here, thinking the small town would be better for his kids. And then his eldest son got mixed up with meth. The sheriff remembered Maury as contrite and sincere, but you sensed it was an act. And personally, the sheriff thought detention would have done the kid good. But Maury Trumble was the only one who got off. The others, including Kurt Baxter and Jerry Trailor . . . not so lucky. And the main guy got away. They never saw the main guy, even though they'd set a trap. At first, he'd suspected one of the kids had tipped off the ringleader, which is why the sheriff didn't step up to help prevent the kids—all of them except Maury—from serving time in juvie. But if it was one of the kids who had tipped the ringleader, the sheriff couldn't figure out how they'd done it. And there didn't seem to be any love lost between the kids and the leader, an older guy with a record.

"When your brother was busted over the meth lab business," the sheriff said, "His name was Kurt. Where'd he pick up Suthy?"

"Nickname he had as a kid. Then he went to that detention center and there was another Kurt Baxter, so he started calling himself Suthy again, just to be different."

"Old family name?" Sam said.

"Southpaw. He was a left-hander," Ronnie said.

Ronnie reiterated the two hadn't been close. But still, he was shaken by his brother's death. He told Sam and the sheriff how the meth lab business just about killed his mom. Then she died a year after Suthy got out of detention. Their dad had passed 10 years ago.

"I'm glad they didn't have to live through this," Ronnie said.

"Anyone else? Any other siblings?"

"Just me. And this house. I'm down in the Cities."

They asked Ronnie for more names or anything he could think of, but since he and his brother hadn't been close, he couldn't say. He suggested checking out the others from the meth-lab business but repeated that Suthy had told him he didn't have much to do with any of them anymore. When Ronnie found out how Sam had tracked Suthy through Jerry Trailor's phone, and the message Jerry had texted Suthy, he was surprised.

"Maybe Suthy wasn't being straight with me because he knew how I felt about Jerry. And the others. But that's what he told me. And I believed him because nursing is a tough degree, and he was doing okay. Unless he was lying about that too," he said, shaking his head.

Sam could tell the brother was stunned. The full impact of his brother's death, even though they hadn't been close, was starting to register. At least on an emotional level.

Sam told him to let them know if he thought of anything else, anything at all he might consider important. Ronnie told him he would, and they exchanged phone numbers, just in case.

When the last tech came out of the house, he was carrying a plastic bag with Suthy Baxter's iPhone and laptop with a power cord.

"Password protected," he said. "Take these to the college?"

The sheriff thought about it.

"I got a guy," Sam said. "He's pretty good. He got into Jerry Trailor's phone. If there's a way in, he'll find it."

During the couple of hours they'd been working together, Sam appreciated Sheriff Broom, and the sheriff appreciated Sam.

"You think he can get to it soon?" the sheriff asked.

"Today."

The sheriff handed over the phone and laptop. "Let us know what you find. Meantime, as soon as I get back to the office, I'm going to check out the file on the meth lab deal, maybe get some more info. Maybe some names too."

"That'd be good, sheriff. And I've got a colleague, Agent Mac McCollum, who's been helping out. You okay if Mac comes up and noses around a little, maybe visit the school and talk to some of the victim's classmates and teachers? Just to get a feel for the kid?"

"That'd be fine," the sheriff said. "Just let us know what you find."

Sam said he would. "And I'll bring Detective Marschel up to speed too."

The sheriff appeared thoughtful. "Probably should call the DEA, now that there's two victims." He didn't sound happy about it.

"I think Marschel was going to call them about issuing a press release," Sam said.

"That'd be Scott Pepper," the sheriff said. He frowned. "Let me talk it over with Marschel. But you might be hearing from the guy." He peered at Sam, looked like he was about to say something, then thought better of it and looked away.

The head of the techs told the sheriff they were pretty much done. The two EMTs had been waiting outside, ready to take the body to the city morgue.

"Before you close up," Sam said, "we should let Gray have a sniff, just to be sure there isn't a stash we missed."

The sheriff thought about it. "You guys okay waiting just a few more minutes?" the sheriff said to the EMTs. They were. Besides, both the sheriff and the lead tech were interested in seeing the hybrid work.

Sam turned to his jeep, opened the door, and brought Gray down into a heel. Then the two of them started back to the house.

CHAPTER THIRTEEN

N ow there was a crowd. The sheriff, Deputy Hardy, Sergeant Campenelli, Officer Caldrot, the lead crime-scene tech, and the two EMTs were all trailing after Sam and Gray. When they reached the front step, Sam turned to see the others behind him.

"Probably better if we keep the crowd small," Sam said.

"Oh, sure," the sheriff said.

Earlier, Sam had noticed Officer Caldrot's interest in Gray. Understandably, Caldrot had also been interested in Deputy Hardy. Sam was pretty sure he'd seen some glances exchanged. "Maybe just the deputy and officer?" Sam suggested.

The sheriff and the sergeant nodded, and the deputy and officer stepped forward and followed Sam and Gray into the house.

Once inside, Sam had Gray smell the leftover baggie of heroin and then set him loose with the single command, "Find."

Gray immediately started sniffing. He made a quick circuit of the living room, then went into the bedroom. He checked out the kitchen and the bathroom and the second bedroom, which didn't appear to be used. But Sam could tell the minute he entered each room there didn't seem to be anything, any substance or scent engaging his nose.

When he finally entered the TV room, where Suthy's body still sat slumped in the chair, his attention intensified. He sniffed at Suthy, pausing. Sam shook him loose and he sniffed in the ashtray where they'd found the marijuana remnant. Then he turned his attention to the cooking paraphernalia. But other than the obvious, Gray didn't seem to find anything.

Then he turned to the couch against the back wall, in front of the TV. Something interested Gray, but he didn't become excited in the way he did when he discovered drugs. It was natural curiosity, as though he was on the trail of an interesting, organic scent he had never smelled.

Sam watched him sniff around the bottom of the couch.

"What is it, boy?"

Gray was sniffing under the couch by the near corner, his nose all the way under. He suddenly growled and jumped back, startled. His massive head made a quizzical turn. Then he pawed his nose, as though he'd been stuck by something. When he kept pawing, Sam made him sit and examined his muzzle.

Nothing. But Gray's eyes were watering.

"You hit a nail, boy?"

Gray immediately stuck his nose to the carpet and kept pawing it. Then he peered at the space under the near corner of the couch. Then he whined and pawed his nose again.

Sam got Officer Caldrot to help him lift and move the couch back. Near the corner where Gray's nose had been, Sam saw something move, something small and spider-like. He stepped over to have a closer look. Its small pincers were raised in defiance and its tail appeared ready to strike.

"What the hell?" Sam said.

Deputy Hardy said, "What is it?"

"I think it's a scorpion."

"Scorpion?" Hardy said.

"Looks like a bark scorpion," Sam said, suddenly worried. "They're venomous."

"I don't know if I've ever seen a scorpion," Caldrot said.

"Just watch it," Sam said. "Don't let it move." He went into the kitchen and started opening drawers. He finally found what he was looking for and pulled out a 2-cup-sized Tupperware container with its lid and came back into the living room. By now the deputy and officer were staring at the scorpion, which wasn't moving, but its small pincers and tail were still raised, ready to strike. They had the little bug surrounded, but they were giving it plenty of space, as though they feared it might spring up and sting their foreheads.

Sam moved in close and coaxed the bug into the 2-cup container, snapping the lid shut.

Gray was whining and Sam had another look at his nose, but he couldn't see anything. He had no idea if Gray had been stung, but he knew bark scorpions could be lethal, so he was worried. And he knew who to call.

In 30 seconds Carmel Rodriguez was on the phone.

When she answered Sam told her about Gray's nosing around and that he thought it was a bark scorpion.

"Couldn't be. We don't . . ."

"Yeah, yeah, I know, no scorpions in Minnesota. But I'm telling you, I think one just stung Gray on the nose. I caught it and I'll show you, but for now I'm worried."

"How's his nose look?"

"I can't see anything, but he keeps rubbing it and his eyes are watering."

Carmel could hear the heightened concern in his voice. She admired that in a man.

"Bring him down here and I'll have a look. Meanwhile, if anything changes, let me know. Bring him right now."

Sam hung up and put Gray on a leash and explained he had to take off.

"Aren't you going to take these?" the deputy said, holding the phone and laptop.

Sam grabbed both, checked on Gray again, and headed for the door. He said goodbye to the others and hurriedly got into his jeep.

After he entered in the clinic address on his phone, he selected the quickest route and took off.

Gray appeared fine. His eyes looked good and his breathing was normal. His nose was a little drippy. He whined and pawed it. *The wetness could be from pawing,* Sam thought. *Probably nothing. Probably poked himself with a nail.*

On the way to Carmel's, Sam called Mac.

"You had lunch?" Sam said.

"Margie packed me a spinach wrap. Says I need to lose weight. So, yes, if you're asking can I meet you for lunch and it involves proper food and is in the line of duty so our tab is paid by the federal government. Where are you?"

Sam explained he was still in Cambridge and brought Mac up on current events, including the chance that Gray had just been stung by a scorpion.

"A what?"

"A scorpion. He was nosing around Suthy Baxter's house and found a bark scorpion and I think he got stung."

"I don't think I've ever seen a scorpion," Mac said. "I didn't know we had them in Minnesota."

"We don't."

There was a pause. "So what the hell does that mean?"

"No idea."

"Scorpions?"

"I don't know. Right now I'm just trying to get Gray to Carmel's place. Bark scorpions, if that's what it is, are dangerous. He seems okay," Sam said, glancing over to Gray. "But I want her to have a look."

"You got the victim's phone?"

"His phone and his laptop."

"I'll get Wheezo. We can meet you at Carmel's clinic, maybe go have some proper food while the kid scans your equipment."

Sam thought that was perfect and hung up.

He glanced at Gray, whose eyes were still watering. Otherwise, he seemed normal. Just in case, Sam kept his speed exactly 9 miles over the speed limit until they hit 694, the beltline freeway around the Twin Cities. When they approached the entrance onto 694, Sam thought he saw a little froth near the corner of Gray's lip. He turned onto the ramp and accelerated.

"Good boy," Sam said.

There was a little bubbling on the corner of his lip and Sam thought maybe his breathing had kicked up a notch.

In another few minutes, starting the turn south, still 10, maybe 15 minutes from Carmel's clinic, he glanced back at Gray and watched a dollop of froth fall from the wolf dog's lip, like toxic flotsam. Gray looked at him then, breathing a little faster, and Sam thought he saw something he'd never seen in his partner's eyes.

Fear.

Suddenly Sam punched it, hurtling south, pushing it close to 90, praying he got lucky with the patrols.

CHAPTER FOURTEEN

Jon Lockhart didn't talk about it because he didn't think about it, but he'd spent two years in St. Paul as a kid, when he was 10 and 11. At the time, he and his alcoholic mother were living with Mitch O'Connor in a broken-down, Westside two-story, down off Cesar Chavez Street. Lockhart could recall plenty of bad childhood scenes. One that stuck was the night he ended up in the ER. He'd stepped between his mother and Mitch's fists, and the man's knuckles landed on the kid's scrawny arm and there was a crack the likes of which Lockhart had never heard. Or felt. And certainly never forgot. More broke than just that bone, especially when his mother told the ER doc he'd been jumping on the bed and fell.

Lockhart's mother told him his real father was a miner, a lawyer, a farmer, a politician, and a bank president, trying on role models the way she tried on men. His old man, whoever he had been, had a lot of different names, though none that lasted. The only thing Lockhart knew about "daddy" was that Jon needed to "make him proud" because his daddy was a big shot, and he was watching.

Once Lockhart understood the whole biological thing, he understood there was a man who was a big shot, but it wasn't from his job. Lockhart doubted his mother even knew the donor's identity, other than a guy up on the Iron Range who needed to get laid. Lockhart's mother wasn't a whore, but her affections were easily purchased for a few drinks and a roof over her head.

The final incident happened when Lockhart was 12, if he remembered correctly. But it was difficult to recall details because that was the night Mitch put his mother in the morgue. Mitch went to prison on a 25-year manslaughter charge, eligible for parole in 12 years. Jon Lockhart swore he would be waiting for him. It was the first time Lockhart felt the power of dark purpose, something to guide his days and give them meaning.

After his mother's death, Family Services farmed Lockhart out to an uncle up on the Range. The uncle combined his mother's alcohol problem with Mitch-like fists.

When Lockhart was 15, he stole his uncle's car from a back-woods bar and had a joy ride all the way to the western edge of North Dakota, before a Smokey jumped him just shy of the border. Then it was one juvie camp after another until he was 17 and served two years in prison for grand theft auto. Prison was the place he first tried meth and learned how to cook it. But watching his mother, and then his uncle, destroy themselves with drink soured him on the taste for alcohol and drugs. The only time Lockhart used was if a woman was involved and he needed to cloud her judgment.

During Lockhart's incarceration, he heard that Mitch O'Connor had died in a prison fight, the son of a bitch. And for a very short while, he was robbed of dark purpose. But his informal tutoring at the North Dakota State Penitentiary taught him how easy it was to cook meth. When he was released, he got a job in a gas station up on Highway 95 between Cambridge and North Branch and started to plan.

Life behind bars also put eyes in the back of his head, where he could see things. Or feel them. *Prison sense.* His prison sense had saved him on more than one occasion, including the meth-lab farmhouse trap set outside of Cambridge.

His entire life was a lesson in tooth and claw, and the verity of the Old Testament perspective regarding an eye for an eye. The only thing that made any sense to Jon Lockhart, that made him feel even remotely like the world had order, was revenge. His unwavering belief in retribution was why Jerry and Suthy had paid the ultimate price, and Lonnie and Maury were up next. You did not steal from Jon Lockhart, unless you wanted to suffer.

Since meeting up with *Las Monarcas* three years earlier in Mexico, Lockhart had conjured another plan out of the protoplasmic soup of his life, a black purpose that guided his days step by step until this, here, now.

"Straight ahead," Lockhart said.

Domina drove another block to Broadway, waited until the light turned, and then drove to a parking lot entrance, where she steered her car in front of a tone arm and took the proffered ticket. She parked in a space across the street from an old redbrick building. A large "Pilsner Artists Lofts" sign hung on the outside corner, where Lockhart's next contact, Tim Casselmire, lived.

Tiburon sat in the back, quiet, the backpack beside him.

"So where are we at with our next shipment?" Lockhart said.

Two more pounds of brown heroin had arrived yesterday in a box of monarch pupas. At Lauderdale Elementary in Lauderdale.

"It's here. I told you. Tommy texted me as soon as the shipment came in."

"So did you confirm the pickup time?"

"Tomorrow. Early. I let him know."

"Did you hear from him?"

"Not yet."

"We've got time. Call him and let him know. First thing tomorrow. Before dawn."

Domina pulled out her cell. She thought it was unnecessary, but since coming into St. Paul, Lockhart had been as tense as a cattle prod. The whole trip to Minnesota had started with Lockhart on edge, and then yesterday Jerry and that kid in Cambridge had ratcheted him up a notch. Domina thought the night might settle him, but it had only wound him tighter.

Domina dialed Tommy. When his voicemail came on she hung up. Then she texted him: "Tomorrow morning @ 5."

After Domina sent the text, Lockhart said, "Tomorrow's a school day. Tommy got a good reason to be there that early?"

"I guess. When I mentioned it before, he seemed okay with it."

"Cop drives by, sees us at a school side entrance in the dark, looks pretty damn suspicious, doesn't it? Especially on a school day?"

"It's protected. We park on a street, walk up the sidewalk, cross the yard, and go around back. Nobody sees anything in the back."

"If there's a utility light over that back entrance, we need it out. Tell him. And make sure he's got a good reason for being there early. You trust this guy?"

"Sure. Tommy and I did some time together in juvie. I know him."

"Did he know Jerry?"

Domina shook her head. "Different juvie."

"Does he know what's in the box?"

"Not exactly."

"Will he look?"

"No."

"That's what you thought about Jerry."

At first, Domina didn't respond. Then she said, "Tommy's not Jerry."

"He wasn't a user, was he?"

"Tommy used a little. We all did. But Tommy's cool."

Lockhart didn't like it, but he knew if things didn't turn out he could use it, so he let it go.

Domina thought, *If Lockhart is worried about being careful, maybe he should stop killing people.* But she didn't say anything.

Casselmire wasn't expecting them for more than an hour.

"Couple blocks over there's a park, I think," Lockhart said. "Has some places to eat around it."

"Drive? Or walk?"

"Let's walk. We got time. Besides, you already paid for the parking."

Domina thought it was only $5, so it wouldn't be a problem. But she didn't want to argue with the man. "You want Tibby to put the shipment in the trunk?"

"Fuck no," Lockhart said. "As long as we have it, we keep the product in sight. Besides, my friends are in the pack. Might get too hot in the trunk."

Domina told Tiburon he should bring the pack with them. Tiburon shrugged, comfortable with Lockhart making the call, even though the man's only friends were scorpions.

CHAPTER FIFTEEN

B y the time Sam entered Carmel's office, he was cradling Gray in his arms, struggling with the wolf dog's weight. There were two receptionists behind the desk, wearing what looked like green surgical scrubs. A parrot sat on a perch behind them. A cat wearing diapers was walking across the lobby floor. There was a woman seated with a small, mop-headed dog on a leash. The dog looked up and barked, just once. Then he noticed Gray and backed up between the woman's legs.

Normally, the scene would have been interesting. But Sam didn't acknowledge any of it because Gray's breathing was labored and irregular and he could feel him starting to slacken.

"Carmel Rodriguez," Sam said to the receptionists. "Now!"

Before the girl turned, Carmel swung out a rear door and said, "In here," stepping into a nearby exam room. The room had a stainless-steel table and Sam laid Gray onto it while Carmel called out, "Peggy, where's that Anascorp and syringe?"

"He's reacting," Sam said.

"Careful with him," she said. Once he was settled, Carmel bent over his head and lifted one closed eyelid. A yellow eye stared back, the pupil narrowed to a knife point. She lifted his lip and saw foamy gums and wolf canines. He was having trouble breathing, and when she listened to his heart it was irregular.

"How long has he been like this?" She kept her eyes focused on Gray.

"He seemed fine in Cambridge. Then before we got to the jeep, when he was still walking, he relieved himself. A little diarrhea and lots of urine. And then after we hit 494, he laid down and basically didn't get back up."

"He's going into shock."

"A bark scorpion," Sam said. It was surreal.

"Did you bring it?"

"It's in the jeep."

Peggy entered with a small vial and sterilized syringe. Carmel grabbed it, tore the paper, pulled out the needle, and took the vial in her free hand. While she worked, she said, "Are you positive it was a bark scorpion?"

Sam nodded. "I've seen them before. Out in the field. Pretty sure."

She nodded. Then to Peggy, "Get me another syringe with 5 milliliters of epinephrine."

Peggy left while Carmel lifted some skin on the back of Gray's neck. She cleaned it with an alcohol swab, holding the skin taut. Then she stuck in the needle and used the plunger to empty the liquid into Gray.

Peggy entered the room with another syringe. The needle was already out of the paper. It held a thimbleful of liquid. Carmel took it and repeated the process she'd done with the previous syringe.

"What is it?" Sam said.

"Epinephrine. It'll increase his heart rate and we should see a pretty dramatic recovery. But Gray's going to have a hangover. I'll need to keep him under observation."

"He'll be okay?"

"Should be fine," Carmel said. For the first time since bringing Gray in, she noticed Sam Rivers. He had profound concern. Sam obviously loved Gray, and she admired that in anyone, particularly a grown man. Her ex could be that way with their daughter, Jennifer, but never anyone or anything else. Never an animal. It had been one of their issues.

During the entire drug delivery process Sam stroked Gray's side, and it helped. They were strong hands, ropy with veins.

"How long will he need to be here?" Sam said.

"Definitely through the afternoon. Maybe longer, depending on how he comes out of it."

Gray's breathing was beginning to normalize.

"He looks like he's improving," Sam said.

Carmel glanced at the hybrid. "He's going to be fine. Epinephrine reverses the symptoms pretty quickly. And you're lucky. I'm probably one of the few vets in the Twin Cities with Anascorp."

"What is it?"

"It's the first FDA-approved antivenom for bark scorpions. But not a lot of vets up here have it, for obvious reasons. It's pretty common in Mexico. I go back to Northern Mexico on occasion. I always carry supplies with me, just in case." She turned her attention back to Gray. "I can stay with him if you want to get that scorpion. I'd like to see it."

"You double-checking, doctor?"

"Not a lot of Northerners know scorpions. Just making sure," she said, and grinned.

"If it's not a bark scorpion, I'll buy you dinner."

Something flashed between them.

"If it *is* a bark scorpion, I'll buy *you* dinner," Carmel said.

"Tonight," Sam said. Damn. He surprised himself.

That made her smile. "I can't tonight. I've got my daughter. But tomorrow night I'm free."

For just a split-second Sam wondered if he should invite them both to dinner? *Too soon,* he thought. *But . . .*

Sam looked back to Gray and noticed his breathing was continuing to improve. Clearly the vet knew what she was doing. And now that a serious wager was involved, he wanted to have another look at that scorpion. "I'll be right back."

He retrieved the Tupperware container from the passenger-side floor. It was tipped over from the high-speed ride, but its lid was intact and when he fetched it, he could see the small scorpion scuttle to right itself on the opaque container's bottom.

Part of him was tempted to rattle the small bug's cage, to teach it a lesson, or kill it. But the scorpion had only been following its nature. And there was something else.

"What were you doing in Suthy Baxter's house?" Sam said aloud, staring at the bug.

If Baxter collected them, where were his cages? Then he wondered if it was a stowaway on some kind of shipment from the Southwest. That was possible. Could have ridden on the inside of a piece of furniture, for instance. It was more plausible than the pet theory. Sam remembered a friend who purchased a small cactus and within a day a tiny anole lizard hatched out of the dirt. He'd heard about tarantulas concealed in bunches of bananas. Maybe . . .

But Sam wasn't really feeling it. He didn't remember any plants, let alone a cactus, in the house. And when he searched his memory, he couldn't remember any of the furniture looking new, or Southwestern. It was all second-hand and worn.

But if not a pet or hitchhiker, then what?

By the time he got back to the exam room, Gray was already on his haunches, breathing regularly, though there was still drool hanging out of one side of his mouth.

Sam greeted Gray and the hybrid whined. "You look really good, buddy."

"He does," Carmel said. "It's a great response. And his size helps."

There was a countertop along the side of the room, under the double cupboard. Sam moved over to it and said, "Let's open this over here, where it won't cause any more harm."

Gray was quickly returning to his regal self.

Carmel turned while Sam lifted the lid, carefully, and pulled it away from the opening. Inside, the small scorpion backed up to a Tupperware wall and raised both its pincers and stinger.

"Close it," Carmel said.

Sam closed the lid.

"That's a bark scorpion. Pretty sure," she said. "But it wouldn't hurt to double-check with an expert." Carmel said she knew an entomologist at the U. She had a minute, so she stepped out of the room to call him.

Sam spent the time talking with Gray and stroking the big dog. Gray considered him, his eyes saying, "I'm going to remember scorpions." Otherwise, he had returned from the River Styx.

Carmel took a while, but when she returned, she said, "I called him. When I told him you had a bark scorpion, he said, 'I doubt it. Probably a pseudoscorpion.'"

Sam rolled his eyes. "Did you tell him it's a scorpion?"

"I did, but he said he'd believe it when he sees it. He's got student conferences all afternoon and through tomorrow morning. But he said if you stopped by tomorrow, sometime after noon, he'd make time."

Sam's phone went off and he saw Mac come up on the screen.

"Gotta take this," he said to Carmel. Then, "Mac, where are you?"

"Just pulled into the vet's parking lot. Wheezo's right behind me."

"Good. I'll be out in a sec."

Carmel had written down Dr. Gerald Toynbee's address, building, and office number, and handed the slip of paper to Sam.

"Thanks," Sam said.

"I guess I owe you dinner. Tomorrow night."

Sam smiled. "When can I pick up Gray?"

"Give him an hour. If he continues to improve, you should be able to take him. But I'd keep him quiet."

By the time Sam walked into the parking lot, Wheezo and Mac were both standing in the sunshine next to Mac's car, an aging Impala. There was a little rust along the running board, sort of like Mac.

"You have your gear?" Sam asked.

"I do," Wheezo said. "What kind of phone?"

"Another iPhone."

"Which version?" Wheezo said.

"No idea. An iPhone."

"Let's have a look."

Sam showed him the phone and Wheezo turned it on and said, "Can't do it without Apple's help, and they won't give it."

Sam squinted, but he let it go. "What about the PC?"

"Shouldn't be a problem." Then he paused. "Maybe we should go to some nearby restaurant where we can check it out over lunch?"

"I like how you think," Mac said.

Sam rolled his eyes. "How long is this going to take?"

"Probably a formidable lunch plate," Wheezo said.

CHAPTER SIXTEEN

Around noon Sam Rivers drove into Shirley's parking lot. The place looked busy. He pulled out his cell phone and speed-dialed Mac, who had been right behind him.

"Where are you?"

"We got caught up in road construction. I'm headed west on 494."

For the second time in 10 minutes, Sam rolled his eyes. He'd been careful to follow the signs because he knew if he got headed west, it'd be at least 10 minutes before he made it to Shirley's.

"I'll get us a table," Sam said.

The diner served comfort food on platters. On his way to a booth, Sam passed mashed potatoes with meat loaf and gravy, a cheeseburger with fries, a pork loin sandwich, a few egg plates massive in their yellowness, and more. He'd been preoccupied, so he hadn't noticed, but the platters were making him hungry. His hunger and the food were distractions from the scene back in Cambridge. All morning he'd been mulling the image of Suthy alone in his back room with the syringe in his arm, slumped over, the baggie of white powder, the spoon, the rest of it. It was awful, unexpected, and tragic. And Sam felt again something was not right. It was more than the skidded hands and knees and the bump on the back of Suthy's head.

Sam sat down in a corner booth, facing the window onto the lot so he could focus on his thoughts. Sam put his hand to his pocket and could feel the tissue with dried blood. There were the small, dried drops of blood on the victim's right arm. The same marks were on Jerry Trailor. Probably some kind of bug. Maybe a spider? But the coincidence. Same marks on the same arm?

And the similarity of the scenes. Sam understood it could be the same bad heroin. And there were only so many ways a person would sit at a table and shoot up. But it was almost as though the scenes had been choreographed. Everything except the presence of a small amount of brown heroin.

There was something else. He kept rolling through his first encounter of the scene. There was something he was missing. Something he'd learned.

Like Gray, Sam followed his nose. He had good instincts for the salient detail. He believed that if he had any special skill as an investigator, it was a sixth sense that often began with nagging, some insight hidden behind his rational considerations.

Coffee arrived and he sipped it meditatively. It was strong and good.

Sam had a deep streak of empathy, almost in direct proportion to its absence in his father. He had always been able to look into a creature's eyes, almost any creature, and recognize a sentient being staring back. The latest biological research proved most other animals shared huge amounts of human DNA. Sam had always felt a profound, some might say spiritual, sense of the interconnectedness of all things, animate as well as inanimate. Animal behavioral research also underscored how most species— for instance, dogs—had significant emotional lives. Sam thought all these perspectives were just some of the characteristics that enabled him to read people and form an instinctual feel for who they were and the basic motivations that compelled them. Usually his readings were accurate, though admittedly not always.

Sam took out his iPhone and scanned back through the photos of Suthy and the scene. As he stared at the kid's slumped figure, he had that same bizarre sensation that the kid was trying to tell him something.

He had never met Suthy Baxter, but from seeing the house and knowing about his life and school and past, he formed some opinions. Nursing was a practical degree, but it involved rigorous study and commitment and was not a career you pursued unless you were willing to put in the time and effort. Frequent partying was out of the question. Maybe Mac would find something at the school, with his teachers or classmates? Maybe the kid had a latent wild side? Maybe he dealt drugs to his classmates? But Sam didn't think so.

Sam thought about Suthy sitting in the room, pouring white powder into the spoon. He watched him, tried to feel the kid, flicking the lighter until the flame rose under the large soup spoon, watching it heat the powder to the melting point, and then carefully setting it down and taking up the syringe. He watched him tie off the rubber tubing on an arm that had never seen any needles, far as Sam could tell—no scars, no marks—and then find a likely vein in the under part of his left arm and prick himself with the needle and then . . .

Suthy was *left-handed*. That's what his brother Ronnie said. If the kid was truly left-handed, wouldn't he have used the left hand for the small motor dexterity required to handle tubing, a syringe, and a needle?

If the kid was mildly left-handed, or ambidextrous, it was probably an unimportant detail. But if he was mildly left-handed, why would he have earned the nickname Suthy?

Sam fished Ronnie Baxter's phone number out of his pocket and dialed his number.

"Ronnie," the brother said, muted.

"Sam Rivers," Sam said.

There was a pause. "I still can't believe this is happening. Happened," Ronnie said.

"I'm sorry. There's no easy way to absorb a loss like this."

"I just never saw anything like this coming. He was a good kid. I thought he'd straightened out."

"It's tragic," Sam said. "Again, I'm sorry." After a moment of silence, Sam said, "Can I ask you something about your brother?"

"Sure."

"I'm not sure what it means, but I need to know how left-handed your brother was."

"What do you mean?"

"I mean, the nickname Suthy was because he was a southpaw. Did he do everything left-handed?"

"Everything," Ronnie said. "Everything athletic. He threw left-handed. Batted, shot baskets. We weren't really raised on golf, but we tried it a couple of times. He was left-handed at that too."

"What about writing?"

"That too. Always claimed it made him more of an artist, being left-handed. Why?"

"Just . . .," Sam hesitated. "Trying to get the full picture of your brother."

Sam thanked Ronnie and hung up.

And then Mac and Wheezo arrived.

Wheezo carried his laptop and said, "Did you see that bacon cheeseburger?"

"It's a heart attack waiting to happen," Sam said.

"It's an embarrassment of riches," Mac said, eyeing a nearby plate with turkey, mashed potatoes, and gravy.

"What about your spinach wrap?"

Mac frowned. "As far as Margie's concerned, the spinach wrap was excellent."

Sam ordered a veggie omelet with cheese but had to admit the bacon cheeseburger with fries and plate with meat loaf, mashed potatoes, and gravy had a definite allure.

Wheezo switched up the bacon cheeseburger plate and ordered tater tots instead of fries. And Mac made a surprising last-minute change: steak and eggs with hash browns and toast.

While they waited for their lunch, Sam brought them both up to speed on the scene. Wheezo took the iPhone, saw it was a 5s, and said, "Sorry, no way."

"I thought you could get into anything," Sam said.

"Not an iPhone 5 or higher. Nobody can. Not Israelis, not Russians, not even Wheezo," he said. "But I can get you whatever he has on that laptop, and probably tap his email account."

"Do it," Sam said.

It took Wheezo only minutes, using his forensics application, to get into Suthy's laptop and then email account. Sam got him to download Suthy's contacts to a flash drive, so they could cross-check them with Jerry Trailor's contacts.

Then their food arrived.

While they ate, Sam kept talking and described the scene back in Cambridge, the house, the sheriff, the sheriff's memory of the meth bust five years earlier, what Suthy Baxter had been doing—enrolled in a nursing program at the local community college—and the meeting with Suthy's brother.

Mac and Wheezo were listening, but also intent on their substantial plates.

Sam thought about next steps, and said, "What I need you to do, Mac, is head over to that school. Talk to some of Suthy's teachers. Find out what was going on. See what kind of kid he was."

Mac nodded, chewing.

Wheezo popped a tater tot into his mouth and appeared content. His burger was nearly finished. There was a piece of bacon sticking out of a bite-size section of bun on top of a patty, and he was eyeing it with what Sam thought might be melancholy.

"Sounds like you suspect something other than a couple ODs," Mac said.

"They were definitely ODs. But the paraphernalia and the way they were set out was almost identical. I'm not sure you could accomplish it in the same way even if you were staging it. But why would you stage an OD?"

"Murder," Mac shrugged. "Except Jerry Trailor texted the kid what, yesterday, day before, and told him he'd be coming into some money. I'm thinking he was dealing. Maybe sold a little and kept some for himself and this guy in Cambridge. But they didn't know how strong it was."

"If he sold, where's the money? The crime-scene guys turned Jerry's place upside down."

"So they were getting it from someplace," Wheezo said.

"The question is, did they both deal with the same guy, or did one of them get it—my bet would be Jerry—and then share it, or sell it, to the other. To Suthy Baxter?"

"Or maybe they both got it separately?" Mac said. "But I'm thinking it would be Jerry who got the stuff, sold most of it, made some dough, and kept a little for himself and this kid."

"But where's Jerry's money?"

"Could be anywhere," Mac said. "Buried in his backyard."

Wheezo had finally stuffed the last bit of cheeseburger into his mouth. "Gotta see a dessert menu," he said.

"Not until you do some work," Sam said.

Wheezo thought about protesting, but considering it was a free lunch, second day in a row, and Sam hadn't said no to dessert, he capitulated. He knew a place like Shirley's was going to have some rockin' dessert options.

He re-entered his laptop and quickly cross-checked the contacts in the two phones. There were four names on both phones.

Sam noted them and then had Wheezo check the criminal justice database. "Maury Trumble" popped up.

"Gotta be one of the kids arrested for meth," Sam said.

"The ones the sheriff told you about?" Mac asked.

"Yeah. Run the rest of Baxter's contacts through the database. See if any of them had records."

"Can we at least *see* a dessert menu?" Wheezo said.

"What kind of place you think this is? It's right there on the main menu," Mac said, pointing to where the menu was tucked behind a condiment rack at the end of the Formica table.

Wheezo grabbed the menu before Sam could protest.

"The kid makes me feel used," Sam said.

The waitress came and Wheezo ordered apple pie à la mode, which put a little glint in Mac's eye and caused him to hesitate, but he didn't order. Then Wheezo returned to his screen. He'd created an algorithm to automatically pull the names from the contact list and one by one run them through the criminal justice database. But the only names that popped were Maury Trumble and Lonnie DeLay. Maury was busted with the others but served two years probation, at home, due to "unspecified assistance." Lonnie DeLay was 18, tried as an adult, convicted, and served four and a half years. He'd recently received early probation for good behavior.

Then Wheezo's dessert arrived and he was offline again, at least for a couple of minutes.

Mac still had a fork and he eyed Wheezo's pie, then glanced at his fork, calculating.

Wheezo, who didn't miss much, moved away from Mac, bringing his plate in close, encircling it with a forearm.

"Are we in grade school?" Sam said.

Sam's cell phone went off. He looked at the number, 612 area code, but didn't recognize it. He clicked Accept and said, "Rivers."

"Sam Rivers?"

"Yes."

"Scott Pepper, Special Agent with the DEA."

Sam had heard the name and remembered Sheriff Broom's hesitance.

"Scott Pepper," Sam said. "Sheriff Broom said you might be calling."

"Damn right. How is Earl?"

"He's good."

"So did Earl tell you I headed up the task force that closed down the heroin trade in the Twin Cities for the last six months?"

"The sheriff didn't, but I think Detective Marschel mentioned it."

"Good of Raven to remember. The seven-county metro area's been dry as a dead dingo since we bounced that Asian cartel off the streets. Sixty-one arrests. Damn fine work. And now Marschel's telling me she's found fresh product?"

"Yesterday in Hopkins and today in Cambridge. Looks like a couple ODs."

"And she says it's heroin laced with fentanyl."

"We think so. Detective Marschel has the results on the Hopkins OD. Sheriff Broom's guys are testing the Cambridge OD, but it looked like the same stuff. We also found a couple grams of brown heroin on the OD in Hopkins."

"Uh-huh," Pepper said, preoccupied. "I understand you have their phones?"

"Yes," Sam said.

"Find anything?"

He considered telling him about Wheezo and what they found, but hesitated. "Jerry Trailor's phone led us to Suthy Baxter. That's why I went to Cambridge."

"Uh-huh," Pepper said, again without much interest. "With all due respect, Rivers, we're dealing with drugs and dealers here, not ducks or deer or what have you. No offense."

"None taken."

"You bring those phones down here pronto and we'll have a look ourselves and see what there is to see. Since this happened in the greater metro area, the DEA's taking over. It's an interjurisdictional matter. We'll figure out what we've got. Comprende?"

"Loud and clear," Sam said.

"So it's almost 1 o'clock. Where are you now?"

"Eden Prairie."

"Bring in those phones and we can talk. Should take you about a half hour to get here."

Sam took down the address. 100 Washington Avenue North in Minneapolis.

Sam Rivers was a team player, providing he considered the captain worthy. "See you in a half hour," Sam said, and hung up.

"Who was that?" Mac said.

"Scott Pepper, a DEA agent."

"You gotta go down there?"

"I do, but you don't. You need to go up to Cambridge and track down some of Baxter's teachers and fellow students. Find out about him, especially whether or not he was using and if anyone has any idea about his source. I need to take the phones to Minneapolis." He turned to Wheezo. "Everything downloaded?"

Wheezo nodded. "From the laptop. They're not going to be able to get into his phone."

"Let's let them figure that out. Scott Pepper strikes me as the kind of guy who would tell us to cease and desist, if he knew what we were doing. So for now, I'll just deliver the phones and the PC and make sure my hunches about Pepper are correct." He looked at Mac. "Meanwhile, let's keep following leads."

Mac nodded. "Better 'n my desk."

"I have to go back to the office?" Wheezo said.

Sam considered. "I suspect some of those kids at the community college might be more willing to speak to you than grandpa."

"Hey," Mac said.

"I think he's talking about the ladies," Wheezo said.

"Let me put it a little differently," Sam said, turning to Mac. "At some point Wheezo might want to expand his horizons and get into field work. I need a seasoned pro to show him the ropes."

Mac's face brightened. "I get your meaning."

"And while your natural charm is truly something to behold," Sam said to Wheezo, "It's good to remember you're doing field research. And back home *your lady* is four months pregnant."

"I didn't say I was going to touch anyone," Wheezo said.

"Just figure out who the kid was," Sam said.

"We're on it," Mac said.

It had been an hour since he'd left Gray. Sam swung by Carmel's office and was disappointed she was seeing a patient. But Gray, miraculously, was back to his old self.

"You should let him rest for a while," Peggy, the vet tech, said. Sam assured her he would.

"How much?" Sam said, reaching for his money.

Peggy turned around the corner, sat at a computer screen, and pulled up Sam's invoice. Her eyebrows furrowed. "Hmmmm," Peggy said. "It says 'charges pending.' I guess I haven't seen that before, so I'm not sure what Dr. Carmel has in mind."

"Okay," Sam shrugged. "I can ask her about it tomorrow night."

"Over dinner?" Peggy said. When Sam appeared surprised, she said, "She mentioned you had a date," and grinned.

"I guess," Sam said. The women had been talking.

"Maybe you can work off that charge somehow," Peggy said.

The comment was so unexpected and suggestive, it startled Sam. Still, it was hard not to smile. "Maybe," he said.

CHAPTER SEVENTEEN

Lockhart, Domina, and Tiburon had taken the better part of an hour walking to the nearby park, Mears, and finding a place to eat, Solid Barbecue. Then they returned to the Pilsner Artists Lofts.

"So what is this place?" Lockhart said.

The area had changed since Lockhart last walked the lonely streets. It was upscale now, gentrified. The sign on the outside of the building they were walking toward was big and stylish.

"Looks like the Pilsner Artists Lofts," Domina said.

Lockhart had never had much of a sense of humor. The last few days had only tarnished it. In his world, everything was a threat or an impediment. Now he considered Domina's comment, recognized it was neither, and didn't smile.

"So who is this guy?" he said, putting it differently.

Domina looked away. "Another Fuego connection."

"I know it's a Fuego connection. Any idea how he got it?"

The backpack containing the heroin was slung over Tiburon's right shoulder. They walked up to the red light and waited.

Domina said, "No idea."

Up the street there was some activity. Farther up the block they could see a big opening, what Lockhart remembered as the

St. Paul Farmer's Market, though now it was empty. Since it was around lunchtime there were a few pedestrians. But otherwise the area was mostly residences and small businesses set up in renovated warehouses.

"How in the hell does a guy in Michoacán get a connection in the Pilsner Lofts in St. Paul?"

Domina shrugged. "All I know is what Fuego told us. The guy can move product, so . . ."

Lockhart needed the *Monarcas*. So for now, Lockhart waited for the light to change and then walked into the street. They crossed, found the entrance to the building, pushed the number next to "Casselmire," and waited.

"Yo," a young voice barked through the intercom.

"Tim Casselmire?" Lockhart said.

"Yo."

"We're here for a visit."

"Come on up. Take the elevator to the 4th floor. I'm down on the end. 402."

In the elevator, on the ride to the top floor, Lockhart reminded himself about the first name business, to use it and build rapport. And if Casselmire was anything like Rich Matthewson, Lockhart thought he knew how he could get more info out of him, about how he knew a Mexican drug lord.

But Tim Casselmire wasn't anything like Rich Matthewson. He was skinny. He wore a T-shirt with "Handel's Messiah" on the front and "SPCO" with dates at the Basilica. The shirt was wrapped tight over a bony frame and what you noticed was sinew. Skintight, faded black jeans narrowed down to skinny ankles and bare, bony feet. If the kid was nervous, he didn't show it. He looked like maybe he'd been a dancer. Or a tight rope walker. Or a young Mick Jagger, if Mick had sandy blonde, unkempt short hair with a cowlick sticking up in back. It looked like the kid just rolled out of bed, or maybe he'd just gotten home from an all-night gaming convention.

They all shook hands and the kid's grip, Lockhart noticed, was firm.

"Call me Tim," Casselmire said.

"So we must have mutual friends, Tim," Lockhart said.

"I guess," Casselmire said.

"How'd you find out about us?" Lockhart said.

"I didn't. Somebody contacted me."

"From Mexico?"

Tim Casselmire shook his head no. "Friend of a friend."

The loft was spare with a cement floor and walls and a striking Persian rug, mostly red, in the center of the room. And blonde furniture. There was a poster advertising *Hair*, the musical, on one wall, inside a frame. And a couple of similar posters advertising theatrical events. There was a table in the kitchen with four chairs and a sitting area, probably billed as the living room, with a futon couch in front of a long blonde coffee table and a couple of simple chairs on either side. The whole place was neat and spotless and looked like something out of one of those . . . Lockhart was trying to remember it. Then, *Ikea*. It had been an Ikea catalog he had thumbed somewhere, mindlessly. Casselmire's place looked like Ikea.

There was a single closed door to one side.

"We alone, Tim?"

"Sure."

Lockhart considered it. Then turned to Tiburon and nodded for him to check the place out.

Tiburon walked back to the closed door and opened it.

"Hey," Casselmire said.

"No offense, Tim. But we both know this is serious business and we're just being careful. We know you would be, too, if you were in our position."

The kid didn't like it. "We're alone," Casselmire said.

Tiburon walked into the room and glanced around the one bedroom. The bed was unmade. Clothes were scattered around the room, most of them piled on the floor. The bedroom was as unkempt as the living area was spotless. Tiburon opened a closet, a bathroom, but there was nothing. He came back and nodded, the backpack still on his right shoulder. Tiburon stood, while Domina and Lockhart sat on the two chairs with Casselmire on the couch, his feet on the floor, hands folded.

There was a little edge in the room, now that Tiburon had violated Tim Casselmire's space.

"That's quite a rug," Domina said, admiring the Persian.

"Thanks," Casselmire said.

"You got a nice place," she added.

Casselmire finally figured it was understandable these guys would be tense, so he tried to let the bedroom search pass. "The rug really ties the room together," he said. It was a line from the movie, *The Big Lebowski*.

Domina understood and laughed. "Nice," she said. But the comment was lost on Lockhart and Tiburon.

"Get you anything? Beer? Coffee? Water?" Casselmire said.

"We're good, Tim," Lockhart said.

"Okay," Casselmire said.

"So I'm just trying to understand the connection?"

Domina sighed.

Casselmire picked it up but repeated what he'd said earlier. "Like I said, just a friend of a friend."

"Got a name, Tim?"

Casselmire paused. "Anonymous."

Lockhart thought about it. "You trust the guy, Tim?"

"Yeah, I trust him."

"I hope so, Tim. Because like I said, this is a risky business."

"I get it," Casselmire said. "You've got product to move. I can move it."

"We got a lot of product," Lockhart said.

"There's a lot of need."

"There's always a lot of need."

"Not like the last six months," Casselmire said. "The feds closed down the trade and the street's been like third-world market shelves. Not a smidgen of anything anywhere. Plenty of other stuff. Meth, some Oxy, and prescription stuff. But none of the . . .," he paused, "Good stuff." Then he said, "Did you bring it?"

Lockhart looked at the kid in a way that would have made anyone fidget, but the kid just stared back. He had more nerve than his wiry frame conveyed, definitely more than Matthewson. Lockhart had been ready to push the name thing, see if he could get anything. If it was a Mexican name, that'd be something. But the kid wasn't going to budge on "Anonymous." And besides, Lockhart recognized Domina's irritation, for the time being, registering it as another entry on his ledger under "insolence."

Lockhart turned to Domina and said, "Tell him to set it on the table."

Domina told Tiburon, whose face and demeanor remained implacable. He swung the backpack strap off his right shoulder, unzipped the bag, and carefully pulled out the pound of brown heroin. Then he set it in the center of the blonde table, in front of the couch.

Tim Casselmire blew out a breath that would have sounded like a whistle, if he hadn't been too surprised to put his lips together. "Damn," was all he said, leaning forward to stare at it, as though it might not be real.

"That's a lot of product, Tim," Lockhart said.

"I see that."

"And you think you can move it?"

The kid hadn't taken his eyes off the brick. "I know I can move it," he finally said, looking back at Lockhart.

"Here's what we need to start," Lockhart said. "This first one's on credit. Hard to believe and I've never done business that way, but we're told you're good for it, Tim, so . . ."

Tim Casselmire nodded. "I'm good for it."

"So how long you think it'll take?"

The kid glanced back down at the heroin. "I know people. I do a lot of work in the local theatre scenes. I know people who know people who want this stuff. So first I'm going to call those guys and pass along the wholesale price you're giving me."

But to himself, Casselmire was thinking, *plus maybe 50, 60%. Maybe 100,* thinking markup.

He looked back at Lockhart and said, "Give me a couple days. If you're really curious you can call tomorrow. But this is going to move faster than a white Russian in a room full of Dudes."

Domina grinned.

Again, Lockhart didn't understand the reference, but said, "That'd be good, Tim. And please let it be known there's more where this came from."

Casselmire grinned. He looked like a kid, Lockhart thought, but a tough kid.

Then Lockhart told him about getting in on the ground floor of a new enterprise, one that was going to be distributing a fair amount of product around the Twin Cities. He reiterated how important it was that names and identities stayed out of any discussions with any of his distributors or users.

The kid didn't need to be told. The kid wasn't going to talk to anyone. "The only people I know are right here, in this room. You don't know my people, and you won't. And I don't know yours, and I don't want to," Casselmire said.

Smart kid, Lockhart thought. Unfortunately, integrity was a doubled-edged sword. He wasn't going to say anything, which meant Lockhart wasn't going to learn anything about his contacts. "Just understand, Tim, that if my people ever got wind anyone was given up, names were divulged . . ."

"Never happen," the kid said, before Lockhart could finish.

Lockhart paused. He didn't like being interrupted, but under the circumstances . . . "That's good, Tim." He smiled, but without humor.

Lockhart stood and Domina took his lead. Then Tiburon turned toward the door.

"So tell me, Tim. Shepherd Road?"

"You mean how to get there?"

"Yeah."

"Where you headed?"

Lockhart looked at him. "I heard it was a nice road with good river views."

"You're close. Definite views of the river, if you like your rivers muddy."

"Good."

"I wouldn't want someone else moving product who was living off Shepherd Road," Casselmire said.

The kid was smart. A businessman. "For now, St. Paul's your territory," Lockhart said. "But stay out of Minneapolis."

"Not a problem," the kid said.

Casselmire told them how to get to Shepherd Road, and that you could take it almost all the way to the airport. Lots of good river views along the way.

Lockhart thanked him and tried to smile in a friendly *we're-going-to-do-a-lot-of-business-together* way, but given Lockhart's misshapen face, it looked more ghoulish than friendly. After they stepped into the hallway, Casselmire's door closed and the bolt lock snapped shut behind them.

CHAPTER EIGHTEEN

S am had a love-hate relationship with urban centers. They were always interesting but difficult to navigate. The new GPS apps made finding places easy. But once you'd arrived, where did you park? Particularly when your partner was a nearly 100-pound wolf dog sitting in the front seat, who needed to be somewhere quiet for a while. From what Sam could tell, Gray had made a full recovery. But he wanted to find the right parking spot, where Gray would be comfortable lying down and sleeping off what Sam assumed felt like a bad hangover.

The DEA offices were in a white square pillbox with what appeared to be embrasures for windows. The place looked like it had been designed by a 17th-century Spanish fort architect, with 8-foot-thick walls and wide slits big enough to fire a cannon. Sam drove by, checked it out, and began looking for the right place to park. There was an inside space in the nearby Minneapolis Public Library's open lot. Because it was an interior space, Gray wouldn't be bothered by pedestrians, and he'd be able to see several feet in any direction. The wolf dog liked to be able to look around.

Sam walked into Scott Pepper's office carrying the two cell phones and laptop. He was surprised to see Detective Raven Marschel sitting in one of two chairs in front of Pepper's desk.

Marschel introduced Agent Rivers to Agent Scott Pepper and Sam nodded, passing over the hardware and taking a seat.

"We love to get a junkie's tools of the trade," Scott Pepper said. He stood to reach across the desk and shake Sam's hand, and then took the equipment. He remained standing as he speed-dialed someone, glancing away.

The DEA agent was short and stout and wore a dark blue suit with a starched white shirt and red necktie. His neck bulged around his collar, and his crew cut was stiff enough to balance a plate.

The office was a narrow rectangular stone quadrant with a black steel desk and a couple of certificates on the wall. There were two pictures: one of a much younger Scott Pepper shaking hands with President George H. W. Bush, and another shaking hands with President George W. Bush.

Sam glanced at Detective Marschel, who grinned and turned back to Pepper.

"Glen, can you send someone up to get these phones," Pepper said over the phone. "Let's crack 'em and see what they bleed."

Pepper hung up and sat down behind his desk, picking up a paper clip and playing with it while considering Sam Rivers.

"You know anyone at the DEA, Mr. Rivers?"

"Not really," Sam said. Among law enforcement officers it was customary to address each other by title. Agent Pepper. Agent Rivers, the way Sam had been introduced by Detective Marschel.

Sometimes, when you were addressing someone from another office, using the title "Mr." was a subtle put-down. Sometimes.

"That makes us even, 'cause I don't know anyone at Fish & Wildlife. What kind of work do you do there? Mostly outside stuff? Chase down poachers, that kind of thing?" Pepper asked, only half interested.

"We do some of that. We do a lot of everything, including drug interdiction at the border and in wild places all over the country."

"You remember that murder last year?" Marschel said. "In Savage?"

"Can't say I do," Pepper said.

"Corporate guy was allegedly attacked and killed by a cougar?"

"Oh, yeah. I think I remember. And the murderer got away?"

"The murderer was killed," Sam said. "His accomplice is in prison. The ringleader got away."

"Damn. Hate to see 'em get away. Particularly with murder. Wasn't it his wife? Made off with millions?"

"She did," Sam said. "For now."

"Agent Rivers was the one who helped Sheriff Rusty Benson understand what really happened there," Detective Marschel said.

"Benson," Pepper said, shaking his head. "How'd you like working with that jackass?"

"At times it was challenging," Sam said.

"I bet. And I bet when he finally figured it out, he was all over it, from a PR angle."

"That's Rusty Benson," Sam said.

Pepper laughed a little, out his nose. "Thing is, we don't have cougars or wolves or snake skins involved in this case. Just heroin," Pepper said. Then he paused, considering.

Sam didn't react, but he thought the agent was waiting for something.

"Detective Marschel here tells me you're someone who can be trusted. That a fair assessment?"

"I appreciate that," Sam said. "Truth is, I've only just met Detective Marschel. But yes, I can be trusted."

Marschel said, "I did a little research, made some calls. Talked to his boss. She thinks Rivers here is the best field operative in the Service, that he has an innate knack for investigating, when he isn't going rogue and pissing her off."

Sam smiled and reminded himself he owed Kay, his boss, an update call.

"We don't need rogue," Pepper said,

"Agent Rivers has been a big help so far," Marschel said.

Pepper considered it. Then, "I'm going to let you in on some inside dope, Rivers. I'm sure you'll treat it with care."

Of course, that was a given.

Pepper breathed heavy, glanced at Raven Marschel, and then back at Sam. "I was telling Detective Marschel here we've heard from some of our Mexican informants that a cartel is trying to bring in product. Right now, no idea how. Probably tunnels, could be by boat. Last March we seized a pound of heroin covered in coffee grounds and axle grease buried in a shipment of boat motors from Vera Cruz coming into New Orleans. Mercs headed for Minnesota. Pretty good cover, considering the upcoming boating season.

And the dogs were no good. The dogs are being outsmarted here, which figures, 'cause they're dogs."

He snorted again, happy with his comment.

"Did any of it contain fentanyl?" Sam said.

"Nope. Pure as the wind-driven snow."

"Any brown heroin?"

"Nope."

"Last March?"

"Yup. We're thinking maybe some of it got through and they've been sitting on it, waiting until things settled down before trying to move it on the street."

"Sounds like a different batch," Sam said.

Pepper shrugged. "Could be. Could be somebody local cutting the stuff with fentanyl? Point is, this is my territory, and no one pisses in my territory. So these dingos are goin' down."

Sam nodded. "Okay."

"Damn straight."

"So what's the plan?"

"Detective Marschel told you about our task force?"

Sam nodded.

"We're resurrecting it, putting out a notice to our partners who helped us last year. Everyone's going to be made aware we've intercepted some new product. Even Rusty Benson."

"And the ODs?"

"We'll put out a release."

"Today?"

"Not quite yet."

Sam looked at Detective Marschel, then back to Pepper.

"Probably want to avoid more ODs," Sam said. "Might make sense to put out a press release, have it hit the local channels? Preferably before the afternoon news cycle. Sooner the better."

Another grin accompanied by a snort. "They're ODs, Rivers. Just another junkie off the street. Don't get me wrong. We'll get the word out soon enough. First, we need to quietly alert the task force, see if they can shake anything loose without startling the kangaroos. This latest kid was in Cambridge, so who the hell knows where it's coming from. Could be Duluth. Maybe Fargo. Our guys need a little time to work their informal networks."

Sam turned to Marschel. "Didn't you say the heroin that killed Jerry Trailor contained enough fentanyl to put down an elephant?"

"Yeah."

"And we can only assume, given the connection between Trailor and Baxter, that Baxter used the same stuff."

"Toxicology hasn't gotten back to me yet, but I'd say that's a fair guess."

"Just a guess," Pepper said.

"If anyone else uses this stuff," Sam said, "we're likely to have another OD."

"Can't be helped," Pepper said.

"We've had two deaths in 24 hours," Sam said. "This new stuff is dangerous."

"Short-term pain for long-term gain," Pepper said. "We play our cards right, we find out the source, we can clear it all off the streets before we have an epidemic."

"Meanwhile, you may lose more people."

"Junkies," Pepper said. "Can't fix stupid."

"What if it's a mother trying to get off Oxy?"

Pepper rolled his eyes. "We've had two ODs by two felons with records, and personally, I don't have a lot of sympathy for illicit drug users breaking the law for a good time. If they're gonna taste the stuff, they're gonna go down one way or another. Better to save taxpayers the time and money it takes to house and feed these reprobates. And the recidivism, particularly for heroin users, is higher than a kite, no pun intended." Pepper grinned. "These two served time for meth, and four or five years later, they both OD. Not a bad outcome for the state, in my book. But maybe it's different in Colorado, where your great state legalized marijuana, making one hell of a problem for the DEA."

It wasn't the first time Colorado's recent decriminalization surfaced during a law enforcement conversation.

"We're not even sure they were heroin users," Sam said.

Pepper glanced at Marschel and frowned. Then back at Sam. "They went to juvie for producing and selling meth. Now they're caught with needles up their arms. If it walks like a duck and talks like a duck, it's a fuckin' duck."

"They haven't found any other indications of needle use," Sam said. "Correct, Detective?"

Marschel nodded. "Doesn't look like it. At least with the first victim."

"So they were smoking it or snorting it." Pepper was annoyed. "I understand you excel at investigation, Rivers, but let's not make more of this than it is. Two meth dealers OD on laced heroin. End of story. Period. We need to find their source."

Sam thought about pointing out some of the anomalies, but only for a second. "Agreed," he finally said. "And it's your show."

"Damn straight," Pepper said.

"So whatever we can do to help," Sam said, leaving it out there. His tongue sometimes got the best of him, and he was expecting Pepper to blow him off. That would be the simplest thing.

"Just take your direction from Detective Marschel here, who tells me she's up to her crack in crocodiles. Don't do anything without first clearing it with Marschel. Understood?"

"Okay," Sam said. "Whatever I can do. Me and Gray."

"That your dog?"

Sam nodded. "He's a drug sniffer."

Pepper shrugged. "Might be useful, unless they've covered it in axle grease and coffee grounds."

This time it was Sam's turn to shrug.

With not much more to say, Agent Scott Pepper stood, letting them know this meeting (or from Pepper's perspective, audience) was over. Sam and Detective Marschel thanked the agent and within a minute they were out on the street.

"Guy's a piece of work," Raven Marschel said, once in the sunlight.

Sam was glad to hear her perspective. "Interesting choice to head up a metro-area task force."

"Politics," Marschel said. "Pepper's comments about Rusty Benson are the pot calling the kettle black. In fact, his grandstanding skills are about the only thing he's really good at. After the last drug bust, he was the first to speak to the media, the first to be out in front. There were several people who were co-leads of the task force, but it was Pepper who, once the big busts happened, made sure he was available and identified as the head of the operation. That news got back to Washington. He was promoted. Did a six-month assignment in Australia, where we were hoping he'd stay down under."

"But he's paddled back like a quacking platypus," Sam said.

Marschel grinned. "Exactly."

"I've got another lead or two to follow."

"You do that, Agent Rivers. Just keep me in the loop. Politics. I've got to get back to Hopkins."

"Crocodiles?"

"Nipping at my ass," Marschel said.

CHAPTER NINETEEN

After saying goodbye to Raven Marschel, Sam got a coffee at a Dunn Bros. and thought about Jerry and Suthy. Both their deaths were incongruous, but in different ways. Presumably Jerry, who had been responsible enough to keep his job working at an elementary school for at least three years, decided to shoot up a couple of hours before the teachers and kids arrived? And everything he had learned about Suthy made the scene at his house illogical. Suthy would have fit in with the young people sitting in the coffee shop. He was a twenty-something college kid with a bright working future. Sam knew the kid should have been sitting here beside them, and it made him all the more aware that there was nothing, nothing about Suthy's death that felt correct, valid, proper, or right. There were many more questions than the mystery of Suthy and Jerry's supplier, and that made Sam both fascinated and unsettled.

While he was mulling over the two ODs, a striking woman entered the shop, maybe early thirties, Sam guessed. She wore a red hoodie over black yoga pants with a pair of red and white sneakers. Her long blonde hair fell over her shoulders like a yellow waterfall.

So maybe he was overdue for a relationship, Sam thought. Not with the striking woman in yoga pants, but with someone who was more likely to wear hiking boots. He was definitely overdue for the endorphin dose that came from touching and being touched, providing it was the right partner. But finding the right partner had never come easy to him. When a relationship with a woman was good, as it had been with his wife their first few years, there was a sense of comfort and belonging unlike anything he had ever experienced. And then there was the physical contact, regular and excellent. From Sam's limited experience it didn't take long to figure out a partner's preferences, and to convey his own.

While he sat there, sipping coffee and mostly spending time contemplating the details of the two ODs, he also occasionally thought about Carmel. Her name and image popped into his head like a bubble from the bottom of a deep lake. He couldn't deny there was an attraction, but the possibility they could have relations of one kind or another? The idea was as fickle as the weather. Fickler.

Sam shook his head and said to himself: *Rivers, get a grip. Because you've got business that needs your attention and most of all we don't want another OD, especially since the DEA isn't going to be any help getting the word out, at least for the foreseeable future.*

He took out his notepad and stared at the blank rectangle of paper, thinking.

Monarch butterflies, he wrote, looking at the phrase and thinking about it.

From the beginning there was something about pupas being shipped from Central Mexico, and most especially about Gray's fixation with the shipment, that raised some red flags. If there were trace elements of heroin on that box, was it because the white or brown heroin or both had been shipped in it, along with the pupas? Or was it because the victim, Jerry Trailor, had touched it with tainted hands?

The monarch butterfly life cycle.

There was more to the monarch pupas than just the box from Mexico. As Sam recalled, when the butterflies were in Mexico, particularly over the cool winter, they entered a state called diapause. It was like hibernation. In the spring, when it warmed, they began to stir and mate, but they wouldn't lay eggs until they could find milkweed, their host plant. And there wasn't any in Central Mexico. A Mexican outfit could have grown some milkweed or shipped some in, but Sam guessed the cost would have been prohibitive if monarch pupas were available where milkweed and monarchs naturally bred. Texas, for instance.

Mexican cartel.

Scott Pepper said his informants heard there was some cartel wanting to get back into the Twin Cities. Sam had seen some USFW reports about increased brown heroin interdiction at the border. He remembered reading the cartels were having trouble competing with the new domestic US marijuana cultivation. In response, many of them had planted their Mexican fields in poppies. Heroin production had increased all over Mexico, including in Michoacán, which meant more of it—no one knew how much more—was being intercepted at the border.

Sam's cell phone rang. Mac.

He picked up. "How's it going?"

"If this kid, Suthy Baxter, was a user, a regular user, none of his friends knew about it," Mac said. "Or his acquaintances. Actually, the kid sort of kept to himself, but he knew a lot of people. And a lot of people knew him. Including two of his professors who said they were shocked. Dumbfounded, really; that's what one of them said. He was *dumbfounded* the kid OD'd on heroin. Never saw it coming because Suthy Baxter was a pretty good student. And you have to be clear-headed to study nursing. There's too much science involved. I couldn't do it."

"You'd make a great nurse."

"I'd make a great everything," Mac said. "Up here, talking to all these students, some of them pretty coeds, I think I'd make a pretty good swinger too."

"Margie would cut your balls off."

That sobered him a little. "It's not me you have to worry about. Wheezo's a natural. He builds rapport in seconds; the cute ones, milliseconds."

"You need to remind the kid that there's a Mrs. Wheezo."

"It's just kind of amazing to watch him work. Who would've thought?"

"He has a good teacher."

"Good point."

"So Wheezo found the same thing?" Sam said.

"Nobody we talked with believed Suthy would ever use heroin. Everyone who knew him had the same story. Straight kid with his head down. Mostly in books. Maybe an occasional reefer, couple beers in the bar Friday and Saturday, or over a weeknight hockey game, but otherwise a serious student. And Wheezo cross-checked everything he's got on all the databases, but he didn't find anything more than he told us about at the restaurant."

Sam flipped over his notebook page and saw the name *Lonnie DeLay*. "So, Lonnie DeLay was the only one on both phones who also had a record?"

"Prison record. The last four years and change in Stillwater. He's been out for a few months."

That was interesting. Sam would need to double-check with the sheriff, but DeLay must have been part of the gang.

"Tell Wheezo to get me an address for Lonnie DeLay. Just have him text it to me. I'm going to call the sheriff, try and get him before he leaves for the day."

"Sheriff Broom?"

"Yeah. He remembered some of those kids and was telling me about them. DeLay was probably one of them. I need to double-check."

"You thinking this DeLay could be selling?"

"Could be. They got it from someplace. The best predictor of future behavior is past behavior, and if this guy, DeLay, was involved in the meth business, he's got a drug record, so . . ."

"Maybe," Mac said, and signed off.

Sam found the sheriff's number and dialed. He had to work through the sheriff's receptionist, telling her who he was. After a minute, Broom got on the line.

"I was just about to call you, but I'm busier than a mad dog in a meat locker."

"A sheriff's work is never done," Sam said.

"It started with that business in town and went on from there. I'd need another four hours just to clean up the mess from this day."

"Sheriff, if there was any other way to get the information I need . . ."

"Hold on, son. You'll be glad to know my priorities are in order. Got the file right here. And I was just sifting through it. There were five of them; four we caught and prosecuted. The head, a Jon Lockhart, got away."

Sam wrote the name down. "So there was Jerry Trailor, Suthy Baxter, and . . .?"

"Kid's name was Kurt Baxter back then. No Suthy, but that was him. And Trailor. And, let's see." The sound of shuffling papers. "There was Lonnie DeLay. He's the one who served time. He was 18. Just turned, poor sucker. And there was Maury Trumble. Trumble I told you about. He was the only one who walked."

"What about Lockhart?"

"Got nothing on him except what those kids told us. He had a record, when we looked him up. Grand theft auto. Served some time, as I recall. We set up a sting for him, but the guy never showed. We think somebody tipped him off, but it would have been a hat trick if it was one of those kids because they were all in lockup at the time. We kept them separated and monitored their phone calls and visits."

"Got any addresses?"

"Old ones. I know Trumble moved away. So did the others. Everyone except Kurt Baxter. To tell you the truth I forgot about them, after the case was done. They got what they deserved.

Everyone but Trumble. And DeLay—the kid never should have done hard time."

"Anything else?"

"That's about all I got."

Sam told him he appreciated it.

"Got Socials, if you need them."

"Sure," Sam said, and took them down.

"Anything on your end I should know about?"

"I don't know. According to my guys, Suthy Baxter was a pretty straight kid. A beer, now and again, but otherwise a pretty serious student. Nursing."

"I remember him. He seemed the youngest of the bunch, though they were all close to the same age."

"I had a meeting with Scott Pepper. Me and Detective Marschel."

After a moment, the sheriff said, "How did that go?"

"Probably like you imagine," Sam said.

The sheriff snickered over the line. "Sometimes I'm not sure Pepper could find his ass with both hands. But he plays the media like a swami in front of a basket of cobras."

Sam smiled.

"I guess he's worthwhile," the sheriff said. "If you need that kind of thing. But if I were you, I'd try and stay out of his way and play dumb. That way you can keep doing what you think makes the most sense."

"Good advice," Sam said.

"If you can do that, you could be a sheriff some day. The only other skill you need is the ability to spend half your life with riff raff, scumbags, and scallywags. And then there's the criminals."

Sam grinned again, said goodbye, and hung up.

A text had come in while he was speaking to the sheriff. It was Wheezo with Lonnie DeLay's address. Hudson, Wisconsin, just across the border from St. Paul. Sam checked his watch, saw it was nearing 5 o'clock, and knew Gray was waiting back in the jeep. He finished his coffee, noticing the blonde had already departed.

Then he thought about Carmel.

Then he remembered he had a pretty good place where Gray could stretch his legs.

CHAPTER TWENTY

By 6 o'clock Sam was pulling into the Anderson Lakes Park Reserve lot. Tonight, there were four cars in the lot. When he recognized Carmel's Expedition, he smiled. Sam had hoped to find Carmel in the park, where she mentioned she ran her dogs most evenings. He was looking forward to meeting her daughter.

"Ready to say hello to our friends," Sam said aloud. Gray was perched on the front seat and clearly recognized the place, judging by his demeanor and whine. He was definitely back to normal. Maybe Gray was thinking about Frank and Liberty, though for pack play, not romance.

It had been a long time since Sam had felt a spark around a woman. Sam had spoken with enough single men and women to know the factors that contributed to relational chemistry were beyond inscrutable. The plethora of books, podcasts, talk shows, and songs devoted to love was testament to its mystery. Clearly no one had yet cracked the code. It was like trying to decipher an ancient language without the Rosetta Stone.

From Sam's perspective, in order for the possibility of a relationship to be viable, there were basic factors that must be met: age, availability, occupation, emotional and spiritual perspective, basic likes and dislikes. For example, Sam had already figured out he and Carmel were approximately the same age. Clearly she wasn't married or dating anyone. So, decidedly single. Beyond that, she loved animals in general and dogs in particular. And she enjoyed spending time in the woods. There were lots of other factors to chemistry, Sam knew, some known, most not. But for his purposes, Carmel was definitely a person of interest.

And from Carmel's perspective, he assumed she shared similar criteria, with the added responsibility of a daughter. In the past, Sam had dated women with kids. At his age, it came with the turf. One of the most important lessons he'd learned was how a parent-child relationship could tell you more about a person than a month's worth of dinner dates. More importantly, kids had no filters. They were often an excellent source of information.

Sam parked, leashed Gray, and locked his jeep. Then they started on the trail they'd taken last night.

Something had happened on the previous night's hike. All day he had been busy with the Cambridge business and its aftermath. But now he had a moment to take in the verdure, the trail, and recall how different it had felt. And the dinner with Carmel afterward. It was comfortable *and* intense, an unusual combination.

Fifty yards in, Sam and Gray came to a fork. Last night they'd gone into unfamiliar territory, following Carmel's lead. They'd taken it because she thought it would be the trail less traveled, so they could have their animals off leash. Sam appreciated it for the same reasons. As soon as they turned around the first tree-covered bend, he unleashed Gray and the happy wolf dog began hunting along the trail, nose down. Sam couldn't be sure, but judging from the occasional excited wag and prolonged stop near the base of a tree or old stump, where he raised his leg and pissed, Gray appeared to sense his new friends.

The evening was perfect. The trees and hillside were resplendent with early spring growth. The air was warm, and Sam noticed the start of a hatch, a few small bugs buzzing through the golden air. It was still too early for the bugs to be annoying, but in another 24 hours, all bets were off. Their presence, the alive sound, deepened the evening's green. He felt nostalgic about the Minnesota spring, the land's unfettered awakening from a long, cold winter. Winters this far north, in the heart of the continent, were dark, long, and difficult. The penance inhabitants were forced to endure made the spring opening more intense and profound. Tonight's green evening struck some kind of chord, as though the grass was singing.

Sam and Gray kept walking, suffused with the waning light of day. The trail's disappearance into the woods, a hundred yards off, was clearly illuminated in the sunset.

Sam's cell phone suddenly vibrated. Reluctantly, he slipped it out of his pocket and glanced at the number. His boss, Kay Magdalen. She knew he was in Minnesota, that he had originally planned to take a few days off, when Diane had been in the picture. Detective Marschel had called his boss, so she knew he was working on a case. He also knew she wouldn't be happy with his silence.

"Rivers," he said.

"So glad you could let me in on current events." Her voice was gravelly over the phone. She had a truck driver's tongue. Demeanor too.

"I was going to call you," Sam said.

"Bullshit."

"I mean, eventually."

"Rivers! When were you thinking you might clue me in? After you spent a few thousand out of our interdepartmental resource allocation budget?"

Sam had never been good with bureaucracies or budgets, which is why he liked working with Kay, who had a knack for running administrative interference. "The what?"

"Don't play dumb, Rivers. If you use personnel from another department, we get charged. Did you read the Commissioner's memo about being a good steward of the public's money?"

"Normally I commit them to memory. But I was getting ready for this trip and it was hectic. I may have skimmed it. Can you give me the CliffsNotes?"

Sam had read it. Reading between the lines, the Commissioner was getting pressure from those "whackos in Washington" (Kay's term) to not overspend. The economy was coming back, the coffers were refilling, but it was no reason to run through Service funds as though they were your personal bank account. The bean-counters out east could see the overall Service spend was, year-to-date, more than 5% over budget.

But regarding bureaucracy and budget, it was definitely best to play dumb.

"Rivers! Those Washington whackos are breathing down his neck. That means he's breathing down my neck. And that means I'm breathing down yours."

"Does Clarence know about all this neck breathing?" Clarence was Kay's husband.

"Leave Clarence out of this," she said. "Here's what you do, Rivers. You drop everything and get me a summary of your activities since arriving in Minnesota. I'm not looking for a novel—just something to put in the file when the bean-counters come asking for some background on why the Denver office commandeered two Minnesota assets for a day and a half. And you know they'll come asking, because your old buddy Carmine Salazar loves to stick his Mont Blanc into an accounting irregularity."

Carmine Salazar was living with Sam's ex-wife. He was also a USFW accountant and, incongruously, a reported charmer. He was a climber in the Service and budgets formed the rungs of his ladder. Perhaps worst of all, he was trying to sideline Gray from working in the Service because he thought employing a wolf dog sent the wrong message to the public.

"Are you trying to ruin my evening, or are you just being particularly unpleasant?" Sam said.

"Both."

"Glad we got that out of the way."

"Don't be smart with me, Rivers."

"I'm not being smart. I'm going to head over to my hotel right now and draft a report. It'll be in your inbox in an hour. Three, max. You'll be interested."

"I'm sure it will be riveting, but right now I don't care what it says, just that I get it."

There was a pause, while both of them said nothing. Kay's temper usually blew over like a squall.

Finally, Kay said, "Okay, goddamn it, give me the CliffsNotes."

Sam spent the next five minutes bringing Kay up to date. She asked a few poignant questions. She didn't see the connection with Fish & Wildlife. Sam reminded her monarch pupas were involved, a shipment from Mexico. And the first body had been discovered in the course of a USFW agent making a public presentation, promoting Service work, and that Gray's nose had actually led them to the body. And Sam, all alone, had discovered the second body, so . . .

She asked him if he'd checked out the monarch shipment and Sam said it was in the works.

Then she got personal and asked about Diane. She knew the opportunity to visit Diane was the primary reason Sam had agreed to speak to Minnesota schoolkids. Kay had been careful to provide bureaucratic cover for his trip. She also knew, just days before the visit, Diane had made her "Dear John" call.

Kay knew Sam could turn dark, on occasion, so she worried about him, in an official boss capacity kind of way.

Sam told Kay the whole mess that started at the schools and had taken him to this point was actually a good diversion from his personal life, which was about as dull as a pond fluke. He preferred being engaged in a case, rather than hiking alone on a trail on the north shore of Lake Superior, where his thoughts could easily lead him into a quagmire. He didn't mention Carmel because he had his doubts about where that trail was headed.

"Just keep me in the loop. Especially if you continue using anyone from the Minnesota office. An end-of-day brief would be good."

"Every day?" Sam said. He hated reports as much as he hated bureaucracies and budgets. Reports were the primary food source of large organizations.

"Rivers!" Kay was easily exasperated.

"Okay, okay," Sam said. But they both knew it would more likely be every other day. Or maybe once a week, depending.

After the phone call Sam tried to settle back into the perfect Minnesota spring evening. If Kay's call left him feeling distracted, seeing Frank and Liberty shoot out of the woodland path, followed by Carmel and mini-Carmel, deep in conversation, startled him. When Carmel turned and saw Gray, and then Sam, the megawatt smile that broke over her face made it impossible to be anything but pleased. The woman was radiant. Her daughter looked on with interest.

Gray ran up to Carmel, his tail wagging.

"Sam," she said, as he approached. She was petting Gray and introducing him to Jennifer. Frank and Liberty had taken up stations to either side of Gray, their tails wagging. "Glad you're getting this magnificent animal out on such a perfect evening. How's he doing?"

"I think he's made a full recovery."

"I'm not surprised. His size helps."

After petting Gray's head, Jennifer's wide brown eyes fastened onto Sam like tractor beams. Carmel was peering into Gray's eyes, examining him.

"You must be Jennifer?" Sam said.

Carmel, startled, said, "Oh, honey. Where are my manners?" Carmel's face reddened and before she could say anything, Jennifer said, "And you must be Sam Rivers."

Carmel's face was already red. Now all she could do was laugh.

Sam grinned and said, "Yes, I am." He extended his hand and Jennifer took it like a grown-up.

She glanced at her mom and, from Carmel's red face, must have wondered if she'd said something odd because her face began to redden like her mother's.

"Well," Carmel started, "I was just mentioning you." There was no use in hiding it.

While the dogs started running over the hillside, they talked, mostly about the evening and how perfect it was, or nearly perfect. While Sam and Carmel spoke, Jennifer's eyes remained wide as saucers. After the color in both their faces faded back to normal, Sam thought he picked up a vibe. But he wasn't good at reading those things, so he let it go.

Sam decided to turn and walk with them back to their car. He used the time to become better acquainted with Jennifer.

After asking her a question or two, she opened like a live broadcast of someone who spoke extemporaneously about whatever came into her mind.

"My mom said wolf dogs are bad ideas but that your dog, Gray, is special and she thinks it's because you must have taken really good care of him. She said that's pretty special because not everyone would be able to care for an animal like this one and it meant you must have a gift for animals. Is that true, Mr. Rivers?"

Sam wasn't sure about that, and told Jennifer to call him Sam.

204 | CARY J. GRIFFITH

For her part, Carmel tried to interrupt a few times but eventually could do little but accept her daughter's infectious loquaciousness and smile. There were a couple of times Carmel could have chastised Jennifer. Once Jennifer talked about how her mom never dated, but should, because it was better when people had friends, especially grown-ups with serious friends. "I mean men, because that's the way it is with all my friends' parents. Well, at least most of them."

Jennifer made a reference to her Dad's special friend, who she seemed to have accepted graciously, understanding these things happened and people needed to get on with their lives.

In summary, Sam Rivers was entirely charmed.

At the cars, Carmel said, "What are you doing for dinner?"

"Writing a report," Sam said. He explained how he'd gotten a call from his boss, who told him he needed to keep her apprised of current events. "She doesn't like surprises. Any time anything happens interdepartmentally, accounting must be notified."

Finally, he said goodbye and told Jennifer how much he appreciated meeting her.

"I hope I see you again," she said. "You and Gray."

Sam agreed. He wanted to kiss Carmel, but of course that would have been entirely inappropriate. At the cars she turned to him and before Sam could step away, she'd stepped forward and wrapped Sam in a hug. It was friendly, but still . . .

DAY 3

Friday, May 23

CHAPTER TWENTY-ONE

The school was in a residential neighborhood not far from the state fairgrounds. Domina cruised by the building's front, noticed a flagpole and a curved walk and bushes lining the low brick walls, and continued driving to the next block. The time was nearing 5 a.m., when they were expecting to meet Tommy, Domina's old juvie contact and the receiver of the next shipment from *Las Monarcas*.

"Quiet as a goddamn morgue," Lockhart said. "Pull up near the school, but not in that loading zone. We don't need any trouble."

Domina turned around the block and drove by the front a second time, parking near the building's corner.

It was too early for daylight. Beyond a field and playground, they could see the shadowed backyards of neighborhood homes, their windows dark. They approached the school's corner and paused. Halfway down the school's low brick outside wall, a steel door bar clicked and the door cracked open 2, maybe 3 inches.

Domina walked down the sidewalk adjacent to the building while Lockhart and Tiburon remained at the dark school corner. When Domina was close, the door swung open.

"Hey, Doms," Tommy Cummins said, holding the door. "¿Qué pasa?"

The pair of them bumped knuckles. "Hey, Tommy. Been too long," she said. Then she turned and motioned to Lockhart and Tiburon.

Domina went through the door and Tommy closed it a crack while the others approached. He watched through the narrow opening and when he saw them near, he swung the door open and let them in.

"It's a damn convention," Tommy said. The door closed behind them and they could hear it click shut.

"These are my associates," Domina said.

"It's cool," was all he said, barely nodding in Lockhart and Tiburon's direction. Tommy wore low-hung jeans that crumpled at the bottom over big work boots. He wore a black T-shirt with The Doors emblazoned in faded green lettering across the front. "We got the whole school to ourselves. Nobody's here. Too damn early."

Tommy turned the corner, and they entered a long shadowy hallway, partially lit by overhead bulbs that looked like night-lights.

"Heard from anyone?" Domina said.

"From the Still?" Tommy said.

Tommy and Domina had both served time in the juvenile detention center near Stillwater. Domina and Jerry had done time in the Arrowhead Center, so Tommy didn't know Jerry or about any of the business that happened in Hopkins.

"Yeah," Domina said. "Any of the old gang?"

"No one. Everyone's trying to keep a low profile, know what I mean?" he said.

They continued talking about old times and former friends, while Tommy led them down the long, low-lit hallway and turned at the end. Then they walked down another hallway and down some stairs to a lower utility room, just like in Hopkins.

Lockhart didn't like the easy familiarity between Domina and Tommy. Lockhart had never liked friendship, considering it a weakness. But for now he stayed behind them and waited.

Tommy took out his keys, opened the steel door, and stepped into the room, flipping on the light. Overhead fluorescents blinked on, white and intense. There was a workbench along the back wall with a pegboard above it, all the tools set in orderly rows. Along the right wall there was a full refrigerator/freezer and to the right of it an industrial-size washer and dryer. A large, round table was set in the middle of the room, surrounded by four plastic chairs. There was a bulletin board on the front wall with a couple of labor notices on it, along with a more prominent "Smoke-Free School Zone" sign. The room appeared to be a hangout for nonteacher professionals, like Tommy.

He walked back to the fridge, opened the door, and pulled a box from the top wire rack. It was a duplicate of the one they'd seen in Amber Mansfield's class. He carried it to the rear workbench, opened a drawer, and pulled out a box cutter, handing it to Domina.

"What you bringing in this time?" Tommy said.

Domina took the box cutter, moved forward, and was about to answer Tommy's question and slice through the clear tape covering the top seam.

"Wait," Lockhart said.

Domina paused. Lockhart stepped forward, examining the box. Then he turned it and looked at the seams along the sides. He peered carefully at the tape seal.

No one spoke, but it was obvious why Lockhart was examining the box, which Domina knew was unnecessary and which any normal person, even one with a Juvenile record for B&E, would consider an insult.

But Tommy kept his mouth shut. Tommy was cool.

Lockhart finally backed away and said, "The only thing you need to do is receive the shipment and call us. What's inside the box is none of your business."

Domina thought it was another unnecessary prick move by a confirmed prick and someone who conjured in Domina (and Tibby, for that matter) scorn, though only Domina showed it, sparingly.

Tommy glanced at Domina, who frowned but said nothing. Tommy took Doms's lead, even though he wanted to tell Lockhart, "It was just a question. No need to be a son of a bitch," but he understood that scarface must be the lieutenant, so he shrugged and turned away.

Domina had been in the world long enough to recognize people in positions of authority had different styles of leadership. Some men, like her father, led by brooding silence, so you were always on edge, trying to figure them out. Others, like Ernesto Fuego, led with charisma that made you feel as though you were one of the most important people in the world and part of a family. Fuego rewarded his players with gifts he personally chose because he knew them well enough to know what they wanted. People liked him. But if he was crossed, he acted without mercy or con-science. Domina had seen him shoot a man in the head, point blank, because the man had been caught stealing.

But Lockhart was a narrow, calculating *puta*. No one, as far as Domina could tell, liked or trusted him. He wielded retribution like Fuego but had none of Fuego's charisma.

After Lockhart nodded, Domina slit open the transparent tape, parted the flaps, and pulled out a thin piece of covering cardboard. Emerald monarch butterfly pupas glittered under the workbench light.

Tommy turned to the bench and reached over to a large Tup-perware container, big enough to hold the pupas.

Tiburon moved in to look and said, *"Feo."* Ugly.

"No," Tommy said, opening the plastic bag. *"Muy hermosa por lo que se vuelven."* Very beautiful because of what they become. Then he smiled at Tibby.

Tibby shrugged and said, *"Si te gustan los extraterrestres."* If you like aliens.

Tommy thought about saying "like you?" But he didn't know the big man well enough, and he didn't want him to misconstrue humor as offense. And besides, he didn't like scarface and would just as soon be shed of him, sooner rather than later. He could touch base with Doms after their business concluded.

So he shrugged and carefully poured the pupas into the con-tainer, revealing another square of thin cardboard over a false bottom.

Once the box was emptied, Tommy set it down and carefully removed the cardboard square. A 2-pound brick of brown heroin was tucked into the space. Domina turned the box on its side so she could extract the plastic-covered brick.

Tommy recognized the shipment but didn't acknowledge it. He waited until Tiburon pulled down his backpack and placed the brick inside it. Then he said, "Can you help me get these back in the box, Doms?"

Domina turned and said, "Sure, Tommy." She tilted the box so Tommy could carefully pour in the pupas. Then Tommy replaced the cardboard square, found some strapping tape and reaffixed the flaps, and returned the box to the half fridge.

"You saw it, didn't you?" Lockhart said.

Tommy was surprised because it wasn't a friendly comment. It caused the hair on the back of his neck to stand.

"Yeah," Tommy said. "Brown heroin, I'd guess. Hard to miss."

"You a user?"

"I've tasted. But no, I'm no user."

Lockhart reached into his pocket. He pulled out the roll of bills with a red rubber band wrapped around them, and a smaller quantity of the white heroin. There were small tinfoil wraps of white heroin inside the bag. Lockhart extracted one of the small squares of tinfoil. It was unclear if it was one of the doses laced with fentanyl, but if so, it would kill if used all at once. Lockhart handed it to Tommy with the bills.

Domina straightened. She thought about saying something but knew it was the wrong move at the wrong time. So she just stared. She would call Tommy later and tell him to be very, very careful.

Tommy smiled, but when he glanced at Doms it wasn't recip-rocated, which made him wonder. He pocketed the roll of bills and the tinfoil and said, "Like I said, not a user myself, but thanks. I know guys."

"Then put it to good use," Lockhart said, trying to be friendly, but there was nothing friendly about it.

Tommy was picking up a strange vibe. He told himself to check in with Doms later. For now, he tried to play it cool. "Going to be a perfect weekend," Tommy said, turning out of the room. The others followed him and once they were out, he pulled the steel utility door shut behind him and checked to make sure it was locked.

They continued making small-talk as they retraced their steps, walking down first one hallway, then the other. Then they were at the door and Domina said, "Thanks for the help, Tommy."

They bumped knuckles.

"Any time, Doms," he said, smiling. "Like I said, it's going to be a perfect weekend." And he patted the bills in his right front pocket.

Until now, he had not let himself think about it. But now it was real, and he was already planning a Saturday evening at a Post Malone concert with his girlfriend and one of her girlfriends, and there had been talk of a possible three-way afterward. Their own little afterparty.

But Tommy betrayed nothing, because he did not like nor trust the guy with the puddy half-face.

They all said goodbye at the door and it wasn't until the three had passed through it and the steel latch clicked, locking Tommy safely inside, alone, that he moved his hand down to the front of his pants and squeezed himself. Clearly all that money and the thought of a three-way moved him.

None of them said anything until they got back to the car. Tiburon took up his place in the back seat and Lockhart took the front. Domina got in behind the wheel and started the car.

"You didn't have to give Tommy a dose," Domina said.

"It was a test. If he overuses, we'll know."

"Tommy doesn't need a test. He's a good guy. We can trust him."

Lockhart turned and stared at Domina, but Domina was driving and looking ahead down the road.

"Trust no one," Lockhart said. "If he was lying about not using, we'll find out, because tomorrow he'll be dead. Besides, if he's careful, no worries, he just gets the rush of a lifetime," Lockhart said. "You can't get close to these guys."

Domina resented the comment because it was condescending, and the idea of Lockhart giving her advice about anything was laughable. She'd known Tommy from the detention center and knew he was solid, at least as a courier. No worries with Tommy. Tommy wasn't like Jerry. You liked Jerry, but Jerry was a liar and a punk. Or had been.

"You don't need to worry about Tommy," Domina said.

"That's right," Lockhart said, "because if anything goes wrong, you need to worry."

It was some kind of threat, but Domina ignored it. She kept driving down the side street. *"¿Un poco desayuno?"* she said, glancing in the rearview mirror. A little breakfast?

"Estoy hambriento," Tibby said, for the first time his face brightening. I'm starving.

Lockhart didn't say anything.

The man is an asshole, Domina thought. If there was ever a chance for payback, Domina would not hesitate.

CHAPTER TWENTY-TWO

S am spent the morning running Gray and finishing the report he'd begun the previous night for his boss, Kay. His impromptu visit with Carmel and Jennifer had distracted him, so the report had taken longer than usual.

On his morning run with Gray through Anderson Lakes, Kay called, probably wondering about the whereabouts of Sam's promised report. He didn't pick up. Back at the car, he texted, "Something came up. Report's almost finished. Can't talk now."

Kay responded with an emoji stream of a steaming head with an angry face that looked remarkably like her, though Sam wisely chose not to mention it.

Sam returned to the hotel and managed to put thoughts of Carmel out of his mind and finish the report, though it took until nearly noon.

Sam arrived at the Hodson Building on the university's St. Paul campus around 12:30 p.m. Hodson looked like it had been designed by the same architect who worked on the DEA building. It was a fortress, with embrasure-like openings that ran the length of the building. It was fitting architecture for cannons or archers, but an odd place for bug research, Sam thought.

Professor Toynbee was easy to find; he was sitting at his desk.

"You must be the USFW."

Sam nodded. "Sam Rivers."

Nothing about the professor looked like a guy who had acquired his doctorate studying insects. He was big and relatively young and, judging by shoulder size and muscle tone, a weight-lifter. Toynbee's gaze appeared to be focused on the corner of his office, toward Sam's left. The oblique focus reminded Sam of, well . . . an insect.

Sam stepped forward and extended his hand. Toynbee didn't rise but took the hand, limply, and shook it just once before letting go.

The handshake didn't cause Toynbee's stare to waver. For a minute Sam thought he was blind, but that wasn't it. Maybe some kind of prism vision?

"So do you have the mystery specimen?" he said.

"Right here," Sam said, handing him the container. "I'm pretty sure it's a bark scorpion."

"And where did you say you found it?"

"In a house up in Cambridge."

"Minnesota?"

Sam nodded.

"Pseudoscorpion," Toynbee said.

Sam watched as Toynbee reached into his drawer and squirted some bacterial disinfectant onto his hands and rubbed them vigorously.

"This one stung my dog."

Toynbee appeared curious. "What happened?"

"Nothing at first. But then he started going into shock."

"If it's a bark scorpion, that's understandable. Let's see it."

Sam set the Tupperware in front of him. Toynbee picked it up and cocked his head, considering it sideways, like an interested bird. But the container was too opaque to see anything other than it held some kind of bug.

He set it down and carefully lifted the lid, just a little, to peek inside.

"I'll be damned. *Centruroides sculpturatus,*" he said, demonstrating he was indeed a professor of entomology, though Sam never doubted it.

He reached into a drawer and put on a pair of wire-rimmed glasses with lenses the size of pop-bottle bottoms. It didn't change his sideways glance, but it did magnify his eyeballs to the size of half dollars. *Now Toynbee definitely looks like a bug-man,* Sam thought.

"Where did you say you found it?" he said, turning back to the Tupperware and lifting the lid.

Sam explained about Suthy Baxter's house, but not the OD.

"Some people keep them as pets. Did you see any cages? A terrarium, perhaps?"

"Nothing. We're double-checking, because I left in a hurry, but I don't remember anything like that."

"Sometimes they tag along with shipments of produce out of the Southwest or from Mexico. But they usually find those in grocery stores. Though it's rare." He looked sideways into the container and said, "My, he's a handsome fellow. Just magnificent. Efficient killers in the arachnid world. One of the most venomous. Lots of people die from their stings."

While Toynbee was examining the scorpion, Sam remembered the other question he wanted to ask, to make certain he understood the monarch butterfly life cycle and migration. "Do you know much about monarchs?"

"*Danaus plexipus*. We band them every year. It's one of our feel-good research efforts. I've been down to their overwintering site several times. It's in the Mexican state of Michoacán."

Sam told him he had been there, too, hoping to build rapport, one bug-man to another. You never knew when you'd need a good entomologist. Then, "Do monarchs breed at the preserves?"

"Yes. Before they head north, it's quite the orgy." The professor raised his eyebrows.

Sam ignored the leer and said, "Do they lay eggs in Mexico?"

"No. Michoacán is Central Mexico. You might find some who lay eggs in Northern Mexico, but close to the border. Mostly they start in Texas, heading north. Why?"

Sam explained about the monarch pupas being shipped from San Isidro, in Michoacán, to Hopkins Elementary.

"If so, wouldn't have formed there," Toynbee said.

"That's what I thought. But then, it *is* right next door to the largest monarch butterfly preserves in the world," Sam said.

"It's an overwintering site. Most of the time they're in diapause, a kind of hibernation. Until the place starts to warm, and the orgy begins."

"Are you sure? What if they held the females until they laid their eggs?"

"Northern Mexico. Southern Texas. It has to do with the sun and the latitude and maybe the Earth's magnetic field and definitely milkweed plants, but we're still trying to figure it all out. They only lay eggs on milkweed, and there are none where they overwinter."

Toynbee continued staring into the corner, with his pop bottle–bottomed glasses on. But Sam was sure he was looking straight at him.

"Might be worth double-checking that box," Toynbee said.

"For scorpions?"

"The label. Maybe there's a San Isidro in Texas?"

But Sam could still see it in his head. *De Mexico.* "Okay. I'll double-check."

"So what are you going to do with this handsome fellow?"

Sam hadn't thought about it. "If you would like the specimen, he's yours."

"Just met you and we're already swapping bugs," the professor said. He grinned again.

Sam grinned, but more at the professor than with him. Then he thanked him and started out of the office.

Sam hadn't really wondered if the bark scorpion was a bark scorpion. But he had questioned the origins of their monarch butterfly pupas. In Sam's experience, any time you encountered answers to questions that resulted in more questions, mysteries deepened, suspicions flared, and more time needed to be spent wading through quandary, trying to sort things out.

CHAPTER TWENTY-THREE

S am was back in his jeep in five minutes, but rather than start the car, he sat for a moment, thinking. The professor confirmed Sam's suspicion that monarchs wouldn't lay eggs as far south as Michoacán, particularly when there was no milkweed.

If not from Mexico, then where did they come from?

Sam called Mac.

When Mac answered, Sam said, "Wheezo around?"

"He's right here. The office was getting a little stuffy. We found a Denny's off 494."

"Here's what we got," Wheezo said, on Mac's phone. "Turns out Suthy Baxter had been in touch with Maury Trumble, one of the other juvies in that meth ring. Something about Foo Fighters tickets, but it didn't look like they ever went."

"Did you find any of the others from that meth ring in his contacts?"

"Trailor, a Lonnie DeLay, and Maury Trumble. They were all in there."

"And now two of them are dead from the same kind of overdose?"

"Looks like it." Mac paused. "We gotta check out these other two, Sam, before another one falls."

"Yeah," he said, thinking. "Seems likely one of them is selling. Or they all know the seller. Could be an old member of the meth-cooking club?"

"Could be," Mac said. "Want me to get Wheezo to find the other two addresses?"

"He should be working on it. While he's at it, can you have him check about their employment."

"Their employment?"

"Where they work?"

"Okay," Mac said, doubtful. "What are you looking for?"

"If either of them is selling, they might appear to be unemployed."

"Okay."

"And after that, I need him to check on something else." Sam spent the next few minutes explaining that he wanted Wheezo to check and make sure the monarch pupas were imported from Mexico. If they had been, there had to be a U.S. Customs record somewhere, since it involved something alive. And then he also wanted Wheezo to check and see if anything had ever been shipped down to Mexico, to San Isidro, from the States. Monarch butterfly pupas should be easy to track. Just in case. If they weren't growing them in San Isidro, they were getting them from somewhere.

"Will do."

"I suspect the Customs research will take a while, so just get him started on the addresses and employment info and tell him I want it as soon as he can get it."

There was a moment during which Sam heard a muffled, "Stop eating." Then Mac was back on the line and said, "His mouth is full, but we'll get back to you within the hour."

Sam waited. It was another warm day and there were lots of kids out walking across the campus, some sitting in nearby open green space.

A call came in from Carmel.

"I hope this is about dinner," Sam said.

Carmel started laughing. "I thought maybe Jennifer had scared you off."

"I was completely charmed."

"She liked you too."

Sam thought it was an odd exchange, implying a potentially serious relationship on very short notice. It felt like he was being lifted by a flock of hummingbirds.

"Maybe we should run the dogs before dinner?" Carmel said.

"That'll work," Sam said.

"So the professor confirmed it?"

"Bark scorpion," Sam said.

There was a pause. "I'm buying."

"A deal's a deal," he said.

"Perfect," she said, and hung up.

Sam wondered about the pause and her affirmation. Frankly, it sounded kind of perfect to him too.

As soon as he hung up a call came in from Mac.

"Hey, it's Wheezo."

"You have the addresses?"

"Yup. But that Trumble guy was hard to find. His address isn't a known fact. He's not in any directories. It's like he doesn't want to be found."

"So how did you get it?"

"We got his Social from that sheriff."

Sam remembered. "So you got his address from his Social Security number?"

"I got his taxes from the IRS. They had his address."

"You have access to the IRS?"

"I have access to everything."

Sam took down the addresses for Lonnie DeLay in Hudson, Wisconsin, and Maury Trumble in the St. Croix River Valley. He was going to pay them both a visit, and he figured he'd better do it soon.

"Did Mac ask you about where they worked?" Sam said.

"Yeah. DeLay is a mechanic at Kunz Motorsports in Hudson. But only for the last six months."

"Got a number?"

"No. You didn't ask for a number."

"Okay. Not a problem. What about Trumble?"

"Looks like he runs the Happy Apple Orchard," Wheezo said. "Pretty profitable, too, judging from his returns."

"Is that surprising?"

"How the hell should I know?"

"Can you find out?"

There was a long pause, while Wheezo thought about it or was eating or considering a menu item. *Maybe dessert,* Sam wondered.

Then, "Probably. How about before end of day? I should be able to get you the Customs info by then too."

"Sounds good. And while you're at it, can you check and see if there are any *other* shipments of monarch pupas coming to Minnesota from San Isidro?"

"Sure."

Sam was still trying to figure it out. He remembered what Scott Pepper said about their internal intelligence, that a Mexican cartel was moving heroin into the US inside boat motors. But he also remembered the false bottom that had given a little when he pushed on it. When he'd parted the cardboard, he'd seen newspaper. At the time Sam figured it was to round out the box and make it so the pupas wouldn't shift much in shipment.

He found Amber Mansfield's cell phone and gave her a call. After four rings her voicemail picked up. While Sam listened, he checked the time. It was almost 2:30. She should be done with her class. When the beep sounded Sam asked her if she still had the box the monarch pupas were shipped in, and if so, could she hold onto it? And give him a call. He just wanted to double-check something.

Then he hung up.

Next he used his iPhone's map app to figure out how to get to Lonnie DeLay's place of work in Hudson and then Maury Trumble's orchard in the St. Croix River Valley. From the map it appeared DeLay would be easiest to contact first, then Trumble on his way back to meet Carmel at the reserve. But only if he hustled.

Sam looked up Kunz Motorsports, found the number, and called. When the switchboard came up, he asked for Service. A moment later a woman came on the line.

"I need to bring in my Harley for an oil change and a tune-up. How late are you guys open?"

"Today?"

"Any chance I can get in?"

"Not today. Service is open till 6, but our mechanics knock off at 5 and there's no way they have time to get anyone else in today."

"Okay. Maybe tomorrow? Buddy told me to ask for Lonnie. Said he was pretty good."

"Lonnie DeLay?"

"Didn't say his last name."

"That's the only Lonnie here."

"Okay. He around?"

"Yeah. He's around. But he won't be here tomorrow. It's Memorial Day weekend. If you want Lonnie to work on it, it's best to bring it in first thing next Tuesday."

"Okay. I'll figure out a time and get back to you."

"Okay," the woman said, and hung up.

According to Sam's map app Kunz Motorsports was 32 minutes, 28 miles. This time he hoped to find one of the former meth gang members alive.

CHAPTER TWENTY-FOUR

As soon as Sam got on the road, he made the call.

"My old friend Sam Rivers," Miguel Verde said, with a thick accent, picking up.

"*Hola, amigo. ¿Qué pasa?*"

Miguel answered with a torrent of Spanish in which Sam picked up *vamos* (going), *animales* (animals), and *esta aquí* (to be here), but not much else.

"*Habla despacio,*" Sam said. He remembered the phrase "speak slowly" from his days with Miguel down in Mexico, when his Mexican counterpart was trying to teach him Spanish.

Miguel started laughing. "I thought you were going to keep studying?"

"I had the best intentions, Miguel. Then, you know, life got in the way. And work."

"Is there a woman?"

"It wasn't a woman," Sam said.

Miguel chuckled. "Priorities, my friend."

"I know, I know."

"*Lo se,*" Miguel said, reminding him of the Spanish for "I know."

"*Lo se,*" Sam repeated.

"Muy bién. It is nice to hear your voice. You are in a . . . predicament, and you need Miguel's help?"

Sam laughed. "That's not the only reason I called, but yes." Sam quickly explained about San Isidro De Las Palomas and the butterfly farm, heroin, drug overdoses, and the scorpion. And the old group of meth dealers, from five years earlier, two of them now dead.

"Scorpions are bad," Miguel said. "Clearly there is a Mexican connection."

"Which is why I called."

"I can tell you, in just the way you have told me this, it sounds like revenge."

The thought had occurred to Sam, but he didn't know enough about the living participants to have a feel for it. Lonnie DeLay had the biggest reason to seek revenge, being the only one in the group to serve serious time. Maury Trumble was problematic because the kid's family was rich and he didn't serve any time in a detention center.

"I don't know," Sam said. "I mean, that's the obvious conclusion, but I haven't yet met all the players."

"I will run over to San Isidro. It's a good day for a job and the family is at Puerta for the week, while *Papa* continues working."

Puerta Gomez was on the Pacific coast. It was a pleasant place. Sam once spent a day there with the Verde family and he remembered thinking Miguel was a lucky man.

"About the bark scorpion," Miguel said. "Is Gray okay?"

Gray had accompanied Sam to the Michoacán preserves. Miguel had an instant appreciation and connection with the wolf dog. Miguel claimed his own heritage was both Spanish and native North American. "Probably Aztec," he had said, though Sam couldn't always tell when Miguel had slipped into the fantastical. Miguel's mixed-race heritage made him think of himself as a hybrid, like Gray.

"He was starting to react," Sam said. "But a vet friend gave him Anascorp and epinephrine and he made a dramatic recovery."

"Anascorp is very good. We have it all over Northern Mexico. I'm surprised you found some in Minnesota."

"Got lucky," Sam said, which was true about more than venom antidote.

"I want to tell you something about scorpions," Miguel said. "Bark scorpions are not the worst, my friend."

"I thought bark scorpions were the most poisonous?"

"In North America. But there are two kinds of scorpions: insect and human."

Sam waited.

"There is a group here, a gang, one of the cartels," Miguel continued. "They aren't the largest, but they are active."

"In the heroin trade?"

"Drugs of all types. My brother Jorge is in the *Federales*. He told me a story a few months ago. About a drug runner they found dead. They could not discover how he died, because there were no bullets, knives, or wounds. But they observed small pin sticks, in his cheeks, his neck, back, belly, and lower," Miguel said. "They thought he had been tortured with a needle and some kind of poison. So they tested his blood."

"Scorpion venom," Sam said.

"Precisely. More than enough to cause a terrible end."

"So they tortured him with scorpions?"

"My brother tells me it is not the first time. I will ask Jorge."

Sam thought about the marks in the arms, the pinpoints of beaded blood. "We may have something similar happening here."

"But more likely a scorpion rode into Minnesota on a bunch of bananas."

"It's possible. I've heard it happens. But I found marks on the two overdose victims. Like mosquito bites without the swelling or redness."

"Bark scorpion stings look like that," Miguel said. "But so does the bite of a common flea."

Sam knew it was true. He was hoping Carmel's laboratory would help him narrow the possibilities.

"*Cuidado, amigo.* These cartels are dangerous."

Sam told Miguel it was good advice for both of them. Then he thanked him for his assistance and hung up.

On his way to Kunz Mortorsports, driving across town, Sam contemplated the two victims, the old gang, Lonnie DeLay, Maury Trumble, the monarch pupas, and more. He had pieces of the picture, but they felt torn up and scattered at his feet. It appeared heroin had been shipped in a box of monarch pupas, but where was the heroin? It seemed obvious there was some connection between old meth-lab gang members, but Lonnie DeLay and Maury Trumble had little contact with their former partners and, Sam assumed, didn't know about their deaths. Suthy Baxter was pursuing a nursing degree, which wasn't a typical junkie pursuit.

Jerry Trailor may have been some kind of mule, but why kill one of the key links in your supply chain? If he could be trusted to be a transit hub for a shipment of heroin, it seemed to Sam Rivers he was an insider. Unless he stole some product.

Sam thought about it, stealing. That could make sense. Jerry stole product, shared it with his friend Suthy, and they both overdosed because they didn't know what they had. It was plausible, given Jerry and Suthy were recently in touch. But Sam didn't think so.

If Jerry had stolen heroin, maybe he was being punished? Maybe that would account for bark scorpions, if Jerry had been stung like Suthy seemed to have been. But the timing wasn't right. First he was stung, and then he used and died of an overdose?

Miguel had told him he thought cartels used bark scorpions to torture people, but why would people with no apparent link to anything—not sellers or mules, anyway (in the case of Suthy)— be tortured? Maybe, Sam thought, if Jerry had shared the heroin with his friend, the heroin owner was punishing everyone who took some product without paying for it? But torture by bark scorpions seemed extreme, if they had stolen recreational doses. And if they were tortured, when did they die? They were tortured, then they used, then they overdosed?

CHAPTER TWENTY-FIVE

It was after 3 o'clock by the time Sam pulled into Kunz Motorsports. There were dirt bikes and shiny new Harleys, some crotch rockets, and a handful of new and used snowmobiles and four-wheelers. The place was a playground for motorsports enthusiasts. Sam had never been much of a gearhead, but in the Service they had a fleet of equipment they used to get into remote places fast. He appreciated a good machine and paused over a brand-new, camo-colored four-wheeler with steel-spring suspension and plenty of cargo space.

"Can I help you?" It had been less than a minute since he'd stepped out of his jeep. You could always trust car salesmen for punctuality, especially when you acted like a buyer.

"I wonder if I can speak with Lonnie DeLay," Sam said. "I understand he's a mechanic here?"

"Oh, yeah. He's here."

A big guy in camo got out of a Ford 150, looking much more promising than Sam. So the salesman said, "Check with Service," and moved off toward more productive game.

At the Service counter, Sam asked for Lonnie. The receptionist, a middle-aged, plain-looking woman whose eyes turned nosy and suspicious, said, "Can I tell him what it's regarding?"

"A friend recommended him to work on my Harley, but I've done several customized things to it and I need to ask him a few questions."

"Oh," she said, disappointed. She made the stink eye, not exactly at him. Then she said, "Okay. Just a sec. I'll go get him."

Two minutes later a short, squat man appeared, wearing a gray workman's shirt with "Lonnie" stenciled over the pocket. His sleeves were rolled up and he had thick arms with plentiful ink, brown hair, and a thick beard. He was rubbing his hands with an oil cloth. His eyes were large brown pools of wariness.

The woman took up her position at the desk and Lonnie said, "What can I do for you?" He didn't offer a hand because they were grimy and the cloth wasn't helping much.

"A guy I work with said if I ever needed anyone to work on my FXR, I should talk to you. I've done a ton of customization on it, so . . ."

"Who do you work with?"

"Crady Shepherd," Sam said.

"Don't think I know him."

"He knows you. Said you knew your way around a Harley. *Any* Harley."

The receptionist appeared to be looking into her monitor, but she was listening.

Lonnie shrugged. "What do you need done?"

"Probably easier if I show you," Sam said. "Can you spare five minutes?"

"Probably easiest if you bring it around back and I can look at it there."

"See, here's the deal," Sam said. "Something's not quite right with it, so I'm going to trailer it in. But I was in the neighborhood and remembered what Crady told me and thought, shoot, might as well stop by and see if you're around. I can show you on an FXR out in the lot. Take five minutes, probably less."

Lonnie shrugged again and turned to the receptionist. "I'll be back in a sec," he said, and started around the corner, following Sam.

As soon as they were out the door and walking across the lot to a line of FXRs Lonnie DeLay said, "You a cop?"

Sam turned, still walking, and said, "Not exactly. Why do you ask?"

"Because you don't look like a Harley man and especially not the kind who would customize an FXR. And you're fit and clean and your eyes are paying too close attention for a discussion about motorcycle maintenance. That smells like cop."

"Thanks for the compliment," Sam said. Then, "I thought cops were known for donuts and bellies?"

Lonnie looked away and said, "Some of them look like you," noncommittal, so Sam wasn't sure if it was a dig or he was just fishing. "But not a lot of Harley dudes look like you," he continued, without missing his stride.

"I didn't want to get you in trouble, seeing as how you've been out for what, just six months?" Sam said.

"What's this about?"

"I need to ask you about your old partners."

That made him stop. He raised the cloth to his hands and resumed cleaning.

But it was displacement behavior, Sam thought. He was think-ing about his next move. And that was interesting.

"I don't know nothin' about nothin'," he said, without looking up.

"Two of them are dead."

That startled him, which was also interesting.

"Who?" he said.

"If you go out to that row of FXRs, we can talk and I can tell you, because the deaths haven't been released to the public. And you might be interested, seeing as how they're your former partners. Also, of course, I need to know where you were when they died."

Lonnie DeLay thought about it, was giving serious consid-eration to turning around, but knew, given the circumstances, an informal discussion was better and less public than a formal inquiry by a county sheriff or local black-and-white or worse, a ride to some nearby cop office. So he finally turned and moved toward the FXRs.

"I don't even know your fuckin' name," he said.

"Rivers. Sam Rivers."

"If you're not a cop, what are you?"

"I'm a special agent with the U.S. Fish & Wildlife Service."

"I don't know nothin' about any fish or wildlife."

"You know anything about heroin?"

"Fuck no," he said, still moving. "Is that what this is about?"

After another minute they arrived at the line of motorcycles. There were five in a row, all FXRs with different colored gas tanks and trim. They glittered in the sunlight like Christmas lights.

Sam moved to the nearest one, knelt down, and then turned and looked up at Lonnie. "Maybe if you moved to the other side, I could point out some stuff."

Lonnie walked around to the other side and kneeled opposite Sam. "I got nothin' to hide," he said. "Because I don't know nothin' about nothin'."

"Just trying to be discreet." He looked through the FXR body and said, "Jerry Trailor, Kurt Baxter, and Maury Trumble."

The names made Lonnie's hands stop. "I thought you said there were two dead?"

"Trailor and Baxter are dead. Heroin overdoses. I haven't tracked down Trumble yet."

"When did it happen?"

"Best we can tell early Wednesday morning, and late Wednesday night."

"I was working here the whole time. Early in the morning, I got neighbors who can vouch for me. Wednesday night, I was at the local bookstore until it closed at 8 and then had a beer with the owner at Barker's, down the street."

Sounded like reasonable alibis, Sam thought. Only thing that didn't sound right was the bookstore. "What's the name of the bookstore?"

"Chapter2 Books," Lonnie said.

"Okay," Sam said.

"And I'm sorry to hear about my old partners, but I haven't seen any of them since . . . it's been a while."

"Never called? Never texted?"

There was a moment during which Sam could see Lonnie's wheels turning.

"When I got out," he finally said. "Trailor and Baxter stopped by to buy me a beer. We got together in Hudson. We exchanged numbers, but Trailor," he hesitated. "Not much had changed with him. And I didn't want any part of the old days, so we never talked again."

"What do you mean, 'not much had changed'?"

"I mean . . . he still seemed like he was a player. In the game. And I didn't, don't want any part of it."

"So that's the only time you talked with Trailor and Baxter in five years?"

"First year in Stillwater, Trailor and Baxter came to see me. But that was about it. They never came after that. It was after they got out of juvie and I think they wanted to know if prison was much different."

"Was it?"

"Like kindergarten to high school, if the high school had steel bars and guards and was filled with predators with hard dicks and no women," Lonnie said.

Sam paused. "Jerry Trailor was the first."

"Guess I'm not surprised. About him," Lonnie said.

"Here's the thing. We didn't find anything, except a small amount of heroin laced with fentanyl, which is what killed him, and about the same amount of brown heroin. If he was selling, he off-loaded it before he OD'd."

Lonnie paused. He moved his hands up to the gas tank and said, "Why in the hell is Fish & Wildlife interested in heroin?"

Sam explained about what he was doing and where, when he discovered Jerry Trailor's body.

"They let Jerry Trailor work in an elementary school?" Lonnie said. "Somebody wasn't doing their homework."

"Why do you say that?"

"Jerry Trailor was a sleazeball. Not that he ever did anything with kids. But you make and sell meth with people, you get to know them."

"That's what I'm interested in," Sam said. "What you remember about your old business partners. And given the last two days, you might want to watch your back."

"Anybody tries to sell me heroin I'll kick their ass through their eyeballs. I'm clean and I'm stayin' that way."

"Just sayin', in the last two days, two of your former colleagues OD'd. All from heroin laced with fentanyl."

"So they were using the same junk?" Lonnie said.

"Here's the thing that bothers me: it doesn't seem like either of them were junkies. Did you think so, when you met them after you got out? Or did you ever know, back then when you were cooking and selling, if they used heroin?"

"Never used heroin," Lonnie said. "Might have, if we'd had it. But we didn't. It was all meth back then. And a little pot." Lonnie paused for a minute, still kneeling. "We were kids," he said. "But I can tell you if anyone was selling anything, I'd have fingered Trailor first. He was a scumbag."

"What about Baxter?"

"Baxter was just a wannabe. When he got caught, that jail cell sobered him faster than waterboarding. State wasted its money sending him to juvie. He was a straight kid with bad luck."

"Maury Trumble?"

"Trumble was slick. He was a ladies' man. Got lucky whenever he wanted. He could have kept selling. I could see it. But why, with rich parents? Trumble's family, they had more money than God. And I always thought he was smarter than that."

"What about the main guy?" Sam said.

Sam saw a startled eye peer at him through the FXR trim. "Jon Lockhart. Heard he was dead."

"That's what I've heard. What was he like?"

"He was bad. He got us all goin', back then. And once we were in, he was nasty. Claimed to have some kind of voodoo. Called it 'prison sense.' Maybe did, since he didn't get caught. If he was alive, he'd be the first guy I'd check. When I heard he was dead, I thought, maybe there *is* a God."

"I guess his, what did you call it? Prison sense?"

Lonnie nodded. "Said he could feel things other people couldn't. Things you can't see."

"Guess it didn't help him stay alive."

Lonnie shrugged. "*If* he's dead."

"Five years ago, you think he felt a trap?"

Lonnie paused, thinking. "Maybe. Everyone got caught so quick, there was no way any of us could have tipped him, though none of us would have. Could have been he smelled it, if you believe in voodoo."

Sam knew there were a lot of strange things in the world. Prison sense wouldn't be the strangest. In his own life, intuition, if you wanted to call it that, had on more than one occasion served Sam well. "You felt anything? Lately?"

There was another startled eye through the chrome. Lonnie didn't answer at first. And the eye didn't blink. "Maybe."

"Like what?"

"Prickly. Watchin' my back. Problem is, you spend four years in prison you're always watchin' your back. So it's hard to know if this is different, or just my mind remembering four years of livin' in a cage on a knife edge. Know what I mean?"

"Yeah," Sam said, who had always felt like his childhood with his old man was living on a knife edge, "I think I do." He paused. "So what have you done about it?"

"Nothin'," Lonnie said, returning to the motorcycle, touching its parts. "Yet."

Sam waited because he thought Lonnie wasn't done.

"Last couple days," Lonnie finally said. "I been feelin' too squirr'ly to ignore it. So right before you showed, I figured I'd hit the road. Tomorrow morning. Get out of Dodge." Lonnie stood up. "Now I'm thinkin' it might be sooner."

Sam had always felt as though he could read people. In almost every instance, he could tell a lot about a person in the first five minutes of meeting them. His sense of Lonnie was similar to the sheriff's. The kid had a tough break and paid for it, probably a little too much. But he was okay.

"Probably a good idea, given current events," Sam said. "Sooner the better, if you ask me." Sam reached into his pocket and pulled out a sales slip and tore it in half, wrote his cell number on one piece. "Anything comes up, or if you remember anything, call me. And if anything comes up on my end, might be good to know how to get in touch."

Lonnie took the paper, looked at the number and considered it. Then he extended his hand for Sam's pen and the other half of the sales slip.

Sam handed both over and Lonnie wrote down his number, returning the pen and his number to Sam.

"If this is about the bad ol' days," Lonnie said, "I'd be looking for Jon Lockhart, the dead man. But if those guys were into heroin, could be anyone. But two ODs in two days, same MO, that's not right."

At the service desk the receptionist said, "Do we need to schedule him?"

She was fishing, Lonnie knew. She was one of those people who had been born with her nose so far into other people's business she was cross-eyed.

"Nah," Lonnie said, not wanting the gadfly to know anything about his business. Especially the personal stuff. "Guy just had a bearing loose," he said, and kept walking.

But Lonnie thought, *in less than two hours I'll be on the open road.* The freedom of the idea made him feel better than he had all week.

CHAPTER TWENTY-SIX

After Sam's conversation with Lonnie, he returned to his jeep, made sure Gray was good, and checked messages. There was one from Mac and another from Amber Mansfield. Sam checked his watch. It was 4. He needed to head back to the Cities, via Maury Trumble's place. After he spoke with Trumble, he and Gray would need to hustle to meet Carmel by 6 at Anderson Lakes, which was on the other side of town.

Sam listened to his message from Amber. She affirmed she still had the monarch pupas box, though it was empty now, all the pupas distributed to the kids.

Sam pushed "Call Back" and waited.

"Amber Mansfield," she said.

"You still at school?"

"Just cleaning up before the long weekend. Soon as I finish, we're headed up to Vermilion with the family."

She sounded excited. Sam had forgotten about Mac's commitment. He needed Mac, at least for a while longer.

"That sounds great. I bet you're looking forward to getting away. What about the monarchs, when you're gone?"

"They're at that perfect stage. They'll be growing all weekend and should emerge the end of next week. Maybe you can come back and finish your presentation then?"

Sam thought about it. There were still so many unknowns, all he could say was "maybe," but with enthusiasm. "Can you get your hands on the box those pupas were shipped in?"

"Sure. It's right here beside my desk, next to the trash can."

Sam asked her to tell him everything written or printed on the side of the box.

She reiterated it the way he remembered. Michoacán, Mexico.

"That's it?"

"Other than the address label, to Hopkins Elementary with my name on it. That's everything."

"Can you look inside?"

"There isn't anything inside."

"I think they put some stuffing in the box. Newspaper in the bottom. Filler, so the pupas were all on top?"

"Oh," she said. He heard her open the box's folded top flaps.

"Yeah, there's a piece of thin cardboard," she paused. "And underneath, crumpled newspaper."

"What kind of newspaper?"

"Newspaper," she said. "Like, *Star Tribune.*"

"Is it the *Star Tribune?*"

Another pause. "Hmm."

Sam heard her uncrumple a page.

"That's surprising," she said.

"What?"

"Yes, it's the *Star Tribune.* From last Tuesday."

"You sure it's last Tuesday? Tuesday, May 20?"

"That's what it says."

Sam heard her pull out another page and uncrumple it. "Yes," she said.

"Didn't you get the box on Tuesday?"

"Yes," she said. "Jerry told me before I left Tuesday. I remember because he made a comment about locking it. He said he would put it in my fridge and lock it so none of the kids could get into it."

"Somebody tampered with that box after it arrived, and the only one we know who touched it was Jerry Trailor. What was he like?"

"Kind of," she said, thinking, "a little white-trashy, I guess, if that's not a terrible thing to say. But we all thought he was harmless. He was the janitor."

"Did anyone other than Jerry have a key?"

"No. But I knew as soon as we needed to get into it, I could call him."

"Can you do me a favor and hold onto that box? Put it someplace no one will toss it."

Sam remembered Gray's interest in the box. At the time Sam thought it was probably heroin residue from the victim's hands. Now he wondered.

Sam rechecked the route to Trumble's place. Trumble appeared to live at the end of Mink Farm Road. The front of his property bordered the St. Croix Regional Park. When he checked his watch, it was 4:10. He needed to roll.

Once on the road, Sam dialed Mac.

"Remember my brother-in-law, Vinny?" Mac said.

"The guy who thinks you work for him?"

"One of them. He and his brother, Rob. Vinny wants a ride up to Vermilion. He and his fourth wife are having issues."

"Imagine that."

"Yup. She's not going to Vermilion this year. And he refuses to stay home."

"You can't go," Sam said. "I need you."

"I was hoping you'd say that."

"We need Wheezo too."

"He was hoping for the overtime. With another kid on the way, he really needs to make some extra cash."

"Perfect," Sam said. "Where's Wheezo on the U.S. Customs research?"

"He's working on it now. Both imports and exports."

"Good."

There was a pause. Then, "Thanks for the lifeline," Mac said. "You're going to be on Margie's shit list for a while, but somebody had to step up and take one for the team. I'm glad it was you, buddy."

Sam knew Mac's wife and liked her, even though she had demonstrably bad taste in men.

Sam kept driving and thinking.

Lonnie DeLay suggested Jon Lockhart, but everyone said Lockhart was dead. Scott Pepper had seemed the most definitive. If Lockhart had been on the DEA's radar, as Pepper noted, they probably had intelligence about how he died. *Or knew about it,* Sam thought. The word "intelligence" was poor diction when used in the same sentence with Agent Pepper.

Sam dialed him up.

The receptionist told him Scott Pepper was in an all-day meeting and would be leaving the office as soon as he got out.

Sam left his name and number and asked that Pepper call him. "It's important," he said, then hung up.

He was heading south along country roads when he thought about dialing the sheriff.

"Broom," the sheriff picked up.

"Sheriff, Sam Rivers."

"Agent Rivers. How's the fin-and-feather business?"

"About the same as yesterday, only every time I turn over a rock, something new slithers out."

"Snakes are like that."

Sam talked about his conversation with Lonnie DeLay. The sheriff remembered Lonnie, who he thought got a tough break because Scott Pepper was trying to score a big conviction.

"Nothing wrong with ambition," Sam said. "As long as you don't abuse the privilege."

"With Lonnie, Pepper was more interested in a belt notch than the person. In my book, that's abuse."

Sam agreed.

"What can I do for you?" the sheriff said.

"There was another guy back then. Jon Lockhart."

"Heard he's dead."

"That's what everyone says. Do you know how he died?"

"Sorry. Don't know much about it, except what Pepper told me. House fire, I think. In Albuquerque. Sounded like they had him cornered, and then the place exploded."

"And they found the body?"

"I presume. It's worth asking, though, given Pepper's love of belt notches. He would have jumped at the chance to put another bad guy on his list of 'no longer operational.' And to take credit for it."

Sam thought about it. "Back when you waited for the guy. At the meth house. You don't think one of those kids tipped him off?"

"It wasn't those kids," the Sheriff said. "There was no love lost between Lockhart and those kids."

"What do you mean?"

"Once we got them in holding cells, they were all in for giving Lockhart up. Particularly if it would lighten their own situations, which is how we started out, as I remember." There was a pause. Then, "They seemed to be more afraid of the guy than anything. When we were taking their statements, every one of those kids said they didn't want to share a cell with him. And these were four separate interviews. They hadn't had a chance to compare notes or talk strategy. We wouldn't let them. But every one of them said they didn't want to see him, or to have him see them. In fact, they didn't want Lockhart to know they were caught, and especially not that they'd squealed on him."

"Retribution?"

"All I know is he'd served time. He had a record. And he was about five years older than the rest."

Sam thanked the sheriff and hung up.

CHAPTER TWENTY-SEVEN

M ink Farm Road was not an easy turnoff to find. If there had ever been a street sign marking the place, it was gone. The only sign was "No Outlet."

More than a mile down the road, Sam started seeing heavily budded apple trees, evenly spaced behind what appeared to be an 8-foot-high fence. The fence was for deer, which could decimate a fall apple harvest.

The guy is careful about his orchard, Sam thought, *if this is Trumble's place.*

Ahead there was a gravel driveway that ran 50 yards up to a low-roofed red rambler on top of a hill. The only sign was "No Trespassing," with a small video cam perched above it. There was a black mailbox with no numbers, but according to his app, this was the place. Sam ignored the "No Trespassing" sign and turned in over a cattle guard, also for the deer.

The driveway ran up to a lower-level garage. Sam parked well away from the garage door, cut the jeep's engine, and started to get out. Gray looked expectant, but Sam knew he couldn't let him out onto unfamiliar, private property. When Sam stood, he was startled to see a young man on the narrow porch, standing at the top of a half dozen steps, wearing an expression that would have been a suitable accompaniment to a cradled shotgun, though his hands were empty.

"You're trespassing," he said.

"You Maury Trumble?"

There was a pause. Then, "What do you want?"

Sam shut the car door and started around the front of his jeep.

The kid had short brown hair and looked young enough to be Trumble. He wore a work shirt, jeans, and a pair of Birkenstocks. If he had been working in the orchard, he was taking a break. But Sam guessed this time of year there wasn't much going on in an apple orchard.

Sam started up toward the steps and the man came down toward him, and in a moment they were face to face.

"What do you want?" the man repeated.

"Maury Trumble?" Sam said.

"I'm still trying to figure out why you think it's okay to ignore a 'No Trespassing' sign."

Sam reached into his wallet, pulled out his badge and flashed it. "I'm an agent with U.S. Fish & Wildlife." While Trumble glanced at it, Sam said, "Nice orchard," turning to look at the rows of trees stretching away from his house.

"If this is about my cattle guard or fence, it's all within code."

"I see that. And I appreciate that an orchard owner needs to protect his apples from marauding whitetails. I'd do the same thing." Sam was hoping the comment might loosen up the owner. But it didn't.

"Then I don't think I can help U.S. Fish & Wildlife."

"You're Maury Trumble?"

"I am. And I'm trying to figure out how in the hell you found me."

"Looked you up in the phone book," Sam said.

"I'm not in the phone book."

"Everyone's in some directory."

"Not me."

Sam thought about it. "Can't recall how I found you, right off. But I need to ask you some questions."

Trumble didn't respond.

"Do you know Jerry Trailor?" Sam said.

Trumble paused. "I know Jerry. Haven't seen him for a while."

"He died Wednesday, of a drug overdose."

Trumble's face remained unchanged.

"Like I said, I haven't seen him in . . . in a long time."

"We found Kurt Baxter on Thursday. Both drug overdoses."

Still no reaction.

"Five years ago you were arrested for cooking meth. They were your partners."

Trumble's face darkened. "My juvenile record was supposed to have been expunged."

"Are you curious about how they died?"

"Not really. That's in my past. Now I grow apples. And like I said, it's been a while since I've seen any of them."

"It was heroin," Sam said.

"Okay," Trumble said. "Damn shame. No one deserves to die young. But if you're gonna dance with the devil . . ."

It was a cold reaction. "Seeing as how two of your former partners died in the last couple days, we thought you should know."

"What you told me, Agent Rivers, is somebody's going to have some kind of legal action slapped across their bureaucratic ass. Because there's no way I was supposed to be connected to anything that happened five years ago. I was a stupid kid, end of story. Now I'm a businessman. I'm running a solid enterprise, and you can understand why I don't have much interest in the past or in the people I used to know."

"It's all the same kind of heroin," Sam continued. "It's laced with fentanyl. We assume it's being supplied by the same source. And it's dangerous. Jerry Trailor also had a little brown heroin. Any ideas?"

"I don't know anything about it. Like I said, I haven't seen any of them in a long time. We're definitely not friends, if we ever were."

"What can you tell me about Jon Lockhart?"

His eyebrows raised. "Nothing. I don't know anything about anything. Like I told you."

"Do you remember him?"

"I try not to."

"Did you hear he's dead?"

"I may have heard something like that, now that you mention it. If it's true, I'm glad to hear it."

"You never heard from him again? After your enterprise in Isanti County went belly up?"

That appeared to piss him off.

"I definitely never saw him again. He disappeared. And I don't have much recollection of those days, given I was high most of the time. It was a lifetime ago, and it's behind me. I don't spend much time thinking about it."

"Okay," Sam said. "If you remember anything, anything at all, can you let us know?"

"I won't remember anything," Trumble said.

Sam was going to push his number on him but decided to let it go.

"Look, Agent Rivers. I've spent the last five years trying to put my childhood indiscretions behind me. I run a profitable enterprise here and it's more than a full-time job and it's really starting to get off the ground. I'm not the person I was back then and I'm sorry to hear about my old acquaintances. But like I said, if you're going to dance with the devil, the devil gets his due."

Trumble seemed earnest, but . . .

"Okay," Sam finally said. "But given what's happened, you might want to watch your back."

"I'll be careful."

Clearly, the interview, if you could call it that, was over. Sam thanked him, though he wasn't really feeling it, and returned to his car.

"We'll be getting out soon enough, buddy," Sam said to Gray, getting into his jeep.

There was an open area near the top of the drive. Sam used it to turn around. Down near the cattle guard, when he glanced in his rearview mirror, he could see Trumble still standing at the bottom of his steps, waiting for Sam's jeep to disappear up the road.

When Sam considered the whole interaction—coming out to meet, stonewalling, getting rid of him as quickly as possible—it was like the kid was hiding something. It could just be his past, but Sam didn't think so. It would be good to pay him another visit, this time letting Gray out, who would be able to nose around and see if he smelled anything awry.

Sam's phone rang. "Mac" appeared on the screen.

"That was fast," Sam said.

"I spoke with Margie, and if I were you I'd avoid her for at least a year. Maybe two."

"That bad, huh?"

"That bad. She'll get over it. I have to live with her, so . . ."

"I suspect she knows the truth, that you'd rather skip opening night, maybe two, and drive up to Vermilion by yourself, late Sunday."

"Uhhh, I kind of left it open."

"Left what open?"

"That you might need me the whole weekend."

"No wonder I'm on her list."

"If she calls, don't answer."

Sam just shook his head. "I bet you liked telling your brother-in-law."

"I did. He said, 'Tell him to fuck off. They can't make you work on Memorial Day.'"

"Nice. Isn't he unemployed?"

"Yup. Now you know why."

"How's he getting up to Vermilion?"

"He said he'll drive Margie up, but only if she lets him use her car."

"So he's a freeloader?"

"Always. Never really done much of anything in life, except complain about the government. And marry four women."

"I heard that antigovernment thing is a virus."

"Then a few people in my family are infected. I'm just happy I don't have to ride up with him or sit around a fire and drink beer with him. It's like fingernails on a chalkboard."

"You'll be there for Memorial Day."

"Not if Sam Rivers needs me."

Sam could see he was going to be a scapegoat as long as Mac needed one. "I met Maury Trumble."

"Is he alive?"

"He's very much alive, and not very happy he was found."

"What do you mean?"

Sam explained, and also told him about Trumble's lack of empathy for his former partners.

"Sounds pretty cold," Mac said.

"Definitely. Kind of made me wonder what was in that house."

"Maybe we should have a look. Later?"

"Too much security."

"Guess what Wheezo found?"

"Shipments?"

"Shipments *to* and *from* that butterfly farm in Mexico."

"Give me the *to*."

"The Cedar Creek Butterfly Farm in Cedar Creek, Texas, sends regular shipments of monarch pupas to the monarch butterfly farm in San Isidro Mexico."

"Where's Cedar Creek, Texas?"

"Near Austin."

"I love it when hunches hit pay dirt."

"And the *from* are even more interesting. In May, there were five shipments from that butterfly farm in Mexico. Two went to Kansas City, one to Des Moines, and two to the Twin Cities."

"Another shipment to the Twin Cities?"

"Lauderdale Elementary. Delivered yesterday."

"We need to check it out. Where's Lauderdale?"

Mac explained it was a first-tier suburb over by the St. Paul Fairgrounds. "But if you want to check it out, maybe we should talk to Detective Marschel."

"Good idea. I'll call her. But we can't check it out today."

"No one will be there tomorrow. It's a holiday weekend."

"If we get a warrant, we could find somebody to let us in. Gray could nose around with us."

"Good," Mac said. "How's the pooch?"

"Full recovery, I think. He's ready to run."

"With the veterinarian?"

"That's right."

"I bet you're ready to run too."

"I'm exercising my dog."

"Funny way to put it, but I get your meaning."

"I don't think . . .," Sam started. But then he decided to let it go. Part of Mac's brain would always reside in the gutter.

"So keep me posted on the warrant," Mac said. "I have to go home and help Margie pack and complain about Sam Rivers's demanding work ethic."

"You do that," Sam said, and hung up.

Detective Marschel picked up on the second ring. "There's another shipment," Sam said.

"Shipment of what?"

"Of monarch pupas."

"You mean in Hopkins?"

"No. In the Twin Cities. Lauderdale Elementary."

"So?"

So Sam explained about the box, Gray's interest in it, the false bottom, and the *Star Tribune* newspaper.

"You think . . .?"

"Pepper said the Mexicans are trying to bring in more heroin."

"An elementary school?"

"What better place to receive heroin. Nobody would suspect."

There was a pause while Marschel thought about it. "You may be onto something."

"And monarchs don't breed in Central Mexico. The San Isidro Butterfly Farm imports the pupas from Southern Texas, then exports them back into the US."

Sam explained about the Texas butterfly farm and the tracked shipments.

"Damn. That's really interesting. We gotta check it out, but it's Memorial Day weekend."

"Do you think you could get a warrant?"

There was a pause. "Probably. You mean, like for tomorrow?"

"If we could get one for tomorrow, we take Gray, see if he could track anything down. If they did use these boxes to transport heroin, sooner we get over there the better."

"Before they destroy evidence," Marschel said. "Or move it. Let me see what I can do."

"What about Pepper?" Sam said.

"What about him?"

"You going to bring him into the loop?"

"No need yet."

Sam told her to keep him posted and hung up.

Traffic slowed on the way to Eden Prairie. By the time he crossed the Minnesota River, heading west, he was down to 35 mph in a 55 zone.

Another call came in. Scott Pepper. Uh-oh.

"Rivers," Sam said.

"Rivers, goddamn it. Do you know what crocodile just barked up my ass?"

"No."

"Carl Rodriguez."

When Sam didn't respond, Pepper added, "One of the Twin Cities' most prominent criminal defense lawyers. He gets everyone off. He's barking so far up my ass my teeth ache."

Suddenly Sam recognized the name. "You mean *Carlos* Rodriguez?"

"Carl," Pepper said.

"Is his first name really Carlos?"

"Goddamn it, Rivers. His first name is Carl the Crocodile, and you do not want Carl getting into your business."

Sam waited, but there was silence. "Okay."

"He was calling about Maury Trumble. Ring any bells?"

"Maury Trumble?"

"Are you telling me you didn't just leave Maury Trumble's house?"

"I did, but why is Carl Rodriguez calling you about it?"

"Because we aren't supposed to know that five years ago he was part of a gang who cooked meth and sold it to kiddies. We're supposed to let bygones be bygones. And I fought it for a while, but you don't fight with Carl the Crocodile. If you have enough money—and Maury's family does—you pay Carl the Croc to make it all go away."

"I don't get it."

"Let me spell it out for you, Sherlock. After Maury's innocent little mistake, his old man hired the biggest criminal defense gun in the Twin Cities. Carl got Maury off with probation. He never served a second in juvie, unlike his buddies. And he got his records pulled from public databases. So now I'm supposed to ask you how you found out about him?"

"Can't remember, right off," Sam said, something he knew would make Pepper's blood boil. But Sam liked Sheriff Broom and refused to get him in trouble. "I've talked to so many people about so many things, it's hard to recall where I heard about Maury."

"Are you dumb as a dingo in heat? You had to find out somehow. And I have to let Carl know. And let him know we will *not* be asking Maury any more questions."

"Okay," Sam said. "I'll need to get back to you after I review my notes."

"You stonewalling me, Rivers?"

"No," Sam said. "I'm in the car. I'm sure it's in my notes, but I have to wait until I'm not driving to have a look."

There was another pause. Then, "I'll tell him. I'll also tell him he can tell his client he will no longer be bothered by U.S. Fish & Wildlife. We're perfectly clear on that?"

"Crystal," Sam said.

"Does Raven Marschel know what you're doing?"

"Of course. I always keep Detective Marschel informed."

"Before you do anything else—I mean *anything*—you make sure you have Raven's okay. Understood?"

"Definitely, Agent Pepper. We discussed this. And please pass along my condolences. For what it's worth, the conversation went nowhere."

"Good. Then there's no reason to talk with him again."

"None," Sam said.

The line went dead.

Sam immediately speed-dialed Detective Marschel.

"What's up?" Marschel said.

Sam told him about the call with Scott Pepper. When he got toward the end of it, Marschel said, "Just a second." In a moment she returned to the phone and said, "Guess who's calling?"

"Pepper."

"So the warrant and the school search is just between you and me. That why you're calling?"

"Great minds," Sam said.

"If we find something, that's when we'll bring him in," Marschel said.

As Sam continued down 494, he thought about Maury Trumble. Sam had a feeling about the guy. And unless Sam's intuition had grown tarnished in the last 24 hours, he thought Maury acted far too strange for someone interrupted in the middle of the day. He wasn't passing Sam's smell test, so Sam suspected another conversation was definitely in their future, though it would have to be properly managed.

CHAPTER TWENTY-EIGHT

Domina, Tiburon, and Lockhart had spent most of the day lounging in their rooms at the AmericInn. Domina put on her earbuds and dozed, listening to Brandi Carlile on Pandora. In the adjoining room, Tiburon got into a *Three Stooges* marathon. He could not understand the English, but the Stooges' antics made Tiburon laugh so loud Domina heard it through the wall and her buds.

At 1 they went out for food. After lunch, Domina dropped them both back at the hotel and went out to gas up. Then she took a ride, not wanting to return to the hotel and be annoyed by the Stooges. She found the Minnehaha Parkway and followed it all the way to the park, where she got out and admired the falls.

Her family rarely asked questions about what she was doing in Mexico. It was ironic, she thought, to travel south of the border to make money. But that's what she did. When her parents saw her refurbished LeBaron, her mother was pleased, her father suspicious. When her father asked about her work, Domina told him she was in trade, mostly agricultural products. Domina explained it had something to do with corn and that her Iowa roots helped.

Frankly, they were just happy she was making her way in the world, given her predilection for girlfriends and her youthful gangster days in Storm Lake, when she was known to the authorities and did two stints in juvenile centers in Minnesota.

Even though Storm Lake was just four hours south, she hadn't told her family she was coming to Minnesota. They thought she was still in Northern Mexico, and that was just fine with Domina, who thought she might make an early fall trip back home, when the Iowa cornfields would be tan and ripe and the trees scarlet, yellow, and orange.

Then her cell rang. Ernesto Fuego.

"*Sí,*" Domina said.

"What's happening?"

"Right now I am looking at Minnehaha Falls," Domina said.

"Is it *hermosa?*" Beautiful.

"Very."

"How is the American?"

Ernesto Fuego had always called Jon Lockhart "the American," especially when he wanted to hear Domina's private perspective on the man.

"The same," Domina said. "There have been two overdoses. The American is settling scores."

"Has there been any noise? From the authorities?"

"None. I have checked the papers, but there has been nothing."

"Good."

"But two is enough," Domina said. "The point has been made."

There was a pause.

"For the American," Domina added, "building interest in product is of secondary importance. The overdoses are about revenge."

It took another beat for Fuego to answer. "If our business concerns and the American's private concerns are aligned, then . . .," Fuego said, and Domina knew him well enough to see the ambiguous shrug over the phone. "The overdoses are also about past debts."

"If he kills more the way he's killed the first ones, it'll be three in three days."

"What about the product?"

"Received and delivered."

"And how are sales?"

"It's only been a day, but given what both of them said about how dry it is up here, the product should move quickly."

"Quick is good. We have supply."

"And there is demand."

"Economics," Fuego said.

"*Sí, El Jefe.*"

There was a pause. "*Tu es familia,*" Fuego said. You are family.

"*Sí. Siempre.*" Always.

"So, keep your eyes on the American."

"Always," Domina said.

"*Bueno.*" Good.

Then the line went dead.

The LeBaron sat in the parking lot like an auto at a rally for vintage cars. Domina was careful about burnishing its gleam. She had watched a couple of passersby take a second look at the car. She was proud of the interest.

She took one more wistful look at the waterfall. Then she checked her watch—almost 4—and returned to her perfect set of chrome wheels.

They were in the car, heading east by a little after 5. Lockhart had spent the afternoon in his hotel room, maintaining a low profile. The facial burn scars made him hard not to notice, so he only showed himself when necessary.

En route to Lonnie DeLay's house in Hudson, Lockhart took two calls. The first came from Rich Matthewson. The product was a huge hit and people were clamoring, he said. The rest of his supply would be gone by the end of the weekend or before. Lockhart assured him there would be more and let him know he would get back to him soon.

Casselmire called after Matthewson with the same information. There were rave reviews of the product, and he was running through his allotment, so the sooner he got more, the better. He had also heard about a heroin overdose at a school in Hopkins. A janitor was found dead with a needle in his arm. Pure heroin.

"When did it happen?" Lockhart asked.

"I guess the past couple days."

"And how did you hear?"

"One of my buyers. He knows a junkie who said the cops told him."

"We're not selling pure heroin. Someone must have got careless," Lockhart said, feigning worry.

"It was some kind of pure white stuff, cops said. So far, source unknown, but they think European. Even this guy's junkie, who heard about it and keeps tabs on the market, had no idea where it came from."

Lockhart told him to keep him posted and it was good to hear the product was moving well. He also told him they had more supply and would see him soon.

Next shipment, prices will double, Lockhart thought. But he did not tell Casselmire or Matthewson. They were already getting a deal, and he knew they would pay it and pass along the cost to their network. Besides, even at twice the cost they would still make plenty of money.

While Domina nosed her car onto the I-94 St. Croix River Bridge, Lockhart's phone rang a third time.

Lockhart glanced down, then cursed.

Fuego, Domina thought.

Lockhart explained about the product and the calls from his first two distributors. Fuego asked about his personal business but was careful to keep Domina out of it. Lockhart said two ODs from the pure heroin with fentanyl had helped them build interest in the brown product. The street already knew about it, and that the white product was dangerous.

"*Cuidado,*" Fuego said. Be careful.

"Of course."

"Nothing should interfere with our business. *¿Comprende?*"

"Yes. Of course."

"*Bueno,*" Fuego said, and hung up.

There are two more scores to settle, Lockhart thought. He would take his time with Maury and Lonnie. They were going to tell him about his money. Then they would pay.

By the time they pulled up to the curb around the corner from Lonnie DeLay's house, it was almost 6. The house was a small, shabby one-story—with a front porch and probably less than 1,000 square feet of living space. It may have had a front room, a kitchen, and a bedroom, but not much else. The paint was peeling from the old board siding, and the roof was in need of repair.

They sat, waited, and watched. Over the next hour they saw two neighbors arrive and one kid walk down the sidewalk, wearing earplugs. By a little after 7, the sun was setting and there was still no sign of movement in the house.

"He's not there," Domina said.

"*¿Qué?*" Tiburon asked.

"*No hay.*"

After another half hour they decided to get something to eat, and then circle back.

By 8:30, they had returned and were hugging the curb. Most of the neighborhood homes showed light, but not Lonnie's. They watched for another hour, but nothing changed.

"We need to check," Lockhart said, turning to Domina.

"I can do that," she said.

She stepped out of the car, rounded the corner, and crossed the street. The house was three down; Domina glanced left, then right, then swiveled her head behind her. She climbed the steps and lifted the mailbox and pulled out a piece of mail, checking the address. "Lonnie DeLay."

Then she returned it to the mailbox. There were other items in the box. Apparently, the man hadn't gotten his mail for the day. She decided to knock. She could ask some kind of bogus question about the whereabouts of a nonexistent neighbor. Plausible enough. So she knocked and waited.

Nothing.

Domina knocked again, a little louder, but not loud enough for the neighbors to hear.

When the house remained dark and quiet, she decided to nose around. Domina came down off the steps and walked around the side of the house. She peered into windows, but the place was dark. She could see the outline of a kitchen table and a couple of chairs, but otherwise the place was spartan. There was a detached garage on a back alley, and when Domina looked through a side window, she noticed it, too, was empty.

Nobody home.

She walked down the alley, turned at the corner, and headed back to the car.

"*Nada,*" she said, getting in. "I don't think he's coming."

"He's probably out at a bar," Lockhart suggested. "It's Friday night before Memorial Day weekend."

"Maybe he's taken off. For the weekend."

Lockhart didn't want to entertain the idea. "We wait," he said.

CHAPTER TWENTY-NINE

A little after 6, Sam was in the reserve parking lot. He'd pulled up next to Carmel's red Expedition, and when she turned and smiled, he smiled back and thought, *That is a lovely woman.* Then they were out of their cars. Before he knew what happened, she moved forward, hugged him briefly, and said, "God, what a gorgeous evening."

It was unexpected. He tried to hug back, but he was awkward about it, being out of practice. If Carmel noticed, she didn't show it. And if Carmel was out of practice, he didn't pick it up. What he picked up was the pressure of her body.

"Your patient has fully recovered," Sam said, looking toward Gray. Gray was in the rear of the jeep. Sam could see his eyes through the tinted windows. The wolf dog stared fixedly at Sam, while Frank and Liberty in Carmel's SUV were whining and jumping like kids desperately needing to get out.

"He is so magnificent," she said.

"You better get Frank and Liberty out of there, before they ruin the inside of your SUV."

"Already ruined," she said, turning to reach for the leashes. "Unless you like hair and the smell of wet dog."

"That's not ruined. That's what I call 'lived in.'"

When Liberty and Frank saw the leashes, their energy moved from frenetic to buzz saw. "The craziness starts the minute I exit 169," Carmel said. "They recognize landmarks. That's when the whining and jumping begin."

Sam waited while she leashed Frank and Liberty and the two dogs leaped out of the back of the Expedition, pulling Carmel toward the reserve path.

Gray's tail started wagging. When Sam moved toward the back of the jeep, Gray moved forward and began licking Sam's hand. Once he was leashed and out of the car, Gray stood on his wolf hind legs and stared Sam straight in the face, tail wagging, trying to lick his cheek.

"Hey, hey," Sam said, backing up until Gray dropped to all fours. It was uncharacteristic behavior for the wolf dog, who was obviously excited to be back in the reserve, hunting it up with his new friends.

Frank, Liberty, and Carmel were already on the path, heading into the woods. Gray was clearly interested in pursuit. So was Sam.

There were three other cars in the lot. By the time they came to the turnoff, they hadn't seen anyone. The dogs had settled, but only a little, straining every 5 feet to the left or right, sniffing and pissing on tree stumps and trunks.

"We gotta set 'em free," Carmel said.

Sam reached down and unclasped Gray's leash.

Carmel let Frank and Liberty off-leash and the dogs took off down the path, Gray following. The path opened into a long straightaway with pasture on either side. Carmel's dogs turned into the early spring bush with the long-legged Gray towering behind them. But only briefly. Gray could move much easier and faster through the spring cut and quickly eclipsed them, taking the lead.

"Magnificent," she said again, about Gray. "Just the way he moves."

"I agree. But they all look good."

Carmel and Sam kept walking down the path, catching up to the point where the animals left it. The sun was just settling into the horizon, turning a magnificent orange. It had been another unseasonably warm day, nearing 80. Now it was on the cusp of a cooldown, but neither Sam nor Carmel felt it.

They were witnessing the front end of the early spring leaf explosion, and Sam thought he could see a measurable change in the last 24 hours, since the last time they walked down this path.

"This place is changing all of a sudden," Carmel said.

She turned to consider some trees in the distance and her hand brushed Sam's. Their movement down the woodland path had generated some kind of static electricity and she felt a spark.

"Did you feel that?" Carmel said.

"Definitely. It's like the place exploded," Sam said, referencing the leaves.

Sam was one step in front of her. Maybe a half step.

Suddenly there was a tug at his hand that made him stop. When he turned, he could feel her close.

And then they were together, lips brushing, the touch causing another jolt. Sam realized her comment was about the spark.

But before he could curse his romantic ineptitude, he was overwhelmed by the sensation of lips.

After a long first kiss, they parted. He was startled and felt the kiss high up in his chest. His breathing quickened. "That was unexpected."

"Sorry," she said.

"Sorry?" Sam turned into her.

This time, on instinct, he tasted her and thought, after another minute, if they didn't start walking it was going to be difficult to put whatever this was back into its box. Bottle. Whatever.

Carmel pulled away, but Sam was pretty certain she felt the same way. He felt a glaze across his eyes. Unless he was a poor judge of sensuality—which he could be, since it had been so long—her eyes held the same hazy longing.

"I haven't kissed anyone in . . .," her voice trailed off. She was looking up the path toward her dogs. They were far ahead, working the pasture-covered hillside like a well-seasoned pack, Gray out in front. "Seriously," she finally said, as though the kiss had erased any memory of past sensuality, "I can't remember."

They walked a few paces.

"Can't remember what?" Sam asked.

Then they both started laughing.

Sam and Carmel followed their animals quietly into the woods, along the lake, back around the reserve hills. The evening was warm, and the remnant of sun burned a startling orange, then deep crimson as it settled into the west. They managed to say a few words, but suddenly everything radiated with deeper meaning and ambiguities they sensed and felt. At least Sam hoped it was so.

"So how did you ever find this place?" Sam asked.

"I was looking for a place to walk my pack," she said, "when I was trying to get over my divorce."

That reminded Sam of the one thing he'd heard that day that he had wanted to share with her. "So is your ex-husband a criminal defense lawyer?"

"That's right. Are you checking up on him?"

Sam laughed. "No. But he's checking up on me."

"What?"

"I ran into one of his clients this afternoon. Though at the time, I didn't know he was your ex's client."

She waited while Sam told her about his afternoon, his investigation, and why he had stopped to check on Maury Trumble and speak with him. Then about Trumble's reluctance. And then his subsequent phone call from Scott Pepper, who raised the name of Carl Rodriguez and who let Sam know he was still on the case.

"Scott Pepper called him 'Carl the Crocodile.'"

Carmel laughed. "That's good. He'd like that."

"What about you?"

"I'm done with the Croc."

They walked a few more paces before Sam turned and they kissed again. This time it was Sam's turn to pull away. But he only did it because he sensed it was the precursor for something much deeper and more intimate.

They talked for a while about their ex-partners. Sam described the circumstances of the end of his marriage, and the fact that his ex was now living with Carmine Salazar, a USFW accountant and seeming rising star in Fish & Wildlife, even though he had no field experience. And how Carmine didn't like Gray and was trying to get the hybrid removed from the USFW ranks before Gray had a chance to prove himself.

If Carmel had no opinion about Carmine Salazar before Sam explained who he was, his effort to banish Gray from the force was a kind of character sentence. The man was guilty of letting his political perspective (and possibly ambitions) interfere with obvious better judgment. She gazed after Gray, romping with Frank and Liberty, and said, "How could anyone deny that animal his due?"

Sam agreed and kissed her again.

After dinner at a nearby restaurant, a couple glasses of wine, and just the right amount of personal story sharing (which took place in a bubble in which there existed one woman, one man, and three dogs), Sam knew it was time to go. Rather, he knew the right move was to pay the tab, push away from the table, and say, "Thank you for a lovely night. Now I think it's time for Gray and me to go." But he struggled mightily against it.

In the end his accursed inner gentleman—who, when it came to relations between men and women, always reminded him, like a good angel, to be chivalrous—said, barely audible, "I should go."

Carmel only smiled. Which made Sam think he'd made the right choice, if he was taking the long view.

"Yes," Carmel said, a little sadly. "I should go too." She paused. Before pushing away from the table and rising, she said. "But would you think me untoward if I suggested you not be a Boy Scout tonight? And I will set aside my usual prudence and invite you back to my place."

Later in bed, following their first torrid encounter, Carmel turned to him and said, "Not bad for a first try."

"That was . . ." but Sam had no words for it.

Then she turned to him and said, "It has been more than a year since I have felt like it. And now . . .," her voice trailed off and her mouth found his in the dark. Later, she said, "Practice makes perfect."

Sam thought so too.

DAY 4

Saturday, May 24

CHAPTER THIRTY

The weather on the start of the Memorial Day weekend was resplendent, but Sam and Carmel were oblivious to it. The two of them, coming together as they did on more than one occasion into the evening, well past midnight, created their own meteorological system. Friction and heat. There were moments the histrionics became so intense even the canines were startled out of sleep.

But finally, in the post-midnight darkness, they collapsed and felt the kind of bliss reserved for lovers spending a tantric holiday beside a deep, profound sea. Eventually everyone drifted into heavy, untrammeled slumber.

Sam dreamed.

He was standing in front of Amber Mansfield's class. Everything was as it had been on the previous Wednesday morning, when he had spoken to her students about monarchs and their overwintering sites. Behind him rose two columns of images, each starting at the bottom with magnified yellow, variegated monarch butterfly eggs. Above these images were colorfully striped monarch caterpillars. Above the caterpillars rose the gleaming emerald pupas. Near the top of the column spread the vibrant orange of the fully winged mature adult. And then finally, at the top, a single huge poster depicting a male monarch conjoined with a female. It was a magnificent depiction of the circle of life represented by the butterfly life cycle.

Sam was speaking to the class, pointing out the differences between males and females. The male's underwings had slightly enlarged spots along their black veins. Except for those sex spots, the female image was almost identical. They were both stunning, burnt orange, vibrant, and alive.

And then Carmel was beside him in the classroom. They were standing in front of the monarch images, Sam in front of the female monarch, Carmel in front of the male. He could feel her hand take his, warm and pulsing. Pulsating.

Then the classroom dissolved, and he was in Cambridge, wading into the Rum River. Monarch butterflies were flowing across the water in dispersed orange clouds. When he looked down, he saw a scorpion crawling up his forearm and he shook it, startled, as though he had been shocked by an electric wire. The scorpion flicked off into open air.

And then, dreamily, the river transformed into a section of the Rio Grande where Sam had once stopped to observe the orange butterflies migrating north from Mexico into Southern Texas.

Now there was a huge scorpion rising out of the sand on the Mexican side, beyond the Rio's flat water. The river's current flowed and Sam walked into it. The scorpion unnerved him, but he had to see it and confront the menace of it. He thought the water was shallow, but with every step the water surged around his calves, his thighs, above his waist, until he took one more step and dropped beneath the water's surface, fully submerged.

He was reaching, kicking toward the surface light. He hadn't been submerged long enough to be running out of breath, so he wasn't frightened. He felt more curiosity than fear. He kicked, but the gap of water did not close.

He kicked again.

And then he could see a man through the surface of the water. Miguel Verde, his Mexican counterpart, was reaching for him, and on his forearm was a scorpion. The pincers of the scorpion oozed small drops of blood.

Then Sam awoke.

Carmel was breathing deeply and heavily beside him. He turned his head and saw her bedside digital clock. It was 8:34, about the latest he could ever remember sleeping. He glanced over at the dogs, and they were curled up on dog beds against the wall, apparently exhausted from the night's activities. The memory of it threatened to eclipse Sam's dream. He closed his eyes and tried to focus.

Sam had researched dream imagery and interpretation. At times, dreams had helped him with cases. Sometimes, when dreams followed a narrative, a contiguous beginning, middle, and end, the sequence could be picked apart as one long message. When dreams metamorphosed into entirely different settings, there could be several messages.

If he tried to break up the dream into logical sequences, the first of four, in the classroom, could be things he was trying to discover. But it had been a long time. Since he'd loved, he thought. And that idea *felt* right. He and Carmel were discovering something very old, the ancient opposites, male and female, yin and yang, which had the power to transform and place him, them, squarely in the center of a mystical life flow, a coupling that created a mysterious, powerful transcendence.

He considered the next dream images: Cambridge and the Rum River, the monarchs and small scorpion, and then the Rio Grande and Miguel.

He was struggling to make sense of the images. But it felt like the scorpion threat, the danger and poison, was coming from Mexico. He needed to follow up with Miguel and see what he found. The scorpion on Miguel's forearm and the pincers oozing beads of blood. He needed to get the dried drops of blood he'd collected from Suthy Baxter analyzed. Carmel had access to labs, for her veterinary work. He'd ask her, after she awoke.

Calling Miguel made him think of his phone, which he had placed on the end table next to the bed. They had both muted their phones, for obvious reasons. Now Sam reached over and lifted it off the end table. On his display he could see three calls from Mac and two from Detective Marschel.

Uh-oh.

Carmel stirred. Still in heavy sleep, she turned and with intimate familiarity threw an arm over Sam's chest.

When Sam turned, she cracked an eye.

"Put that thing down," she said. And then her hand moved down to grip him.

You could not make this stuff up, Sam thought.

It was well past 9 by the time they rolled out of bed. It felt as though an endorphin fog had settled around them, suffused with intimacy, good fortune, and grace. And humor. And the dogs had finally stirred, needing attention.

"Can we do that again?" Carmel said.

"Now?"

She approached him then, wrapping her arms around him and kissing him. Sam thought he was incapable of feeling arousal so soon. But it swept across him like billowing cumulous rising in a cobalt sky. He started moving her, both of them, back toward bed.

"Hold on, Romeo," she laughed, twisting away. "I need to have some breakfast, and then I have to run these boys and then go into the office and check on some patients." She glanced at her digital clock display. "I guess I mean brunch. Luckily, Jennifer is with her dad all weekend." Carmel looked at Sam and grinned.

"Let's eat."

"Yes. And I see the dogs are hungry too."

Frank, Liberty, and Gray were all watching Sam and Carmel with intense interest.

While Carmel moved to take care of the animals, including Gray, Sam checked his messages. Mac's first two messages said, "Call me." The third one said, "Rivers, where the hell are you?"

Detective Marschel's messages were simpler.

"Call me when you're online. I'm close to getting that warrant for Lauderdale Elementary. And I think I know a cop who can get us into that school."

Her second message said, "Got the warrant. Call me. We need to move."

Sam checked his watch. It was not yet 10. Carmel had already gone to the kitchen. The smell of coffee was coming up the stairs. He speed-dialed Detective Marschel.

"Where the hell have you been?" Marschel said.

"Sleeping in."

"Figured."

Sam suspected he knew what Marschel meant, but said, "You got the warrant?"

"Didn't take much, seeing as how we have two ODs in two days."

"So how do we get into the school?"

"We knock, for starters. But if you can meet me there by noon, I've got a cop lined up to help us. They have keys."

"I'll meet you there at noon," Sam said.

"Bring the dog."

Sam hung up and dialed Mac.

"What are you doing?" Sam said.

"I'm having second breakfast," Mac said.

"You've been hanging around Wheezo too long."

"Problem is, his exercise routine hasn't rubbed off on me yet. Just the eating part."

"If you're going to eat like Wheezo, you've got to run, swim, and bike like Wheezo."

"I'd rather not talk about it." There was a pause. Then Sam said, "Can you meet me at noon at Lauderdale Elementary?"

"You mean seriously? We're going to work?"

"Yes, we're going to work, if you call nosing around an elementary school work."

"It's Saturday on Memorial Day weekend," Mac said.

"You can always head north, spend time with Vinny."

"Noon. Lauderdale. I'll be there."

"Good," Sam said, and hung up.

Sam dressed and went down to the kitchen. Carmel was sitting at the table, reading the paper. Sam bent over and kissed the top of her head and she reached down and patted his thigh. It felt like they'd been having breakfast like this for more than three decades.

"Hope you like oatmeal and eggs," she said, without looking up from the paper.

"Perfect. Maybe a piece of toast?"

"We've got toast."

They sat and ate oatmeal and soft-boiled eggs with toast. Sam got up and went to the fridge for some juice. Carmel got up and met him with her empty glass and there was a moment, a close encounter, that threatened to pitch both of them back into the bedroom, but clearer heads prevailed.

Carmel was going running with Frank and Liberty. Sam had a hard time with the idea of running, but Carmel said she felt great and needed the exercise. The dogs too.

She offered to take Gray, but Gray sensed Sam's impending departure and was watching him with focused eyes. Besides, Gray was working today.

"Do you have access to a lab?" Sam said.

"Sure. Why?"

"A lab that does blood work."

"Of course. I run a vet clinic."

"Are they open Saturdays?"

"Most Saturdays. I don't know about this one. Why?"

"I have two very small beads of dried blood. I need to know," Sam paused, knowing it would sound crazy, "if they contain any bark scorpion venom."

"Where'd you get them?"

Sam paused. "I'd rather not say just yet."

"You want me to give some dried blood to my lab guys and see if they can find any traces of bark scorpion venom in it?"

"Could you?"

Carmel grinned. "That's the craziest thing I've ever heard. For starters, I have no idea if they can identify scorpion venom, let alone in a sample of dried blood."

"Haven't you seen those shows?"

"Make believe," she said. "And then there's the fact that it's my day off."

"I thought you said you were going in to check on some patients?"

"Rivers, I've got dogs to run. And I thought you'd be going with me."

"I need the help. And it's important. What if I promised you dinner tonight?"

"Not enough."

"I will buy you dinner. The rest of the evening's activities I will leave to your discretion. Whatever you want."

That made her grin. "Okay. I'll call. But prepare yourself for some serious servitude."

Sam waited while she fetched her phone and called. Someone answered. There was a familiar to and fro, and then she asked about the blood sample and after a few moments, listening to the other end, her eyebrows raised.

"Really? So if I brought it by this morning, you could have a look?"

There was a frown.

"What if it was an emergency? Like, involving law enforcement?"

Then, "Okay. Thanks, Carter. I'll see you within the hour."

When she hung up, she turned to Sam and said, "Those guys are good."

CHAPTER THIRTY-ONE

Sam reminded himself to call Scott Pepper. He wanted to follow-up about the death of the old meth gang's kingpin, Jon Lockhart. When and where and how? And he wanted to see if any of the product, the pure heroin laced with fentanyl, or the brown heroin, had been found on the street. If it had, they might get lucky following it upstream to its source. If they found the source, at least locally, they might find some of the missing pieces. But there were still more questions than answers.

It was going to be interesting, Sam thought, to see what they found in the school.

When Sam pulled up in front of Lauderdale Elementary, Raven Marschel stepped out of her Crown Vic. She wore green, iridescent sweats with a maroon stripe down the bottoms and across the top. She had on a pair of Nikes and looked like she'd just come from a pickup game at a nearby park.

"Sam," she said, nodding.

She noticed Sam wondering about the sweats.

"My husband and I are in a mixed basketball league on Saturday mornings. Didn't have a chance to change."

"How'd you do?"

"When Rodney Marschel's on your team, you usually win."

Sam had passing interest in college sports, and the name sounded familiar. "Your husband play college ball?"

"For Minnesota. Me too. It's how we met."

"I had no idea I was working with such a distinguished detective."

"That was a while ago. And college ball doesn't have a lot to do with being a detective. Except maybe keeping me fit."

Clearly, Sam thought. He could see Raven Marschel, Swish, still had game.

"This weather is incredible," she said.

It was in the high 70s, with a few white wisps in the stratosphere. There wasn't a lot of wind.

"Perfect for a Memorial Day weekend," Sam said.

"But not for Jerry Trailor or Suthy Baxter. Pepper told me he's hoping to issue a release next Tuesday."

"The man's negligence in issues of public health is going to come back to bite him," Sam said.

"The PR machine turns slow when it's Scott Pepper and there are junkies involved," Marschel said.

"But they weren't junkies."

"I reminded him of that. But all Pepper sees is two ODs from people with previous drug records."

A cop pulled up in her black-and-white and parked near the curb.

"The only reason he's issuing the release is because he knows it's going to be a press opportunity," Sam said.

The cop, young and clean-cut, with short hair, approached them.

"Officer Lisa Daly," Marschel said. They shook hands, familiarly. "This is agent Sam Rivers, U.S. Fish & Wildlife."

Officer Daly shook his hand and nodded without comment on fish or wildlife, which was refreshing.

"Got that key?" Marschel said.

"Got it. But not sure we need it." She glanced toward the school entrance.

"Why?"

"Supposed to be a janitor on staff."

"On Memorial Day weekend?"

"They had a break-in last Christmas. Got some computers and some petty cash in the principal's office. Never caught anyone, but they decided to begin having someone periodically check on the place, at least during the day."

They heard the front door of the school open, and a man peered out and said, "Officer, can I help you?"

Officer Daly crossed the front walk toward the entrance. Sam and Marschel fell in behind. When the officer grew close, she said, "Did Barb Nelson talk with you?"

The man nodded. "Yeah."

The man was unshaven, with unkempt hair.

"We just want to come in and have a look around," Daly said.

"She didn't say what for," the man said.

Officer Daly turned to Sam and Detective Marschel behind him.

Marschel said, "Do you have a shipment of butterfly . . .," she turned to Sam.

"Pupas," Sam said. "Monarch butterfly pupas."

When the officer and Marschel still looked perplexed, Sam added, "The stage in the life cycle of a monarch butterfly before it becomes a butterfly. We have a Customs notice that you received a shipment from Mexico?"

Sam caught a flicker in the man's eyes.

"Yeah," he said.

"We'd like to see it," Marschel said.

The man paused, for maybe one beat too long. Then said, "Okay. I can show you. Got ID?" Neither Sam nor Marschel were dressed like officers.

When Daly crossed the threshold, she said, "I'm Officer Lisa Daly and this is Detective Raven Marschel from Hopkins and Agent Sam Rivers from . . .," she turned to look.

"Denver," Sam said.

The janitor nodded and waited while the detective and Sam showed him their IDs. Then the janitor shook their hands, limply, and said, "Tommy Cummins."

The man was reserved.

"I should get Gray," Sam said to Marschel.

"Oh, yeah." Marschel turned to the cop and janitor and said, "We've got a dog we want to bring with us."

Tommy hesitated. "Dogs aren't allowed in the school."

Sam stopped and turned. "He's a working dog."

Tommy frowned.

"If anyone finds out the dog was in the school," Marschel said, "we'll let them know the dog was part of the investigation."

"It'll be okay," Officer Daly said.

The janitor, Tommy, thought about it. Clearly, he didn't like it, but he was outnumbered. Finally, he shrugged and said, "Okay."

Sam turned and started toward the jeep. They were still waiting for Mac, but the man was nowhere in sight. Earlier in the year, Margie bought Mac an iPhone and taught him how to use the basics, mostly because she wanted to be able to text him messages without having to speak with him. But he hadn't picked up any of the other useful apps, like Maps.

"What are you looking for?" Tommy asked.

"We've had some problems and we need to take a look at the shipment of monarch . . . things," Marschel said.

"What kind of problems?"

Detective Marschel was beginning to pick up a vibe from Tommy, so she said, "Possible U.S. Customs violations."

Back near the car, Sam heard the exchange and appreciated Marschel's vague response. He pulled out his iPhone and sent Mac a text: "Wait outside." Then he opened the jeep door and leashed Gray. They both started up toward the door.

"That's a big dog," Tommy said.

"He's a wolf dog," Sam said. "Half arctic wolf, half malamute. I can introduce you."

"Ah, that's okay."

Tommy turned behind the door and pulled it open for the officers and Gray. Sam passed through last. Gray stopped at the door and turned, sniffing at Tommy, interested.

Sam pulled Gray back and said, "Come on, buddy, I told him you were well mannered."

Tommy made a dramatic, wide turn around Gray, hustling to get out in front.

The guy really doesn't like dogs, Sam thought.

"It's down this way." Tommy led them down a shadowed hallway.

The school's janitor wore baggy jeans and a too-big AC/DC T-shirt. His arms were tattooed, one with a snake and the other with some kind of long blade tracing the outside of his forearm, maybe a sword. Like many bodies on which Sam saw multiple tattoos, there was no apparent connection or visual theme between the tattoos, supporting the idea they were impulsive acts. Tommy looked like the type who might have been seized with inspiration after an all-nighter.

As they followed Tommy, Gray kept putting his nose forward, not exactly straining at his leash, but keeping a close eye on their leader, sniffing in an interested way. At first Sam thought it was body odor, since by appearances Tommy looked like an occasional bather. But Sam wasn't picking up any particular odor, so he wondered.

"So the monarchs aren't poisonous or anything, are they?" Tommy said. He was fishing.

"We just need to see the shipment," Marschel said.

"Nothing the kids need to worry about, is it?"

"No," Marschel said. "The kids are fine. How long ago did the shipment arrive?"

"Day before yesterday, I think. They said to put it in the fridge right away. It comes refrigerated."

"Is this the first year you've received monarch pupas?" Sam said.

"Nope. I've been here for the last four years. We've gotten shipments every year I've been here. Everything's been fine with them, far as I can tell."

They turned a corner and kept walking. At the end of the corridor was a set of stairs leading down into shadows.

"Good," Sam said. "It's probably nothing. I'm with U.S. Fish & Wildlife and we periodically need to check these things, from a Customs perspective."

"Oh," Tommy said. "I'm not up on the paperwork. I just take delivery. But we've never had an issue before."

"I'm sure it's all fine," Sam said.

"Do you have the paperwork?" Marschel said.

"You mean the Customs stuff?"

"Yes."

"No. If that's what you want, you'll need to talk to Dr. Nelson. The principal."

"Okay," Sam said. "We'd still like to see the box."

They came to the top of the stairs and Tommy started down in front of them. Near the bottom of two flights, they came to a steel utility door. Tommy took out his keys, opened the door, and they all stepped into the room.

The place was clean and square and bright. This room held not only tools and a tool bench, but also a full fridge, washer, dryer, simple table with chairs, and a bulletin board for notices. Clearly, it was used for more than Tommy's work.

Tommy walked over to the fridge and pulled out the box, setting it atop the workbench. The side printing was identical to the Hopkins box: "San Isidro De Las Palomas."

"So you received the box on Thursday and immediately placed it in this fridge?" Marschel asked.

"Uh huh."

"And no one else touched it?"

"Miss Concher came down to the office and signed for it. She's the one who called me. She knew what it was and said it was for her class, but they weren't going to need them until next week. Until then, she said, they needed to be kept cool."

"And you put them here?" Sam said.

"Uh huh."

Sam examined the box. The first thing he noticed was the way the tape had been cut and a new line of strapping tape reaffixed over it. "Anybody open it?"

"The box?" Tommy said.

"Yeah."

He paused. "I don't think so. Maybe Miss Concher?"

"To check on the shipment?" Marschel said.

"Maybe."

"Other people have access to this room?" Sam said.

"Sure. The other maintenance guys. Sometimes the cooks from the cafeteria come down to shoot the shit."

Sam glanced at Marschel. "Okay," Sam said. "Let's open it and have a look, make sure it's what it says it is."

"What else would it be?" Tommy said.

"Nothing in particular. Just, when it's a biological shipment, Customs makes periodic, random checks just to make sure everything's in order," Sam said.

The janitor reached into a drawer and pulled out a box cutter. He carefully sliced through the tape and opened the box.

Sam peered in. A thin cardboard covering was a couple of inches down from the top of the box. There was a lot of wasted space, unless something had already been taken from it. When Sam lifted off the cardboard, he peered into a mass of emerald green pupas. They were alive and resplendent. Sam wiggled his index finger down into them and pushed all the way to the bottom of the box, affirming it only contained pupas.

Sam picked up a pupa and placed it in his palm.

Marschel, the cop, and the janitor all peered at it, and Marschel said, "Creepy."

"Beautiful," Sam said.

"If you say so," Marschel said.

Officer Daly and Tommy just stared.

Sam replaced the pupa on the pile in the box and folded down the flaps. Then he turned to Gray, unleashed him, and waved his hand forward in the quick gesture that let Gray know he should begin searching the room. "Find."

Unexpectedly, Gray immediately turned to Tommy and moved toward the man's front left pocket.

"Hey," Tommy said, stepping back and turning away.

"What's in your pocket?" Sam said.

"Nothing. Money."

Gray was still staring at Tommy's pocket, intent and unwavering, ready to lift his paw.

Tommy reached in and pulled out a roll of bills. "It's just money."

"Can I see it?" Sam said.

"It's my money."

"Of course it's your money," Sam said. "We just want to look at it."

Reluctantly, Tommy handed over the roll.

"That looks like a lot of cash," Marschel said.

"After work I'm going to dinner with my girlfriend and then a concert. Might do a hotel. Could be a pricey evening."

While Sam held the roll of bills, Gray followed it with his nose and eyes. Sam lowered the roll of bills and Gray's tail made one wag and he peered at Sam, to let him know the money had scent.

"Interesting," Sam said.

"What?" Tommy asked.

"Sometimes my dog smells things," Sam said. "I guess he likes the smell of your money."

Sam handed the money back and Tommy pocketed it.

"How much is there?" Marschel said. It was an impudent question, but Sam was curious too.

Tommy considered it. "Enough for a pricey evening," he said, vaguely.

Marschel didn't push it.

Sam gave Gray the signal to keep searching, but Gray didn't move. He kept staring at Tommy's front pocket, the one with the money. He was intent.

"Got anything else in your pocket?" Sam said.

"No."

But Gray didn't move.

"Let's see that money again," Sam said.

Tommy pulled it out and handed the roll back to Sam.

Then Sam told Gray to search again, and Gray returned to Tommy's pocket.

"Can you just turn it out, so Gray can see it's empty."

Tommy paused, and then shrugged. He started reaching into his front pocket, to turn it out, and then suddenly, unexpectedly pivoted and put a shoulder into Officer Daly. She fell back into the door frame and Tommy sprinted through it. Before Sam or Gray could do anything about it, Tommy Cummins was out of the room.

By the time Daly regained her footing there was a traffic jam at the door. Sam managed to burst through first and saw Tommy's feet disappear over the top edge of the steps. Sam could feel Officer Daly behind him, followed by Gray, and then Marschel.

"Halt," Sam yelled, but it sounded stupid, given the circumstances. He turned to Gray and said, "Go!"

The hybrid didn't need to be told. Gray was in wolf pursuit. He ran around the officer and then Sam. Sam briefly worried about what Gray might do once he caught up. But given Tommy's head start, he didn't worry much. By the time Sam rose past the top of the stairs, Gray was two steps ahead. The fit Raven Marschel passed Sam and was closing in on Gray. But Tommy was fast, his pace hastened by hearing a wolf pound down the hallway behind him. And the detective. Twenty yards ahead, Tommy turned at the hallway corner and disappeared.

Sam's cell phone went off and, on the run, he picked it up and saw it was Mac. He pressed it and said, breathless, "Where are you?"

"I'm at the school. What's wrong?"

"There's a guy running your way," Sam said. "Don't let him out of the building."

"What?"

"A guy on the run. Don't let him out."

"10-4," Mac said, and the line went dead.

Gray rounded the corner, sliding hard and hitting the far wall but focused on Tommy like a wolf on a whitetail. Raven Marschel slowed enough to pivot, her Nikes making a high-pitched squeak as her shoulder bounced into the wall, barely breaking stride. By the time Sam rounded the corner he could see the janitor's lead had shortened to 10 yards, followed by Gray, who was closing in, and Marschel.

Up ahead were the glass front doors, but where the hell was Mac? In a split-second, Sam realized Tommy was going to breach the doors before Gray could catch him. Once through the doors, there was a chance Tommy could reach a car, if it was close.

Marschel, behind Tommy, yelled, "Stop! Goddamn it, stop or I'll shoot!" But everyone knew Marschel wouldn't shoot in a school, especially when there wasn't a clear shot and she was sprinting. Besides, she didn't have a weapon.

Gray kept closing in on Tommy, who was almost through the glass double doors.

And suddenly, a figure came out of nowhere, the other side of the glass. There were double doors and Sam watched Mac hold one side and knew Tommy would blow through the other. Sam started yelling as Tommy veered and blew through. Then suddenly, Mac's leg dodged in front of Tommy and, while he tried to jump it, his toe caught the inside of Mac's knee. Tommy's momentum sent him tumbling. Mac grunted, heavy, his leg spinning from the blow, and then he dropped like a bag of hammers. In that split-second, both of them were on the ground.

Tommy tumbled onto the cement walkway in front of the school and didn't have a chance. Gray was on top of him, and Tommy's arm came up to protect his face. Gray took hold and the janitor was screaming, breathless, "Off! Get him off!"

Marschel was dancing around the pileup, unsure what to do.

Sam came up and hesitated long enough to make sure there was no way the janitor was going anywhere. Then he said, "Gray! Stop!" and grabbed Gray's collar. Tommy rolled and moved both arms over his head, pulling in his knees to protect his torso. Once he was certain Sam held the dog, he started to rise, quickly. But by that time, Marschel and Officer Daly were beside him and they had Tommy corralled, nowhere to run.

"Goddamn it!" Mac said.

Behind them Mac had managed to right himself, but he was favoring his trip leg, trying to walk off the pain.

"You okay?" Sam said, still holding Gray.

"Fuck no, I'm not okay."

But he was up, limping and cussing, which Sam considered a positive sign.

CHAPTER THIRTY-TWO

Gray wasn't sure he was finished with the runner. He was straining to get another piece of him, and everything was happening so fast, Sam wasn't sure if Marschel saw the fear in Tommy's face. But he hoped so, because Sam could restrain Gray in a heartbeat, but if Tommy was afraid of Gray's fangs, fear was a powerful motivator.

Then Marschel said, breathless, with a little edge to it, "I'm not sure the dog is done."

"Keep that fuckin' animal off me!"

Officer Daly moved in, cuffs in hand. Everyone was breathing heavy. Tommy was trying to turn away from Gray. The situation was still tense. Sam said, "Don't know if I can hold him." And then Sam let his grip loosen, just a little, and Gray lunged at Tommy, who twisted and screamed.

Sam snapped forward and caught Gray's collar and Gray strained, making a low whine that rumbled into an ugly growl.

"Goddamn it," Tommy said.

Officer Daly was holding him, but Tommy was squirming in fear. After Tommy's hands were cuffed, the officer reached into Tommy's pocket and pulled out a small packet of aluminum foil, flashing it up to Sam and Marschel.

"They moving heroin in that box?" Marschel yelled.

Tommy tried to squirm away, but Officer Daly had a strong grip on his cuffed hands.

"Fuck!" Tommy said.

Officer Daly recited Miranda.

Gray was straining and Sam kept his arm stretched, making it appear as though his grip was insecure.

Gray's jaws gnashed and the guttural sound coming out of him was startling and primitive, sounding more wolf than malamute.

"The box?" Marschel said.

"Heroin," Tommy said. "Two pounds."

"Who?" Marschel yelled.

The wolf dog lunged.

The janitor, terrified, tried to spin, but Officer Daly tightened her grip, keeping Tommy between her and the wolf.

"Three of them. Only one I know is Domina."

"Who are they?"

"Mexican, all I know. 'Cept one."

Gray lunged a third time and the man tried to rear back as Sam stepped and reached forward at the last second and caught Gray's collar.

"When did they come?" Marschel said.

"Morning," the janitor said, in a kind of hoarse whine. "Yesterday. I ain't sayin' another word unless you put that animal away."

Marschel paused. Then, "Okay."

Sam located Gray's leash, bent down, and affixed it to Gray's collar. Then he stood up, straining to hold Gray back. The wolf dog began to settle but stared at the man with his eerie eyes, ready to attack if given a chance.

"What kind of heroin?" Sam asked.

"I don't know," the janitor wheezed. "Brown."

Tommy Cummins was clearly shaken by the chase and tumble and Gray. They continued questioning the janitor but only got bare descriptions of the three people, the most noticeable feature being the "American's scarred neck and face." Once the janitor realized he'd said too much, that there might be repercussions for being a snitch, he asked for a lawyer and grew quiet.

"We can do that," Marschel said. "We can get you a lawyer. Doesn't look good. Particularly with heroin in your pocket."

They all let it sink in.

"I didn't know it was heroin," Tommy said.

"You can try that on the judge, and see what she thinks," Marschel said.

"I need a lawyer," he said.

"We know you need a lawyer," Sam said. "But if we can tell the judge that you cooperated it'll be better for you. Because right now it's murder."

"Murder?!" the janitor said, still breathing hard. He was red-faced and starting to get his ire back.

"Murder," Marschel said.

"I didn't murder nobody."

"If that foil contains white powder and it's what we think, almost pure heroin laced with fentanyl, the same stuff that killed two men in the last three days, you bet your sweet ass you'll be tried for murder. In the first degree," Marschel said. "Premeditated."

"I don't know nothin' about murder."

"If we find the same kind of stuff that killed those men, it's not going to look good," Sam said.

"I don't know nothin'. I told you."

"I hope the jury sees it that way, but it doesn't look good, Tommy," Marschel said.

"Looks like murder," Sam said. And he laid out what happened the previous three days, explaining how two men had died from heroin they'd taken that Sam guessed was the same stuff Tommy had in his pocket. "If you didn't know anything about it, and if the same people gave the same stuff to you, and the shipment was brown heroin, not white stuff, I'd say these three might be hoping you ended the way the others did. Dead."

"No tomorrow," Marschel said.

"Make it look like an overdose and get rid of an eyewitness at the same time," Sam said.

"Dead men don't talk," Marschel said.

Marschel, Sam, and the cop could *feel* Tommy thinking. Hard.

"Those guys were trying to kill you, Tommy," Marschel said.

"I don't know Minnesota," Sam said. "What do you get for first-degree premeditated murder?"

"Life without the possibility of parole," Marschel said.

"A pretty dark hole," Sam said.

Officer Daly was still holding Tommy, but she could feel him sag a little.

"I'm tellin' you all I know," Tommy said. "There were three of them. There was a really big guy, the guy with scars, and a woman I knew from the juvenile detention center outside of Stillwater, few years back. Domina. I don't remember her real name, but if you asked at the Still, they'd know. She was still serving when I got out. Domina was the one who contacted me."

"And they gave you the foil?"

"The guy with the scars gave me the foil. He was in charge." Tommy was sweating.

They questioned Tommy for 10 more minutes and found out as much as they thought they were going to. The scarface appeared to be in charge, but judging from how Tommy conveyed it, there appeared to be some dissension in the ranks. The other one was clearly Hispanic, Mexican, Tommy said, remembering the big man. Domina too. But Mexican-American.

"The big guy barely spoke," Tommy said. "And only Spanish."

"And the other guy was American?" Sam said. "The main guy. You're sure?"

"Positive."

"Did he have an accent?" Marschel said.

"You mean, like Mexican?"

"No, like, was he from Jersey, or did he talk like he was from Alabama?"

"No," Tommy said.

"So he sounded like he was from around here?" Sam said.

Tommy thought about it. "Yeah. Like he was from here. Maybe up North?"

They noted the descriptions of the three people. Finally, they asked Tommy if he'd seen how the three had arrived, what they were driving, or if there were multiple cars.

Tommy shook his head. "They came to the side door at 5 yesterday morning, like we'd arranged."

Earlier Sam had noticed video monitors set up along the school's roofline, and on the building's front corners. "These set up around the school?"

Tommy nodded. "They're motion-triggered, but whatever triggers it needs to be close enough before they work." Tommy explained they'd set up the cameras after they'd been robbed and that the recording devices were in the principal's office.

"You're going to say something?" Tommy said. "To the judge?"

"When the time comes," Marschel said, "we'll say a good word, Tommy. But you might have to testify."

"That could get me killed."

Sam thought about it.

"We'll talk to the prosecutor and try and figure something out."

"I need a lawyer," Tommy said.

"We'll get you one," Sam said. "But you've been a big help and we'll let 'em know it."

A shade passed across Tommy's face as the cop tucked him into the back of the squad car and shut the door.

After Tommy was in the car, Sam turned to Mac and said, "Get on the phone and get Wheezo over here. Tell him it's important."

Mac's face still looked pained and a little pale. But he said, "I'll call him."

Then Sam turned to Marschel and said, "I got a hunch."

"What?"

"The sheriff told me the guy who was the head of that meth gang, few years back, died in a house fire. In Albuquerque."

"You think scarface is that guy?"

"I don't know. If they ID'd him with dental records, I don't see how it could be. But if it was something short of DNA or dental records, could be our guy. We need to talk to Pepper."

Marschel shrugged. "I can call him."

While Marschel pulled out her phone, Sam glanced at his watch. It was already early afternoon. He was thinking about calling Carmel to both check in on the lab analysis and talk to her about tonight. He was starting to get a bad feeling about how the rest of his day, especially the evening, might unfold. The idea he'd have to postpone the reoccurrence of how they'd spent last night was giving him heartburn. You didn't walk away from that kind of evening. And Sam was certain they'd be enjoying each other's company again, only better, now that they had their first night behind them.

Damn.

But this was a serious lead in a serious case, and if he was right about the former head of the meth gang, it would mean Jerry and Suthy had been killed, probably for revenge. If there were still two people left, Lonnie DeLay and Maury Trumble, the guy was going to finish what he'd started. Particularly if he still believed he was under the radar.

Bait.

It could be a busy evening, Sam thought. But then, *Carmel, naked, in bed* . . .

There was a whole lot of him that said, *screw it, Marschel can follow the leads.* But there was a whole lot more that felt like a hunter in search of dangerous prey. If Sam was right about what the man had done, he needed to be taken down, if not out.

It was hard not to think of Carmel. But it was harder to think the chase might continue without him and Gray.

Then his cell phone went off.

"*Amigo,*" Miguel Verde said.

"Miguel."

There was a pause. "You sound like you have been stung by a scorpion?"

"I feel like it."

"Be happy, my friend. I have interesting news."

"Give it to me."

"The butterfly farm you mentioned is a place where they make ceramic pieces, for the stores in Delores Hidalgo."

Sam remembered Delores Hidalgo. It was a city renowned for a style of Mexican ceramic tile called *Talavera.* It was around four hours north of San Isidro. "Do they raise monarchs?"

"There is nothing live there except *señoras* painting dishes and pots and small figurines, some of them butterflies."

"So it's a front?" Sam said.

"*Probablemente,*" Miguel said. Probably.

While Sam was chewing on the news, Miguel said, "And the other I mentioned, the one who uses scorpions to enforce?"

"Yes?"

"His name is Ernesto Fuego. He is one of the highest-ranking members of a cartel called *Las Monarcas.* Monarchs, like the kings. My brother tells me it is known that *Las Monarcas* have been trying to build a distribution network into the northern part of the United

States. They are smaller operators and do not want to compete with the big cartels in California or in the East."

"Are they working with any Americans?"

"They don't know. Only that they are interested in the area."

Miguel told Sam he would let him know if his brother found anything else of interest.

While Sam was speaking with Miguel, Marschel had dialed a number. In a second she was talking, but Sam had moved off to finish his conversation with Miguel, so he couldn't hear how the conversation started. When he walked over, Marschel thanked whoever she was speaking to and hung up.

"Pepper?" Sam said.

Marschel grinned. "He wasn't happy about being called on a holiday."

"Where's the man's sense of duty?"

"He didn't know anything about the details on that house fire, where the guy died, or how they ID'd him. Just that he died in a house fire in Albuquerque. But he can find out how it all went down because he remembered the local DEA agent who had the place staked out when it blew."

"Can he reach him? Today?"

"Said he'd try. Told me something else pretty interesting."

"What?"

"Said yesterday, before he left work, he got a call from his Minneapolis liaison. Said there was a street cop who heard some talk from one of his locals about heroin on the street. Brown heroin."

"Could be our stuff," Sam said.

"Could be."

"Okay. We need a plan. If somebody is moving pounds of brown heroin, they have contacts, somehow. And if this is tied up with revenge, there are still potential victims left. We need to stake out their houses and see what comes. And if we could figure out what whoever is moving the product is driving, even better."

"We need more people."

"I can get Mac, and Wheezo's on his way. As soon as Wheezo has a chance to check out the school's video, we can get together and figure out how to get it done."

"Sooner, rather than later, if we can trust Tommy that they were here yesterday."

Sam thought about it. According to Customs, the only shipments of monarch pupas to Minnesota were the Hopkins and Lauderdale packages. If they were in receipt of their last shipment, what were they doing with it? If Pepper's information was good, they were moving it, but where and to whom? And if they were from Mexico, maybe they were members of *Las Monarcas?* How the hell did they have contacts in Minnesota? Unless this Lockhart still knew people? But he was killing his old partners, if it was him. Didn't make sense.

The best thing they could do would be to huddle and try and sort out some of the details, come up with a plan. And it better be now.

Mac was leaning against the school doors. He still looked pale, but the color was returning to his cheeks, along with wariness.

"You about ready to help out again?" Sam said.

He thought about it. Carefully. Then nodded. "Yeah."

Sam turned to Marschel. "Let's process this guy. Mac can wait for Wheezo. If he finds anything, do you think you can convince your judge to issue us a broader warrant?"

"With what we've got? If Wheezo can ID a car, better yet a license number, we put out an APB. Even if we have just a description, if whatever's on that tape is clear enough, the judge should give us a warrant."

Sam left Mac with directions for Wheezo. Once Wheezo finished his work, they could all find someplace nearby to sit around a table and talk.

"We need to contemplate all the angles and figure out next steps. Tell Wheezo we'll also need him for brainstorming and research."

"We're a little short-staffed," Marschel said. "How do you think the kid would be on a stakeout?" Marschel said.

"He'd do it," Mac said. "The missus wants him out of the house, and they could use the cash. But he doesn't have a weapon."

"If he's with you or me, he doesn't need one," Sam said.

CHAPTER THIRTY-THREE

Mac waited for Wheezo back at Lauderdale Elementary, and with his help got lucky with the video. They watched what they identified as a Chrysler LeBaron pull up to a curb and park near the corner of the building. Three people got out and disappeared into the shadows along the side wall. There was no lighting along the school's side, so other than a flash when the door opened, they saw nothing. A nearby streetlight helped illuminate more of the parked car, but even that image was grainy, blurring the details of the three. They could see one of them was large, and the other two medium height, but little else. And they could not see a license plate number. The images were black and white showing a two-toned LeBaron, colors unknown.

Mac phoned the information to Marschel, who used it to extend their warrant to the car. Without the license or car colors the judge was reluctant, but given the fruits from their initial warrant, she was willing to play along. Marschel also used it to post an APB but knew it would be doubtful they'd get any play without additional information, especially the license plate number.

Because it was after lunch and they were hungry, Mac lobbied Sam to meet at the Paulie's restaurant in downtown St. Paul. It was near enough to all of them and he'd heard they had an excellent burger bar, but it was expensive, which meant Margie would never allow them to visit the place. Besides, she frowned when he ate burgers, so he usually didn't order them.

They all arrived about the same time and got a corner booth, set back into a section of the restaurant where they could have some privacy. Sam told the hostess they preferred being out of the way. Given their appearances—Sam, Marschel, Mac (with a grim limp), and Wheezo, wearing tattered khakis and a loose-fitting flannel shirt with a hole in the pocket—the hostess agreed and seated them in the corner.

"I hope we didn't get you out of bed," Sam said to Wheezo.

"Nah. I was in a serious game of Wii Sports Resort. Me and the old lady."

"Where was the kid?" Mac said.

"Grandparents. There all night so we could get some rest. Only Anika wanted to play." He flicked his eyebrows.

Mac shook his head.

A waiter brought menus.

"I'm starving," Wheezo said.

"$14 burgers?" Marschel said.

"Grass-fed beef," Mac said.

Marschel rolled her eyes. "What else are they going to feed them?"

"You know, like, corn," Mac said.

"What's wrong with corn-fed beef?" Marschel said. "I always heard it was the best."

"They say that in corn-belt states, like Iowa and Nebraska," Wheezo said. "But corn gives them indigestion and it affects their meat."

Marschel stared at him and said, "You some kind of food critic? I bet you eat organic too."

"What's wrong with organic?" Wheezo said.

"Can we just order?" Sam said.

"All that organic shit is a conspiracy," Mac said.

"I don't know about that," Marschel said.

"It's a fad," Mac said. "I'll eat organic when they make organic Cheetos."

"I eat organic veggies," Marschel said. "I use them in our smoothies."

Mac stared at her, thinking about asking, but then thought better of it.

Their waiter returned to the table. He had wild black hair and a close-shaved, dyed-purple temple. He nodded to Wheezo as though they were kindred spirits. "Can I take your order?"

Wheezo ordered the grass-fed beef burger with a salad. Mac and Marschel also ordered the grass-fed beef burger, both with fries.

"Can I also get some fries?" Wheezo said.

"They're good," the waiter said.

Sam was thinking low-fat vegetarian and asked about the soup of the day, but it was cream of broccoli, which he suspected had more cream than broccoli, so he ordered the bison burger.

"You always gotta be a little different," Mac said.

"What?" Sam said.

"Bison burger?" Mac said. "And what was that shit about the vegetarian soup?"

Sam was almost as tall and lean as Marschel, in part, because he tried to eat vegetarian when he could. But he also ate lean. Bison was a very lean meat.

Sam ignored Mac's comment, and while they waited for their drinks, he covered next steps.

"Here's what we know. Or at least suspect," Sam said. "Judging from what this janitor told us, there's three people, two men and a woman, driving an old Chrysler LeBaron, pushing brown heroin and maybe committing murder. Sounds implausible, but we think the main guy who's doing it has some kind of vendetta. He's getting even for a bust that happened five years ago. Or maybe he lost some cash and is looking for payback, both revenge and to recover his money."

"Murder?" Wheezo said.

"We think," Sam said.

"We suspect," Marschel added. "It's a little outside the box, given both victims were ODs. But it fits with some of what we've learned."

"Just so I'm clear," Mac said. "We think there's a guy who was the ringleader of a group of meth heads five years ago in Isanti County. Everyone got caught except the main guy, so there was a stakeout to capture him, but he got away. That tells me somebody, most likely one of his old gang members, was watching out for him and let him know the net was about to fall. And now he's killing them?"

The three others considered it, thinking the way Mac described Sam's theory made it sound problematic.

"Sheriff Broom didn't think any of his former partners tipped him off," Sam said. "He said there was no way they could have. They came down on all of them like an iron curtain. And they were scared of him. They wanted to see him caught. But they didn't want him to know they'd worked with the cops to make it happen. They were afraid of what the guy would do."

"But murder them? Where's the motive?"

"Inject them with lethal doses of pure heroin and fentanyl."

"Why not just walk away?"

Sam shrugged. "Money? Maybe they owed him?"

"Back when they did the bust, did the sheriff find any money?" Mac said.

"Pocket money," Sam said. "Not enough to count for much. The big stash, if there was one, disappeared."

"Even more of a reason to just walk away. The main guy had the big stash and took it with him."

"But what if one of his old partners took the money?" Sam said.

Mac shrugged. "That's about the only thing you've said so far that makes any sense. That could be a reason. But it's a big if. *If* they had a stash, and *if* one of the other partners stole it, and *if* this main guy . . .," Mac looked at Sam.

"Jon Lockhart."

". . . Jon Lockhart is still alive and five years later crosses paths with Jerry Trailor and Jerry doesn't tell him what he wants to know, he kills him?"

"And then he tracks down and kills Suthy Baxter?" Marschel said. "Same way. I admit, it's a reach."

"So give me an alternative theory," Sam said.

"Two ODs, plain and simple," Marschel said.

"I agree," Mac said.

"But what about the coincidences?" Sam said. "Two former meth lab partners are in contact. They both die in the exact same way, from heroin that hasn't been seen in the Cities in at least six months. And neither one of them appears to be a frequent user. When was the last time you saw two ODs in a row, all happening with former meth gang members, all apparently clean, and only a couple of them in recent contact? Doesn't make sense."

"Does heroin use ever make sense?" Marschel said. "Especially when it's mixed with fentanyl?"

"From everyone we spoke with, neither of these guys was using," Sam said.

"That's true," Mac said. "Nobody we talked with thought they were using."

"Definitely nobody I spoke with at that community college," Wheezo said. "From what I heard, I'd be shocked if the Baxter kid was using heroin."

They all sat and thought about it for a while, and finally agreed that the most plausible theory was Sam's: two guys murdered for revenge or by a guy who was looking for stolen money. Murdered with heroin laced with fentanyl. But they also agreed they needed to be open to other possibilities.

Then their burgers arrived and they were, for the moment, occupied. Everyone agreed the food was pretty good, except

Marschel, who kept talking about a $14 burger and the fact she could cook one at home, using organic beef, for about two bucks. It was a rip-off.

Mac just nodded and ate. So did Wheezo.

Then Sam's phone rang. It was Carmel.

"Gotta take this," Sam said. He got up out of the booth and started for the restaurant door.

"Your lady friend?" Mac said.

Sam waved him off, pressed Accept and said, "Hey."

"Hey," she said.

Sam thought there was a smile in it. He started outside, to where the front of the restaurant looked out over the area that normally held the St. Paul Farmer's Market.

"My guys are done with that analysis," Carmel said.

"What'd they find?"

"Where'd you get that blood?"

"What'd they find?"

"Scorpion venom. Probably a bark scorpion. The lab guys didn't believe it at first, so they double-checked."

"They had enough in those drops for two tests?" Sam said.

"They're good. But they still wonder about it."

"Did you tell them we found a bark scorpion?"

"Sam. What the hell is going on?"

"We're not sure, but it's useful to know it was venom."

Sam told her where he'd gotten it; small beads of residue from the right arm of Suthy Baxter. And there were similar marks on Jerry Trailor, though they never got samples.

"Really? You think . . . ?"

"My contact in Mexico tells me there's a cartel down there that uses bark scorpions to punish and instill discipline."

"More like torture," Carmel said. "I didn't need to hear that, that there's that kind of evil in the world."

"I know. But it's the only thing I can think. Somebody's up here using the same tactic."

"They brought scorpions with them?" Carmel said.

"Only thing I can think. And one of the scorpions got away. The one that stung Gray."

"What'd these guys do to deserve that?"

"Not sure. Trying to figure it out."

They tried to make small talk. Sam asked about Jennifer. Carmel reminded him that she was at her dad's again tonight. All weekend. The next question they could both feel, but neither one of them said it. There was a pause, during which both of them recognized that, under the circumstances, they weren't good at small talk, and Carmel finally said, "Sam," in a way that meant fish or cut bait.

The problem was, Sam knew ignoring an evening like the one they'd just spent would have been sacrilege in just about any world religion that recognized the sanctity and transcendence of physical coupling. So he said, "Ahhh."

"Sam! When are you coming over?"

If desire could be conveyed in a voice, Carmel's question came across his phone like a dusky Sade ballad. Only more urgent.

"Sam?" she said.

"Ahhh . . ."

"Sam. It's a simple question."

But it wasn't, and they both knew it.

"Here's the deal," Sam said. "I need to figure this out."

"Figure us out? What's there to figure out? Either you want to come over or you don't." Now her voice had a little heat.

"Carmel. I've never had a night like last night. Period. Nothing like it."

"So what's to figure out?"

"This case. Something's going on. And we're at a point where things are starting to happen. I have the feeling they're going to start happening very fast and it's like riding a bull—you've got to stay on top of it or it just might kill you."

"Interesting analogy," she said. "So, no dinner? No evening? Jennifer is still at her dad's."

"Goddamn it, Carmel. You know if there was any other way."

Carmel, who understood the seriousness of Sam's work and respected his commitment, because her own work was just as important to her, finally said, "Here's the other way, Sam. Do whatever you need to with that case, no matter how long it takes. Even if it takes until tomorrow afternoon. As soon as you're finished, you come over to my place. You and Gray. Frank, Liberty, and I will leave a light on."

She was as perfect as a partner could get. Smart. Accomplished. Funny. Willing to flex a little for a mess like him. He didn't deserve it, but he'd take it.

"Thanks, Carmel," he said. "You know I'll be there."

Then she hung up.

Back inside everyone was finished. When he sat down at the booth Mac said, "You getting lucky again?"

"You gotta go?" Marschel said.

"I'm not going anywhere. We've got work to do."

"What?" Mac said, incredulous.

"We can handle it," Marschel said.

"I'm sure you can, but we need the bodies. Besides, I can't walk away."

"Why not?" Wheezo said.

"Because this is what I do. Because if I walked away right now, some very bad people might get away. Though I understand my colleagues," he added, looking around the table, "are more than equal to the task of continuing without me."

"We can and we will, and you can have the night off," Mac said. "You shouldn't say no to a woman like Carmel."

"I appreciate that. But I didn't say no to Carmel. I told her I had to do this."

Mac wasn't going to argue the point. Marschel understood, though probably because she'd been married for a while. She loved her husband, but no way she'd walk away from a day and possibly evening like this one. Wheezo thought Sam Rivers was crazy but couldn't help but feel a twinge of respect.

"Carmel told me something that's like another puzzle piece falling into place," Sam said, coming back to it. "Along with my Mexico contact earlier today, Miguel Verde."

"What?" Marschel said.

Sam explained about the call with Miguel, the Monarchs cartel, their use of bark scorpions to torture and kill, and the results from Carmel's lab: scorpion venom. Then he reviewed current events.

"So it's possible the ringleader could be coming back to set up shop selling Mexican brown heroin," Sam said. "He learns one of his main distribution links, Jerry Trailor, is his former business partner. He starts questioning him. Jerry doesn't tell him what he wants to know, and things get out of hand."

"Kill your distribution guy?" Marschel said. "Still seems short-sighted, even for a heroin dealer."

"I know. It does. But when you consider all the pieces, it's the only thing that fits. Revenge. And maybe trying to get his money back, if there was some."

"Again, a lotta *ifs*, Rivers," Mac said.

"I'm open to other suggestions."

But nobody had any.

Finally, Sam said, "Okay. Here's what we do."

CHAPTER THIRTY-FOUR

By the time Domina, Lockhart, and Tiburon arrived in Hudson, it was well after noon. This time they parked on the corner behind Lonnie DeLay's place, maintaining a clear view of the rear of the house. The shades were still drawn on the near side and back windows. *But maybe,* Domina thought, *Lonnie is a private guy who always keeps them closed?*

They watched for a couple of hours, but nothing changed. They saw no one on the street or in any of the yards. It was a warm late-spring Saturday, Memorial Day weekend, and Domina assumed everyone was down at the river or up at the lake.

Finally, Lockhart told Domina to check it out.

Domina got out of the car and took a circuitous route toward the house. She strolled down the walk and turned at Lonnie's, walking up to the front door like they'd been friends forever and she was just stopping by to say "hello." But the house still felt empty. She glanced at the mailbox. More mail had been added to what had been there yesterday. Lonnie DeLay was gone, at least for the weekend.

Lucky man, Domina thought.

She walked around the left side of the house and double-checked the kitchen window, but everything was unchanged. Then she returned to the car.

"Nothing?" Lockhart said.

"*Nada.* The guy hasn't been home since at least yesterday, maybe before. Just more mail. I bet he's gone for the whole weekend."

"Maybe the weekend," Lockhart said. "But he can't be gone forever."

"Where to?" Domina asked.

"Maury's place. We need to check out that orchard, maybe do a drive-by."

Maury's orchard address was one of the few pieces of information they'd gotten from Suthy Baxter, before Lockhart used the needle to end his pain. Domina plugged Maury's address into her map app. The orchard was only 15 minutes from Lonnie's house. They followed the app until they came to an unmarked road.

Lockhart turned to Domina and said, "Take it, but go slow."

Domina turned down the gravel road. They passed a farm and a couple of homes and two turnoffs that went toward the river. After a few more minutes, about a mile, they came to a steep climb before reaching the corner of the apple orchard, apple trees beginning to flower. They crested the hill and then drove down the other side, skirting the roadside edge of the property.

"*Simpático,*" Domina said. "Nice."

Lockhart said, "I think I see my money."

"Didn't you say his parents were rich?"

"Yeah, he came from a rich family. But if you wanted to launder money, my money, an apple orchard business might be a good way to do it. He gets a loan from his rich parents and cleans up the money by selling fruit. Thing is, nobody knows how much fruit he produces. Every year he brings in another 10 or 20,000 by selling phantom fruit. Fuckin' Maury," Lockhart said, remembering. "I never figured him for an apple orchard. Not enough action."

"So maybe it's not just an orchard," Domina said, indicating with a nod the entrance far up ahead, where they could see a cattle guard and a small camera lens perched atop an 8-foot-high deer fence.

"Keep driving," Lockhart said. "Pick it up a little, like we're thinking the road goes through and we just took a wrong turn."

They drove past the property, passing the driveway with its tall fence and camera. The gravel drive turned up to an underground garage. Lockhart toyed with the idea of heading in and parking behind the garage, after dark, when they were ready to make their move. If Maury saw them coming, the LeBaron would block his exit. But the cameras, if he was watching, and the car's engine would be announcement enough. Maury would have time to slip out the back into land he knew and they didn't.

The only thing Lockhart saw that he liked was the steep hill before the start of the property, which they would be able to hide behind when they returned.

Definitely a night job, Lockhart thought. *And bring wire cutters.*

CHAPTER THIRTY-FIVE

S am and Wheezo turned into the St. Croix Bluffs Regional Park
entrance. Sam saw the park's hours posted at the entrance; the
gate closed at 10 p.m. for everyone except registered campers. He
also noticed plenty of space around the gate, if they needed to exit
after hours in a hurry.

Wheezo held his map app and was following the drive and had
zoomed out far enough to determine that the best place to park was
the upper picnic area. From there it was only a quarter-mile bush-
whack through the woods to the perimeter of the park property and
a tree line, up on a hill, directly across from Maury Trumble's drive.
From what Sam recalled, it was a thick tree line and they should be
able to stay well concealed but still have a clear view of Mink Farm
Road, Trumble's orchard, his driveway, and his house.

Wheezo could also see the rear of Trumble's property abut-
ting the St. Croix River, though it was at least 100 yards behind
the house. And the orchard trees were set back well from the river's edge. He couldn't tell, exactly, but it looked like between the
orchard edge and the river, the trees and brush were thick right
down to the water. He switched to Satellite view, zoomed in on
the river's edge, and noticed there wasn't much beach along the

property, which might account for why it hadn't been sold off for development.

"That's a helluva piece of property," Wheezo said. "It runs right up to the riverbank."

"What do you mean?"

"I mean, it's right on one of the widest, most scenic parts of the river, if he owns that whole thing. He doesn't have a beach. Looks like a shallow bluff. But it's still gotta be worth loads."

"Definitely expensive," Sam said.

They parked in the picnic area lot. There was a playground and kids playing on swings and ladders and big prehistoric-looking animals with holes in them and places to climb through and on top.

"Sweet," Wheezo said, getting out of the jeep with Gray. "Gotta bring Liam here."

"Get that pack out of the back," Sam said. "I'll take Gray."

Wheezo fetched the pack while Sam told Gray to heel, and they started around the playground.

"Never had kids?" Wheezo said.

"Not yet. Not any humans, anyway."

"How old are you?"

"37."

"You got time."

"Here's the problem," Sam said. "It takes two."

"They got surrogates," Wheezo said.

"I'm not exactly the surrogate type."

"In the not-too-distant future they're going to genetically select for the best traits," Wheezo said.

In addition to playing a lot of video games, Wheezo read a lot of science fiction.

"Maybe," Sam said. "But not me. If I meet the right person and if we decide to have kids, I'm tossing the dice."

"Course, that's what me and the missus did. Turned out pretty good, I think."

"How old is Liam?"

"Three."

"Sweet age," Sam said, but wondered if Wheezo would say that when the kid turned 16.

"Makes a difference if you start out with good dice," Wheezo said.

As they turned the corner of the playground and went into the woods, Sam said, "So, Liam takes after his mother?"

They were less than a quarter mile from the park's perimeter. It took 15 minutes to make their way with Gray to a rise directly across from Maury Trumble's orchard. They looked down a steep hill filled with wild pasture all the way to Mink Farm Road—no fence—and then across the gravel to Trumble's driveway. From this height, they had good visibility of Trumble's house, orchard, and more than a mile down Mink Farm Road. They could see the road crest on a series of rises, then disappear in low spots. Sam took a pair of binoculars out of his pack and scanned the front of the house, and then down the length of the road.

"Perfect," Sam said.

Once they were in position, he called Marschel. "Where are you?"

"Looking at Lonnie DeLay's house."

"See anything?"

"Nothing. Went up and knocked, but nobody answered. There's a lot of mail in the mailbox and nothing moving inside. The guy's still gone, just like you said."

"Good," Sam said.

"So, it's a ghost stakeout."

"They don't know he's a ghost, if they're planning on paying him a visit."

"Maybe they already have."

"Maybe. But if they did, they didn't get Lonnie, cuz I saw him yesterday and he was heading out right after work, straightaway."

"Well, I hope you're right and I hope they come. Hope something moves because it's damn boring sitting here with Mac and his bum knee."

"Hey," Mac said. "Watch your phraseology." There were two bags of potato chips, one Cheetos and a small sack of pork rinds, with a couple of cans of soda sitting between them. Mac reached down and opened the bag of pork rinds.

"Mac isn't going to be much help, if they show up," Sam said. "So don't be a hero. Call me if anything moves."

"He says you're not going to be much help, if they show up," Marschel said.

"I've saved Rivers's ass so many times, I practically own it," Mac said, around the pork rinds.

Sam heard the comment and said, "Uh, it was the other way around. But don't mention it. He sleeps better this way."

They agreed to check in on the half hour. If either saw anything, they'd contact the other via text messages, their phones set to vibrate. They knew they were only 15 minutes apart, less if they needed to hustle.

Then they waited.

Back in the tree line, they made small talk. Wheezo wanted to talk about video games, but Sam didn't know anything about them. Then he wanted to talk physiology, particularly involving triathletes, which was only marginally more interesting. But at least Sam could follow the physiology.

Sam told Wheezo about a stakeout he did in Florida, when he was tracking a Key deer hunter. It took a while to explain about the Florida Keys, rare Key deer, the stakeout, and how he found the hunter and used threat and interrogation to track him back to developers. The discussion of the Keys included a brief description of Key West, the southernmost point of the United States, just 50 miles from Cuba. Wheezo had heard of Key West but didn't know anything about it. Sam told him about Ernest Hemingway's house, where Hemingway had lived for a while with his second wife and boys. Wheezo had read Hemingway in high school, but only a short story about trout fishing in Michigan's Upper Peninsula.

"'Big Two-Hearted River,'" Sam said.

"What?"

"That was the name of the story."

Wheezo shrugged. "Maybe. All I know is it was sort of interesting, the fishing stuff and setting up camp and stuff. But it was just one guy in the woods. There wasn't anybody else in it."

"Exactly. He'd been to the war, and he was using the woods and a meditational camping and trout-fishing trip to heal and reclaim himself."

Wheezo looked at Sam and said, "You an English professor? Because I don't remember anything about any of that, especially a war."

"I just remember the story. I was in the same place once, emotionally. I love that story."

"As I recall, it was about camping and fishing."

"The war was there, in the place he started from, the burned-over town of Seney, where the train stopped, and he threw his pack off the rails. But you had to be reading carefully. It helped to know the other Nick Adams stories."

"That was the guy," Wheezo said. "But you remember a hell of a lot more about it than I do. No offense, but except for the fishing parts it was kind of boring."

"No offense, but that was a great American short story. A great story about the ability of nature and the natural world to heal the spirit."

Wheezo looked at him. "If you say so."

So they talked about the kinds of books Wheezo liked, science fiction, *Ender's Game* being one of his favorites.

Sam was familiar with *Ender's Game* and could understand why Wheezo would like it, even though Sam didn't know anything about video games.

"That's what I'm saying," Wheezo said. "You didn't have to. Whereas with Nick Adams, it helped if you were a camper and trout fisherman."

"That's where you're wrong. Like *Ender's Game,* Hemingway's story wasn't just about fishing and camping," Sam said. "At least not entirely."

"I don't know about that deeper meaning crap, if that's what you're talking about."

"Maybe you haven't lived long enough."

That commenced an argument about what constituted experience leading to maturity and wisdom, which was about as far out of Wheezo's league as sand-lot baseball from the majors.

By the time dusk settled in, the mosquitoes started buzzing and all Wheezo could say was, "Fuck me. It's a goddamn swarm," waving his arms around his head.

Luckily, Sam had repellent, which they both spread over their exposed skin. It helped a little. Sam and Gray both remained still as stone, ignoring the pests. Wheezo couldn't stop flailing his arms and complaining, particularly after he inhaled a few.

He managed to cough and spit and curse without making much noise.

"Good protein," Sam said.

"I don't know if I can stand it."

"They're attracted to your carbon dioxide. The more you wave your arms and move around and exert yourself, the more they can sense you, smell you. It's better to stay still."

He tried to sit still but only managed a couple of seconds. Then he started flailing again. "Fuck me."

There was still a hint of light in the western sky, to the right and behind them. Then they saw headlights coming down the gravel road, more than a mile away. They watched the headlights, moving slowly, top a hill and then disappear into a low spot, and then rise to the next hill.

"This looks interesting," Sam said. He raised his binoculars and focused on the car, but it was too far away to see details.

"I hope it's them, so we can get out of these goddamn trees and away from the bugs."

"If it's them, we're not going anywhere until Mac and Marschel arrive."

Sam got on the phone. "Someone's coming," he texted Marschel.

"Keep us posted," came back in text.

"1 minute," Sam texted.

"Quiet as morgue here," appeared on Sam's iPhone screen.

The car was still a half mile away when it topped another rise and suddenly its headlights darkened. There was still enough twilight to see the shadow of the car continuing down the road.

"Did you see that?" Wheezo said.

"Get over here," Sam texted. "Fast as you can. Come in quiet and dark. Stay back. Text me when you turn onto Mink Road."

"You think it's them?" Wheezo said.

Sam lifted the binoculars and focused. "Looks to me like our two-tone LeBaron. And the only reason you would cut your lights a half mile from the house is if you wanted to sneak up on a place. It's them." Sam handed the binoculars to Wheezo.

He took a moment to focus and then said, "Yeah, that's the car that was at the school."

They watched as the car slowed, just a shadow in the gloaming. It crested one more hill and then came off a rise that was maybe 200 yards from Trumble's drive. There was a low spot in the road after the rise, then one more rise, and then the gravel road made a long descent to the edge of Trumble's property and then his drive.

They were moving slowly now, 5–10 miles per hour, approaching the last rise like a predator. Near the top, at the point where they could look out onto the orchard trees and farther down, to the house, it stopped, like a snake waiting for something to move. The car stayed mostly behind the road rise and maybe 50 yards before the fence with its camera. They were watching, far enough back to be out of view of the camera and house.

"What the hell?" Wheezo said.

"Give 'em a sec. They're thinking what to do."

In another moment the car appeared to back up, slowly. From Sam's vantage point, if he listened carefully, he could hear the slow crunch of gravel as the car retreated down the hill. It backed up until its grillwork disappeared.

"What the hell?" Wheezo whispered.

"They're parking where they're not visible from the house and still far enough away from the perimeter fence to be invisible. I bet they're going in on foot."

Now it was getting dark fast. Sam raised the binoculars and fastened on the road rise beyond the place, where he assumed the car was parked. They did not hear any car doors. In a moment he discerned three figures cresting the hill on foot, well back from Trumble's driveway, walking along the road's shoulder in single file. They turned into the nearby field and began making their way through a pasture, approaching the edge of the orchard property and the deer fence, where they would be concealed behind the trees.

"They're going in from the side, through the trees," Sam said. "Take a look."

Wheezo peered through the binoculars and said, "Three of them. Definitely. One of them is pretty big and looks like he has a pack. The other person is medium height. And then there's a smaller guy, out in front. Looks like the same people in the video."

Good eyes, Sam thought.

There were a couple of lights on in the house. There were only two front windows, and Sam remembered the front porch, which didn't appear to be a frequent sitting place. It was facing north-northwest, so it didn't get much sunset. It overlooked the gravel road and drive. There wasn't much to see.

"Best if we wait until they get into the house," Sam said. "Then we need to check out that car."

They were whispering very low now. Gray sat behind Sam, mosquitoes buzzing around his head. But he, like Sam, just watched, quiet as stone.

"You think they're going to bust in?" Wheezo said.

"No idea. Maybe just knock? The guy doesn't have any neighbors close enough to hear anything. They could bust in, but why?"

"Element of surprise?"

"You've been watching too many movies."

The three figures approached the fence and paused, but they were only shadows and Sam and Wheezo couldn't make out what they were doing. They paused for more than a minute, and then seemed to move through the fence and disappear into the orchard.

Wire cutters, Sam thought.

Then it was a couple more minutes before they saw the three shadows emerge from the trees, approaching the house from the side. One of them, the medium-size figure, turned away from the other two and disappeared around the far corner, circling around to the rear of the house. The other two approached the front.

"Covering the back," Sam whispered.

The big man and smaller one approached the front porch. Right before they stepped onto it a flood light triggered, probably a motion sensor or from an inside switch, Sam couldn't tell. The two men appeared startled but kept moving forward.

At the door, the smaller of the two men knocked, loudly, while the big man reached around behind him, lifted his shirt tail beneath the pack, and pulled something out of his pants.

"Gun," Wheezo whispered.

CHAPTER THIRTY-SIX

Jon Lockhart and Tiburon stood at the front door and waited. Tiburon held a Glock G27 in his puffy fist, aimed about mid-level. They heard someone approach and then the door opened.

Maury Trumble stared back with a startled look. He glanced at both men and then down at the gun. Then, before Lockhart could speak, Maury opened the door and said, "Jon Lockhart. What a surprise. I heard you were in town. Come in."

Now the surprise was Lockhart's. Maury was the only meth gang member who had immediately recognized him. Given the burn scar across Lockhart's face, the recognition was unnerving. And Maury was affable, not scared. He was treating them as though they were old friends. And who the hell told him he was in town? Jerry and Suthy didn't have time to do anything but give him information and die.

"Where's your car?" Maury asked, peering out at the empty drive.

Lockhart, still startled, said, "None of your goddamn business."

Maury shrugged. "Come on in," he said, ignoring the gun.

Maury is fuckin' with our heads, Lockhart thought.

"If he does anything stupid, shoot him," Lockhart said to Tiburon, who didn't understand, but nodded.

"You don't really need the gun," Maury said to Tiburon, friendly.

Tiburon kept the hollow black eye pointed at Maury's stomach.

"You want to holler to your colleague in back?" Maury said. "I'd rather she came in the front. I don't want her breaking a basement window."

Maury Trumble had always been smooth. They called Lockhart the ice man, but Maury was the one whose veins were filled with antifreeze.

Lockhart was considering what to do about Domina, when Domina appeared out of the darkness, around the opposite corner of the house.

Domina was startled to see the three of them. Then she said, to Lockhart, "No way out in back."

"Not entirely true," Maury said. "There's an opening off the kitchen onto a second-floor deck. But it's easily missed." And then he opened the door wide, saying, "Come in, come in. It's been too long."

Maury held the door, letting Lockhart pass, then Domina, looking more suspicious than Lockhart. Tiburon peered at the friendly man and waved his gun, indicating Maury should walk in front of him.

"Suit yourself," Maury said, and turned and followed Lockhart and Domina into the hallway. "Got a living room, but never use it," Maury said, nodding to the unused room. "Why don't we go into the kitchen, in back. It's more comfortable and I can fix you guys a drink, if you want."

"Basement," Lockhart said.

"I got a basement. But it's unfinished."

"Basement," Lockhart said.

"Now why would you want to go into the basement when we have a nice kitchen to sit in? And talk."

"Because if I don't hear what I want to know, I would hate to see you bleed all over your kitchen floor," Lockhart said.

Maury shrugged. "Okay. But I'll tell you what you want to know."

At the end of the hallway, before turning left into the kitchen and right into what appeared to be a comfortable family room with a big flat-screen TV, there was a door. Maury opened it and started down the bare pine plank steps. Lockhart turned and indicated he wanted Tiburon's gun.

Tiburon nodded and handed it over. Lockhart waved the barrel, letting Tiburon know he needed to search the rest of the house. Then Lockhart turned and followed Domina and Maury into the basement. At the bottom Maury threw a light switch and they stepped onto a bare cement floor. There was a washer and dryer tucked back to the left and an open half-basement space to the right. There was a card table with four folding chairs poised at different angles around it.

"If I have guests who smoke, we come down here," Maury said.

The half-basement had two large bay windows that started about 4 feet up a cement wall, at outside ground level. The window shades were pulled up high and the basement light shown onto a small backyard.

Lockhart turned to Domina and said, "Close those blinds."

Domina moved to the nearest one and pulled the cord.

"Nobody's out here, Lockhart. Even if the windows were wide open, there's nobody to see in. That's one of the things I liked about the place."

Lockhart didn't acknowledge the comment.

"I think you need to know . . .," Maury started.

"Shut up. The only thing we need to know is what you did with my money."

"What makes you think . . ."

"Shut up." Lockhart said.

Maury grew silent, but the start of a grin was creasing his lips, which made Lockhart's face turn uglier than it already was.

Domina moved to the second window and dropped the blind, thinking Maury was a stupid *gringo* kid who did not know the wickedness of which some men were capable.

"Sit," Lockhart said.

Maury shrugged and moved to a nearby chair.

They heard Tiburon come down the stairs. When he reached the bottom, he said, *"Está solo."* He's alone.

"Tape him," Lockhart said.

"You don't need to do this," Maury said.

"Shut up," Lockhart said.

Maury's chair was angled away from the table. Lockhart stood to his left.

"But, Lockhart," Maury said.

Lockhart pivoted and back-handed Maury's face with his gun hand. Maury twisted and grunted and almost fell off his chair. His head remained down, stunned. After a moment he seemed to shake it off and looked back at Lockhart. A little blood marked the corner of his mouth.

Clearly, Domina thought, *Lockhart now has his attention.* But while Maury wasn't smiling or talking, he was surprisingly cool.

"Talk again until I tell you to, and you lose your dick," Lockhart said, moving the pistol's eye toward Maury's groin.

This time Maury didn't comment.

Domina moved to Tiburon and said, *"Cinta."* Tape.

The big man unshouldered the pack, carefully reaching around the jars to pull out the tape.

Maury sat quietly while they taped his ankles to the chair legs. The chair did not have arms. Lockhart told them to tape Maury's arms behind him, a move Maury was reluctant to accommodate, at first keeping his hands in front of him, until Lockhart started wagging the Glock at his groin. "Tape his mouth too," Lockhart said.

CHAPTER THIRTY-SEVEN

After Sam received Marschel's text that they'd turned onto Mink Farm Road, Sam, Wheezo, and Gray moved quietly out of the trees, cutting down across the field through the dark pasture grass.

It took them a few minutes to reach the car. It was definitely an older model LeBaron, with some obvious retro work. Sam approached the car carefully. There was a very faint glow from a utility light up near the front corner of the orchard property. It cast just enough light through the car's windshield to see inside. Across the front seat, there was a large duffel, unzipped and open, with two 1-gallon jars inside, one standing upright, the other on its side. Sam squinted, but couldn't discern anything about the jars, other than they were clear glass with tightened lids.

"See anything?" Sam said.

Wheezo peered into the front seat. "Can't see much," he said. "But I see a couple big jars in that duffel. That one that's on its side," Wheezo moved to within an inch of the passenger's side window, squinting, "it's got something in it. Looks like bugs."

"Could they be scorpions?"

Wheezo moved his head a little, continuing to squint. "I guess," he whispered. "Can't say I've ever seen a scorpion up close, but it could be," he shrugged. "Creepy."

Sam peered through the driver's side window but noticed the ignition was empty. He looked over the dash for any signs of a more modern installed security system but didn't see anything.

"This is a damn nice vintage car," Wheezo whispered.

"Any idea on the year?"

"I'd guess mid-90s. But they've done some work on it."

"Think it has a security system?"

"Definitely no security. We'd see the gear, and probably a blinking light to show it was armed." Wheezo peered in again but couldn't see anything that looked like an alarm. "You thinking about getting inside?"

Sam was definitely thinking, but his sudden idea didn't only involve entering the car. Given Wheezo's distaste for bugs, he said, "Let's wait for Marschel and Mac."

After a couple of minutes, Marschel's Crown Vic, headlights off, drove down the last rise, moving carefully onto the shoulder. She parked just yards behind the LeBaron. Then Marschel and Mac slipped out of the car.

Marschel approached, while Mac hobbled around the front passenger side of the car.

"This the car?" Marschel said.

Sam nodded. "There were three of them. They hiked through the pasture up to the fence. Then they cut a hole and approached the house through the orchard."

"Ambush," Marschel said.

"And then they knocked on the front door," Wheezo said.

Marschel looked at Sam and he shrugged. "Big guy in front had a gun."

Marschel nodded and then Sam said, "There's a bag in the front seat. I think we need to check it out."

"If we can do it quickly and quietly," Marschel said.

Sam took a minute to open the car door. Marschel watched for a light to come on, but there was nothing. She peered over Sam's shoulder and saw the large workout bag. Sam leaned behind the steering wheel, reached in, and pulled out the near gallon jar. Once it was out, they used the ambient utility light to peer inside.

"What the hell?" Marschel said, startled, taking a step back.

"Scorpions."

Sam peered back inside the bag and saw a second jar filled with the ugly arachnids, lying on its side. "Here's the source of our bark scorpion."

The jar Sam held contained at least a half dozen bugs. He held it up close and peered inside.

"What are you doing?" Mac said.

Marschel took another step back. Wheezo had come around behind Marschel, but as soon as he saw Sam holding the jar up close, he, too, stepped back. Mac had never gotten close enough to do anything but consider them from a comfortable distance.

"Just checking to make sure," Sam said. "And counting them. Seven. They're not going to jump out of a jar."

"We can see," Mac said. "They're scorpions."

Sam returned the jar to the workout bag, careful to set it upright, in the same position it had been in when he pulled it out. Then he managed to shut the door, silent and tight.

"When the action starts," Sam said, "we'll get Mac to block that drive with your car. There are three of them, and if they split, Mac can make sure they can't take whatever vehicle Maury Trumble has in that garage. Wheezo, can you let the air out of the rear tires?"

Wheezo made a wide berth to the rear of the car, bending to deflate the driver's side rear tire. When it was done, he moved to the passenger's side rear.

Sam turned to Mac. "Just be ready with Marschel's car. When you hear the commotion, get down to the drive and block it. You might have your weapon handy too. Just in case."

Mac nodded.

Sam peered back into the car. The bag, the jars, everything looked undisturbed. If someone tried to use the car in a hurry, they probably wouldn't notice the flat tires until they tried to drive it. Then they could easily be overtaken.

Sam and Gray started up through the pasture toward the fence hole, Marschel and Wheezo following.

CHAPTER THIRTY-EIGHT

After Maury's mouth was taped shut, Lockhart handed the gun back to Tiburon. Then Lockhart spent some time with Oscar, the large emperor scorpion designed to kindle fear. He moved Oscar close enough so Maury could see the tiny whiskers growing out of the scorpion's shell. Maury twisted his neck, struggling to look away, whining beneath his tape gag. He pushed against his bonds, his wrists trying to break free. But the tape was stronger.

Maury was starting to squirm.

Lockhart grabbed a fistful of Maury's hair, pulling his scalp tight, lifting his eyes, forcing him to look at Oscar. "When I rip this tape off your face you will tell me what I need to know."

Lockhart started talking about five years earlier, what he had lost, and how he figured it was Maury who ended up with his cash. Lockhart spent a few minutes detailing those last hours and how, when Maury answered the phone from their farmhouse, Lockhart's prison sense told him something was wrong. He explained how he'd hiked to a nearby rise and watched a cop come out of the back of that farmhouse.

"On that day, I had to bleed back into the country and disappear," Lockhart said, inches from Maury's face. "I had to walk away from all that money. It was in my hidey hole, Maury. I waited two months before going out to check. Gone. What happened to all my money, Maury?"

Lockhart's last words were delivered with spittle. The gag prevented Maury from responding with anything except an anguished moan. For the moment, that was just fine with Jon Lockhart. Because Lockhart enjoyed watching Maury Trumble squirm. And Lockhart wasn't finished.

He handed Oscar back to Tiburon and indicated it was time for his other friends.

Tiburon pulled the larger jar out of the pack, this one with much smaller creatures scuttling across its bottom.

Maury was trying to check his rising panic, but it wasn't easy, given the small scorpions piling over each other in the jar. Even if you didn't know they stung, the spider-like bugs looked like they'd crawled out of a horror movie. If Lockhart wanted to shake Maury's earlier composure, he'd succeeded. Maury struggled, trying to keep in mind that when the moment came, he needed to be ready.

"These guys aren't very big," Lockhart said. "But what they lack in size they make up for in deadliness."

Lockhart continued explaining about the venomous animal and its power to inflict pain, especially when victims were stung twice. "Double the pain, half the life expectancy," he said. "If they were still around, you could ask your old friends." Lockhart grinned.

The mention of Maury's former partners, and how they had been tortured prior to being murdered with an overdose of heroin, made Maury's stomach flip-flop. But he swallowed and tried to stay focused on the moment Lockhart *had* to take the tape off his mouth and let him speak.

"Now all I want to hear from you is what you did with my money," Lockhart said.

He opened the jar and Tiburon handed Lockhart a pair of forceps. Lockhart managed to catch one of the writhing bark scorpions, holding it carefully so it would not waste its stinger on the gleaming chrome pincers. He held the scorpion an inch from Maury's twisting face.

"All I want to hear," Lockhart repeated.

Then he nodded to Domina and she moved in and managed to lift a corner of the tape covering Maury's mouth, using the edge to rip it from his lips.

Finally, Maury's moment had come.

"Ernesto Fuego! Goddamn it!" Maury screamed, his lips burning and free. "Ernesto Fuego has your fuckin' money!"

This time it was Lockhart's turn to be stunned. Hearing the name of his Mexican employer startled him. "What?"

"We have a deal," Maury said, talking fast. "I'm the one who located your contacts in St. Paul and Minneapolis. I found them and partnered with Fuego to bring in the dope. I'm a fucking Monarch, you moron."

Jon Lockhart struggled to digest it.

Domina was staring with shock and surprise.

The sickening reality of Maury's words swept over Lockhart like a red tide. If it was true, and Maury Trumble was Ernesto Fuego's secret Minnesota connection, that meant the lying, cheating, stealing son of a bitch must be spared.

But Lockhart had planned his revenge for so long he did not think he could turn away from punishment and retribution.

He took one step forward and said, "No!" as though in a trance, moving in millimeters with the writhing scorpion, its stinger flicking back and forth, trying to find purchase.

Then Domina moved, just a step. "Don't!"

It was enough to make Lockhart pause.

"If what he says is true, you can't," Domina said.

If Lockhart had a gun, he would have killed them all. For now, all he could do was try and absorb Maury's news, the way a fighter in the last round tries to absorb an unexpected blow. Lockhart peered at the writhing scorpion, poised to sting Maury's face. There was madness in Lockhart's eyes.

"No!" Domina said.

Maury's get-out-of-jail-free card was having its effect. But Lockhart was near a dangerous edge.

Maury turned his face, arching to keep away from the twitching bug.

"If you do," Domina said, "Fuego will take his time pulling you apart."

"Listen to your friend," Maury said, through clenched teeth, his face crimson.

In a burst of anger Lockhart flung the forceps across the room. The silver clamp struck one of the window blinds and the impact caused its top right side to fall, revealing a gaping corner of open black windowpane.

Peering out of the dark was Sam Rivers.

CHAPTER THIRTY-NINE

Tiburon had set the gun down to help with the pack and scorpions. Now he turned to the weapon, picking it up. *"¡Hay hombre!"* Indicating there was a man at the window.

Maury's chair was turned away from the window, so he couldn't see what startled the others. But he understood there was someone outside, and for the moment he felt lucky.

Tiburon raised the pistol to Sam's face, but he was gone. Then, from outside, Sam Rivers said, "We followed your bodies, Lockhart! Jerry Trailor and Suthy Baxter. It's over!"

Lockhart was as stunned to hear his own name as he had been to hear Maury invoke the name of his employer.

"Shoot him!" Lockhart said.

Tiburon fired twice through the window. The gunshots blew out the glass and shattered the blinds, reverberating through the room.

Tiburon held the gun and turned to the stairs, running, followed by Domina.

Lockhart stood frozen, but only for a moment. He turned and yelled, "Give me the goddamn gun!" But Tiburon was gone.

By the time Lockhart reached the top of the stairs, Tiburon and Domina were blowing through the front door.

The first thing Tiburon saw was the Crown Vic blocking the bottom of the drive, with Mac's head and shoulders standing above and behind it. Tiburon fired wildly, sending Mac into a crouch. Then the big man turned to his left, heading for the orchard.

The minute the two fled the basement, Sam turned to Marschel and Wheezo and said, "Cover the other side," and he and Gray turned around the near corner.

By the time he reached the corner of the house, Tiburon was in the clear and heading for the trees.

Sam ducked, startled. Then he turned to Gray and said, "Attack!"

Tiburon heard it and started turning the Glock toward the sound. But Gray was a wolf blur in the dark, rising like a shadowy demon. Before Tiburon could angle the gun and shoot, Gray's fangs sunk into his forearm. Tiburon screamed, terrified, as Gray jerked the man's arm down. The gun fired once, harmlessly, and then Tiburon let it go, too terrified to notice.

Domina took one look at Gray and started running in the opposite direction, her own Glock in hand, firing wildly toward the Crown Vic.

It was dark in front of the house, but Mac, behind the car, could see the blur of someone change directions, heading for the opposite side of the orchard.

"Stop!" Mac yelled, but it had no effect on the fleeing figure. Mac aimed his weapon in advance, hoping his leading shots would give them pause, and fired twice.

But the figure ducked and didn't slow and in a second vanished into the trees.

Lockhart had not yet cleared the front door when he heard Gray's guttural growl—definitely not human—and turned back into the house toward the kitchen. He found a rear door that led to a small deck, and then he was down the stairs and into the back orchard before anyone saw him.

Wheezo let Marschel take the lead, but by the time the pair of them turned the corner they heard Mac's shots, which caused them to hug the house wall. They could see a figure nearing the trees, holding a gun, running, and then Mac's shots and two tufts in the grass in front of the fleeing suspect. And then the figure was gone.

"Mac!" Marschel yelled.

"Into the trees," he yelled back.

And then Marschel was running, fast, her weapon drawn, following Domina's footsteps. Wheezo, without a gun, hugged the house wall.

Tiburon struggled with the demon, screaming unintelligibly, trying to shake him loose. Gray held long enough for Sam to step forward and retrieve the fallen gun. Then he pulled Gray off. Tiburon would have run, but the minute he looked up from the struggle, Sam Rivers's Glock was pointed at Tiburon's leg. Sam thought he needed to get the man's attention, so he moved the pistol a few degrees and fired, once, into the ground, close enough to nearly graze Tiburon's knee.

Tiburon froze, but it was almost as though he hadn't heard the weapon fire. He stared at Gray and said, "Chupa . . . chupa . . . chupacabra," breathless with fear.

Sam remembered stories of the chupacabra, a Mexican were-wolf, from when he had visited the monarch preserves. The beast had snarling fangs and was part wolf. Clearly Gray, who was straining against Sam's collar grip, ready to finish the big man if he was given a chance, fit the chupacabra description, or was at the very least its demonic cousin.

Wheezo came over to where Sam was holding Gray and his gun. Mac hobbled up, another gun on Tiburon. Mac had cuffs and was able to get the big man's arms behind him and fasten the bracelets to his wrists. It wasn't easy. The man's wrists were like tree limbs, and the way he was breathing, clearly shaken, made Mac think he was going to have a heart attack.

"Marschel followed one of them into the orchard," Mac said, excited.

"And the other?" Sam said.

"No idea."

"Could still be in the house?" Wheezo said.

"Stay here and help Mac keep an eye on this guy."

Wheezo nodded, and Sam and Gray started back toward the house.

By the time they cleared the main level, walking into the rear kitchen, Sam saw the opened back door and figured Lockhart was gone. The front door was open, and he was starting toward the basement door when he heard Mac yell from out front.

Sam and Gray came running and the second they burst out the front door, Mac said, "He's taking the LeBaron!"

"Give me Marschel's keys," Sam yelled.

Mac reached into his pocket and tossed them to Sam as he fled past. Sam caught them midstride and then he and Gray tumbled into Marschel's Crown Vic, started the engine, backed and turned the car around, hitting the road in a tailspin, gravel kicking behind them like the rooster tail from a speedboat.

CHAPTER FORTY

A s soon as Lockhart reached the car, he popped it open. Earlier they had turned off the interior lights, so now he could only see the faint illumination from Maury's distant utility light, casting an opaque shadow on the car's front seat. Domina had a second set of keys above the visor. Lockhart climbed in, dropped the visor, caught the keys, and started the engine. It took him a few seconds to get the car turned around. It was sluggish and turned hard and Lockhart wondered about it, but he had heard shouts and voices back by the house, and then something about "keys" and he knew he had to move. He accelerated and sped down the gravel road, sidewinding as rocks scattered behind him.

In another 10, 15 seconds the rear tires started fishtailing, and as he continued to accelerate the car's tail shifted back and forth. Flat tires! He braked to keep from skidding into the ditch. The car veered right over the shoulder, hit a hard pile of gravel, and suddenly the upright jar of scorpions jumped out of the bag as though it was spring-loaded. The jar struck the dash, hard, and the lid popped off. It tumbled down, hit the seat, and rolled before dropping to the passenger side floor. Lockhart, both hands on the wheel, righted the car, veered back onto the road, and accelerated.

There was a sharp pain on the back of his neck near the hairline. He reached back and slapped and could feel a scorpion moving under his hand! Feeling the sting and the bug on him made him swerve and scream. As soon as the car slowed enough to straighten, he started flailing his hands wildly through his hair.

The scorpion was gone, but its sting felt like someone had lit a match and held it against his skin.

Lockhart glanced in the rear-view mirror and saw headlights crest a rise behind him, maybe a quarter mile back. He accelerated and as the car surged forward, the rear tires began fishtailing again. As Lockhart struggled to keep the car on the road he felt another sting, on his Achilles.

He screamed, lifting his foot off the accelerator and banging it against the bottom of the driver's seat. The car began slowing, but Lockhart only half noticed, the burn now spreading behind his right ankle. He slammed his foot back onto the gas and the car lurched forward. At the crest of the next hill, he glanced and saw headlights gaining on him, shifting to the left and right in the rearview because his tires were causing him to fishtail across the road.

Lockhart kept his white-hot foot on the pedal and piled down the last hill toward the blacktop, the car threatening to pitch from one ditch into the other. As he approached the turn, he knew he was moving too fast to make it. So he braked and the car skidded, slowing just enough to angle onto the dark pavement.

By the time he reached the blacktop a third scorpion stung him on his left ankle. He managed to keep the pedal to the floor, stomping his foot. But it wasn't fast enough, and he could feel the bug strike again.

Lockhart veered onto the shoulder, then over the lip of the ditch. One of his rear flat tires caught the blacktop's edge and the car spun sharply to the left. He twisted the steering wheel to compensate and the car straightened, hitting the bottom of the ditch hard before the car's momentum shot him up the other side and straight into a recently planted corn field. His tires rumbled over the rows. He wasn't sure but he thought he felt another hot sting on his right thigh, through his pants. The steering wheel was pulling so hard to the left that when he moved his hand to swipe at the scorpion the wheels turned and suddenly the car lurched to a stop, Lockhart's forehead striking the steering wheel.

Adrenaline and a rapid heartbeat were pushing the hot venom inside him, spreading his burns like a deadly fire.

Dazed, Lockhart knew he had to abandon the car. He managed to open his door and tumble out. The world was starting to move.

There was a firebrand on the back of his neck. Fire in both feet. Fire rising up his legs.

He tried to get up but was broadsided by a wolf, a werewolf.

Lockhart screamed, but the wolf had his arm. Lockhart's terror and Gray's growling attack made primeval sounds in the dark, as though some deeply animal battle was being pitched across the field.

And then there was Sam Rivers, beside Gray, pulling him off.

When Gray was clear, Lockhart did not rise. He rolled and tried to get up but felt suddenly disoriented.

Through the open car door Sam saw the jar of scorpions with its top popped off. "Don't move," Sam said.

Lockhart heard it through a fog. The venom was taking hold. Too many stings.

Sam Rivers was over him, starting to realize Lockhart was down and writhing from the stings. He glanced carefully over Lockhart's clothes, hair, and face but didn't see anything. Then Lockhart suddenly quieted.

Sirens started in the distance. Marschel, Mac, or Wheezo must have called.

Sam slapped Lockhart's face, "Lockhart!"

But the man was starting to drift. Sam wondered if he'd been stung more than once. If so, with toppling out of the car and being run down by Gray, then fighting for his life, Lockhart's blood would have rocketed whatever venom was inside him, pushing it into his heart and brain.

Jon Lockhart had delivered enough scorpion strikes to know that four, maybe five—he couldn't remember, exactly—was the end. He was beginning to fade, and he knew it. Somewhere in his addled mind he thought, *goddamn Maury*.

He tried to move his lips, but nothing came out.

"What?" Sam said. "What?"

He was trying to make the sounds.

"What?"

"Tremble," Lockhart managed, though he wasn't sure. "One of them," he said. "Mexicans."

And then there was nothing.

Tremble, Sam wondered. *Mexicans?*

Sam Rivers had been bitten twice by rattlesnakes. He'd once suffered a venomous spider bite in Costa Rica. While diving off the Yucatan Peninsula he'd been stung by a venomous sea fish. Those had all been painful, and he remembered how their poison could creep over the body, quieting the pulse, threatening the heart, clouding the mind. But they had been survivable bites and stings.

He did not know how many times Jon Lockhart had been stung, but it must have been several, because now he watched Lockhart drop quickly into oblivion, his breathing rapid and shallow.

Two black-and-whites pulled into the ditch. As soon as their deputies neared him, hands resting on their weapons, Sam explained what happened and told them to close and secure the LeBaron, that it was dangerous, filled with venomous scorpions.

Under the circumstances the cops did what they were told and let Sam keep doing CPR, because they figured Sam's account was too bizarre to be made up and besides, who wants to mess with venomous bugs.

Marschel had called the EMTs so they were on the scene a couple of minutes after the deputies arrived. By then Sam had been rapidly pressing on Lockhart's sternum for at least that long, artificially pumping the blood through the man's system, hoping to keep him alive. Though it occurred to him he might be hastening the man's demise.

When the EMTs appeared, Sam told them about the bark scorpions, and they quickly administered epinephrine. But it was like sticking a needle into a side of dressed beef.

Sam and Gray left them working over Lockhart, but Sam was pretty sure it wouldn't make any difference.

On the way back to the farmhouse, Marschel called.

"We got the big guy. He's a little bitten up, and he keeps mumbling about a choopacompadre or something. Pretty shook. I think Gray did some kind of number on him."

"Chupacabra?"

"That's it. The big guy's kinda freaked out, like he's seen a ghost."

"It's a Mexican werewolf."

"They have werewolves in Mexico?"

Sometimes Sam was stunned by people's ignorance of flora and fauna.

"We got Lockhart," Sam said. He explained what happened, but he didn't say anything about Lockhart's last words, because Sam thought he knew what he heard and it fit, given what he'd heard through the basement window. But he needed to be certain. It would be better if Marschel, Mac, and Wheezo were left out of it for now. If they knew Maury was a suspect, and if they tried to question or move on him before Sam had a chance to figure out a way to surface Maury's involvement, the orchard owner might go free.

"What about the other guy?" Sam said.

"Looked like a woman," Marschel said. "She took off into the woods and I went after her. At the edge of the orchard, she got caught up in the brush and I could hear her going through it. But she was maybe 50 yards out in front. I stopped and listened, because she had a gun. And then I heard a huge splash. She jumped off the bluff! By the time I reached the edge I could hear her spitting water."

"She jumped? How high's the bluff?" Sam said.

"I'm guessing 10, 15 feet, but in the dark no way to tell for sure. The whole area is so choked by weeds there's no way left or right. She had one way out and she took it."

"You sure?"

"Positive. Get back here and we'll take Gray into the woods. If she jumped, her trail should end at the cliff. But she's gotta come ashore somewhere, downriver. We'll pick her up."

By the time Sam returned to the orchard house, Tiburon was handcuffed and sitting on the ground near the bottom of Maury Trumble's drive. When Tiburon saw the chupacabra step down from the car he managed to stand up, ready to run.

Mac grabbed him while Sam leashed Gray. A sheriff's cruiser pulled into the drive and Mac moved the big man into the back of the cruiser, where he was happy to go, his wild eyes fastened on Gray.

Sam and Gray approached the others in front of the house, where Sam made Gray sit.

Maury Trumble pushed through the front door and walked straight to Sam, hand extended. "Agent Rivers, I want to thank you for saving my life."

It was a serious attitude change from Sam's previous afternoon visit, but given the circumstances, Sam waved him off and said, "We'll talk later. Right now we're in the middle of a manhunt."

CHAPTER FORTY-ONE

S am turned to Mac, who was keeping an eye on Tiburon in the cruiser. But with a chupacabra on the prowl, the man wasn't budging.

The orchard owner moved back up to his porch.

Sam called down to Mac and said, "Hey, Mac," and waved him up.

Wheezo was up on the porch, talking with Maury, who was about the same age. Sam thought Wheezo should be in on this, so he called him over too.

When the four of them were assembled, Sam said, "We need to go after the other one while the trail's fresh. Me and Marschel and Gray."

"I called the local sheriff and he's sending over more deputies," Marschel said. "A few more can't hurt, if we need to search down the riverbank."

"Good. You okay until they get here?" Sam said to Mac, Wheezo, and the deputy.

"Does the pope shit in the woods?" Mac said.

That caused the others to stare for a moment, having to think about it. Wheezo might have smirked, but Sam just said, "Okay."

"How long ago did you return from that cliff?" Sam asked.

"Maybe 7, 10 minutes. No more. It's close, through those trees in the back. I could hear her searching for a way off that cliff before she jumped."

"Get us in the right direction and we'll turn Gray loose."

The three of them—Marschel, Sam, and Gray—took off through the side yard and went into the trees, Marschel leading. A couple of minutes and they were at the orchard's border.

"Let Gray take it from here," Sam said. Sam let Gray know the scent he should be following, the broken trail through the grass.

"Gray," Sam said. "Search!"

The big animal's training kicked in and he took off through the thick underbrush.

Sam and Marschel pulled out their phones and lit up the path in front of them. They followed the recently trampled line through the weeds. In less than 30 seconds the trail broke out onto an opening, and they could see, 10 yards ahead, the cliff edge. Gray was already at the edge, head down, leaning into darkness.

"Gray!" Sam called.

Gray's pursuit gene was so powerful that Sam could tell he was thinking about following the trail scent over the cliff edge into the still night air. Gray held, but kept peering into blackness, excited, anxious to follow his nose.

When Sam glanced out across the river he saw lights on the distant shore, but it was at least a half mile of wide water. When he glanced to his right, over the bush, he could see lights down the bank, probably a quarter mile through the trees. Except for this small opening, upstream and downriver, the dense weave of bushes grew to the rock edge, seemingly impenetrable.

"You heard the splash?" Sam said.

"Big splash."

"And then what?"

"Sputtering. Hard breathing. A woman's deep voice. She sounded scared and cold. Who wouldn't be, jumping for your life off a cliff edge into the dark? And that water's gotta be colder than a gravedigger's ass."

Sam approached the edge and shined his light. He thought he saw the river's surface, not too far below. He picked up a rock, tossed it over the edge, and in about a half second heard a splash.

"I'd guess 15 feet," Sam said.

"You can tell that from a rock?"

"Physics."

There was a pause while Marschel wondered what in the hell Sam was talking about. Sam and Gray peered into the darkness, Gray close to the edge.

"Let's head back, go downriver, hunt along the shoreline," Marschel said. "No way she's gonna try and swim across. She'd freeze to death. I bet she's down at those lights." Marschel indicated the house lights a quarter mile down the shore. "We'll get her."

Sam shined his light along the dense bushes to the side, seeing if there was a way around it, but there wasn't.

"Let's roll," Marschel said, turning.

"Dammit!" Sam said. He knew Marschel was right. The only way was to head back and hunt along the road. "Let's go!" he said, starting to turn.

Gray had been so eager to follow the air scent, he misunderstood Sam's command. Suddenly, he was off the cliff edge, sailing through the air toward the river.

"Gray!" Sam said, stunned, yelling down after him.

He heard a splash and then waited, holding his breath, until he heard Gray surface and then start chuffing toward the near shore, following the scent across the water.

"Goddamn it!" Sam said. It took a split second to consider his options, none of them good. The woman had a gun. If Gray tracked her and that gun was operational, he could get shot.

"Goddamn it!" Sam repeated, pulling dog baggies out of his pocket, double bagging his phone.

"What the hell?" Marschel said.

"Gotta go after him."

"Are you batshit crazy?"

"Head back. Get in your car and try to find a way down to that house with lights."

"You could kill yourself."

"You heard the woman splash and swim away. Gray just did the same thing. As soon as Gray hits that shore, he's going to find the trail and take off. No choice," Sam said. And then he jumped, without thinking, with no other notion in his head but worry for the animal that had seen him through good times and bad. He remembered abject despondency, when sometimes Gray's touch, presence, and bicolored eyes reminded him life was precious and good.

For the half-second Sam plummeted through darkness, his stomach rising, he also remembered to keep his mouth shut. Then he hit the water hard, going under, deep and freezing cold.

The cold was a shock.

But it was a shallow jump and he came up quick, feeling the current push him downstream.

"Gray," he called out.

"You're a crazy mother, Rivers."

"M-m-m-meet you at the lights," Sam managed. He hiccupped for breath but managed to follow Gray, knowing he had to get to the shoreline fast if he wanted to catch the wolf dog and avoid hypothermia.

By the time he hit the shore, the current must have pushed him downstream 20 or 30 yards. It was enough distance to get beyond the bluff to where the riverbank came down to the edge, the thickness of the bushes receded, and there was 5 feet of open bank. Sam kept following Gray, who thankfully had worried in both directions over the bank, trying to pick up the scent. He moved a little farther downriver and then took off in that direction, fast.

Normally Sam would have screamed for him to stop, but if the runner was nearby, she'd hear them. At this point Sam's only recourse was to stumble after his partner, hoping the perp's movements would be loud enough to drown out any sound of Gray's.

The riverbank was sand and dirt and mostly clear of weeds. Sam hurried over it, still within hearing distance of Gray. Gray turned off through a stand of river willows. Sam followed, occasionally stopping to listen. They were nearing the house lights and Sam figured the woman had taken off for them, maybe hoping to steal a car or get some kind of help. If she was in there, or somewhere nearby, Sam wasn't sure what they were going to do. She might have lost her gun in the jump or the river or the water could have disabled it. Sam had nothing but his iPhone. And a chupacabra.

The willows broke open and he was in some kind of big side yard with huge oak sentinels and a side window light, up by the house. Sam watched as Gray, head down, wound back and forth over the grass, following a trail.

"Gray," Sam said, in a harsh whisper.

Finally Gray paused, looked around to see Sam catching up. Then he turned back to the trail.

"Gray," Sam repeated, and his partner finally stopped.

As Sam approached, he could hear him whining, softly. Sam came up beside him and let him know he'd done a great job. But Gray had no time for praise.

"Sit," Sam said. Reluctantly, Gray sat.

They were at the side of the house and Sam approached the corner, peering around it. There were lights on in the front. They cast a glow over a row of emerging hostas and then a walk that ran from the driveway to the front door. There were wet footprints on the sidewalk that led to the door. When Sam crept to the window edge he could see a woman inside, jet black wet hair, wrapped in some kind of blanket; whether forced or invited, Sam couldn't tell.

The outside temperature was still warm and Sam's hustle through the woods had heated him enough to minimize the effect of his cold plunge. But he was still wet.

He turned to Gray and in a whisper put him in another sit, just short of the corner of the garage. He told him to wait and keep an eye out. If the garage door opened, he would be concealed by the edge of the house.

As usual, Gray seemed to understand.

Through the window the woman looked tired, cold, and wet. As Sam watched, a white-haired woman appeared, handing her a steaming cup of something. Sam could see it was friendly. If the woman had a gun, she hadn't used it. *Smart,* Sam thought.

Sam approached the front door and knocked.

In a moment the door opened and the woman looked out, stunned there would be a second person on her front step who had fallen off a boat. She was in a robe and had an aged, friendly countenance. Sam wondered if she lived alone.

"Are you okay?" she said.

"Yes," Sam said. "Just fell into the river."

"Oh, good gracious," the woman said. "Come in. Did you fall off the same boat as this nice girl?"

The woman opened the door and Sam walked into the house and the woman's gun was drawn, pointing at Sam Rivers.

"I'm sorry, ma'am," Domina said. "I don't want to hurt anyone." She wondered about Sam Rivers, who wasn't wearing a uniform. But she figured anyone wet like her probably got that way in pursuit. That meant the law. "I just need to borrow your car," she said, turning to the woman. Her gun was still pointed at Sam. The homeowner appeared startled, but not shaken.

"Oh," she said.

Sam didn't move.

"Car," Domina said, with more urgency. "Do you have a car?"

She nodded.

"Get the keys. I need to borrow it. Just borrow it."

"Better do as she says," Sam said.

She started toward the kitchen. Domina nodded with the gun for Sam to follow. Once in the kitchen, they watched her get into her purse, pull out her car keys, and approach Domina. Hesitant, she handed her her keys, at arm's length.

"It's in the garage," she said.

"Good." Then to Sam, "Move over, closer to the nice lady."

Most guns are still operational after being doused in water. There was a chance it could still hold a water plug, which could blow up the barrel when shot, but you never knew.

Sam stepped over to the woman.

"Now let's all go out to the garage," Domina said.

They shuffled toward the garage door, Sam following the woman, with Domina behind both of them. They moved through the kitchen to a side door, and then she opened it and turned on the light. They could all see a car sitting in the single-stall garage.

"Open the garage door," Domina said.

The homeowner moved through the doorway and pushed a button and the garage door started up.

Sam hoped Gray was still in a sit and would stay that way until he heard Sam give him the command.

The garage door finished opening. No sign of Gray.

"Move through the door to the right, out of the way. Get into the back corner," Domina said. "Don't get smart or try anything. If you stay cool, everything'll be fine. I just want out. I'll leave your car in the city, ma'am. It'll be found. You'll get it back."

Sam and the homeowner shuffled into the back corner.

Then Domina stepped forward, locking the kitchen door. Locking them out of the house would slow them.

Domina started backing down the passenger side to get to the rear of the car, keeping an eye and her gun on Sam and the woman. She backed around the rear fender, eyes and gun still pointed in the direction of her captives and began shuffling quick to the other side.

"Attack!" Sam yelled.

Startled, Domina looked back at Sam, the gun still raised. There was a blur and suddenly Domina's gun hand went down as Gray's bulk exploded into her. Domina felt Gray's jaws on her gun arm; as she went down, a shot fired and the woman screamed. Gray clamped hard onto Domina's raised wrist and the gun tumbled across the ground.

Now Domina was fighting and twisting, trying to break free. Sam rushed forward. The homeowner tried the door, found it locked, flipped a mat at her feet, groped for a key, used it, and disappeared into her house, slamming the door.

Gray was on top of Domina, who was still trying to free herself, but the chupacabra was focused on her upraised arm like a furious hellhound.

Sam picked up the fallen gun and said, "Gray! Gray!" He grabbed his collar and pulled.

Domina rolled and managed to rise, and Sam said, "You move and I let my friend go. Understand?"

The woman nodded, once, quick and afraid, staring at Gray.

Sam turned and called back through the closed door, "Call 911! Tell them to get some people out here. Now!"

Domina was still breathing heavy. "I wasn't going to hurt her."

"What?"

"The old lady. I'd never hurt an old lady."

"There are two corpses in your trail."

Domina flashed Sam a look, still breathing hard. "That wasn't me," she managed. "That was Lockhart."

Sam wondered about it. "Jon Lockhart?"

"Yeah," she said, her breath starting to normalize. "Jon Lockhart." She bent over with her hands on her knees, still staring at Gray.

Domina knew she shouldn't talk. But she had never signed on for murder, and now she was in way over her head.

"Where's the brown heroin?"

Domina looked up. The animal, now that she could see it, appeared to be a wolf, or maybe a mix. It was under control, but she knew if she took off running the animal would chase her down.

Domina was trying to think.

"What's your name?" Sam said.

"Josefina," Domina finally said. "Josefina Domínguez, from Storm Lake, Iowa. But everyone calls me Domina."

"You American?"

Domina nodded.

"But you're part of a Mexican cartel? ¿*Las Monarcas*?"

Domina looked surprised but didn't say anything because she was still trying to figure out her best move.

"Thought so," Sam said. "But since you're Mexican-American, seems to me you're the logical link to *Las Monarcas*. Not Jon Lockhart. I'm guessing you're behind the ODs? And the scorpions."

Another startled look.

"That's not right," Domina said. Then she paused.

"You know how this works," Sam said. "We gotta run with what we know. We know you're Mexican-American. The big guy is already back at the house. He's definitely Mexican. But Jon Lockhart looks like, he looks like a Minnesotan. My money's on you as the leader. Not the Minnesotan."

The white-haired woman came out of the house and said, "They're coming."

Sam nodded and said, "Thank you. You should probably wait inside."

She nodded and returned, but not before Domina said, "I'm sorry," to the woman's retreating back. "Thank you."

The woman turned before she opened the front door. "I hope you sort things out. You seem like a nice young woman." And then she disappeared into the house.

Tough old lady, Sam thought, *to have been threatened by a gun and still see something good in the person who held it.*

"I'm in trouble here," Domina said.

"You are," Sam said.

"I'm trying to figure out my options."

"Not many."

"I never killed nobody. It was all Lockhart. He's the main guy."

"Accessory to murder, if not murder," Sam said. "We don't know how any of it went down. We're just left trying to sort out the pieces."

"Lockhart will talk out his ass. Lockhart will tell stories and blame us. He's fucked up."

"So what happened?"

"I can tell you everything."

Domina was getting started now. She'd turned some kind of corner.

"I can even tell you where they manufacture it and how they get it across the border and what happened here, in Minnesota," she said. "But it's not free."

"I'd like to help you," Sam said. "But I need some details."

"I don't see how I get out. I talk and the Monarchs'll kill me, if Lockhart doesn't first. I talk and I'm dead."

"You come clean and give us what we need, and I can talk to the prosecutor and judge. But you need to know your rights."

"Yeah, yeah," Domina said. "I know my rights."

But Sam said it anyway, the whole thing, making sure Domina understood Miranda.

"I can give you everything, but I don't see what you can give me."

Sam thought about it. "Enough, I think," he finally said. And then Sam explained how—if the information was good, and there was plenty of it—he could speak with the prosecutor. They could get a sentence that would make it look like she'd received the maximum punishment. Nobody would think she said anything, once arrested. And then, a couple of years into it—she'd have to serve some time, Sam couldn't whitewash that—they'd make up some bogus transfer to some out-of-the-way place. Maybe Canada. And in transit, they could let her off for good behavior. You never knew if prosecutors would go along, but Sam thought he could make a persuasive case.

They'd be careful with it. It could work. At least, it was enough to give Domina some hope.

Domina thought about it. She was fucked, no doubt. Every option appeared to be a dead end with a long stint growing old in a dark cell, save possibly one.

So she talked. She explained everything that had happened since they'd crossed into Texas.

In the distance there were sirens. First Marschel turned down the long drive. Then a deputy's cruiser. But before Marschel pulled up in front of the house, Sam had the whole story.

There was one last thing Sam needed. And if the last piece was going to fall, they needed Domina's help.

CHAPTER FORTY-TWO

Within the next 15 minutes, the rural yard in front of Corinne Johns's place grew busier than at any time in the 22 years Corinne had been living there. Unless Sam was a bad judge of character, she appeared to be thriving with all the sudden, newfound activity, brewing a full pot of coffee and bringing a plate of cookies out to the sheriff's deputies, Marschel, Sam, and Domina. The cookies were followed by a small plate of tri-cornered sandwiches.

Judging by how nice she was to Domina, she seemed to have forgiven her for holding a gun on her and almost stealing her car.

Sam wished there were more Corinne Johns in the world.

Sam stepped away from the deputies and Domina and motioned for Marschel to walk with him. Once they were away from the others, Sam said, "What have you heard about Lockhart?"

"Pronounced dead en route to Hastings. But they think he'd been dead awhile."

"Have you told anyone else about it?"

"No. Just found out myself."

"Good. Don't say anything."

"Okay," Marschel said. "But why?"

"Because we need this perp's full cooperation. If she thinks Jon Lockhart's dead, she might put two and two together and realize we don't have all the evidence we need to get the others, especially Maury Trumble."

"The orchard owner?"

"Looks innocent. Acts innocent. But he's part of it."

There was a pause before Marschel said, "You sure?"

"Back at the house, when I was standing outside that basement window, I thought I overheard his complicity. And then before Lockhart passed out, he said something else that made sense. But I wasn't sure, and it's not recorded, and we got nothing if it came to a trial. So just follow my lead," Sam said. "And if you wonder whether or not you should say something, don't."

"What?" Marschel said.

"I'm not in charge. You're in charge. We're just following current events."

Detective Marschel was irritated. "Something tells me I been following your current events since the beginning. Me, Sheriff Broom, Scott Pepper, everyone."

Sam didn't say anything.

"Okay," Marschel finally said, with resignation. "I'll follow your lead."

After a couple of beats, Sam said, "What do you have in the trunk of that Crown Vic?"

They talked about Marschel's supplies. Besides some additional weaponry and a vest, she had exactly what Sam needed.

"Get it out and set it up. Fast."

By the time Raven Marschel was finished, Sam had explained the plan to Domina. Domina stood beside them, her hands cuffed. But she wasn't going anywhere. She had shifted so suddenly into a co-conspirator that Sam questioned the authenticity of it. But the woman seemed genuine, even so far as to make suggestions for improving the plan.

Detective Marschel didn't like it, and never once made eye contact with Domina. But Sam treated Domina as he saw her, a full-on partner, and someone they needed in order to capture the biggest fish in the pond. All of them.

By the time the four of them rolled back to Maury Trumble's house, Domina was secured in the back with the chupacabra sitting next to her. Maury's place had more bustle than Corinne's house. There were two deputy cars, one holding Tiburon in the back. Their official overhead lights were flashing red across the front of Maury's house.

Marschel rolled down both rear windows about 6 inches, presumably to let a little air into the back, but more importantly in preparation. Sam came around and opened up the back door and let Gray down off the seat. Marschel cut the ignition and got out.

Sam, Marschel, and Gray approached the gaggle of officers near the front porch. Wheezo was off to the side, talking to Maury.

When the deputies were introduced to Sam Rivers, one of them said, "Any idea what's going on?"

"Not much," Sam said, loud enough for everyone to hear. "I'll tell you what I know. There's a guy in the hospital because he was stung by a scorpion. He's not talking. And then we got these two, but they're not talking either. We think the three of them were involved in the heroin trade and some ODs that happened in the last three days. But we're still trying to figure it out."

The deputies considered it for a while. And then one of them said, "Any officer willing to jump off a cliff in the dark into that freezing river is either crazy, stupid, or has atomic balls."

Everyone picked "crazy." Though they all knew it had more to do with instinct, pursuit, loyalty to his dog, and just flat-out chutzpah. And maybe there was a little crazy, but less so since it worked.

Then they wanted to hear his side of the story, especially about the dog.

Before Sam had a chance to explain, Maury approached and said, "Agent Rivers, I want to thank you." He extended his hand.

Sam took it and told him his thanks were appreciated, but unnecessary.

"Is that the other one?" he said, glancing down at the Crown Vic, parked near the bottom of the drive.

"That's her," Sam said.

"Wow," he said, but it sounded contrived.

Sam wondered if any of the others caught it. He didn't think so.

"I am so lucky you came when you did."

"Sometimes we get lucky. But in this case, that Lockhart guy led us straight to you."

"I am lucky," Maury said. "I was telling the others that I recognized Jon Lockhart, from quite a while ago. From when I was a kid. And then I thought I recognized the others. But when I talked to the big one, I realized I was wrong. But that other one?" he paused, a silent question. "Something about her seems familiar."

"She's first-generation Mexican-American, from Storm Lake, Iowa."

"I don't think I know anyone from Storm Lake," Maury said, nice enough. "But she looks like someone I know. Maybe she worked in my orchard? Do you mind if I go speak to her? I'll keep my distance. And who knows, maybe I can get you some more information."

Sam appeared to think about it. "I'm not sure that's a good idea. She seems docile enough, but if she tried anything . . ."

"Is that back door locked? And she's in handcuffs?"

"Yeah," Sam said.

"I'd definitely keep my distance. I can see the back window's half open. And like I said, maybe she could tell me something that would be helpful, from a connection point of view. Maybe helpful for your case?"

Sam appeared to think about it.

Mac was in the periphery of men. "I can go down with him," Mac said.

Maury flashed a look and said, "You know, if there's more than just me, might make her nervous. If I was alone, she might be more willing to ease up and talk."

For a third time, Sam seemed to consider it. Then he nodded. "Okay, but keep your distance. Mac, stay back with us, but keep an eye on them."

Mac nodded. Maury thanked Sam and started down to the car.

The vehicle was far enough down the drive to be well out of earshot. As soon as Trumble approached, he bent down, keeping 5 feet away from the car's side, but with his back to the gaggle of officers by the front of his house.

"Don't say a fuckin' word," Maury said.

"I ain't said nothin'," Domina said.

"You listen to me. I can help. I got a lawyer who can cut the balls off any prosecutor."

"Lockhart killed people. Made it look like ODs," Domina said.

"If I know Jon Lockhart, he was careful about it."

Domina paused, thinking. "He was. We never left any prints, if that's what you mean."

"Just don't say anything about anything. Right now, they're nothin' but ODs."

"But Lockhart stuck 'em. With scorpions and then needles with some bad shit. Like he was going to do you."

This time it was Maury's turn to pause. "That fuckin' Lockhart," Maury hissed. "Scorpions are one thing. There's nothing to say the guys didn't OD after Lockhart stung them. On their own."

"What if they get to Lockhart? Try and swing him a deal?"

"Don't worry about him. Sounds like he was stung, and it was bad enough he's in the hospital. Some of them don't think he'll make it. And if he's in the hospital, he's vulnerable. I'll take care of Lockhart."

"What do you mean?"

"Never mind."

"What about Fuego?"

"Ernesto will see reason, after I explain the situation."

"So you're the contact?"

Maury glanced at her. He turned and glanced back at the gag-gle of men, considering. But even Mac was bent into the circle, probably listening to Sam Rivers talk about what it was like to jump off a cliff into the dark.

Maury had always known how to play people. He had an instinctual ability to say the right thing at the right time, regard-less of truth or consequence. And at this moment, his gut told him he had to let Domina in on some inside information, just to make her know she was part of the team. This moment called for a smile and a little glad-handing and we-put-it-to-the-boss chagrin.

So Maury turned back and grinned. "I thought Lockhart was going to shit himself."

"He thought he found his money. Instead, he found you."

"You know what's funny about his money?"

"What?"

"Your boss, Fuego, charged me $250,000 up front. Said it was to help finance the operation. We both knew it was commitment money. A test. But since I had it," Maury smiled. "I used it. And to think it was all because of Jon Lockhart."

"There's something definitely sweet about it."

When it came to reading people, Maury was practically a magician. But Domina hadn't survived the Storm Lake gangs, the local public schools, two stints in juvies, and then the South-of-the-Border Monarchs without also being able to read people. So she played along, and she played well.

Maury could not see the recording device under the driver's side head rest.

Maury, for his part, had correctly identified Domina as the most balanced among the group of three who had come up to deliver heroin to the Twin Cities. He knew if the operation was to survive, he'd have to bring Domina in, make her a part of it, or at least feel enough a part of the whole Minnesota operation so she'd keep her mouth shut. Domina would need to serve some time for accessory to murder, but they could pin the big stuff on Lockhart, after he was gone. If Domina had a reason to keep her mouth shut—a serious nest egg she could count on, after serving time—Maury was pretty sure Domina could be convinced it was in her best interests to keep her mouth shut and play along.

So Maury told her a few details, just to bring her in. Especially how Maury's lawyer would get her the lightest possible sentence. A few years, max. Definitely less than 10. And meanwhile, her share of their blossoming organization would be growing.

It sounded so good, Domina was having second thoughts.

But not many.

EPILOGUE

Despite the holiday weekend, it had been a busy two days. But not so busy it eclipsed Sam's promise to return to Amber Mansfield's class and help with her student's monarch project.

Over the long weekend, an enterprising *Star Tribune* reporter caught wind of the two connected ODs, the death of Jon Lockhart by scorpion sting, and the effort to resupply the Twin Cities with heroin. Scott Pepper tried to intercede and claim—on behalf of himself and the DEA—that they'd been working the case since intercepting that heroin shipment concealed in boat motors a few months back. And even though the reporter was under deadline, she interviewed Sheriff Broom and Raven Marschel, several of the deputies involved, and Wheezo and Mac. Everyone explained the DEA and Scott Pepper were involved, but only because of the hard work and sharp eye of USFW Special Agent Sam Rivers, who, in the course of the investigation, not only stopped heroin from returning to the Twin Cities but also solved two murders.

The real story ran Memorial Day, along with photos of the dead victims, Jerry Trailor and Suthy Baxter, and the perpetrators, including Domina, Tiburon, Jon Lockhart, Maury Trumble, Rich Matthewson, Tim Casselmire, and Tommy Cummins. *Las*

Monarcas, the drug cartel from Michoacán, was implicated, in particular Ernesto Feugo. The authorities were trying to extradite him. But first they had to find him. Not surprisingly, he'd disappeared.

The use of bark scorpions as weapons, truth serum, and torturing devices made the story sensational. Readers were shocked, but they could not help following along, morbidly fascinated.

Amber Mansfield's class was packed. The reporter was there, doing a follow-up story on Sam Rivers and his penchant for wild places and wild things, including monarch butterflies. She was attractive and interested, but Sam's attention was clearly focused on Carmel Rodriguez, who also stood in the back of the room, smiling like the Cheshire cat.

Sam had been busy last Saturday night, setting and springing the trap on Maury Trumble. He never had to use the recording that was made with Domina's assistance. He testified about what he'd overheard outside Maury's basement window, and about Jon Lockhart's final words, as he lay dying across the earthen furrows. Sam added several other details he'd picked up investigating the two ODs, so it sounded to Maury as though Jon Lockhart, on his deathbed, had sold Maury out. Had sold everyone out. And when Maury recalled the rage that broke across Lockhart's face when he discovered Maury was Ernesto Fuego's contact, he wasn't surprised by Lockhart's dying wish for revenge.

Sam and Gray did not arrive at Carmel's house until the wee hours of Sunday morning. But true to her word, she left a light on. And after Gray said hello to Liberty and Frank, and was fed, and finally led off to bed, Sam retired to Carmel's.

'Nough said.

The Memorial Day front page feature that helped pack Amber Mansfield's class was "Agent's Knowledge of Monarch Butterflies Helps Solve Two Murders." Sam's boss, Kay Magdalen, loved the story, but was still a little miffed about Sam's dearth of reports. She'd only received one. But the commissioner was pleased with the positive USFW publicity and said, "I told you so," and she could only say, "Okay, Rivers, take a few days off. But don't get comfortable."

It was the best Sam could expect and he took it, looking forward to spending the time with Carmel.

Back in class, on Tuesday morning, Sam Rivers flashed the photo of an oyamel fir onto the screen. The tree was 70 feet tall, and every branch, twig, and frond was covered with monarch butterflies, transforming the normally deep-green fir into orange-skirted brilliance.

And once again, the kids, and more parents now—some spilled out into the hallway—exclaimed with awe. When Sam showed the photo, he heard a "phenomenal" and "beautiful" and "what a shot" among the numerous "oohs." And then, over the chorus, Mac's "whoa!" was loud enough to eclipse everyone.

Some things don't change.

Sam had excused Mac from the three-ring circus that commenced after Saturday night. Sam's near-retirement colleague was able to make it to the Vermilion gathering before dawn. And once Margie read the news accounts and heard how her husband had acquired his limp, she softened toward Sam, though it would still be a while before she forgave him enough to speak to him.

Sam showed the kids more photos of the swarm of orange over the trees. Then he showed them some aerial photos of the Michoacán region where the monarchs overwintered. He explained there were several preserves in this part of Mexico, where the monarchs and the oyamel firs were protected so the monarchs could spend their winters in peace, as they had for millennia. Sam showed an aerial photo of one of the most remote preserves, the same one in which Miguel and he discovered the stumps. His first photo had been taken 20 years earlier and showed a mountaintop thick with trees. The next photo, taken last year, showed how much of the land had been deforested, cut down for lumber and firewood.

Sam explained how the region was very poor and how woodcutters had been felling trees for generations and how some, barely literate, didn't understand where the preserve boundaries started and where they ended.

"Natural resource dollars are scarce, so the park boundaries aren't well marked or fenced, and without a GPS it's difficult to tell where you're standing."

The two wildlife agents had revisited the mountaintop and with Gray began tracking the trail of felled trees. Once cut, they had been hauled out of the forest by horses. It had been easy to follow the trail to a distant logging road. Then, with the help of Gray's nose, they followed the tire tracks to a remote woodcutter's hovel.

Sam showed a picture of a tiny farm with a dirt floor and a stack of firewood next to an outside garden. The woodcutter's family stood beside him, a wife and four young children, all wearing threadbare clothes. There was a nearby field that had been trampled and covered with sawdust. Sam explained the illegally cut logs had been processed here by some kind of portable sawmill and hauled to another location for storage and drying.

"As you can see, this part of Mexico is very poor. These woodcutters were not arrested. They did not understand they were cutting trees in a protected preserve. So they were educated and warned that if they ever felled another oyamel fir on that mountaintop, they would be prosecuted to the full extent of the law."

Then Sam showed the stunning wooden beams of a kitchen. The beams were straight and dark, and the grain was striated in different hues of brown and white. "This was the end of the trail of the oyamel firs," he said. Sam explained that any time natural products were shipped across the border, a customs declaration must be completed. This oyamel fir lumber had been concealed and shipped inside a container with regular pine lumber. It took some detective work, but eventually they tracked the exotic wood to this kitchen, which was the home of a Mexican immigrant who had grown up in Michoacán and recalled the unusual grain of it.

"He's now an American citizen and made a lot of money in the plumbing business in Los Angeles. He paid for the firs to be felled and cut into lumber and beams he could use to build this Michoacán kitchen in his Pasadena home. It was beautiful," Sam said.

Sam showed a picture of the man in his kitchen, appearing grim.

"He didn't know it was illegal. He worked through informal channels and paid enough money to obtain the exotic wood. Once he understood how the felling of these oyamel firs had killed thousands of butterflies he felt awful. He paid to have his kitchen dismantled and its special wood shipped back to his childhood home, in the

Michoacán mountains, where it was used to build the entryway to a forest preserve interpretive center, up in the forest of butterflies, so people could be educated about the threat to monarch butterflies and the key role oyamel firs play in their survival. He also agreed to partially fund reforestation efforts, and fully fund the interpretive center for the next 10 years, hiring the woodcutter to be a guide."

Sam showed an image of a simple structure, nestled in a stand of fir trees. The Pasadena plumber stood in front of it, beaming. It wasn't the kind of interpretive center typical of preserves in the United States, but it was a start.

"Most people want to do the right thing," Sam said. "One of the jobs of a USFW special agent is to educate the public about flora and fauna, the plants and animals, that inhabit our world. Sometimes plants and animals need our protection and help, so they can continue to survive and hopefully thrive."

As Sam's hour wound down, the kids began asking questions. Once the kids were done, the adults raised their hands, including the *Star Tribune* reporter.

"What's next for Special Agent Rivers?" the reporter asked.

"First I'm going to help these kids release some monarch butterflies into the wild. Then I'm heading up to Isle Royale. I'll be there for a while, consulting on their wolf repopulation efforts. The Isle's wolves need new blood. With too few wolves, the moose population rises. With too many wolves, the moose decline. It's a constant battle to strike the right balance of codependence and coexistence."

"Will you be back?" the reporter asked.

Sam glanced at Carmel and said, "You can count on it."

ACKNOWLEDGMENTS

In 2017 Minnesota's *The Loft* (www.loft.org) began offering a year-long writing course called The Novel Writing Project (NWP). After finally stepping away from the corporate cube permanently, I enrolled in that first class. It was officiated, taught, managed, therapized, and more by novelist Peter Geye. I cannot use enough accolades (or words) to thank Peter for his insight, advice, and guidance. He's a serious novelist and a phenomenal instructor. I know the final version of *Killing Monarchs* was significantly improved by his—and the class attendees'—careful reading and commentary.

I am also profoundly grateful for my year-long NWP classmates, who as part of our mutual efforts read and commented on large portions of each other's work. I not only benefited from their remarks and advice on *Monarchs,* but also on reading and critiquing their work as each of their titles evolved. Many thanks to Amit Bhati, Judy Borger, Brian Duren, Margaret Hartman, Richard Lentz, Drew Miller, Tamrah O'Neil, Sakki Selznick, Sue Telander, Sara Williams, and Rebecca Wurtz. Novels in progress need dedicated, careful readers, and these classmates and now friends all improved my manuscript and helped make *Killing Monarchs* possible. A simple thank you is insufficient. I look forward to continuing to work together to make all our works shine.

Back in 2009 my wife, Anna, and I visited San Miguelle De Allende, in north-central Mexico, during the Day of the Dead celebration. It's an interesting place, especially during this celebration (November 1), which typically marks the time monarch butterflies begin returning to their overwintering grounds in Michoacán, three hours south of San Miguelle. At the time I was unable to visit the monarch butterfly preserves, but our nearby stay kindled my imagination, and over the subsequent year I began thinking about and writing *Killing Monarchs*.

Anna was not only along for the San Miguelle trip but has also had a lifelong interest in monarch butterflies. She was the first to read an early version of the novel, and she weighed in on setting, characters, the gruesome details involving bark scorpions, and more. Her assistance and insight were, and are, invaluable.

After changing the entire novel's setting to the Twin Cities, friends Steve and Laurie Sauerbry, Anne Torrey, and others read and commented on the new versions, making several helpful suggestions for improving the story. Laurie in particular has a proofreader's sharp and careful eye and found numerous errors that required fixing.

When I first approached AdventureKEEN Acquisitions and Developmental Editor Brett Ortler with the idea of publishing my Sam Rivers Mysteries, I believed the possibility of working with this excellent publisher was a long shot. AdventureKEEN publishes almost entirely nonfiction, several titles of which sit on my own bookshelves or accompany me into the outdoors on various nature hikes. But they decided to gamble. They hedged their wager by supporting these mysteries/thrillers at every stage of the writing, editing, marketing, publication, and distribution process.

First, they hired Mary Logue, an outside fiction editor, to review the Sam Rivers Mysteries, including this one. Mary is the author of more than eight mysteries and numerous books of poetry, and she is an experienced, well-known writing teacher and editor. She had excellent suggestions and edits, all of which I took.

Second, the manuscript was carefully edited by Adventure-KEEN editors Holly Cross, Jenna Barron, and Emily Beaumont. *Killing Monarchs* went through many revisions, and these three were instrumental in making sure the entire text was painstakingly proofed. They also flagged several revision discrepancies and had numerous excellent suggestions for making the book better.

Third, AdventureKEEN Director of Marketing and Media Relations, Liliane Opsomer, has been and continues to be a tireless promoter of the Sam Rivers Mysteries. She managed to get numerous book reviewers and outlets to cover the mysteries and booked countless public appearances for the titles. She managed reader campaigns, wrote letters, sent out advanced review copies, and worked on everything from social media banners to appearance posters. In summary, her participation has been indispensable and magnificent.

Finally, AdventureKEEN produced a quality paperback with an excellent cover design, while managing creative book distribution efforts. When my niece was on vacation with her family near Rapids City, South Dakota, she sent me an image of *Wolf Kill,* the first Sam Rivers Mystery. I learned, to my surprise, that she pulled it from the store shelves at Bear Country USA! That's distribution.

All monarch biology that is referenced in the novel is accurate.

When accounting for early *Killing Monarchs* versions and the work done in Peter's NWP class, I suspect the novel has been revised at least 20 times, give or take. Hopefully, everyone's participation and input into these revisions has helped create a novel worth reading. Again, many thanks to everyone who had a role in bringing it to press.

ABOUT THE AUTHOR

Award-winning author Cary J. Griffith grew up among the woods, fields, and emerald waters of eastern Iowa. His childhood fostered a lifelong love of wild places.

He earned a BA in English from the University of Iowa and an MA in library science from the University of Minnesota.

Griffith's books explore the natural world. In nonfiction, he covers the borderlands between civilization and wild places. In fiction, he focuses on the ways some people use flora and fauna to commit crimes, while others with more reverence and understanding of the natural world leverage their knowledge to bring criminals to justice.

DISCUSSION QUESTIONS

1. *Killing Monarchs* opens with Jon Lockhart, a diabolical drug runner, questioning Jerry Trailor, a former business associate. Lockhart is picking up a shipment of heroin. But he also wants to know what happened to his money, stolen five years earlier. In what ways does Lockhart's treatment of Jerry presage Lockhart's fate? If Lockhart had shown mercy, would the smugglers still be in business?

2. Sam Rivers shared his knowledge about the monarch butterfly migration with sixth graders at Hopkins Elementary. How does Sam's knowledge of that migration and the monarch life cycle eventually help him understand the chrysalises shipped from Mexico may be conduits for illicit drugs?

3. When Sam first meets Hopkins Detective Raven Marschel, she treats him with suspicion. Like many law enforcement officers, she is unfamiliar with the USFW and its mission, and doesn't think Sam is qualified to investigate a drug overdose. How does their relationship evolve over the course of the novel? By the end of the novel, how does Detective Marschel feel about Sam?

4. Sam first learns about Suthy Baxter, another former Lockhart business associate, on the day Jerry Trailor is found dead from an overdose. Sam cannot visit Suthy until the following morning.

How is that delay fortuitous? What physical evidence does Sam find at Suthy's house? How does that evidence help Sam with his investigation? Does Sam learn anything else important about the connection between Jerry, Suthy, and others?

5.   When Sam and Carmel walk their dogs in the woods, how is what they see and experience poignant? How does their hike contribute to a growing interest in each other?

6.   In what ways are Carmel and Sam similar? How do their likes and dislikes, personal histories, interests, and the other things we learn about them contribute to their mutual attraction?

7.   When does Sam learn the identity of the Mexican drug cartel's Minnesota contact? How does that knowledge change the course of his investigation? In what ways is the Minnesota contact different from his former meth partners?

8.   In pursuit of a drug runner, Sam jumps off a cliff into a cold river in the dark. Do you think this was a reasonable risk to take? Why would Sam make such a crazy leap? Given similar circumstances, would you?

9.   Toward the end of the novel, scorpions escape from a jar inside Jon Lockhart's getaway car, several stinging him to death. For the moment, Sam wants to keep the news of Lockhart's demise quiet. Why? If Lockhart's death would have become known, would it have changed the end of the novel?

10.   Technically, Jon Lockhart is drug runner Domina's boss. When does the tension in their relationship first appear? Over the course of the novel, how does their relationship change? By novel's end, how do their different perspectives influence their different fates?

READ ON FOR AN EXCERPT FROM CARY J. GRIFFITH'S NEXT NOVEL

Praise for *Killing Monarchs*

"Griffith's third Sam Rivers mystery, *Killing Monarchs,* moves with the speed of a bullet train. A gripping tale of greed and vengeance, drug cartels and murder, scorpions and butterflies. Not to be missed."

—Jeffrey B. Burton, award-winning author of *The Finders,* *The Keepers,* and *The Lost*

AVAILABLE SUMMER 2024
WHEREVER BOOKS ARE SOLD

CHAPTER 1

Holden Riggins lay in the bottom of his boat, still as a stone-cold corpse. The day had dawned clear but sharp. There was a light breeze out of the northwest, causing Lake Vermilion's surface to riffle. The breeze kept the fishing boat's anchor rope taut.

Holden wore a faded black down coat with oil stains blotting its front. He liked to fry whitefish in Crisco, and he worked part-time as a small motor mechanic, so the stains could have been Crisco or engine oil or both. The coat had been patched in two places, obvious because the patching tape was a shade too dark. His Carhartt work pants were worn to a faded taupe, with their bottoms frayed over a pair of scuffed leather work boots.

Holden's feet were splayed out, and his arms flung from his sides like a pair of catawampus windmill blades. The palm of his right hand was face down, with a crudely fashioned S-I-N-K tattooed on the top knuckle bone of each finger. The palm of his left hand faced the sun. You could not see it, but atop his left-hand fingers, cleaner, more stylized, and recent, tattoos spelled F-I-S-H. His face was round and puffy, and beneath a pair of black plastic-rimmed glasses, his eyes were shut tight as a toad. Most people would have thought the tattoo off the corner of his left eye was a mole. It could have been a teardrop. Holden had done prison time, and in convict parlance, a teardrop meant either a long sentence or testament to having killed someone. But it also had the shape of a crudely fashioned, 2-ounce split shot sinker. Regardless, lying in the bottom of his boat, his body had the kind of terminal flaccidness of someone who had been pole-axed in the middle of the night and left for dead.

Holden was in his late 30s but had the wizened appearance of someone much older. In his early 20s, he had learned to appreciate the day's first beer buzz. By his mid-20s, he followed the beer with harder chasers. By the end of his 20s, he had become intimately familiar with most controlled substances. Growing up in Northern Minnesota, he had always been an outdoors guy, and the sun, combined with hard living, had turned his skin leathery with occasional age spots appearing on his face and across the backs of his hands.

Less than 3 feet from his prone body, an empty bottle of Old Crow rested against the boat's livewell compartment. Near the bow lay a half-filled fifth of Jack Daniel's.

If not for the above-freezing embrace of Vermilion's red waters, and the sun, which an hour earlier had crested the boat's gunwales, the man would have been covered in a patina of hoarfrost, already dead from a heart attack triggered by hypothermia. But Vermilion had kept Holden Riggins alive, though it was uncertain it could keep him alive much longer.

In the distance, the faint sound of an outboard motor cut through the mid-morning like a chainsaw felling trees. Holden, of course, could not hear it. The sound did not reach over the boat's gunwales. Besides, his body temperature was nearly 95 degrees.

If he had been conscious, he would have been shaking like a man with delirium tremens.

On the leeward side of the boat, 20 yards into the lake, a pair of empty white jugs anchored each end of a 40-foot whitefish gill net. Minnesota DNR regulations were very specific and strict about fishing with nets. Except for a few weeks in late fall, netting was forbidden. Holden knew all about the regulations, in part because he had been fishing his entire life. Also, more than once, he had been arrested and convicted for poaching. The most severe penalty had been eight years earlier, when he was caught selling illegally netted walleye to local restaurants. Technically it was a violation of the Lacey Act, and because he was selling the fish commercially, he was convicted of a felony.

There had been other violations, although none recently. For the last seven years, Holden had been clean, or at least had not been caught committing an illegal act. There were a few people who believed Holden was a changed man. He had turned over a new leaf, so some said. There were many others, less sanguine, who believed he had finally figured out how to avoid getting caught. These people opined the Holden Rigginses of the world don't change; they just get smart, or lucky.

Regardless, today, October 14th, there was nothing untoward about Holden's gill net. It was strung 3 feet deep across familiar shallows. The net was perfectly situated to catch whitefish, which in late fall swam up out of Vermilion's depths to spawn. There was nothing illegal about Holden's net because last Thursday had been the whitefish netting season opener, and Holden had a license.

The motorboat was growing closer.

Beyond Holden's whitefish net, the lake bottom dropped to a rugged, well-known 25-foot-deep rocky bottom. Locals knew it as prime walleye habitat and a great place to fish. But again, walleye could never be taken with nets. Minnesota's walleye had to be caught the old-fashioned way, with hook, line, sinker, and live bait or lures or both. Or any one of a huge number of variations involving fishing poles, reels, and tackle.

Walleye fishing in Minnesota was big business. New boats similar to Holden's Lund 1600 Renegade easily sold for tens of thousands of dollars, and were outfitted with fish finders, GPS, livewells, rod storage compartments, swivel pedestal seats, steering wheels, gauge-filled dashes, and more. And providing you only used some variation of hook, line, sinker, and bait, whatever boat and fishing technology you could leverage was legal.

But Holden's boat was old. Years earlier he had purchased it used, and now its hull was scraped and dented. He had none of the newfangled electronics typical of boats purchased today. In many ways Holden's boat was a counterpoint to the Minnesota DNR runabout, whose gleaming hull rested 30 yards shoreward, tethered to an overhanging cedar branch. Affixed to the boat's aft was a shiny black 150-horsepower Mercury outboard motor, now drifting up and down in the chop, its propeller occasionally scraping against the lake's boulder-strewn bottom.

Twenty yards farther out into Vermilion, beyond Holden's legal nets, bobbed a pair of faux pine branch floats. If you boated by you would think they were tree debris, to be avoided if you did not want your motor to get caught up. The faux branches anchored each side of a 15-foot-long, 25-foot-deep gill net, set in a way designed to produce a maximum walleye harvest. Pound for pound, a single catch of walleye in that net would fetch enough money to keep a grown man stocked with Old Crow for a year. Maybe Jack Daniel's too.

Annually, Minnesota restaurants sold 25 million dollars of the prized fish, none of it commercially harvested in the state. Most restaurants and grocery stores purchased their walleye from Canadian fisheries or the Red Lake band of Chippewa, the only Minnesotans who could legally harvest and sell the fish.

Because of the cold and time of year, there was almost no one on Lake Vermilion. The lake contained more than 40,000 acres of water, dotted with 365 islands. It was strung across Northeastern Minnesota in a series of channels and bays that were so ragged and jagged it had 341 miles of shoreline, the most of any Minnesota lake. There were a lot of places to lose oneself on Vermilion, which is why the distant sound of the motorboat, growing closer, was surprising.

The index finger on Holden's left hand, the one tattooed with an elaborate "F," twitched.

If Holden had not been nearly comatose, he would have recognized the sound of the approaching outboard. Like the patrol boat tethered to the nearby shoreline, the distant drone was definitely a 150-horsepower four-stroke Mercury, standard issue for the Minnesota DNR. From the approaching noise, he might have suspected the authorities were on their way. If he remembered or had been aware of any of the things that happened the previous night, he might have worried. But he was just beginning to regain consciousness, and besides, he would have never guessed that the reason for the patrol's approach was because five hours earlier a call was made to Minnesota's Turn-in-Poachers (TIP) line.

"TIP line," Dispatch answered, before dawn. "Can I help you?"

"Uhhh," the caller began, not unusual for TIP line calls. "Think I got somethin' to report."

"A violation?"

"Well, don't know. Exactly." The voice sounded old, but with that inflection that identified a Northern Minnesotan. A man.

"What did you see?"

"On Lake Vermilion. Out across Big Bay. Near that big island. Two boats, one of them DNR, pretty sure. But nobody in sight. Leastways, that I could see."

"And you think there was some kind of violation happening?"

"Looked fishy, know what I mean? Where the hell was they? And there were net floats. Could a been whitefishin', but looked like there were two nets. That ain't legal. Is it?"

"No sir. Unless there were two people with licenses. Are you sure one of the boats was DNR?"

"Two empty boats. One of them DNR. I was a ways out, headed to my car. But when I seen the boats I come up close and hit them with my high beam. When no one popped up, I yelled. But . . . nothin'."

"Can you tell me a little bit more about where exactly you saw them?"

The voice paused and then said, "North of the casino water tower. Clear 'cross Big Bay. Just 'bout a straight line, I'd guess. Up close to that long island."

Dispatch repeated the location. She had been to the Lucky Loon Casino and was familiar with that part of Lake Vermilion. She didn't know the island he referenced, but there were a lot of islands on that big body of water, and she thought she remembered seeing a map that showed a long island, due north of the water tower.

"What made you think the boat was ours?"

"It was . . . new like. With a big black Merc on the back. Pushed up to shore, just sittin' there empty. But I seen that DNR sign on its bow. That yellow and blue map?"

"Map of Minnesota with M-N-D-N-R in big letters?" Dispatch said.

"That's it."

Lake Vermilion was in District 5, which was Conservation Officer Charlie Jiles's territory. Dispatch had the rosters for all the COs, since they were typically the first to respond to TIP calls. But Charlie had the weekend off, and COs were forbidden to use their official boats for anything personal. She knew Charlie Jiles. He had a reputation. He was a good officer, but he didn't always follow the rules.

"Can you describe the other boat? Was it against the shore too?"

"Nope. Bout 30 yards out, I'd say. A Lund. An old Lund. Just anchored there."

"We'll check it out," she finally said. "Would you like to leave a phone number in case we have any other questions?" Dispatch had already captured the number from caller ID. But something about the caller sounded a little off. She wanted a name and was leading up to asking for it, thinking the phone number would be a good first step.

Then the line went dead.

Most people were reluctant ratters. DNR regulations could be ambiguous, and most were willing to give fellow outdoors people the benefit of the doubt. Others who might recognize a larcenous act refuse to get involved because they are acquainted with or related to the perpetrator. And then there were a minority who thought if someone could get away with a little larceny, especially when it involved Minnesota's abundant natural resources, more power to 'em. This caller's voice sounded like it belonged to one of those guys—*a Northern Minnesota good ole boy, she thought. And if the caller was coming across the lake before dawn, to get his car, he most likely lived in a cabin you could only reach by boat. And if he lived on the lake, surely he knew the name of that big island.

Something was a little off, but one thing was certain: they needed to check it out.

TIP calls were dispatched out of Brainerd, and it had taken nearly four hours to marshal two neighboring COs—Jennie Flag out of Grand Rapids and Bernie Olathe from Two Harbors—and get them over to Vermilion to follow up. Flag trailered her boat. They had put in at the Lucky Loon Casino docks, feeling anything but lucky. The late morning was sunny but cold. Not ideal for being on water that in another three weeks would be solid ice.

They both knew fellow officer Jiles. He lived alone in Eveleth, and Dispatch had told them he had the weekend off. Dispatch had called his cell as soon as they'd received the tip, but it rolled over to his voicemail. Must have had it off. Each of the COs tried him on their way over, and then Flag had tried him again from the dock. But again, no answer, which was regrettable because the day was bracing. Flying full throttle across Vermilion's red surface in 26-degree cold was going to be, well, frosty.

Once they motored out of Hemingway Bay, they cut due north, starting across the big open water. Flag pushed the throttle all the way down, and the runabout surged forward. The riffle on the lake's surface was mild enough, so the boat almost immediately planed level, flying like a hockey puck flung across a mile-long expanse of smooth ice. Both officers wore tight wool stocking caps pulled down over their ears, heavy down coats, and wool gloves. All of it DNR khaki green. To avoid the windchill and keep their hats from blowing off, they kept their heads hunkered behind the boat's windshield. Once into Big Bay, Officer Olathe raised a pair of high-powered binoculars, scanning far out over the huge expanse of water, searching along the distant shoreline.

This part of Vermilion is more than a mile across, so it wasn't until they neared the middle that Olathe thought he saw two boats, one of them silver, tucked up close to the opposite shore. He pointed in that direction, and Flag corrected their course.

There was movement, back in the bottom of Holden Riggins's boat. Following the finger twitch, his hand had seemingly come alive. It trembled in the cold. Holden slowly awakened. Almost immediately he felt cold. In direct proportion to his rising consciousness, his body began to shake. And apart from the bone-rattling nature of the shakes, it was a good thing. Intense shivering is the body's way of creating movement and heat. The ambient temperature didn't help, but the overhead sun did.

Now he could hear a boat approaching. He had a vague notion of hope, thankfulness, maybe even luck. But what he felt most was awful. In fact, he was pretty certain he was going to be sick, if he didn't freeze first. He was disoriented and nauseous and trying to regain consciousness and body heat all at the same time, and it was taking a toll.

When he was finally able to sit up, with a touch of vertigo that made the world unstable, he thought he recognized the motor's sound, a 150-horsepower Merc. DNR, if he had to guess. He hoped whoever it was had a bottle of aspirin and blankets or some kind of heater and something to drink. His mouth felt like someone had stuffed it with a dirty sock and wired his lips shut. Sitting up, he could barely peer over his boat's gunwale. He looked out into Big Bay and saw a boat, definitely approaching, maybe a quarter mile out.

Then he had to lay back down, his hands bracing himself for support. His hands felt like a pair of ice chunks. He knew he had to move. He had to get up and move.

He rolled to one side, coiling into a fetal position. He stayed there for a moment until he was able to push himself up.

He was shaking, but not like a leaf. More like the start of an epileptic seizure. Only Holden's shaking didn't stop, and he swore his teeth were rattling as rapid as a woodpecker's thrum.

He was certain he was going to be sick, and just about the time the approaching boat drew close enough to see him, he managed to place his knees on the boat's side bench, hang his head over the gunwale, and heave.

It was a mix of solids and liquids, something that had no business seeing the light of day. He had a vague memory of last night's dinner at the casino restaurant, a recollection that triggered a gag reflex. He paused long enough to catch his breath, and then . . . this time he choked up bile, accompanied by a low-throated growl. He wavered a little, afraid he was going to pass out, still coming awake.

The two COs were within 20 yards.

"You okay?" a man yelled.

Holden barely looked up. No, he was not okay. He was sick. But he was alive. He was at least regaining consciousness enough to both hear what the man said and understand it. He wasn't yet thinking clearly, because otherwise he would have realized it was a stupid question. Neither could he speak yet, so for now he just shook his head. Once. No.

The other officer was at the helm, and Holden squinted to see her throttle down, edging the boat forward so that in another minute—Holden's head still precarious over the gunwale—the runabout's bow kissed the edge of Holden's Renegade.

Holden couldn't move anything but his head. He bent it and squinted at them sideways, recognizing khaki green DNR uniforms, one man and one woman, but not much else.

"Water," he said, dry and squeaky, like a frog. Making an effort to talk threatened to precipitate another expulsion. This time he managed a dry swallow.

Officer Flag reached down into her pack and brought out a water bottle. She handed it to Olathe, who was gripping the side of Holden's boat. He took the bottle and stepped into the Renegade and sat down next to Holden, noticing the empty Old Crow and half-filled Jack Daniel's resting on the boat's floor. No wonder the man was sick.

"You been out here all night?" Olathe said, unscrewing the water bottle cap.

Holden didn't look at the officer. He stared at the water, still shivering, and said, "drink," whispered and raspy.

Olathe started to hand the bottle over but quickly realized there was no way Holden's shaky hands could grip it. He was still leaning over the gunwale, partially prone. Olathe managed to bring the bottle to Holden's lips and tilt it and Holden sipped, some of it dribbling down his chin.

The three-day beard growth on Holden's face was coarse enough to sand the chrome off a trailer hitch. His hair was salt and pepper, short and greasy. Given the F-I-S-H and S-I-N-K tattoos, his raggedy attire, the booze bottles, and disheveled demeanor, Olathe thought the man looked more Skid Row than Lake Vermilion. He looked like a drunk on an all-night bender, just coming around, lucky to be alive.

While Olathe was giving Holden water, Officer Flag stepped back to a rear compartment. She pulled out a DNR-issued wool blanket and handed the folded blanket to Olathe, who spent the next few minutes unfurling and wrapping it around the shivering drunk.

After another couple of minutes and small sips, Officer Olathe said, "What's your name?"

Holden finally looked up at him, as if starting to wake from a bad dream. "Holden," he said. "Riggins," the name squeezing out of him.

By now Olathe and Flag had scanned the area and absorbed the scene. They needed to get over to the DNR boat, tethered against the shore. They could see a standard-size whitefish gill net, strung 100 feet along the shallows, near Holden's boat. Out beyond the whitefish net, Flag recognized the faux pine branch floats. She had seen them at an outfitter's supply store over in Ely. They were supposed to be natural looking floats used to anchor duck and geese decoys, and while those seasons were open, there were no decoys in sight. She wasn't sure how they were being used here, but judging from the fact they hadn't drifted an inch in this light breeze, she wanted to see what kept them anchored.

The COs had also registered a violation of the open container law, given the bottles in the bottom of Holden's boat. Probably drunk while boating. Possibly illegal netting if he didn't have a license. Hopefully, nothing more. But it didn't look good.

And where was Charlie Jiles?

The whole scene was a clusterfuck, as Officer Flag liked to say. She was one of a handful of women COs in the state, so she felt like her language needed to be a little salty. She also grew up the middle child, a girl, in a family of four boys, so she learned rough and tumble and how, when necessary, to land a blow. But both officers remained silent, because if Holden was a perp, they didn't want to piss him off. They wanted him to cooperate.

By the time Holden's hands finally settled enough to grip the water bottle on his own, Officer Olathe took another turn looking around. His eyes followed the same objects and jumped to the same conclusions as Officer Flag. They needed to get over to the runabout. They'd checked the numbers and verified it was Jiles's boat. Now they needed to make sure Jiles wasn't lying in its bottom.

When Olathe finally turned to consider the shoreline, he said, "Any idea why there's one of our boats tied up to the shore?"

With some effort Holden swiveled his head and glanced at the nearby shoreline. Then he peered back into the lake and said, "First I seen it."

Olathe caught Flag's eye, and they exchanged a wordless comment, part irritation, part concern, mostly disbelief.

"We gotta have a look at that boat," Olathe said. "Stay put."

Holden nodded, clearly in no shape to do more than drink water and shiver more heat into his hands and limbs.

After Olathe was back in the runabout, Flag pulled away from the Lund, steering toward the shoreline. She nudged the gunwale up close to Charlie Jiles's DNR boat, and Olathe grabbed hold of its edge. A red fire extinguisher was out of its side bracket, laying on the boat's bottom. There was no sign of fire. A DNR officer's hat lay near the extinguisher. Beside the captain's chair they saw a Styrofoam cup stuck in a cup holder, frozen coffee dregs in its bottom. It was Jiles's boat, but where was he?

They took another moment to radio Dispatch and tell them what they had found. Other than Holden Riggins, who needed medical care and who they still needed to question, and an empty DNR runabout, nothing.

Dispatch told them they had been unable to reach Officer Jiles by phone. They should secure his boat, search the area, and if they were unable to find him, one of them should drive the boat in.

It was all very strange. They would need to search this part of the island. It was Pine Island, they had seen, finally consulting a map. From Jiles's boat, the shoreline rose rocky, steep, and poplar-covered to a granite overlook. There was a towering white pine way up on top. From there they figured they could get a better view of the entire area, but neither of them was looking forward to the climb.

They still needed to check on the faux pine bough floats, which they both suspected were probably attached to an illegal net. They had decided to check on the floats first, when Holden called over to them.

"Hey," he said, the word still scratchy in his throat, but sounding stronger. "Somethin'," he managed, "in my net," pointing to the net's middle.

Flag pushed away from Jiles's boat, put her motor in gear, and puttered to where Holden had pointed between the two white buoys. But it wasn't until they were right on top of it that they recognized, through Vermilion's red water, a body caught up and submerged in Holden's net. When they squinted through the lake's choppy surface, they noticed the body was dressed in khaki greens.

PRAISE FOR *WOLF KILL*

"Griffith's prose makes you feel the winter chill . . . and the twisty plot delivers a chill down your spine. This is a Minnesota mystery with razor-sharp teeth."
  —Brian Freeman, *New York Times* best-selling author of
  The Deep, Deep Snow

"*Wolf Kill* is a terrific read! The writing is so good that you can feel the frigid winds blowing through this dark and masterfully crafted novel even as the suspense heats up. And the wolves are as magnificent and frightening as you could hope.
  —David Housewright, Edgar Award–winning author of
  What Doesn't Kill Us

"In northern Minnesota, winter is full of dangers that can kill: hard cold, hard men, and hungry wolves. Cary Griffith brings the menace of all three into play in his riveting new thriller. Returning to the childhood home he fled 20 years earlier, Sam Rivers finds himself battling a group of scheming reprobates and struggling against an avalanche of painful memories. Griffith's intimacy with the territory he writes about comes through in every line. I loved this novel and highly recommend it. But I suggest you enjoy it under a warm blanket. Honestly, I've never read a book that evokes the fierce winter landscape of the North Country better than *Wolf Kill*."
  —William Kent Krueger, Edgar Award–winning author of
  This Tender Land

"Up here in the North Country, we have a bounty of fine mystery writers. Krueger, Housewright, Eskens, Freeman, Mejia, Sanford . . . Add to that list Cary Griffith, whose *Wolf Kill* thrills for its plotting, superb writing, and unforgettable characters, not least the brutal Minnesota winter. Sam Rivers is not only a fine sleuth, but a complicated man with a complicated history and a fair family grudge. Taken together, he's a force, both on the page and long after you finish reading his story. Good thing there's more of him to go around, and I'll be first in line for the next Sam Rivers novel."

—Peter Geye, author of *Northernmost*

"Cary J. Griffith defines the savage, howling beauty of a Northern Minnesota winter in this taut, compulsively readable mystery. I want more Sam Rivers!

—Wendy Webb, author of *The Haunting of Brynn Wilder*

"Fans of Paul Doiron's *The Poacher's Son* or the Joe Pickett books will appreciate this descriptive novel with an intriguing plot and well-written characters."

—Lesa Holstine, *Library Journal*

"Involving, fast-paced . . . [Cary J. Griffith's] writing is so vivid the reader wants to bundle up and enjoy the beauty of the landscape, even at 20 below zero."

—Mary Ann Grossmann, *Pioneer Press*

"The latest from accomplished Minnesota author Cary J. Griffith brings us a new North Woods hero to join the ranks of William Kent Krueger's Cork O'Connor and Allen Eskens' Max Rupert. He even gives Brian Freeman's Minnesota-to-the-core Jonathan Stride a run for the money."

—Ginny Greene, *Star Tribune*

PRAISE FOR *COUGAR CLAW*

"*Cougar Claw*, the second installment in the Sam Rivers series, sends the U.S. Fish & Wildlife special agent to the scene of a grisly cougar killing on the outskirts of the Twin Cities. As usual in Sam Rivers's world, all is not as it seems. Griffith doubles down on his strengths in this series, giving us another vibrant cast of allies, suspects, and a misunderstood predator, while navigating a path between animal rights and human fears of the natural world. I can't wait for Sam Rivers's next assignment.

—Mindy Mejia, author of *Everything You Want Me To Be* and
Strike Me Down

"A deadly threat from the wild comes far too close for comfort when an urban bicyclist is found mauled to death by a cougar. In this second book in the Sam Rivers mystery series, Cary Griffith takes this U.S. Fish & Wildlife special agent on a hair-raising hunt to find the cougar—and the truth. Mixing deep knowledge of the natural world with the twists and turns of the best suspense novels, *Cougar Claw* is a thoughtful and thrilling story."

—Mary Logue, author of the Claire Watkins mysteries and
The Streel

"From the first page to the last, *Cougar Claw* blends high suspense with the quiet observations of the predator's predator, Sam Rivers. Between Griffith's descriptions of Minnesota's natural beauty and the human nature of his characters, this is a book you won't want to end."

—Debra H. Goldstein, award-winning author of the Sarah Blair
mystery series